THIEF'S HONOR

A DAK HARPER THRILLER

THE RELIC RUNNER
BOOK 6

ERNEST DEMPSEY

138 PUBLISHING

For Kunal.

1

MADRID

Dak's legs were on fire. He knew there was nothing that would stop the burning, so he kept pumping his legs, running as fast as he could.

Sprinting across the slanted tiles of a rooftop didn't make things any easier.

The warm air did little to cool the heat in his muscles, or the ache in his lungs as it blew past him, slightly tousling his thick dark brown hair.

He reached the end of the roof and leaped without hesitation. For a second, his body felt weightless as he sailed across the narrow gap between buildings. Then gravity won, as it always did, and Dak's soles hit the flat space of a patio on the next roof. Without the slightest pause of movement he kept running, his balance unaffected by the slight drop and landing.

Dak kept his eyes firmly locked on his quarry—a young man, probably in his late twenties. The guy's red button-up shirt flapped around his belt as he ran. The black dress pants and matching leather shoes weren't doing him any favors, either.

Which was one reason Dak always preferred jeans. Though he

would have swapped those out for some shorts or beach pants here in the oven-like heat of Madrid in summer.

The runner disappeared around what was either a small storage shed or the housing for a water heater twenty-five yards ahead.

Dak wanted to yell at him, to tell him he just wanted to talk, but he'd already tried that back down on the street level in the nightclub where he'd found the man.

Manny Lopez had covered his tracks pretty well—as well as someone like him could do. He clearly enjoyed attention—thus the flashy clothes, the Ferrari Dak had seen him arrive in, and the penthouse mansion he had in the wealthiest part of the city.

For someone who made their money the way Lopez did, Dak would have thought the man would be a little more low-key with how he spent it.

Youth, Dak had thought as he'd looked over the guy's file.

He loathed to call it a dossier. That term, Dak felt, was reserved for military or agents. Lopez owned a nightclub and ran heroin out of the back. The only thing Dak could figure that kept him out of prison was the level of corruption that gripped the nation of Spain. As long as Lopez could grease the right palms, he'd stay out of trouble.

Learning about Lopez had been an easy enough task for Will Collins—Dak's friend with more underworld connections than anyone he knew. Thanks to his time running guns to underground militia and freedom fighters, predominantly in Central African nations, along with his most recent funneling of weapons to the war in Ukraine, Will had nearly as many contacts as the CIA.

Lopez seemed like someone Col. Cameron Tucker would have nothing to do with. In his pictures, he looked like a wannabe celebrity, always posing with models and showing off his money.

But guys like him had solid connections, too, and through a fair amount of digging, Will discovered that Lopez and Tucker had been doing a little business together.

It seemed Tucker had decided to diversify his financial portfolio and gone into heroin—either for profit or simply to wipe his dirty money.

Three months had passed since Dak last saw Tucker. Dak thought the man had been killed, but he never found the body. It had been a cat-and-mouse game ever since. Everywhere Dak went, Tucker was a step ahead.

This was a nice change of pace for Dak, being the hunter instead of the hunted. He'd spent the last few years of his life running and hiding, doing his best to lie low and keep his head down.

Now he was on the offensive. But he knew that could change in a heartbeat. The second you felt comfortable was when the tables would turn.

Dak had no intention of letting that happen.

He was, however, surprised by how fit his mark appeared to be. To Dak's surprise, Lopez had made him the second he spotted him across the crowded room in the club. Lopez had been passing out shots of tequila to a gaggle of women and men that composed his entourage. Only two bodyguards—both large guys with broad shoulders and huge chests—stood just behind him.

The second Lopez saw Dak and awkwardly excused himself from his friends, the two bodyguards stepped forward, wading through the crowd toward Dak.

Evading them had been easy enough. Dak had simply skirted around the dancing, seething mob of clubgoers and disappeared in the blinking, colorful lights.

Amateurs.

He'd expected to encounter more men when he reached the stairs next to the elevators. By the time Dak got to the lifts, the one on the left had already reached the fourth floor at the top.

He considered taking the elevator up but thought better of it. The second Lopez noticed the other lift heading his way, he'd simply go back down to the ground floor and make his escape. No doubt he'd already called the valet desk and ordered his Ferrari to be brought around to the front.

So, Dak called both lifts down to the main floor, stepped inside, and pressed the emergency button for each.

Doing so would bring the fire department out, and maybe a few local cops, but it would cut off Lopez's exit options, leaving him only the stairs. Which is exactly where Dak found him.

Lopez must have thought Dak would try the elevator, and believed he could slip by using the stairwell. When Dak rounded the corner on the second floor, he heard footsteps above and looked up to see Lopez making his way down with his hand on the rail.

The Spaniard stole a glance down through the shaft and saw Dak leaning out into the opening. The two froze for a second, then Lopez took off in the other direction, heading back up.

Dak made quick work of the stairs, though the last flight and a half took the same amount of time as the first two.

By the time he reached the fourth-floor landing, his legs felt heavy. Lopez would have the advantage for the moment, having only climbed a single flight before getting back to the top.

Dak stopped at the door and paused. He wished he had his pistol with him, but there hadn't been a good way to get that into the club with all the security and metal detectors at the doors. While he knew they were searching for knives, his pistol would have set things off.

So, he'd come in unarmed.

After a quick look out into the hallway on the fourth floor, Dak realized his quarry had gone through the other door at the landing—a rooftop maintenance access.

Now, he found himself in the open air, chasing Lopez across the tops of apartments and condos.

Dak kept himself in good shape—sticking to a strict workout routine five days a week, and that was probably the only thing keeping him close to Lopez.

Fear was a heck of a motivator when it came to the flight portion of a fight-or-flight response. He'd witnessed people normally incapable of running more than a quarter mile without stopping, somehow able to run four times their max capacity simply because they feared for their lives.

Eventually, though, he'd always caught up.

He reached the shed and started to dart past it when he caught movement from just beyond the corner. Dak managed to duck to the side just enough to avoid being struck in the head with a board. Instead, the plank hit him in the shoulder and glanced off, but it stunned him enough to slow him down for a second.

He retreated back a step, instantly bracing for another blow. He didn't have to wait long.

The board swung around again, this time aimed at the other side of his head.

Dak ducked below it, then surged forward at Lopez, who was still in the middle of his follow-through.

Raising his right arm, Dak plowed ahead, clotheslining Lopez before he could finish swinging the oversize piece of wood.

Dak caught his target's neck with the crook of his arm, and used his momentum to slam Lopez down onto the hard rooftop.

The club owner's head hit hard and instantly sent him into a dizzy haze. His eyes rolled around, searching for balance.

Then he felt himself being dragged by the collar.

"What... what are you doing?" he managed, kicking his legs around wildly in protest.

"Seemed like you were trying to get somewhere," Dak answered, barely looking back at the slender Spaniard. "I'm just helping you get there."

"Wha—" He couldn't finish the question. Overwhelmed with nausea and the world spinning around him, he tilted his head to the side and vomited.

Dak cringed and shook his head in disapproval. "That's disgusting. Seriously. Get ahold of yourself, man. You don't even know what I want."

"I... know who you are," Lopez spat after emptying his gut of tequila and ceviche. "You're the one looking for him."

"Oh. So you do know what I want," Dak corrected. "Go figure."

He stopped at the edge of the building and pulled Lopez up onto the two-foot-high concrete wall, then leaned him over so his torso hung above the alley below. No traffic occupied the dark, quiet side street, and no pedestrians lingered around to witness the two men just over four stories above.

"Now," Dak said, "seeing how you do know what I want, how about you give it to me?" He panted for air between words but was already catching his breath.

"I don't know where he is," Lopez blurted. "He was here two days ago. He didn't say where he was going next."

"What's so special about you? Why does Tucker have you on his payroll?"

Lopez searched Dak's eyes for a second. "Really? You really don't know much, do you?"

Dak pushed the man's torso back a little more, arching his captive's spine the wrong way in the process.

Lopez screamed, but that sound cut off in an instant as Dak squeezed the man's throat tighter.

"Nuh-uh-uh," Dak said, shaking his head. "No screaming. We don't want to draw any attention. Well, you obviously do with that shirt and the car you drive. Not smart, Manny. Not smart at all. A man who does what you do should keep a low profile. Enjoy life on a beach somewhere. But that's not how you roll, is it? Now, what did Tucker want from you?" He pushed down a little harder, forcing most of Lopez's weight over the edge.

"Money," Lopez grunted through clenched teeth. "He just wanted his take from the last month. That's it. I swear. He didn't say where he was going next. You have to believe me. He never tells me anything."

Dak nodded as if accepting the explanation. "I do believe you. Why would a man like Tucker trust someone like you? I'm surprised he does business with you. Then again, not much surprises me anymore."

Easing his grip on the man's throat, Dak used his left hand to search Lopez's pockets. He found a phone and a wad of cash but nothing else.

"You know," Dak said, "I really should turn you over to the cops. Your drug-running days are over, Lopez. Shoulda retired when you had the chance." He loosened his grip further, and the Spaniard took the respite to suck in several gulps of air.

Once he'd regained his composure, he laughed. "The cops? Go

ahead, Harper. Call the police. I own the police around here. Maybe no one told you."

Dak instantly resumed choking the man. "You don't know when to shut up, do you? Taunting a guy who is considering killing you isn't a great plan."

Lopez snickered. "If you kill me, you won't know what he's going to do next."

That caused Dak to pause. What did that mean?

"Okay, Manny. I'll give you thirty seconds to tell me what's going on, what Tucker is up to."

"I'm sure you'd like to know. But the second I tell you, you'll kill me."

Lopez moved his right hand toward his pocket. It was a subtle movement, and anyone standing ten feet away might have missed it even if they were paying attention.

"Sounds like something a desperate person would say. You're bluffing."

"Am I?" Lopez's eyes shifted back and forth from left to right as he had trouble focusing on both of Dak's eyes at the same time. "Are you willing to risk her life on that?"

The question surprised Dak, but it only took him a fraction of a second to catch on to Lopez's meaning.

"That's right. You'd be wise to release me, Harper. One call from me, and she's as good as dead."

The second threat felt hollow, truly empty. There was nothing in the words other than false bravado. Lopez held no sway over Tucker's actions any more than he did over the ebb and flow of the tide. But the fact he'd even brought her up was enough to send a chill through Dak's spine.

"What do you know?" Dak snarled, pulling his prisoner so close he could barely stand the all-consuming scent of overused Italian cologne on the man's chest and neck. This punk had bathed in the stuff.

The Spaniard grinned. It was a smug, toothy expression—one that didn't sit well with Dak, and he immediately got the distinct impression that this was a spoiled brat who'd never been spanked in his life.

"She's going to die," Lopez sang in a creepy, *nah nah nah boo boo* tune.

Dak's nostrils flared, and he glowered at the man through slits for eyelids. A warm gust of air blew over them, and Lopez took the opportunity to make his move.

He'd been slowly, carefully, making a play for the blade sheathed on his belt, and with the handle in his right hand, he jerked it out and slashed at Dak's neck.

Dak sensed the move a blink before the blade's sharp edge swiped through the air. Instinctively, he let Lopez go.

The club owner shrieked as he lost his balance, no longer supported by Dak's grip. His feet flipped up into the air and over his head as he toppled across the short wall's edge. Dak stretched out his arm to try to catch the man, but it was no use.

Lopez yelled—a terrified, high-pitched sound—until he hit the pavement below. Then his voice cut out abruptly, leaving only the echo to fade at the end of the alley.

Dak stared down at the man, bracing himself on the wall with both hands. He breathed heavily even though he'd already recovered from the rooftop run. Now, the effort came from the storm of emotions brewing inside him.

"What did he mean?" Dak wondered out loud.

Only one answer made any sense. And it squeezed Dak's gut until he felt sick. Somehow, Tucker knew where Nicole was.

2

Dak waded through the crowd amassed on the sidewalk. No one seemed to pay any attention to him as he worked his way through the marching throng, all seemingly headed the same way.

He wondered if a concert had just let out, or some other event. It was unusual for a herd of people this size to be congesting the streets at this time.

Dak didn't mind it, other than the fact the mass of people was slowing him down. He needed to put as much distance between himself and the crime scene as possible, not that there were any witnesses who could connect him to the death of Manuel Lopez—none except his bodyguards from the club.

But they hadn't seen what happened, only that Dak was in the club. It could have been anyone who killed Lopez, and with the burgeoning list of shady deals the club owner used for personal gain, Dak felt certain there were no end of characters eager to put an end to him and take the reins to his operations.

The bodyguards were nothing more than hired help. With their employer dead, it was doubtful their allegiance remained intact.

More likely, they were already looking for the next gravy train to babysit.

Sure, they'd have to answer questions from investigators when the body was discovered, but Dak doubted that had happened yet. Best he could figure, he still probably had another ten to twenty minutes, maybe more, before anyone stumbled into the alley and found the dead man.

Then it would be another ten or so before the cops got there, ten more to rope it off—maybe twenty. Initially, they'd consider it a suicide, so there would be no manhunt—at least not right away.

All that said, Dak felt the need to get out of Madrid—and Spain in general—as quickly as possible.

After swimming through the mob, he finally reached the other side and crossed the street at the next intersection. There at the corner, he found the source of the throng. He'd been right about a concert. One featuring a world-famous DJ had just ended in an opera house halfway down the block. People still spilled out of its doors, flowing in all directions, seemingly unaware of vehicle traffic on the streets.

The sounds of thousands of people talking all at the same time filled Dak's ears.

"I can't get out of here fast enough," he muttered as he stepped up onto the curb on the other side of the street.

His heart raced, even though he wasn't going that fast. The rapid beat had nothing to do with physical exertion.

It stemmed from the conversation he'd had with Lopez just before the man fell to his death. Dak felt no guilt over the killing. If anything, Lopez had done it to himself. If he'd only stopped running and told Dak what he wanted to know, the guy might still be alive.

The real source of Dak's worry was what Lopez had alluded to— that Tucker somehow knew where Nicole was. He picked up his speed. The sooner he got to the airport, the better.

Five more minutes passed with Dak skirting along the sidewalk, picking his way around the thinning herd of pedestrians. Many of them filtered into the cafés or bars lining the street, stopping in to get a late-night snack or a few drinks.

In a country where siestas were the norm, it wasn't unusual for some of the locals to stay up until the early morning hours. Dak had a few friends who lived like that, staying awake until three or four in the morning during a vacation.

Dak preferred not to tamper with his already sketchy sleep schedule and delicate circadian rhythms. It was hard enough as it was for him to get a decent amount of rest.

During his time in the military, he'd slept well enough. Part of that had been knowing that despite the imminent danger in the theater of war, he had brothers-in-arms to watch his back, always keeping a vigilant eye open for danger.

That security blanket burned like dry tinder when his team betrayed him in the Middle East, leaving him to die in a cave after they'd pilfered priceless treasures from it.

Ever since then, sleep had come at a premium for Dak. Most nights, he lay awake, fearful that every little sound was an intruder— a stealthy assassin come to take him out. Usually, fatigue eventually won out and pulled him into slumber, only for him to awaken at some unwelcome hour of the morning. Then falling back asleep proved nearly impossible.

Certain supplements had helped alleviate those problems in recent months, but there were still nights when things went bump, or scratch, or squeak, that roused him from his dreams and left him lying in bed, unable to tame the paranoia.

He looked back over his shoulder toward the general area where Lopez died. "That should be far enough for now," he said and immediately looked for a taxi while still walking away from the crowd outside the opera house. Hundreds of people were doing the same thing, hailing cabs or checking their rideshare apps to schedule a pickup.

Good night to be a driver, Dak thought, noting the row of cars lined up along the sidewalk. Patrons climbed in, the drivers drove off, and the next in line moved up to collect their passengers, as if orchestrated by some unseen conductor.

Dak kept walking toward the end of the line, then crossed the next street until there were only a few people loitering on the sidewalk. None of them seemed intent on finding a ride.

A couple of cabs sat near the corner, waiting their turn to move up in the line. Dak waved at the one in front, and the guy behind the wheel nodded.

"Skip the wait," Dak mumbled. "Amazing what the tiniest amount of effort can do."

He hurried over to the back passenger door and climbed in.

"Where to?" the driver asked in Spanish.

"Airport, please," Dak answered in English. He knew enough Spanish to be dangerous but figured if he responded to the guy's question in that language it might spark an entire conversation, which Dak may or may not have understood.

The driver nodded, turned on the meter, and pulled out into traffic. "Many people out tonight," he said, reverting to Dak's native tongue.

The slender man wore a lightweight linen shirt and brown trousers. His dark blond hair, pulled up into a tight bun, bounced with every bump the car's tires struck.

"I hear there was a concert," Dak offered, looking out the opposite window. To the untrained eye, he'd appear as any other passenger, merely gazing absently through the glass at nothing in particular. But Dak was hardly absent. He scanned the sidewalks for potential threats.

"Yes," the driver answered. "Famous DJ. Tickets sold out in minutes."

Dak accepted the response with a low hum. He doubted Lopez's men were after him. Not yet anyway. But there could be others. If Tucker had been here recently, it wasn't outside the realm of possibility that he may have left someone behind to keep a watch on things—just in case Dak happened to show up.

The driver turned left, and traffic opened up enough to hit the speed limit before stopping again at the next intersection.

Dak took the phone out of his pocket and looked up Will's last message. He read it again, then typed out a quick note to his friend and hit the Send arrow.

"Contact expired," it read.

The driver accelerated, but Dak kept his eyes on the phone screen. Within twenty seconds, three dots appeared next to the text bar.

In another five, Will's message popped up. "What happened? Can you talk?"

Dak smirked, looked up at the driver, and then tapped out his response. "You at the airport?"

He waited patiently until Will's answer came through. "On my way there now. I lost track of you at the club, then when the contact's associates started snooping around, I dipped. Just like you said to."

Dak nodded. He appreciated Will's ability to stick to a plan. Initially, Will had been stationed outside the club to cover Dak's exit, and to watch for trouble. But his instructions were clear—if he saw bouncers or bodyguards leave the building, looking confused or like they were searching for something, he should get out and return to the airport.

"We'll talk at the airport," Dak said in his message.

A few seconds later, "Ok" showed up on the screen, and he slid the phone back into his pocket.

"You travel light," the driver noticed.

He maneuvered the car through the thinning traffic and onto the freeway. Dak recalled the drive from the airport to this area and knew it was only another ten minutes. It may as well have been hours. Now, not only was Tucker after him, but the Spanish police might be too if anyone connected the dots.

He reminded himself that that was unlikely, and that the body still might be undiscovered in the alley.

"Just in town for a quick visit," Dak said, keeping his answer simple and obscure.

"For a friend or business?"

So much for being vague. "Business."

Dak knew what question was coming next.

"What kind of business are you in?" His eyes searched Dak's extremely casual attire. He probably also wondered why there was no briefcase, laptop bag, or messenger bag.

"I'm a consultant," Dak answered semi-honestly. He didn't feel like conjuring a lie for the stranger, but the guy was prying. The truth was, Dak's job really was much like consulting—except he often encountered people who wanted to kill him.

He hoped the driver wouldn't ask what variety of consulting, but he sensed that would be the follow-up question.

Before the man could say anything else, Dak felt the phone vibrate in his pocket. He twitched a quick frown at the notification, thinking he'd said enough to Will for his friend to know their next communication would be in person.

He pulled the device out again and looked at the pop-up on the screen. Dak didn't recognize the number. The driver must have noticed the bright glow of the phone in the back seat and decided not to press his line of questions any further. At least the man was polite. Dak had to give him that.

Dak tapped on the message, and it opened in the app. Only two words, "Call me," filled the line.

Suspicion shrouded Dak like a gathering storm. He knew, of course, about phishing scams and other such methods digital grifters used to hack people's devices and their accounts. This number was an international one, though he couldn't recall which country code it applied to.

Then again, he'd become accustomed to cloak-and-dagger-style communications over the years. Dealing with shady characters ranging from former mob bosses to underground casino owners, cartel thugs, and even Russian military had somewhat blunted what little shock may have lingered in the innocent recesses of his mind.

He hesitated—thumbs hovering over the screen as he deliberated whether or not to respond.

Then he tapped on the keys and sent the message. "Who is this?"

The driver sped past a cargo van on the right, then merged back into the lane. Up ahead, Dak saw the airport off to the left. Airplane lights blinked in the air in the distance as the aircraft lined up for landing.

He waited until he felt the phone vibrate again, then looked down at the screen. "I have something that belongs to you."

That's cryptic. The thought did little to shake a growing sense of concern in Dak's chest. He decided to send one more text to feel out the other person. "I don't have much in the way of possessions. Could you be more specific?"

The cab driver turned on his blinker and exited the freeway. Dak barely noticed. His attention was on the phone in his hand.

"No." The one-word answer surprised him.

He sighed. "Fine."

Dak looked out the window at the neighborhood surrounding the car. Apartment buildings lined the streets in every direction. He'd forgotten how huge Madrid was. Dak had never visited the city before, though he'd been to Spain on a few occasions with Nicole.

The thought of her pricked his heart like a needle. With a sigh, he tapped on the number at the top of the screen and waited as the device connected.

He put it to his ear and listened. One ring. Two. Then the ringing stopped.

Dak waited, but the person on the other end of the line didn't say anything. He didn't even hear them breathing.

"Hello?" Dak said, breaking the silence after a few seconds. "Who is this?"

A deep inhale cut through the speaker. Then Dak heard a voice he hadn't expected, and loathed with every fiber of his being.

"Hello, Dak," Cameron Tucker answered. "It's so good to hear your voice again."

3

Dak's jaw tightened on its own as a tidal wave of emotions ripped through his mind. His muscles tensed as if a threat followed them on the road, ready to pounce the second he set foot on the curb.

The fight-or-flight instinct was something he'd learned to control over the years. It had served him well in many instances. In others, it had caused undue anxiety.

Right now, that instinct threatened to break loose and run wild like a deranged animal, along with a million things Dak wanted to say to his former commanding officer. He'd practiced many of them in his head, and occasionally out loud when he was in a quiet space and thinking into the future.

Over the course of his career in the military, and since, Dak had killed people. The first part for business, the second part for... well, personal business.

But he'd never wanted to. *Not really.*

In the case of his mutinous team, he'd felt a certain level of satisfaction in ridding the world of bad eggs. But only because justice had been done. He was big on justice and had tried to live his life according to an honorable creed.

"Cat got your tongue, Dak?" Tucker teased. "I expected you to at least offer up some wisecrack like you used to do when we were in the Middle East."

The mere mention of that place brought back an onslaught of memories Dak would rather not have relived. He'd handled it like the pro he was, but there were nights—those precious few and far between ones when he achieved deep, dream-filled sleep—when visions of the cave returned, visions of his team abandoning him, of the narrow escape, and those visions would pummel his brain.

He felt himself fortunate not to have to endure the seemingly never-ending nightmare of PTSD. He'd known a few guys who weren't so lucky, and were trying everything in their power to salve those wounds. He didn't know why the events of his past failed to haunt him in the same way, but those rare dreams of the events in the Middle East, and the hunt for his former friends, did torture him from time to time.

"I'm not sorry to disappoint you," Dak replied. Even the cab driver picked up on the change of tone. Dak's voice carried a sinister quality to it—a darkness that cast shadows through the car interior.

"There he is!" Tucker boomed with laughter. "That's the wise guy I used to know." The laughter slowed, and he sighed. "Ah. Dak. You always made me laugh. You ever think you missed your calling as a comedian?"

Dak didn't feel like responding. He realized he was squeezing the phone in his hand, subconsciously wishing it was Tucker's neck.

"No?" Tucker pressed. "Eh. Maybe you're right. Seems like those guys who do the observational comedy do better anyway. The ones who always say you ever notice blah blah blah?"

"Tell you what, Colonel," Dak said, spitting out Tucker's title with a pile of disdain, "why don't you meet me, and we can talk about all the comedy you want."

Tucker chuckled, but the darkness in Dak's tone stretched across the miles separating them and caused the colonel to hesitate.

He inhaled audibly, and when he spoke, his voice also took on a sinister quality. "I'm sure you'd like that, Dak."

"Yeah." Dak lowered the phone to just below his chin and quickly minimized the call so he could access the text message app. He found the last note from Will and sent a rapid message. *I need you to track this number. Fast.*

He entered the number from the call's ID and sent the note.

Tucker didn't miss a beat. "None of this would have happened if you'd just played ball, Dak. We'd all be rich. Your buddies would still be alive. And you wouldn't be running from shadows."

The driver hung a left at the next light. The airport appeared through the windshield.

"Who said I'm running?" The cab driver's eyes flashed a quick look at Dak in the rearview mirror. A flicker of fear streaked them.

An uneasy laugh hiccupped through the earpiece. "Yeah, well, I figured you'd end up there in Madrid sooner or later."

Dak wasn't entirely surprised the man knew where he was. In some ways, he'd assumed it. But it still unsettled him, and his skin crawled at the statement.

"Not creepy at all," Dak joked, partially to calm his nerves.

"Again with the wit."

"What do you want, Cam?"

"And always direct. I liked that about you, Dak. I really did."

"I don't care what you like or don't like about me, Cam." He knew using the shortened version of the man's first name irritated Tucker. He'd heard what happened when another officer of lower rank thought he could use it due to a misperceived friendship. That guy ended up in some far-flung, barren station for the rest of his deployment.

"You really should show more respect to your superiors, Dak. It's bad form to call me by my first name."

Dak sensed the man's clenched jaw through the statement. He could feel the colonel's irritation swelling with every breath.

"I'll be sure to do that whenever I encounter a superior."

Tucker sighed, forcing himself not to fall into the trap of playing Dak's game. The truth was, Dak wanted to know where Tucker was, and if he could keep the man on the line long enough, Will might just be able to triangulate his exact location.

Dak held the phone away from his face for a second to see if Will had sent a response. He had. It simply read, "On it."

Pressing the phone back against his ear, Dak stared out the windshield at the airport ahead.

"Funny you should ask what I want," Tucker drawled.

"Oh? And why's that?"

"Because I have something *you* want."

That was unlikely. Dak didn't want much in life anymore, except to be left alone. But the statement also roused a terrifying suspicion, one he absolutely would not voice.

"What would that be?" Dak asked, keeping the question simple while he prayed internally the answer would be something trivial.

"Do you really want me to say it, Dak? Is that really necessary?"

Dak swallowed, choking back rising fears. "Stop playing games with me, Tucker. Meet me like a man, and let's settle this once and for all. The last time I saw you, you were playing possum on the ground in the middle of a firefight. If you have a shred of honor left in you, you'll face me. And you'll do it alone."

Tucker laughed. It was a sharp, sickly sound that would have made a hardened criminal shudder. "I'm a survivor, Dak. Cemeteries are filled with the honorable and brave. I got no interest in being in the ground."

"So, you admit you're the one who's inferior here."

"No," Tucker snapped, his momentary good mood gone. "I just don't trust you. I show up some random place to duke it out with you, and one of your little cronies takes me out with a sniper round."

"You know that's not how it would be. You're just afraid."

"Heh. Maybe I am, Dak. Maybe I am. But never underestimate old-man strength. It's a real thing."

Tucker was far from old. The man was in his mid-fifties if Dak recalled correctly, and in great shape. That said, in a fistfight, he was no match for Dak Harper.

"You wanted to know what I have that you want so badly," Tucker went on. "I would think it obvious by now."

"Enlighten me."

The cab driver slowed down as the car approached the terminal ahead.

"Sounds like you're going somewhere. You're in a car."

"Deduced that all by yourself? I wasn't trying to hide it."

"No. I didn't think you were. And why would you? After you killed Lopez, I imagine you want to get out of Spain as quickly as possible. You and your friend."

How had he known about Lopez? Had they already found the body? And my friend? Did he know about Will being there, too? And if so, how?

"Oh, I'm sure you're wondering how I know all that, aren't you? I can tell from the stupefied lack of a response. By the way, speaking of your friend, seems like he's trying to triangulate my location. You can text him back and tell him that's not necessary. I'm happy to tell you where I am, seeing as I won't be here much longer anyway. You're welcome to come and take a look, though. I suspect you will."

Dak's jaw clenched so hard he could have cracked a walnut with his teeth.

The cab driver pulled up to the curb and slowly brought the car to a stop. He looked back at Dak and politely pointed to the amount shown on his fare screen.

Dak nodded and fished the wallet from his pocket, pulled out the amount the man required plus a little extra for a tip, then passed it to him with a thankful nod.

The driver quickly counted the money and offered a grateful, and surprised, smile at Dak for the tip.

Dak opened the door and stepped out onto the curb to the sounds of car engines and jets taxiing on the runways.

He shut the door and waved to the driver to signal that the man could leave and watched as the car drove away.

Standing there in front of the airport, Dak looked around, half lost in a vortex of thoughts.

"At the airport already?" Tucker surmised. "That was quick. You really do want to get out of Spain."

"No sense in sticking around if you're not here," Dak countered. "Now, you were about to tell me where you are so I can come and beat you to a pulp for trying to kill me."

"Oh, Dak," Tucker laughed. "You are an interesting one. I suppose I could do the whole two-birds-with-one-stone in my answer."

"Come again?"

"It's simple, really. Where I am will tell you what I have that you want."

"I'm waiting."

Another cab pulled up to the curb, and Dak stepped to the side to allow the driver to make the drop-off. A brunette woman in gray leggings and a white designer T-shirt climbed out, followed by a man in tapered soccer warm-up pants and a flashy leather jacket.

"I would have thought you'd guessed it by now, Dak. I'm in Istanbul."

4

It felt like someone had shoved a broadsword down Dak's throat when he heard the words come from Tucker's mouth.

He tried to play it off, despite the heart-wrenching fear squeezing his chest and gut. "Istanbul? What made you go there? In the mood for some baklava? I gotta be honest. I prefer Greece's."

Tucker didn't respond.

Dak waited a few breaths.

"Cam?"

Still nothing.

Dak checked the phone. A faint reflection of his face stared back at him from the dark screen. He touched the glass, and his fears skyrocketed. The call had ended.

He tapped on the recent calls—about to call Tucker back, when the device vibrated and cut him off. The preview on the screen was from the same number as before.

Dak hesitantly touched the glass, and the new message appeared. "You will have one week to get me what I want. Don't call me unless I tell you to."

Dak's breath quickened, and soon it was at the rate of someone who'd just run a quarter mile.

He stood there panting and felt a wave of anxiety crash over him. A minute passed before he realized it, then his phone buzzed again.

"In case you couldn't put two and two together, here's proof. I will send you further instructions tomorrow morning at eight, Istanbul time. One week to get me what I want. Or she dies."

An image appeared below the text. And it confirmed every one of Dak's worst possible fears.

Nicole was bound with her wrists behind her back and duct tape over her mouth.

"See you soon," a new message read beneath the picture.

In that instant, Dak felt more pain and more rage than he'd ever felt in his life. His instincts begged him to hit something—the wall of the terminal, a silver trash can standing near one of the columns, the taxi still idling a few feet away.

None of those things would serve any useful purpose and would either break one of his bones or raise unwanted attention—the last thing a guy trying to flee the country needed.

Out of sheer impulse, he tapped the number attached to the message and pressed the phone against his ear. It only rang once before it went to an automated message telling him the user of that device had not set up a voice mail yet.

Dak grimaced, ended the call, then tried again with the same result.

After his second attempt, it vibrated, and another message glared at him from the screen.

"Temper, temper, Dak. I said I will send you instructions tomorrow morning. Don't call me again."

A feeling Dak was unaccustomed to trickled through his entire body. And there was nothing he could do to stop it.

He was utterly helpless.

For—he checked his watch—the next nine hours, he was unable to do anything to change the situation. For nine hours, and probably more from the sounds of it, Nicole was the prisoner of the biggest monster Dak knew. Worst of all? The proverbial clock was now ticking. He'd have to play this according to Tucker's timetable.

He shuddered to think of what Tucker might do to her, and that thought threw jet fuel onto the already raging fire in his mind.

Dak paced back and forth on the sidewalk near the terminal entrance. Two men behind a curbside check-in counter watched him with curious fascination—as they would a caged bull stomping around in its corral before a rodeo.

Thinking about Nicole being Tucker's prisoner wasn't doing any good. That didn't halt the visuals from flooding his mind's eye. His unbridled imagination seemed to have a will of its own, and he desperately tried to rope it in.

Think about the facts, he thought as he pivoted at the end of the curb and stalked back the way he had come. *Tucker has Nicole. For the next nine hours or so, there's nothing I can do about it. So, what can I do?*

A single idea dangled in front of him like a sign from above. Literally.

The sign for the entrance to the Turkish Airlines check-in counters hung from the airport overhang a hundred feet away.

Without hesitation or even thinking, Dak marched toward the entrance and the bright red-and-white sign above it. He gripped his phone in his right hand as he moved, passing strangers on the curb as they exited their vehicles and unloaded luggage for their journeys.

He tapped the screen on the device and pulled up Will's last message. Focusing on the phone, he nearly bumped into a middle-aged couple with University of Miami Ohio sweatshirts on as they dragged bags out of a shiny new sedan.

With a tap of the finger, the phone dialed Will's number as Dak raised the device to his ear in time to catch the first ring.

Will answered after two.

"Hey, man. Did you make it to the airport?"

"Yeah," Dak said, still storming down the sidewalk, his eyes firmly locked on the new destination.

"You okay? You sound like you're out of breath. And like you're moving in a—"

"I need to get to Istanbul," Dak interrupted. "Tonight, Will."

"Um... what? I thought the plan was—"

"The plan changed. Tucker has Nicole."

"What? How do you—"

Dak interrupted a third time.

"Where are you?"

"At the lockers. Where we left our gear." Will sounded at a loss.

Dak had to push through his concerns and the paranoid thoughts about Nicole. Will didn't know anything about it, about the messages or the call from Tucker.

"Sorry to come out of left field with this," Dak offered. "I know we had a plan."

"You don't have to apologize to me, man. Plans are fluid. Only thing we can do is adapt."

"I'll meet you at the lockers. When I get there, I'll explain what's going on." He stopped under the Turkish Airlines sign and looked inside. The line at the check-in counter wasn't too bad. Only six people waited, though they were checking bags. Dak needed two tickets, and had a bad feeling it was way too short notice to get them.

"Was there something else you were going to say?" Will asked.

"No. Just thinking. I'm going to check the ticket situation, then meet you at the lockers."

"You think they'll have any tickets left?"

"I doubt it," Dak said honestly. "But I have to try. See you in a few. Grab my bag if you don't mind."

"Already doin' it, my friend."

"Thanks, Will."

He ended the call before he could hear Will finish saying "You're welcome."

Dak walked through the automatic doors to the sound of a swoosh and a rush of cool air wrapping around him as he entered the airport terminal.

He hurried over to the line just as a couple of Japanese travelers finished checking in and stepped out of the way for the next passengers.

Dak wished he could hurry them along, or break in front, but he knew that wasn't going to happen. He'd be escorted out of the building—or worse, arrested for causing trouble in an airport.

He looked back over his shoulder and found a self-check-in kiosk and considered getting out of line to use one, when he remembered what year it was.

"What am I doing?" he asked himself. "This isn't the 1990s."

He took out his phone and opened the airline's website. Dak preferred to go direct with airlines and hotels when booking travel accommodations. There had been a few negative guest experiences when he used a third-party booking app, and after the second time decided he'd never do that again.

At the counter, a mom and dad with their kid and multiple bags seemed to be having a difficult time with their check-in. They were American from what Dak could gather—accents from the Northeast, it sounded like. Their lengthy stay at the counter only reaffirmed Dak's decision to use his phone to try to find a flight.

He entered the date and waited—fully prepared to see an Unavailable message pop up on the screen.

To his surprise, two flights appeared. One was set to take off in an hour. The other at six the next morning.

Dak couldn't risk taking the early morning flight. Even if the only seats available on the sooner one were in first class.

He tapped on two of the three remaining seats left for purchase, entered in the details for him and Will, and bought the tickets.

Two more passengers entered the line behind Dak, and he quickly excused himself and stepped past them, leaving the queue.

He checked his phone and added the boarding passes to his wallet, then looked up at the nearest sign to recalibrate where he was in the airport. He recognized some of it from before and cut to the left, passing between a collection of shops and newsstands.

It was the first time he'd been in this airport, and found it a little confusing at first glance.

Dak had done everything he could to protect Nicole. He'd always hoped that the simple fact she worked in Istanbul, and had never had a lot of public interaction with him, might keep her off Tucker's radar.

But the colonel had learned about her somehow. There was no point in fretting over how it happened. Dak couldn't change the past —no matter how much he wanted to.

He walked by a few food stands where the smell of bread, pastries, and meats wafted through the air. Dak's stomach grumbled, but he had no intention of eating. He could think of only one thing, no matter what his stomach was thinking about.

He found the locker area and his friend standing out front holding a pair of book bags. Dak thought it better not to travel with their usual rucksacks, as he'd drawn unwanted attention a few times with his—the most recent in a bar, of all places, where the bouncer told him no military-style bags were allowed.

The reasoning had escaped him, though he figured the only explanation could be that security had connected those kinds of bags with potential threats.

Either way, ordinary book bags would do for their purposes. It wasn't like they were trying to smuggle a bunch of guns and ordnance into Turkey.

Dak wore a grim expression on his face as he approached Will. It wasn't a frown, but he wasn't smiling either.

Will held out Dak's bag as he approached.

"Thanks," Dak said, snatching it and slinging it over his right shoulder the way the cool kids in the 1990s had. He wished he could chuckle at the second '90s thought he'd had in the last ten minutes, but only one thing was on his mind. And it wasn't funny.

"What's going on?" Will asked, hurrying to catch up as Dak spun around and started speed walking toward a security gate off to the right.

"I got us two first-class seats on the next flight to Istanbul," Dak explained, barely looking over his shoulder as Will pulled up next to him.

"You're sure he has her?"

"I'm sure. I saw."

"If that's true, you realize we're walking into a trap by going there —assuming you're planning on going to Nicole's place."

"I know. But I can't do nothing."

"Look, Dak. I can only imagine what you're feeling right now. But a flight to Istanbul from here is—"

"Four hours. I know." Dak proceeded through the precheck queue and walked up to the stopping point to wait for the security person to call him forward.

"I'm just saying, by the time we get there, they'll be long gone."

"I've thought of that, Will," Dak said. He stepped forward when the person behind the computer motioned for him.

Dak took out his phone and opened the boarding passes and handed his passport to the uniformed fifty-something man perched on a stool. The guy wrinkled his nose, which twisted the thick, black broom of a mustache under his nostrils. He adjusted the round wire-frame glasses on his nose with a thick finger, and leaned forward as Dak scanned the two boarding passes.

"He's with me," Dak said, jerking a thumb at his friend by his side.

Will passed his ID over the counter to the man as well.

The man studied the two passports, checked the screen, then gave them both a nod, and instructing them to proceed to the next checkpoint.

"What's the plan?" Will pressed.

Dak took his bag and placed it in a plastic bin to send through the scanners. He looked over at Will as his friend set his bag into a similar bin.

"I don't know yet. But we have four hours to figure that out."

5

ISTANBUL

Despite the amenities—free drinks, good food, and the most comfortable airplane seat he'd ever been in—Dak couldn't relax for what felt like the longest four hours of his life.

Even Will had trouble resting, but he eventually passed out in the luxurious seat—leaving Dak alone with his own thoughts.

He must have run through a million scenarios before the jet touched down in Turkey, and a few thousand more as he and Will made their way out of the terminal and to the rental car counter.

They said little until they were in the car and driving away from the airport. The waxing moon hung low on the horizon, but sunrise was still a few hours away. Seeing Earth's lone satellite only served to sap Dak's energy further.

He needed to sleep. But how could he slumber when Nicole was being held by that monster? Dak could think of nothing else save the myriad things he wanted to do to Tucker if—no, when—he got his hands on him.

"You okay?" Will asked as he steered the car out of the airport parking lot. He already knew the answer, but he still had to ask. That's what friends did for each other. Even when they knew what was coming.

"Nah, man. I'm pretty far from okay. But you know that."

"I know."

Will didn't say anything for another minute as he navigated the streets, following the GPS directions with the voice turned down so he and Dak could hear each other.

"What's the plan?" He asked the question, not sure his friend had an answer, though he felt fairly certain Dak had been mulling over some ideas on the flight.

"We're going to her apartment. And before you tell me they'll be gone, I know that. I still have to go there. Maybe she left a clue. Or maybe he did by accident."

"Clue?"

"Where they might be going next."

Will decided not to argue the point, even though he didn't think there was a chance in Hades that was possible. He nodded.

"Understood. Any ideas what we might be looking for?"

Dak kept staring blankly out the windshield. His face had lost most of its color, and dark circles hung under his eyes like a pair of shadows mirroring the moon. He barely noticed the city passing by outside. He'd seen it dozens of times on his visits here, and usually he took in the sights even if they weren't new to him. He loved this city for all its history, culture, food, and the people.

Now, it felt like he was riding into a tomb. All the colorful lights and smells wouldn't shake the despair in his heart.

"No," Dak answered finally, realizing his friend had asked a question. "I don't have any idea what I'm looking for. I'm just hoping there's something."

Will let out a long sigh. "We both know this is probably an ambush. So, I suggest we split up. Let me cover your back from outside the building in case Tucker has a shooter on a rooftop somewhere."

Dak only made a slight humming sound, as if to say "Who cares at this point? Let him kill me."

"Hey, man. You gotta shake this off. You hear me? Nicole is still out there. And we're going to get her back. Okay? So, snap out of it."

Dak's teeth ground together. The muscles in his jaw tightened, but he knew his friend was right. Moping, pensively stewing over what he'd lost before it was really gone, was not how he would rescue Nicole. And it wasn't how he normally operated.

"Good idea on the watching-my-six idea," Dak offered. "You're right. We're walking right into an ambush. Your guy is good for a couple of guns, yeah?" He looked over at Will, who glanced across his shoulder at Dak and first replied with a mischievous smirk.

"Oh yeah. He's got us covered."

"When are we meeting him?"

Will twitched his nose and scratched the back of his scalp.

"What?" Dak insisted.

"He said he can meet us at nine."

Dak glanced at the clock, then stared at his friend. "That's too late, Will. What, is one of your gunrunning buddies keeping banker's hours now?"

Will chuckled, but the sound was uneasy—a feeble attempt to play off what he knew would be a tense conversation. The pale-yellow streetlights coursed across his dark brown skin in waves with every post they passed. He didn't answer immediately, knowing his friend wouldn't like the response.

"That's when he said he could meet us. It's the best I could do."

Dak shook his head. "No. Just head to the apartment. We'll figure it out from there."

"Unarmed? Are you nuts? Dak, you're not thinking straight. You already said you know this is probably a trap. We'll be going into an ambush naked."

"I realize that," Dak snapped. "But I can't sit around waiting for three hours for some local arms dealer to open his shop. Tucker has Nicole. And I have to get her back."

Will kept quiet for a few tense moments. He knew Dak wasn't thinking straight, which was out of character for his friend. Dak always kept his cool, even under the direst of circumstances. But this... this was different.

Will was fully aware of how much Dak truly loved Nicole, and why he'd gone to such lengths to keep her safe—even if it meant he couldn't see her. Dak's angry response didn't have anything to do with Will. It was entirely fueled by illogical emotion—which was the kind that almost always resulted in bad decisions.

But what could he do? Dak was dead set on going straight to the apartment. Telling him it was a bad idea wouldn't change Dak's mind. Arguing wouldn't do any good.

Will let out a long breath, blowing air through his lips at a low whistle. "Okay, Dak. We'll go to the apartment. But I don't think it's a good idea. I just want to be on record saying that."

"Noted."

Dak's grim tone ended the conversation.

The rest of the drive went by in tense silence. Will kept an eye on the navigation screen, following the directions until they arrived at Nicole's apartment building.

Will parked the vehicle across the street in front of a coffee shop. He didn't know how many times Dak had sat there, watching her building from a corner to make sure she was safe, or to simply look at her from afar—wishing he could smell her perfume, feel her soft skin, stare into her eyes from inches away.

Dak caught himself stealing a short stare at the coffee house. A light glowed somewhere inside, behind the barista counter. It was in the kitchen, if memory served correctly. For a moment, the smells of fresh-baked pastries, desserts, and hot coffee caressed his thoughts. He liked that coffee shop, even if it seemed like a place that teetered on the boundary between his happiest desires and a life lived on the run.

A random car drove by—one of the few they'd seen on the street at this hour. That would change soon as people woke up and started getting ready for the day, eventually spilling onto the sidewalks and asphalt on their way to jobs throughout the city.

Dak envied them in their comfort. Most of them lived unremark-able lives, certainly, but there was something appealing about that. Simply going to work, doing the tasks required, collecting a paycheck, saving for retirement, all sounded delightfully boring in many ways. But that life was not his destiny. At least not in the near future. Maybe ever.

He knew one thing to be true: As long as Tucker was alive, he wouldn't know peace. That single thought had tortured Dak for the last few years, stalking him everywhere like an insidious shadow, always lurking nearby.

"This the place?" Will asked, as if he needed to.

"Yeah," Dak said with a nod. "This is it."

Will studied the entrance to the apartment building. There was nothing special about it. The place looked like most of the others around it, though there were a few modern refurbishments such as the metal awning hanging over the doorway and a new brushed metal sign fixed to the wall that announced the structure's name.

"You sure you want to do this?" Will asked. "Maybe I should go in first."

"No," Dak rejected. "I'll go. You stay out here and watch for trouble."

"Okay, Dak. Whatever you say."

Dak opened the car door and unceremoniously stepped out onto the curb. A few delivery trucks rumbled by, leaving Turkey's signature diesel exhaust in their wake.

After looking both directions, Dak trotted across the street and stopped at the door. He stared at the call box for a few seconds, remembering the last time he'd used it to gain entry. He knew the code to get in, of course. He'd memorized it while watching Nicole use it even before she'd given it to him. But he always thought it polite to "knock" and had never just assumed it was okay to barge in unexpected.

Now, however, he had no choice.

Dak quickly typed in the code and heard the door buzz then click as it unlocked. He quickly pulled it open and stepped inside without so much as a backward glance across the street at his friend in the rental car.

Across the lobby, the elevators loomed, their metallic surfaces both tempting and warning him at the same time.

He checked his watch, noting he still had a few hours before Tucker said he'd contact him. Dak had no delusions about Tucker still being in the building—no fantasies of rushing in to kill the man who had betrayed him and kidnapped the love of his life.

Tucker was gone. Dak knew he wasn't stupid enough to stick around here. Still, Dak wished he had a weapon of some kind. Even a knife was better than nothing.

During his time in the military, he'd been trained in hand-to-hand combat, like everyone else. But something most civilians didn't know was that the core training taught warriors how to defeat an enemy with the purpose of getting back to their weapon to finish the job.

Dak had learned many of his other skills in private sessions with instructors teaching him various martial arts that weren't taught in the military. As a member of Delta Force, his instruction had been more intense, and when combined with the range of his other skills, Dak made for an extremely formidable opponent. That said, he'd still prefer to have a firearm—especially walking into what he was sure to be an ambush.

He walked across the lobby and pulled open the door to the stairs, only cracking it at first to make sure no one was waiting on the other side. The smell of concrete and steel mingled with a scent of vanilla and cinnamon the apartment complex must have piped into the lobby—a subtle welcome for those who lived there, or a lure to those who might consider moving in.

An empty stairwell greeted him, and he quickly stepped inside and eased the door shut behind without so much as a click.

If there were men waiting for him at the top, he didn't feel like giving them a heads-up.

Dak navigated his way up the stairs, moving so quietly that not even the soles of his shoes made the slightest sound.

He stopped at the door leading onto Nicole's floor, and paused for a second. He expected Tucker's men to be stationed just beyond the doorway, guarding either side of it. If that were the case, they'd attack the second he set foot on the carpet.

The door opened outward into the stairwell, as Dak assumed the fire code dictated. That eliminated the possibility of shoving it open and effectively blocking one of the would-be assassins, leaving him a split second to take down the other.

This way, however, he could invite anyone on the other side in and take them out on his own terms.

The decision made, Dak turned the latch on the door and pulled it gently toward him. Then he released it and let the door close, leaving it slightly ajar without the bolt catching.

He stepped back to the left side into the corner and waited. Nothing happened. Relief tempted him to believe he'd been wrong in assuming there would be men waiting for him at the entrance onto the floor.

That temptation evaporated in an instant as he saw the door budge a few millimeters outward. Dak didn't breathe. He squeezed back the instinct to swallow, as even that might create enough sound to give away his position.

The door inched open a little more, and through the crack Dak saw part of the killer's clothes—a black jacket and pants. *Always in black, these guys,* he thought.

Then, he made his move.

6

Dak barged into the door with his left shoulder, crushing the barrier against the man hovering over the threshold. The door stopped with a sudden thud, and a crunch. The killer shouted at the unexpected pain. Dak knew without looking he'd probably broken the man's forearm. That belief strengthened when the pistol that had been in his hand dropped to the ground with a clatter.

Just to make sure, Dak pulled back the door and shoved it forward again, this time hitting the man's shoulder. The blow knocked the assailant into the corridor. Without wasting a second, Dak spun around into the open door—thinking he'd finish the job, but came face to face with a second assassin who stepped in to block the way.

The guy quickly raised his pistol to finish the job.

Dak reacted like a lightning strike. He ducked right while swiping his right hand across in front of the man, knocking the weapon out of harm's way, just as the suppressor muzzle spit a puff of smoke. The round fired down the stairwell, ricocheting away from the target.

The killer tried to force the gun barrel back at his original target while Dak resisted—locking the two men in a battle of muscle and leverage. The gunman strained, and his tanned face darkened, but with slightly more muscle mass than Dak, he started winning the battle.

Dak grunted and clenched his jaw—his face burning red hot as he fought for his life. The barrel began twisting toward him again, and in seconds the muzzle would be in position to put a bullet through his face.

In a last, desperate counterattack, Dak gave up on the fight for the gun, and instead dropped down, swinging his right foot hard at the gunman's left knee. Dak's heel collided with the joint, and a terrible pop reverberated from within as the knee dislocated along with what Dak was certain were a few torn ligaments.

The assassin fell to the other knee, reactively clutching at the injured one with his left hand.

Now Dak had the advantage, and he torqued the man's gun hand around until the muzzle wavered under his chin. Then Dak squeezed the man's trigger finger.

The round blew through the guy's neck, and he fell prostrate onto the floor. As he collapsed, Dak freed the pistol from him, scooped up the other from the concrete landing, and stepped into the corridor, where the first assassin had scrambled to recover.

He pulled a secondary weapon—a subcompact 9 mm with a single-stack magazine—from inside his pants on the right hip. Dak was already aimed at his enemy, though, and fired two quick shots into the man's chest, and a third through the bridge of his nose.

The guy fell onto his back, splayed out on the carpet.

Dak took two seconds to catch his breath and looked down the hallway toward Nicole's apartment, then back to the body. There was nothing he could do about the bloodstains on the wall and carpet, but he could at least hide the dead man in the stairwell so none of the residents would find it—particularly a younger one. The grisly look of death on the man's face would permanently imprint on a child's mind, and Dak didn't want that on his long list of regrets.

He stuffed the two pistols in the back of his pants, tightened the black belt around his waist, and grabbed the body by the ankles. It only took thirty seconds to drag the assassin through the door and into the stairwell where the other dead man lay in a pool of dark crimson.

Dak unceremoniously dumped the body next to the other and hurried back through the door, hoping no one felt ambitious enough to take the stairs at this hour—but fairly certain that would happen within the next ninety minutes. People would be waking up, getting ready for—he stopped that thought in its tracks when he remembered it was a weekend.

That relaxed him momentarily, but he shook off the calm and replaced it with focused determination as he stormed down the corridor to Nicole's apartment.

He slowed down just before he reached the entrance in case anyone was inside waiting for him—no need to let the sound of footsteps give them the heads-up.

Dak drew one of the pistols from his belt and used his left hand to test the latch. He tugged it down and found it to be unlocked.

Nicole never left her door unlocked, even if she knew he was coming to visit—which hadn't been in a long time. Far too long.

He shook off the memories again. Those wouldn't help him right now. Quite the opposite.

Dak finished pulling the latch down, took a deep breath, and kicked the door open. He rushed through and immediately fired the pistol at an ambusher standing in the kitchen, leaning up against the counter.

The man looked like he'd been eating a handful of nuts, unsuspecting of the sudden attack.

His reward was two rounds in the chest and one through the left eye. A second killer waited in the living room, sitting on the couch with his phone in his hand.

The second Dak burst in, the man snapped out of his digitally-induced trance and stood while his partner was gunned down before he could even attempt to defend himself. Dak saw the guy in the living room at the same instant he spotted the one in the kitchen, but took the closer target first, then redirected his aim at the man who desperately reached for his weapon sitting on the coffee table.

"Don't!" Dak barked.

The assassin paused, hovering over the table in an awkward pose with his arm extended, looming several inches above his pistol.

"If you try to grab your gun, you will die just like your pal back here," Dak said, flicking his head toward the dead man slumped against the cabinets beneath the counter.

The killer said nothing, simply staring back at Dak with dark brown eyes. A shark's eyes. A monster's eyes. The man's naturally bushy eyebrows contrasted with his close-cropped hair, lending him the hair of a wild animal trying its best to appear human.

"Or," Dak continued, "you can sit down, and we can have a conversation. The choice is yours."

Dak had no intention of letting him live, not longer than five minutes into the future, anyway.

"Where is Tucker?"

The interloper swallowed, contemplating his options. Dak saw he was calculating whether or not he could grab his pistol and aim it fast enough to prevent his own demise, but they both knew that reality was far-fetched. Like grasping for quarters in a pile of pennies.

Dak's patience already teetered on the thinnest of edges, and with every fraction of a second that passed, he grew weary of waiting for this guy to make up his mind. So, he twisted the sights ever so slightly on his weapon and shot the guy in the hip.

The impact drove the assailant back onto his tail, twisting in the process so that he fell onto the couch like a client ready to tell their shrink about all their baggage. Except this client was bleeding, and Dak wasn't interested in how the guy hadn't been hugged enough as a child.

The man howled in agony, clutching the bleeding joint with both hands while he unleashed a slur of what Dak felt certain were French obscenities.

Dak stepped across the room in three gaping strides, keeping his pistol trained on the man's head as he rolled back and forth on the couch.

"You're staining the sofa," he said, as if that was his greatest concern.

Splotches of red appeared in several places, and for a second, the guy actually checked before he realized the American was messing with him.

"Now. Be a good boy, and tell me where Tucker is." Dak tensed his finger on the trigger and let the guy see him do it.

"I don't know," the assassin confessed without a lie in his eyes. "He just told us to wait here for you. He didn't say where he was going." His French accent betrayed the man's origin.

Dak wondered what his previous life might have entailed—French military? Police? Perhaps even a career in Interpol gone horribly wrong?

None of that really mattered. He was going to kill the guy anyway. But old habits died slow, agonizing deaths. Part of his process was to always know as much about an enemy as possible, which included a rapid assessment of them in times such as this.

"Why should I let you live?" Dak asked. "If you don't have information about Tucker's whereabouts, you're of no use to me."

"No. Please. Wait. I can help you."

"How?"

The man hesitated, but his eyes gave away the play. They twitched to his left, ever so slightly, toward Nicole's open bedroom door.

Dak stepped back and ducked to the right just as another gunman emerged through the doorway.

The man fired a pistol but hadn't had time to aim and was clearly hoping the element of surprise would throw off his target enough to buy him precious seconds. That hope died with him as Dak returned four rounds—one in the chest, one in the neck, and one through the right shoulder as he twisted from the force of each impact.

He stumbled back against the corner, knocking over the flatscreen on an entertainment cabinet in the process, and feebly tried to raise his weapon for one last, desperate attempt at killing their mark.

Dak shook his head and shot him in the forehead while the Frenchman to his left watched in rapt horror.

The second the bedroom shooter went limp, Dak turned to the guy bleeding on the couch, who'd been gradually moving his hand toward his gun.

When he realized he'd been too slow, he begged. "No. Please. I can—"

A click from the pistol in Dak's hands cut his voice in midsentence, and the man fell still.

"I think I've had enough of your help," Dak said coldly.

But Dak didn't stop there. He refused to allow the temptation to relax settle into his mind. There could still be others.

He gave a quick look into the hallway powder room but found it empty, then carefully entered the bedroom, the pistol in his hands leading the way. He swept left, then right, checking every corner. Then he pushed ahead toward the master bathroom.

The door hung wide open, and the lights burned bright above the vanity and its twin bowl-shaped sinks.

The bathroom, like the master bedroom, offered nothing but vacant space and terrible silence.

Dak would have done anything to hear Nicole's laugh in that moment, to feel her wrap her arms around his waist and hug him from behind. He faced a million regrets for not protecting her better, and questioned if he'd done the right thing by leaving her here to live her life in Istanbul alone.

He shook all of it off. The office she'd created out of the spare bedroom still needed to be checked.

Dak turned and walked through the door and into the living room, crossed it in a couple of strides, and entered the spare room where Nicole worked in the evenings or on days she decided not to go to the office.

It was one of the perks of her line of work—being able to work remotely much of the time.

Being in the cybersecurity sector now, all she really needed was a laptop and an internet connection to perform her tasks. Dak had

dreamed of them moving somewhere warm with a beach view and
no one to bother them.

A scent of lilac and rose tickled his nostrils, and he realized
Nicole's perfume still lingered somewhere in the room. Dak knew it
well. He'd bought her a bottle of it once, and she'd worn it ever since.
The fact she still used it only added another tow cable to the
emotions already tugging on his heart.

He looked around in dismay at the state of disarray of her office.
Normally, Nicole was tidy and organized. Now, sheets of paper, note-
books, bills, and receipts littered the floor. Her desk chair had been
knocked over on its side, and the stuffing ripped out of fresh cuts in
the leather.

Every drawer in her writing desk hung all the way out, with more
bits of paper hanging out over the edges.

Dak had expected to find her apartment ransacked, even though
he wasn't sure what it was they expected to find from the woman he
loved. Her world didn't delve into hunting for lost treasures. It was
rooted on the computer. Like the laptop sitting on the desk a few
steps away from Dak.

The screen remained dark, and would have suggested time had
passed since the computer had been opened or accessed—though he
wondered.

He walked over to it and pressed the power button, holding it
down for a few seconds until the logo appeared in the center of the
black monitor. Dak waited until the main screen bloomed to life, and
then he pushed down on the mouse pad with his index finger.

The screen requested a password.

Dak couldn't guess what her password might have been. Not that
it mattered. They'd come here for Nicole, and she was gone—now
held by Tucker and the other men he'd brought with him.

The thought sent a new pang of pain-filled worry through his
chest, and he forced himself to suppress it, though that didn't come
easy.

Dak shook his head as he took in the scene. He'd failed to keep Nicole safe, and there wasn't a chance in Hades he'd be able to live with himself if anything happened to her. Heaven knew it was probably too late for that. There was no telling what tortures Tucker had made her endure.

Whatever happened, Dak knew the things done to her would pale in comparison to what he would mete out upon his enemy.

There was nothing helpful here, not that he noticed right away, and he wasn't even sure what he was looking for. It seemed obvious to him what Tucker and his men were trying to find in the apartment, though. The disgraced colonel could think of nothing else but finding Dak and killing him, though it was Tucker who'd been the instigator in this entire mess.

Tucker knew all he had to do to flush Dak out was find Nicole and hold her hostage. But how he'd found Nicole's home, Dak didn't know.

He'd taken precautions, stacking layer upon layer of fail-safes to make certain she didn't have anything that could link her to Dak. But his safety measures had failed to do the one thing he cared about most—keeping her safe.

He sighed. He was wasting time standing here, and there were bodies that needed to be disposed of.

Dak turned and stepped out of the office, returning to the living room. He walked over to the door, ignoring the memories that kept poking into his head uninvited, and stopped. With a look back over his shoulder and a dump truck full of regret, he reached out and pulled down on the latch.

He tugged the door open and immediately realized he'd committed a horrible mistake. He'd let down his guard, thinking he'd already eliminated all of Tucker's men, but he hadn't accounted for the likelihood that the former colonel would have one more trick up his sleeve.

Dak stood face to face with the long barrel of a suppressor, attached to a .40-caliber pistol.

The black-haired man holding the gun didn't offer him a mono-logue about how he'd be paid well for eliminating the bane of Tucker's existence. He was there to do one job, and do it efficiently. Dak saw it in the vapid, blue eyes that stared back at him.

The gunman's trigger finger tightened, and a fraction of a second before he put a bullet through Dak's forehead, a footstep to his left interrupted his intentions.

He flinched, lowering the weapon to his side, but it was too late.

A muscular black man barreled into the killer, tackling him and driving him into the floor with a crunch and a thud.

The gunman tried to aim his pistol at his tackler, but Will quickly twisted the guy's wrists into an awkward and painful position so that the silencer's muzzle pointed toward the man's chin.

He struggled, raising his right knee into Will's ribs. Will managed to twist his body so that the blow only glanced off his side, but the defense threw him off balance slightly, and the assassin used his momentum to roll over.

For a second, the plan worked, but the killer hadn't planned on Will continuing the inertia, rolling over a second time to get right back where he was before—on top of the assailant, though on the other side of the hallway floor.

Dak rushed over to help and delivered a swift kick to the man's head, driving the tip of his boot into the man's temple.

The strike knocked the man into a daze, and his arms went limp in the struggle. Will wrested the pistol from the loose fingers and aimed it down at the assassin's face.

"I had him," Will claimed through panting breaths.

"I know you did." Dak forced a grin. "I thought I told you to wait outside."

Will flashed a quick sidelong grin at his friend. "You did. But you didn't say how long."

"Thanks, for the assist," Dak offered.

"What should we do with him?"

"He won't tell us anything. I already tried to get one of the others to talk. They're as stubborn as they are stupid." He stared down at the semiconscious hit man, then nodded. "You know any cleaners in the area?"

"Yeah. I think I know someone close by."

"There are two bodies in the stairwell," Dak said, "and a couple more in the apartment. They can take this one and do whatever they want with him."

The hired gun lolled his head over to the side, barely awake at this point.

"Fine by me," Will said. "We should move those bodies into the apartment. People will be waking up soon, if they haven't already. Might cost a little more to clean the area at this time of day. Middle of the night is when they prefer to work."

"Not a problem," Dak said. "I'll handle the payment. You just get the crew here."

7

D ak bumped the door open with his butt and hurried through, holding the trash bag-wrapped ankles as tightly as he could so as not to drop the body.

He grunted, waddling backward into Nicole's flat-turned-morgue.

This was the last of the dead assassins Tucker had sent. The one Dak and Will had let live remained curled up in a far corner with his hands and ankles bound with duct tape. Another strip of the gray adhesive stretched across his mouth. He didn't struggle, though. Full control of his faculties still eluded him, and all he could do was moan and writhe slowly in his corner.

Once Will was through the door, hooking his hands under the dead man's shoulders, he let the door close behind him and gently laid the body down on the floor.

They'd taken the precaution of using trash bags from Nicole's pantry to cover the bodies and keep most of the blood from making a mess in the hallway, but there were a few spots there, and in the stairwell, that would need professional attention.

Dak slumped the heavy burden onto the kitchen floor, where they'd placed the others, and wiped his forehead with the back of his hand.

He inspected the floor back over to the door near where Will stood, making sure they hadn't dripped a trail of blood all the way into Nicole's home.

There were spots here and there, but nothing the cleaners couldn't handle. Dak checked his watch. Not yet eight.

They'd been lucky not to see any of Nicole's neighbors while out in the corridor, performing the grisly task of moving the corpses.

"That could have gone a lot worse," Will commented, as if reading Dak's mind.

"Yeah," Dak agreed with a long exhale. "You said they'd be here in twenty minutes?"

"That's what he told me."

"You trust this guy?"

"I wouldn't have called him if I didn't," Will said.

Three knocks on the door interrupted the conversation. Will spun around, took a step over to the entrance, and leaned into the peephole.

"That's him," he said.

Will pulled open the door, revealing three men standing beyond the threshold. The one in front wore a black leather jacket, a black fedora, and gray pants. The other two also wore black leather jackets, but with black trousers. Those two were taller and broader than the pasty man in front of them. Clearly, he was the brains, and they were the muscle.

One of the big men looked Samoan. The other bore the look of a Philly nightclub bouncer, with wide, strong shoulders, a huge chest, and a thick neck. Both held heavy duffel bags, one slightly unzipped with cleaning bottles jutting out of the top.

"Good morning," the man in the fedora said. His voice sounded calm and serpentine. "I hear you are in need of cleaning."

"Yes. Thank you for coming so quickly. This is my associate, Dak Harper."

The man in the lead stepped into the apartment and removed his hat, revealing the shaved head underneath. He stared awkwardly at Dak for a few seconds, as if assessing him with his frosty eyes. Deep circles hung under them—a trait Dak figured came with the occupation.

The man in charge extended his hand to Dak and shook it firmly.

Dak noticed the guy didn't take off his black leather gloves. The other two wore similar protection on their hands.

"Thanks again for coming on such short notice, Wilhelm," Will said. He shook the man's hand after Dak.

"You are fortunate we were in the area." The man's German accent was faint, as if he'd lived abroad for so long it had nearly worn off. But there were a few words, particularly the ones that started with the letter *W* that gave it away. "Especially considering the mess you need cleaned." He swiveled to face Will. "You've been busy, William."

"I only took out one of them. Dak handled the others."

His face changed slightly, portraying slight surprise. "Impressive. You must be very good to have done that on your own."

Wilhelm stepped over one of the bodies and studied the situation. He turned and glanced over his shoulder at the bedroom to the left, then the office door to the right. "Are there any in either of those rooms?" He pointed from one to the other as he spoke.

"No. There are a few things that need tidying up, though. Things that require your special skills."

Dak didn't need to ask what his friend meant by that. He knew crews like this specialized in sterilizing a scene, including the blood-stains that seemed nearly impossible for ordinary people to eliminate.

Wilhelm shrugged. "You've already bagged them, but we'll need to put them in our own bags to make sure there isn't any more leakage on the way out."

"I figured. This was just a quick fix."

"Well, it's better than nothing." He flicked his head at the bodies, and the two assistants stepped closer. The one who looked like a bouncer set his duffel bag down, unzipped it, and pulled out a black body bag that had been folded within.

"There's no chance of the homeowner returning while we're working, is there?" Wilhelm asked, his eyes darting from Dak to Will.

"No," Dak choked, clenching his teeth. He didn't want to think about Nicole not returning, but it was in his face.

"Oh good. It will take some time, especially now that it's morning. But we can operate with discretion."

"I appreciate it," Will said and handed the man a white envelope. Wilhelm accepted it and stuffed it into the inner pocket of his jacket without even taking a look at the contents.

In that line of work, Dak figured the guy would be less trusting.

"And we appreciate your business," Wilhelm replied. "Now, if you two will excuse me, we need to get to work. It should take an hour. We already addressed some stains in the hallway."

That part surprised Dak, but he figured these guys were thorough. He'd noticed the cleaning sprays before and now wondered if they'd gone ahead and eliminated the problem on the way in.

"Sounds good. We'll get out of your way," Will said, bowing as he retreated toward the door.

"We will lock up when we're finished."

Dak nodded his gratitude and followed Will out into the hallway. Once the door was closed behind them, Dak rounded on his friend and lowered his voice to a conspiratorial level.

"We can trust them, right?"

Will nodded. The somber expression on his face was all Dak needed.

"I've had to use Wilhelm before. Probably best you don't ask."

"I don't want to know."

The two shared a knowing smirk. Just then, the door to the apartment opened, and the guy with the bag of cleaning materials appeared in the doorway. "Excuse me," he grunted in a deep baritone, wedged between the two friends, then turned down the corridor toward the stairwell.

Dak and Will watched him disappear through the door.

"They know what they're doing, Dak," Will reassured. "They'll handle it. Come on. We need to get out of here. You know a place where we can get a cup of coffee?"

Dak knew of a few, but his favorite would be out of the question.

The shop across the street where he'd sat on several occasions was too close to the scene of the crime—a scene that would be clean soon, but still too close for comfort.

That fact did little to salve the guilt torturing his gut. He had no way to know for certain, but he couldn't dispel the notion that maybe he'd led Tucker to Nicole on one of his visits to check her.

He shook his head and pinched the bridge of his nose. Regrets wouldn't fix this.

"Yeah. I know a place a couple of blocks from here. We can lay low there until Tucker calls me." Dak checked his watch and noted the time. It was still a half hour until the colonel said he'd call. Any hopes of an earlier communication flew out the window.

Eleven minutes later, they sat down at a table in the back corner of a coffee shop. Dak faced the windows as he always did, carefully watching the people pass by on the sidewalk and the cars on the street beyond them.

He raised the cup of Turkish coffee to his lips and took a cautious sip of the strong brew. It tasted like an espresso roast but with hints of caramel and cherry. Will took a sip of his as well, and winced.

He shook off the shock and went in for another drink. After swallowing it, he set the cup down and looked over his shoulder, then back to Dak. "I always forget how strong the coffee is here in Turkey."

"Nothing like it in the world," Dak said from behind the cup held near his lips. He drew another sip, then lowered the steaming cup to the table. "I'm sorry, Will."

Will's face scrunched in befuddlement. "For what?"

"For earlier. When I snapped at you. I shouldn't have. It's just that —" Dak faltered and looked down at the table. His eyes fell on the dark brown brew in the white porcelain cup between his fingers. All he could do was stare.

"Don't sweat it, brother," Will said. "If it was my girl, I'd be acting the same way. I get it. You don't ever have to apologize to me."

"You're just trying to help. And you're always willing to help me out. I don't know that I've ever really thanked you enough."

"You have. And don't worry about it."

"Well, thanks," Dak offered. Then a realization hit him. "How much was the cleaner?" He reached into his pocket to find the wad of euros wrapped in a rubber band. He kept some cash separate from his wallet, another old habit he'd formed years ago to thwart pickpockets.

"Twelve. But don't worry about it. I'm good."

"Twelve grand? That's a lot of money, Will. You been pulling bank heists lately?"

Will chuckled. "No."

Dak sighed. "I'll get you the money. I don't have that much on me at the moment."

His gig with the eccentric and wealthy video game millionaire Boston McClaren had provided him enough money to last a few years with how cheap Dak typically lived. He didn't have any bills to pay except for when he traveled, so everything he made from recovering artifacts for the kid went straight into the bank, or into investments. He'd purchased a couple of rental properties that more than paid for themselves each month and gave him a steady income between jobs—which could be months.

"I'm not worried about it. You've helped me out more than you know."

Dak wasn't sure what his friend meant by that and couldn't think of any possible way he'd done any actual favors for Will. "I feel like it's the opposite of that. I've gotten you into more trouble than anything. I mean, the chair bomb in Portugal?"

Will bellowed so loud the sparse collection of early morning weekend patrons looked over at him, startled by the sudden noise. After a cold glare by Dak, they went back to their coffee and breakfast.

He resumed drinking his own beverage and glanced at his watch. *Five more minutes.*

"He's calling you at eight, yeah?" Will asked.

"Yeah. That's what he said."

Will shook his head, a look of disgust painted on his face. "I would love to beat Tucker to a pulp and then drop him out of a plane."

"A plane, huh? Why a plane?" Dak mused.

"Because," Will shrugged, "it would be terrifying to be so helpless, beaten, and falling thousands of feet to your death."

Dak appeared lost in thought for three seconds. "Now that you put it that way, I think I'm on board with it. But I get to be the one to beat him and push him out."

"Understood."

The door swung open with a slight squeak, and both men looked back to the entrance out of habit. A young Turkish woman in a white sundress and open-toed sandals walked over to the counter and stopped in the short line to wait her turn.

Dak checked his watch again. *Two minutes.*

"You want me to go outside or something while you do the call?" Will asked. He shifted as if about to stand.

"No," Dak rejected quickly. "Stay. It's fine. Unless you want to. You aren't bothering me, man."

"Cool."

Dak set his phone on the table and kept an eye on it, semi-worried he'd somehow miss the call.

"A watched pot never boils," Will inserted with a smirk.

"I know. I know. I just...." He stopped in the middle of the sentence, and had to choke back the emotions.

"I'm going to step outside," Will said, picking up his cup. "I'll keep an eye on things from there. Just in case."

Dak nodded. He knew it was more about his friend giving him space than anything else.

By the time Will was at the door, the phone started vibrating on the table, right at eight o'clock.

Dak scooped it up and answered, pressing the device to his ear. "Glad to see you're on time, Colonel."

"One ring. Impressive. I hope you weren't hovering over the phone like some desperate schoolgirl waiting for a boy to call."

"I want to speak to Nicole," Dak said, ignoring the statement. "I need to know she's okay."

Tucker scoffed with a laugh. "I'm sure you do. But I understand, Dak. You need assurance. Anyone would in your shoes. So, here's a crumb for you." He paused, and then Dak heard him order her to say something.

"Dak?" Nicole's voice sounded feeble and frightened. "Are you there?"

Hearing her that way nearly broke him. "Nicole. Are you okay?"

"I'm... okay. Please, tell me what is going on. Who is this guy? What's happening?"

"Don't worry. I'm going to get you out of there. Everything's going to be all right."

She choked a sob back. "That sounds like something you'd say to someone to convince them not to panic."

That's my girl, he thought. Even in the midst of her darkest hour, she could find that wit.

"No. You're going to be okay. I promise. It's me he wants. Not you."

"Very good, Dak," Tucker interrupted. The sound of her struggling in the background, and then being muted, drove a stake through Dak's heart. "I do want you. But you're going to have to dance for me first, monkey. You remember how to dance, don't you?"

"I'd love to dance with you, Cam. Just you and me. Preferably next to a cliff so I could throw you off it and listen to you scream all the way to the bottom."

"That's a little dark," Tucker chuckled. "But I get it. You blame me for all your troubles. The reality is, if you'd just played ball—"

"I'd be a criminal. Like you. Now, are you going to keep chitchatting, or are you going to tell me what it is you want me to do? I've already dispatched all the men you sent to ambush me. I thought we had a deal."

"Yes, I figured you'd handle them, but a guy's got to try, right? I mean, if you couldn't eliminate them, then I doubt you'd be ready for the job I have for you."

A sickening feeling crept into Dak's gut. He didn't like where this was going. "If you think I'm going to kill someone for you, you have another thing—"

"I don't want you to kill. Well, that's not true. I do have a list, but I can handle that myself. No, the job I have for you doesn't have any killing involved. At least, it doesn't have to."

The statement sent a frown across Dak's face. His forehead wrinkled with lines across it, and his eyebrows tightened closer together.

"Go on."

"It seems you have a penchant for finding artifacts and priceless missing items from history. I want you to find one for me."

That confession caught Dak off guard. "You. You want me to find an artifact for you?"

"Not an artifact. A masterpiece. More specifically, a painting."

"I didn't figure you for an art aficionado, Cam."

"I'm just full of surprises," Tucker countered. "But this is less about the art and more about the buyer."

"Oh, I see. You want me to find a lost painting and bring it to you? And in exchange for said painting, you'll return Nicole unharmed?"

"Close. First of all, I'll let Nicole go unharmed. But not return her to you. You, I'm going to kill myself."

Dak found himself dreaming of the chance to go face to face with Tucker, but he knew those visions were delusional. No way Tucker would fight fair with him. More likely, Dak would show up and get shot in the head. And maybe, maybe Nicole would be set free.

In Dak's mind, that was still a win. At least for her.

"And you're wrong about one other thing."

"Oh? What's that?"

"The painting isn't lost. It was stolen."

"Stolen? So, you're thinking I can steal it back for you? From the thief that took it in the first place?"

"Exactly."

Dak looked around the room, barely noticing everyone sat at their tables talking or searching their phones for the next hit of dopamine delivered through funny videos or pretty pictures. Will sat at a table outside one of the windows, watching the street and sidewalks for potential threats while taking intermittent sips of his coffee.

"Okay, fine. Who has it?"

He received another laugh through the speaker. "You think I know? If I knew that, I would have already retrieved the painting myself."

Probably not.

"No," Tucker went on, "you're going to have to figure out that on your own."

"Great. I don't suppose you're going to tell me what painting I'm looking for, are you? Or are you just going to leave it vague and hope that I can guess correctly?"

"Come on, Dak. I wouldn't do that to you. Out of millions of works of art out there, that wouldn't do me much good, now would it? Of course I'm going to tell you."

"Then spit it out, and quit wasting my time."

"Funny you mention time. You have five days to get me the painting."

"But—"

"When you have it, we'll arrange a rendezvous. No excuses, Dak. I want that painting. I have a lot of reasons—several million, in fact—for wanting it. And a buyer who's ready to pay."

"Thanks for oversharing, Cam. Can we get to the part where you tell me what the name of the painting is? Apparently, I'm on some kind of deadline."

"Oh, you are on a deadline. If you don't have the painting by this Friday at midnight, UTC, your little girlfriend here dies."

Dak caught himself breathing harder. He swatted away a dozen witty and threatening comebacks. They would do no good anyway. Better to get this job done, and maybe get a chance to let his fists do the talking—if Tucker didn't shoot him first.

"What's the painting, Cam?"

"*The Sea of Galilee*. It's a Rembrandt. Good luck."

8

D ak was about to ask if Tucker had any hints as to where he should start searching for the painting, but the call ended as soon as the man finished speaking.

Despair and fury tore at Dak's brain. It was rare for him to feel so lost, so incapable of dealing with something.

For a minute, he did nothing but stare at the phone, his mind stewing with a million crazy ideas. He considered calling Tucker back and demanding he show up here at the coffee shop so the two of them could handle things in the alley out back. That, along with all the other fantasies that raced through Dak's imagination were neither realistic nor helpful.

He needed a plan. *But where to start?*

He looked out the window again at his friend still waiting patiently on the sidewalk. Dak didn't want to rope his friend into another dangerous scenario, but Will had connections—and resources. And Dak needed all the help he could get.

Customers continued to sip their coffee and consume their pastries around Dak. Their concerns seemed trivial to him, whatever they might have been. It was unlikely any of them were facing a situation like his.

It was all he could do to drink the coffee in front of him, much less eat a bite of anything. He wondered if his appetite would ever return.

"Snap out of it, Dak," he muttered to himself. No one around him seemed to notice, and his thoughts began to clear from the fog.

Tucker had given him the name of a painting—*The Sea of Galilee* by Rembrandt. It wasn't one he was familiar with, but that didn't mean much. Dak had never been much of an art guy. Not that he didn't appreciate it. He'd been to museums and galleries on a few occasions, and enjoyed what he'd seen. His particular interest in art lingered on the historical aspects of both the creations and their creators. He marveled at the works made by human hands so long ago, and when he found himself in the presence of a master's craft, Dak always felt a profound sense of respect.

Still, he'd not heard of the Rembrandt Tucker wanted him to locate and recover, so he did what anyone in the digital age would do—he tapped on his phone and entered a search.

Several links appeared on the screen within seconds, and he tapped on the first one.

He read the article in under two minutes, then found another that corroborated the first.

The story about the missing Rembrandt turned out to be an interesting one, and would have been more fascinating had Dak's current situation been less dire.

The Storm on the Sea of Galilee was created by the famous Dutch artist Rembrandt van Rijn in 1633.

The painting, as the name suggests, depicts Christ and his disciples in the famous story in which they set sail across the Sea of Galilee to take a break from their journeys and ministry. In the image, their boat is being tossed around by huge, powerful waves. The disciples are shown struggling against the surge. One is seen vomiting over the side of the boat. Dark clouds encroach on both sides of the vessel.

On the right, however, Christ can be seen as the only one aboard who remains calm during the bleakest, toughest of moments.

Dak also found that experts believe Rembrandt actually painted himself into the picture as one of the disciples.

The history of the painting, and its maker, were only the beginning.

In 1990, *The Storm on the Sea of Galilee* was on display at the Isabella Stewart Gardner Museum in Boston when it was stolen. Since then, no one had been able to find the painting—or the culprits responsible for its theft.

Dak continued scanning the documents for more to the story.

According to reports, on the morning of March 18, 1990, two thieves disguised as policemen broke into the museum and stole the painting along with twelve other master works. It turned out to be the biggest art theft in United States history.

Three years after the heist, the FBI declared that they knew who'd committed the crime, but no arrests were made, and the paintings remained lost.

"Two thieves," Dak mumbled. He'd heard of master thieves pulling off unbelievable jobs. Some of his favorite movies involved those kinds of plots. He'd also heard of teams of criminals who did stuff of that nature, and of course dozens of movies featured thrilling, suspenseful stories based on this sort of thing. But even in the movies, art thieves usually worked with teams to help them pull of their heists.

But two. Only two?

Dak figured there was a reason most heists, both real and fictional, involved either one master thief or a group of them.

With a larger team, the proceeds from a theft would have to be split more ways but could be easier to pull off with multiple people handling various roles. With one person, the profits only went into one pocket, though slipping by security and accompanying systems could prove exponentially more difficult.

Two people, however, seemed an illogical way of doing it. At least to Dak's somewhat ignorant mind on the subject.

Aside from all the advantages and disadvantages of leveraging more or fewer people to get the job done, the biggest issue in Dak's mind was splitting the loot.

Thieves, from what he understood, were inherently greedy. It seemed to go hand in hand with who they were—an obvious, natural characteristic of people who stole things for a living. And he'd seen more than a few movies where one person got stabbed in the back by their "trusted" partner in the end, because why split things fifty-fifty when you could have it all?

That kind of logic permeated the criminal mind, and Dak knew it. While the thought dangled in his head, he found himself wondering if that was what happened, if one of the thieves had eliminated the other so they wouldn't have to share the spoils.

Dak figured he'd left his friend outside long enough. And the first moment Will looked in through the window, Dak motioned to him with a flick of his fingers.

Will acknowledged by tipping his chin upward and immediately returned to the door and stepped inside.

While his friend walked back across the shop floor to the back corner, Dak looked over the last article again but didn't find anything else new that would be helpful.

"Well?" Will asked as he eased back into his chair again. He left his empty coffee cup on the edge of the table for one of the servers to take when they walked around.

Dak appreciated the way his friend asked about the call. He didn't ask how it went, or if everything was okay, or what Tucker said. Will may have just been using brevity for the sake of time and energy, or he might have known asking the question in any of those ways listed could upset Dak.

Either way, Dak was glad for Will's distillation of words.

"Tucker does have Nicole."

Will nodded. Again, instead of saying something like "Oh, good, she's alive" or "Does she sound okay?" he offered an understanding gesture.

"I couldn't figure out where he is," Dak went on. "Wherever it is, there were no audio cues to give away his location."

Finally, Will asked a specific question. "What does he want?"

Dak sighed and set down his phone, then spun it around like a fidget spinner and slid it across the table.

"That," Dak answered, jabbing a finger at the device as he leaned forward, propping himself up on his elbows.

Will frowned, staring at the screen. He read the article, looked up at Dak, then back at the text again.

"Wait a minute," he said, raising his eyes to meet Dak's.

"He wants us to find *The Storm on the Sea of Galilee*," Dak said, finishing the thought. "Actually, he wants me to do it. He didn't say anything about you. Which might be a good thing. Means it's possible that he doesn't know you're around right now."

"Probably better to assume he does know."

"Agreed. But still, that could help us out down the road."

"What's down the road? How are you going to find this? The article says the FBI claimed to know who the culprits were, but the names were never released, and as far as this suggests, no one was ever arrested. Does that mean they were full of it?"

"You mean, were they bluffing?" Dak shrugged. "Maybe. I'd have to wonder why."

"Agencies like that don't want to lose face. They had to say something, right?"

Dak didn't seem so sure about that. "Yeah, but you'd think they would release the names even if it was BS. Seems like they never really had anyone to begin with."

"This article," Will said in a conspiratorial tone, "claims there were two people responsible for the theft."

"Correct."

"What if one of them turned on the other and decided to turn his partner in?"

"That's possible, except the one who got turned in would reciprocate against the other."

"True."

Dak thumbed his chin. "I think the agency was full of it."

"There is one more possibility," Will suggested. "It could be the

FBI found the suspects, arrested them, and then sold off the artwork for their own profit, or they never found the thieves. Seen that sort of thing happen before."

"Interesting hypothesis, Will. I hadn't considered that."

"Yeah, agents are just people after all. Think about it. Say you're an underpaid, overworked cop or fed. You and a few of your colleagues are tasked with the impossible job of finding a couple of thieves who ripped off a museum and vanished like a fart in the wind.

"No one really expects you to find the guys who did it, but if you can, great. Then what? You get some accolades at work. Maybe an employee-of-the-month sign on your floor and one to hang on your cubicle. Or you find the culprits, take care of them"—he raised his hand in the shape of a gun and pretended to fire at an imaginary target—"and then you and your partner or whoever is on the case with you makes off with the art, sells it on the black market, and you get an early retirement."

Will's theory was incredibly well considered. And Dak couldn't punch any holes in it. Not yet.

He'd seen something similar happen near his hometown once. A lady had gone out to get her mail when she noticed a brown paper grocery bag sitting in the ditch in front of her yard. She went over and looked inside and to her surprise found bundles of cash hidden within.

When the money was counted, the bag contained over two hundred thousand dollars.

In her ignorance, the woman called the police and turned the money in. Of course, they claimed that traces of drugs were found on the money, and that it would be kept as evidence.

She received almost nothing as a reward.

Dak had always thought it stupid of the poor woman, though he doubted she knew better. That money would have been easy to clean with a few trips to a casino and a couple of other cash-only places. She would have thought something like that to be a crime, but the real crime was letting someone else do exactly that instead of doing it herself.

"It's worth looking into," Dak said after thinking on it. "You wouldn't happen to have any connections in the Bureau would you?"

Will blurted out laughing. "Who? Me? Yeah, no. I stay as far away from them as humanly possible. The last thing I want is any feds breathing down my neck. It's hard enough to do what I do as it is."

The last sentence distracted Dak for a second. "Speaking of, how is it you're running your business when you're spending all this time with me? I wouldn't have thought gunrunning to be a seasonal thing."

"Very funny. I have people that handle the day-in-and-day-out stuff. I handle making the deals. The rest is all part of the machine."

"Look at you," Dak said, impressed. "I had no idea you were so organized."

"Have to be. Now, let's get back to the issue at hand."

For a minute, Dak had almost forgotten about the problem of locating the thieves and the stolen art. Almost. It felt good to laugh and think about something else, even if only for a handful of seconds.

Will prodded a little more. "You know anyone who might be able to help us track down the artwork? Might be easier than finding the thieves. Or the buyers, assuming they sold it. Wouldn't make much sense to steal art worth so much just to keep it in a private display in a basement."

"You'd be surprised. But I agree. Criminals like that do it for the money. They have visions of selling loot and taking off to a beach somewhere in a country with no extradition agreements. That's probably what happened. I'd say they're long gone by now."

"Okay." Will folded his hands on the table. His face took on a serious look. "So, how do we track down illicit art that was stolen more than thirty years ago?" He chuckled. "Heck, the thieves might be dead now for all we know."

"Oh, we're not going to track down the artwork." Dak kept his poker face on, giving away no hint of what was on his mind.

"No? Then what's the—"

"As luck would have it, I know someone who does this kind of thing all the time."

For a second, it didn't register with Will who Dak was talking about. Then it hit him, and his eyes widened. "The kid? Look, Dak, I know your job with that boy is... Okay, actually, I don't know much about it, and I'm not sure I want to know. Like how in the world a twelve-year-old—"

"Fourteen."

Will's chin retreated into his neck at the surprise information. "Fourteen? Already?"

"I hear they grow up fast."

"Fine." Will shook off the shock. "Fourteen. How in the world does this fourteen-year-old kid find all these missing artifacts and pieces of art?"

"Where most people do nowadays, Will. On the dark web."

"I can't believe his parents let him do that. Have you seen what's on the dark web? It's not a nice place for adults, much less a child."

"Teenager," Dak corrected. "And I agree. But I'm not sure his parents know precisely how he finds these things. To be honest, I don't know how it all works, either. All I know is he pays me. And I find them in the real world."

"And almost get killed doing it. The last one we did took us face to face with the Russian army."

"A unit of their army. And you didn't have to come along. Still don't if you're not up for it."

Will scoffed, unfolding his hands and planting his palms on the table. "Yeah, right. Like you could do this without me."

"Probably not. You do make it easier. Nice to have someone to talk to." He cracked a smile at the joke in the last sentence.

Will fought off the urge to laugh. "Fine. You going to call the kid and see if he can figure out who bought the painting?"

Dak pulled his phone back to his side of the table, rotated it around, and tapped the screen. He paused, looking thoughtful as he hesitated.

"What?" Will wondered. "What are you waiting for?"

"It's like three a.m. in the States. I'll text him. But we'll have to wait for an answer. At least it's not a school day."

Will chuckled and shook his head. "I still can't believe you work for a fourteen-year-old."

"I like to think of it more as a partnership than an employee/employer kind of deal."

"Whatever helps you sleep at night." Will stood up and set a coin down on the table for whoever was going to come by and clean up after they left. It wasn't customary, but American habits die hard.

Dak typed out a quick message and sent it as he rose from his seat, and the two words zipped across the planet through cell towers, undersea data cables, data centers, then more cell towers, to reach the phone sitting next to a teenage boy sleeping in his bed in Chattanooga, Tennessee, in mere seconds.

"Call me."

9

S pending four hours in Istanbul was an easy thing to do for visitors. The open-air market was one of Dak's favorite spots to frequent when he came to the old city. He loved seeing the stalls overflowing with fresh fruits and vegetables, herbs, spices, and meats.

It was the way people had sold things in this part of the world and elsewhere for millennia. No fancy packaging. No additives or preservatives. Just real food sold by real people.

Other sellers hawked tunics, pants, and beautiful dresses.

Several spots offered tea and coffee.

Dak appreciated all of it, especially how crowded the market was. He wished he could spend more time there but knew that he and Will needed to keep moving for now. Losing a tail in the marketplace was easier than in other locations, and was their primary purpose for this visit.

Still, two hours in the market was more than ample time to confuse anyone who might be following them and to take a look at pretty much everything on offer.

After leaving the market, the two headed across town to the

waterfront in the Besiktas neighborhood, where an open plaza offered a clear 360-degree view of their surroundings.

Dak noted the famous tomb of the great Ottoman admiral and former pirate Hayreddin Barbarossa to the left as he and Will walked across the plaza toward the water. Huge sixteenth-century cannons propped up on platforms adorned the square.

The centerpiece—a monument to the great sea commander— towered over the area. The sculpture depicted Barbarossa standing erect, facing out toward the sea with a hardened, courageous expression on his face. Turkish flags flapped gently around the memorial to further remind visitors of just how important this incredible admiral had been, and still was, to the Turkish people.

Dak noticed a group of people within the cemetery surrounding the tomb—a two-story building with several angles and windows. An overhead view would confirm, but he suspected it was an octagon or hexagonal shape. The people within the confines of the fence surrounding the graveyard and tomb wore official badges hung from lanyards around their necks. Some donned lab coats. Others wore ordinary, everyday clothes.

Two uniformed police officers stood at either side of the taped-off entrance, keeping watch of passersby in case someone might try to trespass and interfere with whatever was going on in there.

Dak frowned at the sight, curious as to what they were doing, but not so much that he'd risk annoying the cops by walking over and asking. Besides, he had other, more pressing things on his plate.

He checked his watch and noted the time, figuring the kid was still asleep at this early hour back in the States but also hoping that Boston was a morning person.

Will walked alongside his friend, inspecting their surroundings with a careful and sweeping gaze.

"Why'd you pick this spot to kill time?" Will asked, noting the smattering of people gathered in the plaza. Some sipped coffee on park benches. Others enjoyed pastries atop blankets they'd set up on the ground in makeshift, city-based picnics.

"Because you can see an enemy coming from a few blocks away,"

Dak explained. He pointed at the buildings beyond the tomb and cemetery. "Those are shops, restaurants, cafés, and markets. Lots of people, and exposed, so it would be difficult to take a sniper position on one of the rooftops without being noticed. The mosque over there provides an adequate barrier, too." He indicated the enormous place of worship by rotating and pointing back toward the area where they'd just come from. "And it's unlikely we could get attacked from the waterfront. Sure, someone could put a shooter on a boat, but the water is choppy right now, and taking a shot from that distance would prove extremely difficult."

Will's blank and impressed expression said what he was thinking, but he still complimented Dak anyway. "You've really thought this through."

"Always."

"You that worried Tucker is going to make another play at you? I thought he wanted the painting."

"He does. And for now, I think he's probably done trying to kill me. For now. But given the opportunity, I think he'd take me dead over having the painting. You can always make more money."

"You can't always kill Dak Harper."

Dak offered a weak chuff. "I guess."

"So, we're just going to sit here like a couple of tourists with nothing better to do until your young boss calls?"

"Seemed the wise thing to do. We're safe here for the moment. And there's no point in going anywhere else until we hear back from Boston. I don't like the idea of heading to the airport because who knows if Tucker will have guys waiting for us there."

"But we are going to have to go there at some point, right?"

"Well, yeah. But I'd prefer to cross that bridge when we get to it."

Dak spotted a bench thirty yards away and veered in that direction. "Come on. Might as well sit down while we're waiting."

They plopped down on the seat and stretched out their legs as the sun climbed higher into the midday sky. White clouds offered shade now and then, but only enough to tease the two Americans with dramatically cooler temperatures before the sun peeked out again and baked the plaza.

At least there's a steady breeze, Dak thought. *Even if it is a warm one.*

The two didn't say much in the hour that passed, both wary that getting too casual could cause them to slip up and miss approaching danger.

With their backs to the cemetery, and any view from the buildings beyond blocked by the tomb, Dak felt comfortable enough to focus his surveillance on the other three-quarters of the area.

"Braves are looking good this year," Dak commented, cutting the silence like a shovel through gravel.

Will hummed. "Yeah. They could use a solid closer, though. And the injuries. And having a season where all their key players didn't get hurt would help, too."

"Seems like the bullpen has always been an issue. Like all the way back to the nineties."

"Heh. Yeah, that's true."

Talking about baseball relieved the tension for both of them. More importantly, it gave Dak a sense of normality, if only for a few minutes. Since he learned of Nicole's abduction, he'd thought of nothing else.

Dak sighed and looked out over the water. A sailboat cruised by out in the bay. The top of the hull was black, with a white underside. The huge white sales puffed out in a rigid balloon shape, driving the vessel ahead.

"How did you know about this place?" Will asked, interrupting his friend's thoughts. He glanced around the plaza.

"Nicole and I came here a few times. She liked it here close to the water. It's peaceful. Not too many people, usually. That cemetery behind us is where a famous Ottoman admiral is buried, along with one of his more important commanders—if I remember correctly. The Turkish Navy still pays tribute to him when they pass by during new sailors' initiation. I've never been here for one of those days." His voice grew distant, and the respite of baseball fell away like a no-hitter to an infield single in the bottom of the ninth inning. A maelstrom of memories gripped him once more and sucked him down into the swirling dark waters of fear.

"I can't lose her, Will," he said after a minute. "I already lost her once."

"Yeah. I don't think I ever asked you about that. What happened with you two?"

Dak rolled his shoulders and kicked his right leg out, straightening it as he tried to relax.

Will shifted, too. Regret scratched at his skin, and he wondered if he'd gone too far asking about Nicole.

"Sorry, Dak. I shouldn't have asked. You don't have to tell me. That's your business."

"No. It's okay. No one's ever asked. Other than my parents." Dak only stretched out for a few more seconds before pulling his feet back under him and leaning forward, planting his elbows on his knees.

"My job with the military always put me in the middle of danger," Dak started. "Spec ops, as you know, handles the toughest missions. My group was no different. I could have been one of those guys who got married, got my wife pregnant, and then been deployed, but that never sat right with me. I didn't want to end up dead and leave Nicole and a child alone like that. I don't judge anyone who does it that way. I just thought it was the best way to protect her."

Will allowed an understanding nod. "Is it possible that breaking up with her for your job might have hurt her just as much, if not more?" He ventured the question, knowing he was on thin ice with it. But he wanted to help his friend.

Dak simply sat there breathing slowly for a minute, contemplating Will's question. "I guess I never thought of it like that before. I mean, I know it hurt her. And I'm pretty certain she saw it as me choosing my job over her. But it was more than just a job. It was my calling. I wanted to serve my country. And I was good at it."

"Same," Will agreed. "Maybe I wasn't as good as you, but I like to think my time made a difference in the world for the greater good."

"Sometimes I don't know if it did," Dak confessed. "What if everything we did was just a sham, just part of a bigger game?"

"Pawn theory."

"What?" Dak rotated his head to look at his friend.

"Pawn theory. That's what I call it. We're all just pawns in a bigger game run by players with no faces. We sometimes know the names of their puppets: politicians, financial leaders, media, big tech CEOs. But knowing who really moves the pieces is nearly impossible."

"Except in my current situation. I know who is moving the pieces right now."

"I guess that's true."

"Tucker's such a bloody coward," Dak spat. "I can't believe I let him get away before."

"You thought he was dead. Can't blame yourself for that, man. His body was there on the battlefield."

"Yeah," Dak bobbed his head in disgust. "Ten cents' worth of metal would have made sure he never got up."

"Well, we don't have a time machine, so there's no point in looking back. No one's going that direction anyway."

Dak's brow furrowed at the statement. "What did you say?"

"I said we don't have a time machine."

"No. The other part."

"Oh," Will thought for a second. "There's no point in looking back. No one is going in that direction?"

"That," Dak said. "Where did you hear that?"

Will shrugged. "I don't know. Picked it up somewhere, I guess. I doubt I made it up. Nothing new under the sun, right?"

Dak offered a half laugh. "Yeah. I guess not."

His phone started buzzing in his pocket, ending the conversation abruptly. He hurriedly pulled it from his pants and looked at the screen. "It's the kid," he said.

"You need me to—"

"No. Stay here. Keep watching the plaza. I don't want to get ambushed while I'm on the phone."

"Understood."

Dak pressed the green button on the screen and raised the device to his ear. "A little early for someone your age to be up, isn't it?"

Boston McClaren yawned through the speaker. "No. I get up kind of early. I might be one of the only gamers who can say they're a morning person."

Dak didn't know much about that world, but he assumed most video game professionals kept late hours, often sleeping in until the middle of the morning, if not later.

"Well, you're still in school. So, there's that."

"Yeah. That's probably it. So, your text message was a little cryptic. Call me? Nothing else? Sounds important."

"It is. I hope you don't have a busy Sunday lined up."

"Oh," Boston said. "You had my curiosity. But now you have my attention."

"Okay, first of all, you are way too young to watch Quentin Tarantino movies. Second, when you are old enough, you should start with *Reservoir Dogs*, then *Pulp Fiction*, and so on."

"What are you talking about? Also, I'm fourteen."

"The quote you used. You had my curiosity? You know what that's from, right?"

"I guess it's from a movie? I've just seen the GIF."

Dak rolled his eyes. "Okay, well, someday you are going to sit down and watch all the Tarantino movies. He's one of the greatest directors of all time. But you should probably wait until you're seventeen or eighteen."

"Noted. Did you want me to call you just to talk about movies? Or was there another reason?"

Dak chuckled, but the humor quickly evaporated as the problem at hand returned to the forefront of his mind.

"I need a favor."

"A favor? From me?"

"Yeah. And it's a big ask. If you can't do it, I'll find another way."

"You doubt me that much, huh?"

Dak had to hand it to the kid; he was confident. Not in a cocky, annoying kind of way. Boston knew his abilities, and trusted in them.

"If I did, I wouldn't have asked you to call me."

"Good point. Sounds like you have something challenging for me." He sounded almost excited about the proposition.

"Oh, it's a challenge. My old nemesis kidnapped Nicole."

"What?" In one word, the fog in the teenager's voice disappeared. "Kidnapped? Tucker kidnapped her?"

Once, in a casual conversation, Boston had asked Dak if he had a girlfriend or wife, and Dak had cautiously dripped out a few innocuous details to satisfy the kid's curiosity.

"Yeah. And now if I want to get her back, I have to find a painting that was stolen over thirty years ago."

"Painting?" Boston paused. "Thirty years ago? It's still missing?"

"Apparently so. If it was ever found or recovered, that tidbit missed the front pages. I suspect whoever stole it either still has it or sold it on the black market."

"And you want me to find it."

"I know that's a lot. And if you don't want to have anything to—"

"There you go again, putting words in my brain that I never even considered. I'll just stop you right there. I'm in. My only question is, when we find this thing, are you really going to just give it to Tucker?"

Dak sucked in a long breath and looked over at Will, who sat quietly by his side keeping a lookout.

"I don't really think I have a choice, Boston. If there was another way, I would do it, but I don't see one."

"Hmm."

"What?"

"Nothing. You're right. Doesn't matter. We need to find the painting and get Nicole back safe."

Dak heard the boy moving around in his home. It sounded like he was walking down a hall.

"What's the name of the painting?"

"It's called *The Storm on the Sea of Galilee* by Rembrandt."

Stunned silence filled Dak's ear.

"Sorry. Did you just say we're looking for a Rembrandt?"

"I did."

"Wow," Boston gasped. "This guy really swings for the fences, doesn't he?"

After the question, Dak heard the kid's fingers flying across a keyboard and figured Boston had walked to his studio, where he livestreamed his video games. On a lark, Dak had watched the kid during a session just to get a better perspective on what Boston did. He'd been entertaining, and very good at his chosen game, which didn't come as a surprise since he'd made millions doing it at a very young age.

Dak's young employer had proved just as proficient at locating artifacts and works of art that the rest of the world gave up on. Dak could only hope his skills came through again now.

"I don't know why Tucker wants this specific painting, but I'm certain there's some sadistic reason behind it."

Boston didn't respond immediately. "One second," Boston said. "Just reading about this Rembrandt." Another thirty seconds passed before he spoke up again. "I'm surprised I've never heard of this one before, especially considering how it disappeared from a museum in the city I'm named for."

"I actually never even made that connection. But yes. It was stolen in Boston."

"Says here the investigators claimed to know who was involved. That sounds like a load of bull to me. Or maybe they did, and they found the painting, then kept it for themselves."

"I wondered the same thing."

"Well, if someone *has* moved it in the last decade or so, I'll track it down. But if the thieves sat on it, I'm not sure there is much I could do. I mean, there are rooms for people like that on the dark web, but I don't know how active they are."

The kid's weird expertise on the subject wasn't giving Dak a truck-load of confidence. From the sound of it, the odds looked fifty-fifty at best.

"Just do the best you can. That's all I can ask." Dak nearly choked on the words.

Boston gave it a second before speaking up again. "Don't worry, Dak. We'll get this sorted out. You made the right call."

"Thanks, kid. Let me know if you find something."

"You mean *when* I find something," Boston corrected.

"Right. When."

"Talk to you soon."

"Okay, Boston. Sounds good."

Dak lowered the phone, stared at the screen for a long moment, then ended the call.

"You don't look like that call made you feel better about things."

"He's going to do all he can, Will."

Dak looked off to the right, toward a line of apartment buildings near the waterway. Really, he merely didn't want his friend seeing the tears welling in his eyes.

Will noticed, but he kept that to himself. "You said the kid is good. Right?"

"He's the best there is for this kind of thing. I can only think of one other person who might be able to help."

"Hey, if you think they can make this go faster, call them up."

Dak shook his head and pinched his lips together. "No. Not yet. I don't want to call that one in. That time may come, and when it does, I will make the call."

"Okay, Dak," Will surrendered, throwing his hands up. "You know what's best."

Dak snorted, seemingly hating the comment as if it were a sworn rival. "If only that were true."

10

CHATTANOOGA, TENNESSEE

Boston's fingers zipped across the keyboard at blinding speed. He'd mastered that skill before he was twelve and could type as fast as most seasoned writers.

But he wasn't writing a novel or an article or an essay. He was working his way through a series of security protocols he'd put in place for browsing the dark web.

That shadowy cesspool that lay in the basement of the internet was no place for the weak minded, or those with shoddy security measures. Before he'd ever ventured into that dark place, Boston learned the ins and outs as much as he possibly could. One of the key things to remember when you visit the dark web, keep your focus tight or you could see things that a kid his age, nor any person of any age should see.

He was glad he'd taken the time to learn prior to hopping on. There was truly no telling what kinds of horrors he'd avoided—on multiple levels—because of that prudence.

He'd heard a nightmarish story on YouTube about a guy who'd decided to hop on the dark web browser one night, and ended up ripping the motherboard and everything else out of his laptop when the screen went black and the words *I See You* appeared in the center.

According to the story, the guy never went back into the dark web again.

The least the guy could have done was go through a VPN, which was a pretty basic rule. He'd decided early on that this kind of thing wasn't the sort in which you only did the bare minimum.

So, he set out and learned as much about computer and web security as he could. He'd spent hours on weekends just reading and watching videos—some that were only available through private servers. Books, however, were the more powerful in regard to his studies.

Now, he had a setup that was as impenetrable as any individual's rig, and probably the government's, too.

Boston pored over the contents on his screen, skipping over the insidious stuff that somehow slipped through his filters.

"Okay," he muttered to himself, "where are you?"

He scanned the monitor, scrolling quickly through lists of text on the left and numbers on the right. The digits represented dollars, and the staggering amounts posted still shocked Boston.

Despite having snooped around many times in the dark web, it never ceased to astound the teenager at how much money was out there in the world—dirty money in this case.

He slowed his scrolling and kept an eye out for a specific word.

The seedy individuals populating the dark web practiced inscrutable caution when hawking their goods and services, or when buying—partly because of law enforcement in their various countries. But the real reason for their paranoia had less to do with cops or federal agents and more to do with the fact that the place they operated in was inherently full of untrustworthy people.

You could get robbed, killed, or perhaps even turned in to the authorities.

So buyers and sellers had lists of codewords for their inventory. Boston didn't have much interest in most of them, for more reasons than he cared to dwell on. But over a short amount of time, he'd learned which words were the ones most suited to his needs.

For artifacts, the code word *antiques* was used.

For works of art, the marketplace used the word *crafts*.

It was the latter Boston needed to find. He'd seen it many times before and knew there were usually only a few items, if any, listed. That's how it went in the rare goods markets.

"Come on," he said, "there has to be one."

Another minute passed. A second. A third.

Boston froze when he recognized the code word he wanted. "There you are," he whispered. He noted the number next to the word *craft*. "Two million. You're a big fish, aren't you?"

He tapped the screen on his phone sitting on the desk next to the keyboard, and started the timer he'd opened earlier. If he couldn't find what he needed inside of three minutes, he'd have to bail and come back online after a few hours.

Boston clicked his mouse on a button in the top-right corner of his computer monitor, took a slow breath, and clicked the link next to the asking price.

A chat window opened in the center of the screen, and he checked up in the corner to make doubly sure the cloaking program was running. A little flame icon next to it confirmed the system was doing its thing.

He typed a quick message into the chat window and hit the Send button.

"Two million. What's the craft?"

Boston checked the timer again. Two minutes and thirty-seven seconds.

There was the chance that the seller wasn't able to get online to check the query, but Boston felt like these guys were probably pretty eager to get offers when they posted something.

Two minutes and fifteen seconds.

Every passing breath felt like a month. He glanced up into the corner again at the flame icon. Then text started appearing in the chat box.

"*Giovane.*"

Boston replied. "When and where?"

The seller didn't respond immediately. The pause sent Boston's eyes darting back to the timer again. One minute and fifty-three seconds remained.

The flame still flickered in the corner of the screen.

"Toulon."

"Interesting," Boston breathed. "Somehow, I don't think you're really in France." Possible? Certainly. But Boston figured that was just where the dealer wanted to make the transaction.

"Boston? Time to get up!" His mother's voice blasted through the closed door from somewhere downstairs. Based on the rattles of plates and silverware, he figured it was the kitchen. The smells of eggs and biscuits cooking reinforced that hypothesis.

"I'm up, Mom!" he shouted back, then refocused on the computer screen.

"When?" Boston typed into the chat. He clicked the Send button and checked the timer.

The digits ticked dangerously close to one minute. He knew staying on longer than three minutes wasn't an option. By then, whoever was on the other end might be able to crack his security and locate his address despite the many protocols he'd put in place to avoid such detection. It wasn't likely that would happen. He'd taken no shortcuts to set up his system, but that didn't mean it was bulletproof.

"Come downstairs, then!" his mom yelled again.

He clenched his jaw, pressing his lips together, then releasing them over and over.

"Okay, Mom! One minute!"

The screen offered a reply from the seller. "Wednesday. I need two days to move the craft. Meet on the third day."

Boston nodded, absently sticking his tongue through his lips for a second to moisten them. "Exact location and preferred currency."

He hit Send and peered over at the countdown. "Come on. Only forty-eight seconds left."

"Not one minute, young man! Your breakfast will get cold!"

He rolled his eyes. "I really don't need this right now," he complained to himself, then raised his voice again. "Okay! Be right down!"

Boston's parents were notoriously early risers, which had instilled the same habit in their son naturally. Still, their energy level at this time of day was too much for him, and he wondered often what sleeping in must feel like.

Another sharp glance at the clock.

Every passing second felt like a blacksmith's hammer slamming into an anvil—and Boston was the anvil.

"One moment."

The response sent a chill through Boston's spine. "You're stalling," he said to the screen. And he knew exactly what that meant. The seller was trying to track Boston's location.

He couldn't do anything but wait. If he pressed the other to hurry, they might get skittish and drop out of the chat altogether. Or it might make Boston look desperate. Either way, the seller's suspicion would probably drive them away.

Dak needed this to work. Nicole's life depended on it.

The seconds continued to tick by. Thirty-three. Thirty-two. Thirty-one. Thirty.

Boston checked the flame on his screen again, then the chat window, then the clock, and back again.

With twenty-one seconds left on the timer, a new message appeared in the chat box.

"You can't hide from me."

Boston grinned at the suggestion. "Why would I hide?"

Fifteen seconds left.

"I don't hear you coming down the stairs," his mother warned. Her voice did that thing at the end of the last few words where it raised in pitch, then dropped off. He'd heard it before from friends' moms, too, and figured it was a universal thing they did to add one more layer to the threat of what might happen were kids not obeying.

More text blipped into the chat box.

"I will find you."

The flame in the top-right corner started blinking, and a new box opened underneath it. It displayed the image of a man with curly hair so dark it looked nearly black. The dimly lit room displayed few decorations on the white walls. Behind him, Boston saw a tall, steeply sloping hillside descending down to a blue ocean hugged by a gray pebble beach.

The whites surrounding the man's dark pupils glowed brightly in his computer's screen light. His dark features twitched slightly around thin lips, set on the canvas of a slim, almost birdlike face. The long, pointed nose accentuated the hawkish appearance.

Boston looked over at the timer. Eight seconds remained. He heard footsteps coming up the stairs and knew if he didn't appear in the hall before his mother reached the door, he'd get a stern look at minimum. She was a kind woman, but his mom abhorred tardiness —especially when it involved food she'd taken the time to cook.

He quickly typed out his reply. "I found you first." Then he hovered over the Send button for a second before deleting the message. He smiled as he closed the browser.

The timer dinged on the desk next to him, and he quickly reached over and tapped the Stop button on the phone screen. Looking back to the computer monitor, he studied the image recorded on the screen by his fire chaser tracking application. Below the image, a number stared back at him.

The seller's ISP number.

The fire chaser produced another window to the side of the image and began listing a scrolling sequence of numbers—all proxies the underground art dealer had used to throw off tracking software.

He'd been good. Boston had to give him that. But not good enough. And while the man had seemed confident in his threat to locate the teenager, he'd been unsuccessful. If he had found Boston, the fire chaser would have alerted him to the danger, and he could have shut things down sooner.

But that hadn't happened.

Boston spun out of his chair and hurried over to his bedroom door, twisted the knob, and flung it open to find his mother reaching out to open it herself.

"Hey, Mom. Breakfast smells great." He put on the most innocent expression he could summon, and grinned. "Biscuits?"

"Yes. Now get down there before they get cold, if they haven't already."

"Yes, ma'am."

He slid past her and walked the short distance to the top of the stairs, satisfied that back in his room, he had something Dak badly needed.

A lead.

11

LOCATION UNDISCLOSED

Nicole sat upright in an aluminum chair. The ridges on the seat and back pressed into her skin. It wasn't painful. But it didn't feel good, either. Especially since she was tied to the cold, impersonal thing.

At least her captor had taken the tape off her mouth, which hurt —like ripping off the largest Band-Aid in the world.

She stared into the monster's eyes four feet away.

Tucker sat backward in a similar chair with his forearm resting on the top of the back—the way cool kids did in the '80s.

Streaks of gray in his military-cut hair matched the hoops around his pupils. His weathered and tanned face had a healthy but exhausted look to it—the skin drawn down from under his eyes, hanging loosely like someone who hadn't slept in a lifetime. He wore a long-sleeved, light blue button-up and brown trousers.

She still had on the same clothes she'd worn since they took her.

Nicole felt grimy and desperately needed a shower, but the devil in front of her hadn't offered anything of the sort. She doubted that would happen anytime soon.

"You really think he's going to get that painting for you?" Nicole spat.

"He would do anything for you. Even if it cost him his life," Tucker answered coolly.

"If I were you, I'd hope he doesn't find you."

Tucker rolled his head to the side, as if her words were of no consequence. "I'm not scared of your boyfriend. And I hope he finds me, too. Because when he does, I'll kill him."

She glowered at him as he stood and paced to the wall on his right. The nondescript bedroom's barren white walls matched the lack of furniture. A mattress with a single thin blanket and a flat pillow sat in the corner beneath a blacked-out window. The only light in the room came from the foggy domed fixture in the middle of the ceiling.

One of Tucker's goons stood by the door with his bulging arms crossed over his massive chest. Nicole didn't kid herself with hopeful ideas about escaping. That wasn't going to happen.

Since she'd been abducted, the only time she had been left alone was to sleep. And even then, she knew one of Tucker's guys was always standing guard just outside.

"You know that isn't true," Nicole sneered. "If you could have killed Dak, you'd have done it by now. You're afraid. That's why I'm here. You need a little insurance."

He stood still for a second, staring at the blank wall, deep in thought. "Never hurts to have insurance," he mused without looking over at her. Then his tone grew melancholy. "Dak was my best. Truly. He was a master, a true artisan of killing. He was so good."

The conversation about Dak's penchant for taking lives squeezed Nicole's empty stomach. She didn't like hearing about it, and for their entire relationship, Dak had never brought it up.

Tucker looked over at her, staring across his shoulder as he continued. "Of course, I'm sure he never told you what he did—the lives he took, the way he took them. Most of what he did was classified. I doubt he would have blabbed. A true soldier, dedicated to duty and honor."

"Two things you clearly lack."

He allowed an amused hum. "Duty and honor either get you

killed, wounded, or a mediocre pension for the rest of your life. People say "Thank you for your service" or give a round of applause at sporting events during November. But when you get home, you're stuck with whatever the military gave you. And frankly, it isn't enough. Not for me. Not for what I've dealt with."

Tucker rounded to face her fully. "I'd say it's only fair that I get something extra for doing my duty to preserve the American way of life."

She rolled her eyes, figuring she was about to get a spiel she hadn't signed up for.

"Dak's high and mighty morals stood in the way," Tucker said. "He killed the men who worked for me, although I have to admit he did me a favor. All of them were sloppy. I was going to have to kill them myself. But he handled that part. Of course, for him it was all about revenge."

She looked away from him, flashing her gaze to the opposite corner, where the mattress lay mashed up against the wall. After blinking a couple of times, she rounded back to him. "You talk like Dak killed them in cold blood. Sounds to me like they brought it upon themselves. He's not a murderer."

Derision pushed Tucker's right eyebrow up half an inch. "Oh really? You have no idea what he's done. The horrors he's committed."

"Probably by your command," she fired back quickly.

He could only respond by absently bobbing his head, then he turned and paced to the door, stopped, and ambled back toward her, stopping inches from her toes. He leered down at her and bent over at the waist to get close enough that she could smell his pungent aftershave.

"You have a mouth on you. I'll give you that." He raised his right hand and brushed the back of his thumb against her cheek. She winced and twisted her head away. But he grabbed her chin with his left hand and forced her to look into his eyes.

Nicole had feared it would come to this, that Tucker would—

sooner or later—take her abduction to a deeper, darker level. The worst level. The basement of hell.

The coffee on his hot breath turned her already tumbling stomach.

"Don't look away from me when I'm talking to you." He finished the sentence by smacking her hard on the cheek. With her chin and jaw gripped tightly in his other hand, her head couldn't turn to absorb the blow, and the sharp sting seared across her skin.

Tears gathered in her eyes, blurring her vision.

"Not so clever now, huh?" He spat and shook her face, releasing it hard to the left. He stood up straight and peered down at her with a deranged look of disdain stirred with lust.

Nicole expected the worst. Terrible visions of Tucker ripping her pajama pants and T-shirt off raced through her mind. Only one thought managed to fight off that unrealized future.

"You, of all people should know better than to play games with Dak. If you are truly aware of how dangerous he is, you'd have never done this. And you certainly wouldn't try to make him jump through hoops for you. There's only one way this ends. With you dead."

Tucker inclined his head, but he wasn't threatened. He simply smiled, parting his thin lips in a slight crease as if amused by a child's game.

"You have a good imagination. Though you are right about Dak. He's extremely dangerous. But so am I."

He said nothing else. Instead, Tucker pivoted on his heels and walked over to the door and opened it.

"It's too late, you know," she said before he could step out.

He half looked back over his shoulder. Tucker decided to humor her. "And what might it be too late for?"

"You've set things in motion. Even if you let me go, he will never stop hunting you until you're dead. Your future has already been written. And nothing is going to change that."

He hummed. "Well, I guess we'll just have to see."

Tucker closed the door behind him, leaving her in the room alone once more. She knew the guard would be back in shortly to untie her.

Nicole thought it interesting that the colonel even took the precaution to bind her before visiting. He was being careful—extremely so. She posed no threat to a seasoned soldier. That told her that he wasn't going to slip up against Dak, and that thought flung a wrench into her confidence.

"Please be careful, Dak," she whispered.

12

ISTANBUL

Dak gripped the phone in his hand. He hadn't set the thing down for the last half hour since talking to Boston.

He'd gotten up to pace around a few times, eventually wandering over to the cop standing guard at the wall surrounding the cemetery to ask what was going on.

The young man in uniform didn't seem irritated, as Dak had expected, when being questioned about what they were doing. Dak figured the guy probably had curious tourists and locals coming up to him all day to ask. Turned out, the cop sounded excited to talk about it, though in a hushed tone for fear his superiors might reprimand him.

"Someone broke into the tomb a few nights ago. Investigators are still combing the area to make sure nothing was taken." The man's flawless English caught Dak off guard, though he estimated the cop to be in his early twenties, and probably the product of learning multiple languages including English growing up.

The answer piqued Dak's interest. "You said someone broke into the tomb? As in, Barbarossa's tomb?"

The officer nodded. "Yes."

"Any idea who did it?"

"I'm not permitted to say at this time."

Dak noticed the concerted effort on the cop's face, as if willing himself not to give up the information against every instinct within him begging to do so.

Looking beyond the cop through the iron fence, Dak tried to see what was going on within the tomb, but all he noticed were the people he'd seen before, carrying on with flashlights and instruments he didn't recognize.

Dak decided to leave the cop alone and take the questions regarding the tomb and its apparent break-in with him back to the bench.

"Feel better?" Will asked.

"Not really." Dak glanced back over his shoulder at the cop guarding the gate. "That guy either doesn't know anything or won't share what he does know."

"Did you expect him to? I mean, you are a complete stranger. And an American."

"No. But it's certainly curious. Who would break into a tomb like that?"

"Looters? Grave-robber types?"

"I guess." Dak turned around and looked straight ahead again at the waterfront. "I wouldn't think there'd be anything of value in there other than historical."

"Maybe he was buried with a secret treasure or something," Will offered.

"Maybe," Dak half agreed. "It's odd. That's all I know."

The phone buzzed in his hand, interrupting the conversation. Dak checked the screen to confirm the caller's identity.

"It's the kid," he announced and hit the green button before holding the device to his ear.

"That was fast," Dak said, answering the call.

"Gotta be fast in my sandbox," Boston replied.

"Were you able to find anything about the painting?"

"No."

Dak's heart sank so low he thought it might hit his toes. The wind blowing gently around him offered no air to fill his lungs. His chest tightened, squeezing him like a python.

"But I didn't think I would find info about the painting. That would have been lucky."

The statement eased the anxiety wrapping itself around Dak. "Don't you usually find specific details regarding the things you have me traipsing around the world to retrieve?"

"Yes. That, however, takes time. When I come to you with something, that information is the result of a lot of hours on- and offline. And more often than not, the people who acquired the artifacts or works of art in question have been sloppy. They leave breadcrumbs. It's just a matter of finding the trail. I'll keep checking to see what I can find. I didn't have much to work with this morning. And my mom was pressing me to get downstairs for breakfast."

The humorous dose of reality teased a little of the tension from Dak's chest.

"Well, I appreciate you trying. Let me know if you—"

"I didn't say I wasn't able to find anything," Boston interrupted.

Hope fluttered through Dak's mind.

"Yeah?"

"Sometimes it's easier to find a person than a thing. Especially something as high profile as a Rembrandt. Most people have never heard of, much less considered, something like the sword of Francisco Pizarro. That's a pretty obscure and random artifact to hunt for. Because of that, and the others I've had you track down, those who bought or sold them weren't as careful."

"They were sloppy," Dak said, using the word his young employer had a moment ago.

"Yep. In the case of the Rembrandt, I don't know where it is or who bought it or who sold it. But I was able to get one lead."

"A lead?"

"He's an underground art dealer. Tried to track me down. Even threatened me."

"I'm sorry, Boston. I shouldn't have brought you into—"

"He didn't scare me. I have countermeasures in place for people who try to spook me online. What he didn't realize was that his attempt to locate me worked against him. I have a system that hunts down anyone trying to ping my location. It not only works as a firewall against those kinds of attacks, but as a hunter."

Dak's mind felt a little like it was about to explode. Myriad questions pulsed through his brain at light speed. The one dominating all of them was how this young teenager had figured out how to create such a digital nightmare for potential enemies.

Boston, it seemed, was far more than just a video game savant.

"So, where is this dealer?" Dak asked, chopping his way through the jungle of other questions looming in front of him.

"Direct. I like it. He's in Portugal."

The answer surprised Dak, and he glanced over at Will, who puzzled at the look.

"What?" Will mouthed.

Dak held up a finger to tell his friend to wait.

"That's interesting. You wouldn't happen to know where in Portugal, would you?"

"I would, actually. Looks like he's on the island of Madeira."

"Madeira?"

Will sat up at the sound of the familiar place. Having spent the last few years living in Portugal, it came as no surprise that he knew of the island. Dak figured he probably visited there now and then, if not frequently.

"City of Funchal. I'm sending you a text message now. Looks like he's on the outskirts of the city. You can see the town in the background of the image."

"Image? You took a picture of him?"

Boston laughed. "Yeah."

"Wait. You hacked his webcam?"

Another chuckle. "He was trying to hack mine," Boston defended.

"No. No. I wasn't chastising you for it. I'm just... well, surprised. I didn't know you could do all that."

"I guess I'm just full of surprises."

"No kidding."

"I just sent the pic. That way you'll know when you find him. I can't tell you how to do that. But I figure someone like you can handle that part."

Dak nodded. "I definitely can." He felt the temptation to lower the phone when it vibrated, signaling the image had arrived, but decided to hold off until the conversation was over. "Anything else I need to know?"

"Nope. I sent the guy's address. But be careful. I mean, I know I don't have to tell you to do that. But this dude deals with extremely high-end assets. I seriously doubt he messes with anything less than seven figures."

"Impressive. I would think the market for stuff like that would be pretty tight."

"It is. And they're paranoid sorts. Expect lots of security."

That awoke another question. "You don't think he knows you tracked him, do you?"

Boston sighed. "Oh, Dak. Do you really have such little faith in me?"

"No," Dak blushed. "But anything is possible."

"Don't worry about me. I made sure my end was secure. As soon as I got his location and that image, I checked out. He never knew what hit him."

Dak didn't have a choice but to accept the kid's answer. Who was he to question it? He didn't have experience with anything of the sort.

"Okay. I trust you. I just don't want you to find yourself in deeper than you planned."

"I won't be."

"Do you think this dealer knows where the Rembrandt is?" Dak hedged.

"Hard to say. But if he's dealing in high-end art worth millions, it's likely. But I appreciate the thought. I gotta get going. Baseball practice here in a bit. Let me know how it goes in Portugal. And if you need more help, I'll do what I can."

"Thanks, Boston," Dak said. "This means a lot. And it's a massive help. I'll let you know what I find out."

"Cool. Talk to you soon."

"All right."

Dak ended the call and swiped the glass on the device to open the home screen.

"What did he say?" Will asked, noting his friend was off the call.

Dak opened the text message app and tapped on the picture Boston sent. The image filled the screen and displayed a man with dark curly hair and a slender face with a strong jaw. His black lifeless eyes stared back, just below the camera attached to his computer.

"He found someone who might know what happened to the painting," Dak said, twisting the phone around so his friend could see the image.

Will leaned close, narrowing his eyelids to slits so he could see the screen against the glare of the bright sun.

"That's the guy?" Will asked. Before Dak could answer, he added, "Wait. I know where that is."

"I thought you might."

"That's Madeira." He looked up from the phone. "This guy is in Funchal on Madeira?"

"Very astute. Yes. That's what the kid said. You recognize that place?"

Will shook his head. "Not the house. That would be like a one-in-a-million kind of deal. Looks like he has a nice view, though. That beach is called Praia Formosa. It's in a pretty posh area."

"Well, he sells illicit seven-figure art. So that makes sense."

"Don't have to make that much coin to have a place there." Will pointed at the device. "Cost of living on Madeira is about forty percent lower than where you're from."

"Really?" Dak found the revelation shocking. He'd heard about how the cost of living in many places throughout Europe was lower than back home, but that number caught him off guard. "Why am I living in the States like a sucker, then?"

"I've wondered the same thing about you," Will laughed. "There are some differences, though. Things you'll miss from the States." His voice turned distant for a moment. Then it picked up again. "But I think the trades I made are worth it. You give up a few freedoms to get a few others. It's all about priorities."

Dak shook off the tangent conversation.

"If you know this location, we should be able to isolate which house this is," he redirected.

"Definitely. I doubt it's an apartment. Someone in that line of work doesn't want nosy neighbors asking personal questions all the time, if ever."

"Speaking from experience?" Dak joked.

"Absolutely. Seeing strangers out in town is one thing. Seeing them every day, having them pry into your business; all that is no bueno."

Dak stared at the man on the screen, studying the man's face, his eyes, his features. "Funchal," he said quietly. "I guess we're going to Portugal."

Will grinned. "Good to be going home. Even if it is to find a most likely dangerous criminal."

"Boston said he'll likely have security. So, we'll need to be prepared. You don't happen to know—"

"I'll go ahead and stop you right there. You do remember who you're talking to, right?" Will lowered his head slightly and glared at his friend from underneath his upper eyelids.

"I didn't want to impose."

Will chuckled. "Oh, you should. It just so happens I have a nice stash at my new place. We'll fly into Lisbon, drive up to my new house, grab what we need, then drive back to Lisbon. From there, I have a friend who can fly us to Madeira. We'll avoid security that way."

"Couldn't we take a ferry? I know it would be slower."

"Way slower. Like, twenty-two hours slower. The boats run in season, and take nearly a day to get there. Around twenty-three hours."

Dak whistled a descending tone. "Jeez. We don't have that kind of time."

"Exactly why I suggest we use my friend, the pilot. I'll send him a message to let him know we're coming."

"This friend... can you trust him?"

A half-insulted expression drew across Will's face. "Of course I can trust him. I wouldn't suggest him if I couldn't."

Dak looked out at the waterfront again. The sea rippled beyond the walls. In the distance, a collection of white clouds gathered, turning gray by the minute.

"Looks like a storm might be coming," he realized.

Will nodded. "Indeed."

13

MARSEILLE

Tucker walked briskly along the sidewalk, passing countless cafés, bars, restaurants, boutique clothiers, and shops.

Ghostly clouds smeared long patches of white across the blue sky. High on a hilltop in the distance, Notre-Dame de la Garde pierced the azure backdrop with its white stone tower. The focal point of the majestic basilica, a gilded statue of the Virgin Mary, looked down upon the red-tiled roofs and the harbor of Marseille.

The translation meant Our Lady of the Guard, though many locals referred to the spectacular church and statue as *la Bonne Mère* —the Good Mother.

Tucker had heard about the history of the place. The basilica's construction began in the mid-nineteenth century and took a little over a decade. Compared to many other cathedrals in Europe, it was still in its youth, though it had gone through refurbishments in the early 2000s.

He didn't care about any of that. History wasn't his strong suit, nor was architecture, religion, or any of the other minutiae that went along with old buildings and the people who went to great lengths to visit them.

To Tucker, they were just places. Not things to be revered.

His personal guard, Lee, walked just behind him off his right shoulder. The man was built like a tank, with thick, broad shoulders, tree trunks for legs, and tattoos poking out from under his black T-shirt across his forearms and up to the base of his neck.

Lee's shaved head beaded with sweat that rolled down on either side of his wraparound Oakley sunglasses.

The man said nothing as he followed his employer down the sidewalk. The sounds of people conversing about inconsequential things mixed with the ropes banging against tall masts of sailboats parked in the harbor.

That was one thing that had impressed Tucker—the sheer number of boats in the water in Marseille's harbor. The first time he saw it, the sight took him by surprise. There were thousands of them, bobbing and swaying with the temperament of the water and wind.

He'd always dreamed of owning a big yacht when he retired from the military, but knew that the salary he was paid for his years of service, and the subsequent retirement paychecks, wouldn't come close to how much he would need to buy what he wanted.

All of that was superficial at the moment.

Right now, he had problems to deal with.

He turned right down an alley between two of the beige stone buildings that lined the marina and continued into the shadows.

The sounds of cars, conversations, and the constant dinging from the boat masts channeled through the narrow corridor, then faded as Tucker and his guard neared the door they were looking for.

No signs hung out from the wall to indicate the place of business he sought. No neon lights announced its location. It was one of those spots that could only be found by those who knew it was there, and knew how to get inside.

Just past a green dumpster, Tucker stopped at a black metal door. He took a quick glance back the way they had come to make sure they hadn't been followed. Lee did the same, though both were confident they were alone and unwatched.

A metal plate with a narrow slot cut into it was mounted to the wall next to the door. Tucker reached into his pocket and took out a golden card.

He slipped the card into the slot and waited. A second later, the card popped back out of the reader, and the door opened automatically.

Tucker slid the card back into his pocket and stepped through the opening into the building.

Lee said nothing as he followed but gave one last look in both directions just to be safe before he entered after Tucker.

Once the two men were inside, the door closed behind them.

Their ears instantly filled with the haunting sound of maracas, the drums, the grunts and howls, and then the piano accompanying Mick Jagger's young voice singing the beginning of the Rolling Stones' song "Sympathy For The Devil."

"That's a bit heavy handed," Tucker quipped.

Lee's shoulders lifted as he chuffed once.

The dark antechamber was small, but ten feet away through a black marble archway the room opened up into a bar were a female bartender in her mid-thirties stood pouring drinks behind the counter. Her lipstick was nearly as black as her hair and contrasted with her porcelain-white skin like oil on newly fallen snow. She had a silver hoop nose ring and tattoos up both her forearms. The white tank top stretched down to the center of her chest, giving just enough of a view to pique the interest of the patrons, but not give away the farm.

Tucker walked under the archway and looked down the length of the bar. Another barkeep stood at the other end—this one a guy with quaffed brown hair and a well-groomed beard. He wore a brown leather apron and a black T-shirt. His biceps bulged, inflating the tattoos that covered his skin as he shook a drink in a metal canister.

Seven patrons sat at the bar—four of them men, three of them women, all of them deadly. A row of tables lined the wall to Tucker's right, all occupied by people varying as widely in age as they did in origin.

Black, white, Latino, Asian, and a couple of guys from the Middle East rounded out the roster of demons in the mercenary den.

Tucker had seen it all before. He'd been in several such underworld places around Europe, and had been disappointed every single time.

Assassins-for-hire was a tricky business. Vetting such employees required a certain degree of trust in that the bartenders were the ones who kept score and validated kills, missions completed, and overall effectiveness.

Tucker knew very well that the two pouring drinks were just as deadly as anyone else in this room, and that to piss one of them off could have catastrophic results.

The former colonel knew how to fight, how to kill, and how to survive, but he also knew his limitations. A lifetime as an officer had relegated him to far too much desk work, and not enough hard training or field ops to keep him on the same level with these types, which was part of the reason he'd brought Lee along for the ride. Tucker's bodyguard had served under him for a short time in Iraq before being deployed elsewhere. Tucker had always gotten the impression Lee was the kind of guy who would obey orders from a superior, but was morally flexible—especially if the said superior offered a few extra breadcrumbs.

No one in this place, or in any of the others like it around the world, had allegiances to a nation, kindred, tongue, or people. Every one of them were for hire to the highest bidder and would carry out their contracts to completion, ruthlessly if necessary.

The rules in the mercenary world were simple. There were no rules, except one: you don't steal contracts from another.

That wasn't to say one assassin couldn't kill one of the others. In fact, that sort of thing happened all the time when one employer was pitted against a rival. Sometimes the contracts were for protection against other mercs, and when that happened, someone always died.

These sorts would buy each other drinks one night, kill each other the next.

It was barbaric, Tucker knew, but he doubted he'd ever be a target of any of them. He wasn't high profile, and the only deals he made were with people he could manage—like the German buyer he'd dealt with before the incident in Ukraine.

The thought of what happened there heated Tucker's blood, and he found himself clenching his fists almost unconsciously.

"Who we looking for, boss?" Lee asked. It was the first time he'd spoken since they left the abandoned church where the hostage and the rest of Tucker's hired guns remained.

"Follow me. And stay close," was all Tucker would offer.

He knew Lee had never been in one of these places before, and even though the bulky man could handle his own, these killers were different animals altogether.

Tucker walked up to the bar and took a seat on the stool at the far-left end near the wall. Lee sat down to his right.

"Be right with you," the female bartender said without concern or emotion. Her accent was distinctly French, probably Parisian if Tucker had to guess, but her English was flawless, as he'd noticed with so many Europeans these days.

She finished pouring a round of four shots of Jack Daniel's into clear shot glasses and then nudged them forward to a skinny, pale guy in a white T-shirt, navy-blue vest, and blue jeans. He wore a pair of John Lennon-style sunglasses even though the room was barely lit by the faux candles in two black metal, three-tiered chandeliers overhead. His short blond hair was brushed to one side, with a few strands deliberately tousled—probably with some kind of pomade or gel.

Lee cast a dubious glare at the slender man with the four whiskeys, thinking there was no way someone that skinny could hold down that much liquor in one go.

The man rested his elbows on the edge of the bar without moving, and simply stared down at the four drinks as if to consume them with the power of intention.

"Got a problem over there?" The man asked the question with a sharp Irish accent.

Lee suddenly felt both uncomfortable and affronted. His testosterone-infused instinct was to blow up and ask the guy if he had a problem, but Lee sensed Tucker shaking his head to his left and eased up.

"No. No problem." He still didn't see how that guy was going to hold down the liquor, though the Irish accent partially explained it.

Lee tore his eyes away from the man, but looked back again one more time and saw the Irishman's lips quivering. He was saying something, but Lee couldn't tell what.

"It's a blessing," Tucker said. "And you'd do well to leave him to it."

Lee's head did a 180 to face his employer. "A blessing?" he whispered. "In this place?"

"Everyone has their thing. I'd let them have it. Whatever it is."

The bartender stepped over to where they sat as the Irishman finished his prayer and then downed each of the shots one after the other. "What are you drinking?" she asked.

"Two bourbons," Tucker answered.

"How you want those? Rocks? Neat?"

Tucker grinned devilishly. Before Lee could respond, he said, "There's only one way it should be."

"Unless you're Frank. Then you can take it however you like." She winked at him. "What kind of bourbon?"

"Angel's Envy."

"My kind of man," she said flirtatiously with a curl of the lip and a swing of the hair as she turned around to grab the bottle from the shelf behind the bar.

A wall-size mirror positioned behind the bottles allowed the bartenders to always have eyes on the room in case tempers flared and needed to be extinguished.

She expertly set the bottle down in front of the two men, flipped a tumbler up into her left hand like she'd seen the original *Cocktail* too many times. She placed it in front of Tucker, then did the same with the second and set it next to the other before flipping the bottle upside down and spilling the golden amber liquid into the glasses.

She filled them halfway, then splashed a little extra into the colonel's glass for good measure.

"What you lookin' for?" she asked as she spun around and replaced the bottle where she got it.

Tucker wrapped his fingers around the glass and raised it to his nose, sniffing the aroma's caramel, velvety goodness. Lee just stared at it, uncertain if he was supposed to shoot it or sip it.

"Your friend looks like he needs a chaser," the bartender ventured, arching her right eyebrow in a sultry yet insulting way.

Tucker hummed at the barb.

"I'm looking for a hitter."

She crossed her arms and cocked her head to the side, then straightened it. "That much I knew. Anyone in particular?"

"The Black Lotus."

14

The bartender stiffened. It was a subtle reaction, barely noticeable. But Tucker noticed. Few names would have caused such a reaction from someone as cold-blooded as a den handler.

He didn't check the rest of the room, but Tucker thought he detected a few other people pause their conversations the instant he said the name.

The song ended and was replaced through the speakers with another Rolling Stones tune, "Paint It Black."

Tucker resisted the urge to roll his eyes at the coincidence. Then again, he never really believed in coincidences. He didn't have that luxury in life. Believing in random occurrences was a lazy way to think, to live. Of course, the other side of that coin was total paranoia.

Still, he believed things typically didn't just happen.

He'd never been much of a spiritual guy, despite his upbringing in a strictly religious family. But he'd seen too many things line up in mysterious ways to think the universe was spinning out of control, spiraling toward a random doom where it inevitably collapsed back in upon itself.

"That one isn't cheap," the bartender said.

"I didn't realize this was a discount store."

Her right eyebrow flicked slightly at the comeback, and her cheeks stretched with a subtle, flirtatious grin.

"If you know about the Lotus, then you know they only take certain jobs. They are... picky."

"I'm aware."

Lee watched the conversation like he was at center court of Roland-Garros. He remained uncomfortably, awkwardly silent.

Tucker leaned forward so his face was past the midpoint of the countertop. "This contract will pay one hundred up front. With another hundred after completion."

The bartender pouted her lips and tilted her head to the side. Her hair dangled down past a tattoo of scales on her shoulder, a symbol of justice... and judgment.

"A one hundred percent bonus? Since you're in here, you know we don't do high-level political targets."

"And I also know that handlers aren't supposed to dig too deep into contract negotiations. Can you get her or not?"

The *her* in the sentence caught the bartender off guard, which Tucker figured did not happen often. It told the woman that he knew more about the Black Lotus than the typical employer who passed through these doors.

Many people knew the rumors. But few knew the details.

The Black Lotus was a moniker whispered in the darkest of circles. No one knew for certain where she came from, but there were plenty of stories that circulated throughout these kinds of dens around the world.

One consistent rumor suggested that she only took jobs that had to deal with the worst kinds of people. Some theorized that was because she wanted a challenge. And then there was the other element to it, the part of the puzzle Tucker knew she wouldn't be able to resist.

According to whispers, she had a penchant for rare art.

Tucker slid a piece of paper across the counter toward the

bartender. She lowered her gaze to the phone number written in black ink as the song ended.

Saxophones and brass instruments replaced it with quick staccato notes, and then were joined by Danny Elfman's voice singing "All dressed up and nowhere to go," from the song "Dead Man's Party" by Oingo Boingo.

The number on the paper was for a burner phone, of which he had several, and always rotated out old ones after a few weeks to replace them with new numbers and devices. If someone was going to track down Cameron Tucker, they'd have to do it the old-fashioned way.

It went without saying he wasn't online much, at least not in the ways so many billions of sheep were—posting what they had for breakfast, and where they had it, all over their social media accounts. That seemed like a foreign planet to Tucker. And a ridiculous way to live, not to mention insecure.

His quarry, likewise, had proved to be nearly impossible to track down. Finding Dak Harper had been more difficult than he thought, though Tucker wasn't entirely surprised. Of all the men in his elite fighting unit, Dak had been the most measured, and the least given to emotional twists and turns that could turn even the bravest of men into quivering mounds of pudding.

Tucker had visited nests such as this multiple times in different locations, and each time the hitter he'd hired to take out Harper had failed. That list of failures caused Tucker to start to wonder about the mercenary network's vetting process, of which he knew next to nothing.

Then again, Harper was no ordinary target.

Most of the time, the members of dens like this served as high-end bounty hunters, very often doing the bidding of one wicked organization against another. The mercenaries weren't necessarily good or bad. They could serve both sides, though it seemed to Tucker their primary flow of income came from the bad.

He'd noted how the bartender said "high-level politicians."

Tucker knew what that meant. Their killers-for-hire weren't to meddle with international affairs, meaning no taking out a president, prime minister, or monarch. There was a gray area with members of the legislative branches of government, though no one could ever confirm or deny any killings that may have been made to look like accidents.

As he understood the system, though, most targets were blatantly nefarious. Cartel bosses and underlings, Mafia, mobs of every kind from Russian to Chinese, traffickers, drug dealers, and everyone in between were open season all year round. All for a price.

Tucker didn't consider himself a good guy, or a bad guy, either. He was simply a survivor, doing whatever it took to achieve a life of wealth and calm. He'd earned as much, pilfering treasures and looting banks throughout the Middle East during his time as a colonel. That was his reward for suffering through a never-ending War on Terror, and the intolerable conditions in that hellhole.

The United States military had never learned of any of it. Or if they'd found a crumb, they simply swept it under the rug as so many of their Pentagon "journalists" did on a daily basis for all kinds of things.

The bartender had gone for nearly a minute without saying anything. Tucker figured her blank stare was a ploy to give him time to reconsider his request, perhaps ask for a different hitter. But he wasn't going to back down. He'd tried others. It was time for him to try the best.

"You sure you want to—" she started.

"Can you get me the Black Lotus or not," he finished, cutting her off. He knew the risks of insulting a handler, especially in her den. She had home-field advantage. While cutthroat to their cores, every mercenary in this room would immediately turn on him were she to simply say the word. That was the code. It was one of the few rules they lived by.

Just like in the music business, the advice here was never mess with the sound guy or the bartender. Because if you do, you're going to sound like crap, and your drinks will taste the same.

The Irishman to Lee's right had been keeping to himself, either deep in thought or deeper into a buzz from the four whiskeys. Maybe both. His head twisted an inch toward the men to his left, a subtle show of interest in the conversation he'd been ignoring for the last few minutes.

The bartender sighed and inclined her head, as if appraising Tucker one more time. "I can get her. No idea where in the world she is right now."

Tucker knew she meant that statement literally. Once these contractors dropped into a job, they disappeared like ghosts into fog.

"You have my number. That one goes dead in forty-eight hours."

He stood up, fished a fistful of euros out of his front pocket, and tossed them down on the counter next to his untouched drink.

It would go nicely with the 10 percent fee she'd collect simply by bringing the Black Lotus to him. It was the tithe everyone around the world paid for the handlers' services, and discretion. Some might have considered the required fee to be extortionate to some degree.

These dens operated with almost no risk since there were always local, regional, and even federal levels of government both aware of them and customers of their services.

"You know the additional requirement for her, yes?" the barkeep asked without even looking at the proffered money.

"I'm aware. She has a thing for art. Only takes on jobs that involve it in some way."

"Most of our patrons don't need anything like that."

"Well, I do. And I think she'll be very pleased with what I have to offer." Tucker reached down, picked up the glass, and tossed back the bourbon in one gulp. He didn't even flinch as he swallowed the room-temperature liquor. He looked at the empty glass, tilting it slightly in appreciation, then set it down. "Always smooth."

Lee knocked back his drink as well, but winced at the burn in the back of his throat. The bartender shook her head derisively at him.

Tucker turned and walked away with his bodyguard in tow close behind.

They went back out the door and into the alley. After the door closed behind them, Tucker surveyed the backstreet in both directions and started back toward the harbor and the busy street next to it.

"What did she mean?" Lee asked, speaking up for the first time since they'd entered the den.

"About what?" Tucker replied without so much as a sidelong glance.

"The art thing. This Black Lotus person? What's the deal?"

"She's unconventional. Only takes jobs that involve rare black-market art."

"And she kills people for it?"

"That's the point. Yes."

Lee kept walking for a few seconds before he spoke again. "So, an assassin that has a thing for art. I've heard it all now."

The two reached the end of the alley and turned back the way they had come. The sounds of ropes on masts dinged like deranged church bells, once more melding with the sounds of car motors and people chatting.

"No, Lee. You haven't."

15

DOURO VALLEY, PORTUGAL

Dark, shadowy peaks stared back at Dak through the window. A half-moon cast its eerie glow down upon hillsides and mountain tops of the Douro Valley.

The region boasted some of the best wines not only in Portugal but in all of Europe, though the French and Italians probably had something to say about that.

Will guided the small four-door sedan along the twisty road. The headlights illuminating the asphalt ahead disappeared around every curve, casting their beams out over the perilous drops just beyond the road's shoulder.

"I thought you lived by the beach." Dak said, tearing his gaze away from the late evening vistas. "What happened to Nazare?"

"After what happened there before?" Will asked with a chortle. "I love the beach. But I decided I could keep a lower profile out here in wine country. I still have an apartment there. Well, not in Nazare. About fifteen minutes south in São Martinho do Porto. Smaller area. Smaller waves. Fewer prying eyes."

"You're still messed up about the chair bomb thing, huh?"

"Nah," Will deflected. "I'm good. Just drew too much attention. There were a lot of witnesses there that day."

"Yeah. Not a great time for an audience."

Dak thought back on the incredible scenario, and their unlikely escape from certain death. Such a harrowing incident would have kept a lesser person away from Dak for life. But not Will. He kept hanging around and was always willing to help when Dak called—which turned out to be a couple of times a year or more.

If he didn't watch it, people would start to think Will was his sidekick.

Emptying his mind from the strut down memory lane, Dak peered out into the night again.

Getting a flight on such short notice could have been much trickier than it turned out to be. Dak found a flight out of Istanbul later that afternoon with three seats left. None of them were together, so he and Will sat four rows apart during the five-hour flight to Lisbon. Upon arriving, they rented the sedan and hit the road within thirty minutes of stepping off the plane.

After the long flight, it would have been nice to have a short car ride to the destination, but Douro Valley was another five hours away, which would put the two men at Will's new home sometime after two in the morning local time.

Dak looked at the phone propped up in a cup holder. It displayed a map with their location and directions.

"How many times have you been to this new place anyway?" Dak asked.

"Why? Because I still need directions?"

"That too. But also out of curiosity."

"I've only stayed a handful of times so far, but I look forward to doing it more. This place is really beautiful. The moonlight doesn't do it justice. These hillsides are covered with vineyards, some terraced all the way from the bottom to the top. This time of year is when I think it's at its prettiest. The vines are thick with green leaves, and the grapes are well on their way. And the way the sun shines down across the valley?" He shook his head and whistled. "Spectacular."

"I never knew you had the heart of a poet."

Will blew off the comment with a chuckle. "Nah. Not a poet. But I can appreciate a pretty setting when I see one. On nights the moon isn't so bright, you can see a million stars."

Dak peered out the window as they rounded another in the seemingly unending line of curves. "Beautiful how the moon reflects off the river in the bottom of the valley."

"Yeah. The river winds through the hills all the way through the country and ends in Porto."

Questions about wines and other activities in the Douro Valley bubbled through Dak's mind, but he lost them the instant he saw lights flash around the corner behind them. He stole a short glance at the clock to note the time, and then looked back in the rearview mirror.

A pair of headlights raked around the corner behind them.

"Is it normal for there to be people out on this road at this hour of night?" Dak asked, watching the approaching car speed toward them.

"I haven't driven it enough at this time to know, but based on the fact we've only seen two other cars out here so far, I'd say the answer is no."

"That's what I was thinking." Dak adjusted his position and looked out the back window. "They sure seem to be in a hurry."

Will's breathing quickened, and he gripped the steering wheel tighter. "You don't think that could be some of Tucker's guys, do you?"

"I don't know, but we'll find out in a second. Looks like they're either going to pass us or try to run us off the road."

The black sedan behind them accelerated as the two Americans reached the next curve. Then, in an extremely dangerous move, the trailing vehicle's driver merged over into the other lane, as if about to pass.

"This guy is crazy whoever he is," Will blurted. "He's going to get us both killed if he's not careful."

The black sedan behind them pushed up rapidly until they were side by side with Will and Dak.

"Mercedes," Dak noted once he could clearly see the make and model of the vehicle. But he couldn't see who was inside it until the tinted passenger window lowered.

An Asian man—Dak guessed in his late twenties—stared back at the two Americans. But he was less concerned with the man's age than he was about the pistol in his hand, pointed straight at Will.

"Gun," Dak snapped.

Will took his eyes off the road for a split second, spotted the weapon with a suppressor, and slammed on the brakes just as the guy fired the weapon.

They didn't hear the muted report over the sound of tires screeching and motors revving.

For a second, Will had to fight the sedan as it lurched and leaned toward the railing. The enemy surged ahead of them. The instant they were clear, Will took his foot off the brake and stepped on the gas. The car virtually corrected itself, and he regained control, now pursuing the Mercedes.

Dak felt naked without a firearm to wield against the new enemy, and he knew the only weapon they had was the rental car. He didn't like their chances against a gun-toting enemy.

"Any idea who those guys are?" Dak asked.

Will kept his eyes on the road and the vehicle ahead. The Mercedes cut to the left, then back into the right lane as Will guided the sedan ahead. "Um...."

"Wait. You know those guys?" Dak exclaimed.

Will hesitated, biting his lower lip.

"Will? Do you recognize them or not?"

"Maybe."

"Maybe?" Dak sounded incredulous. "You either do or you don't, Will. Who is that?"

The passenger leaned out the Mercedes window and aimed the pistol. The muzzle flashed multiple times, but none of the rounds struck their mark.

Will responded by yanking the handbrake and cutting the wheel to the left. Dak instinctively reached up and grabbed the handle over the window, bracing himself with his shoulder against the door as the car slid sideways—the back end fishtailing toward the upward slope.

"What are you doing?" Dak nearly shouted.

Will corrected the car's slide by turning into the motion, releasing the handbrake, and stepping on the gas.

Plumes of white smoke shrouded the car, and the smell of burned rubber filtered in through the vents.

The sedan charged down the road, away from the gunmen. In the rearview mirror, Will saw the red taillights flash, then cut hard to the left as the other driver realized what happened and likewise changed direction to keep up the pursuit.

Dak peeked back through the window, then over at his friend. "Well?"

"Yeah, so I may have sold those guys some faulty firearms."

The confession only offered a part of the answer Dak was waiting for.

"You did what?" Dak blurted in disbelief. "Who are they? Because I get the feeling they're not happy."

Will accelerated through a curve, keeping his focus on the road. "They're Koreans," he said.

"Koreans?"

"North Koreans, actually. They found me and tried to tell me they were working on some kind of liberation army to free the people from the totalitarian regime there." Will guided the sedan through the next curve to the left, then back to the right. He glanced into the mirror and saw the headlight beams swelling then dying as their pursuers dipped in and out of the turns.

"Why did you sell them fake guns, then? Isn't that kind of your thing?" Dak felt like he was missing something.

"Because they were lying. I had a bad feeling about them from the start. After a little digging, I learned they weren't putting together a liberation army for the people of North Korea. They were communist terrorists."

"Terrorists?"

"Yeah." Will offered a humored chuckle. "So, I sold them a bunch of guns that didn't work."

"Jeez. How much did they pay you?"

Will grinned proudly. "Half million."

"What?"

"Yeah."

"Well, I can see why they're unhappy with you," Dak realized as he looked back again. "What's your plan? We can't get in a gunfight with them. And how did they find you?"

Will answered by stepping on the brake, turning the wheel, then cutting the wheel to the left. He jerked the handbrake again as he hit the gas and spun the tires. The sedan whipped around, and once facing the other direction, repeated the move from before to accelerate back down the road.

"What are you doing?"

"Using the only weapon we have," Will growled.

The headlight beams from the other car grew brighter around the curve ahead. In a few seconds, the Mercedes would come into view.

Dak didn't like where this was going, but he had no choice. Their options were to either try to get to Will's place, arm themselves, and shoot it out with these guys, or run back to one of the villages or cities where there were more people and hopefully police that could end the chase. The problem with the latter was that he and Will would also be considered dangerous by the cops. They'd be arrested along with the North Koreans, and that would not do.

Innocent or not, Nicole didn't have that kind of time.

"Hold on," Will said as the lights from the other car grew brighter. He didn't slow down as he steered the sedan around the curve to the left.

The instant the Mercedes appeared directly ahead in the other lane, Will flipped on the high beams.

The lights blazed through the other windshield, illuminating the driver and the gunman. Both men instinctively raised their arms to shield their eyes from the searing lamps.

A second later, Will and Dak raced by, narrowly missing the Mercedes by mere inches. The cars passed with a whoosh. Dak looked back through the rear window while Will watched in the mirror as the Mercedes jerked left and right for a second before slamming into the rock retaining wall. The vehicle's momentum flipped it up high, as if it might topple over the wall. A second later gravity smashed the tail end back down to the pavement. It bounced on its rear tires twice before settling.

They didn't see what happened to the vehicle's two occupants, but dead or not, Dak knew the gunman and the driver would at the very least be unable to continue their pursuit. Even if they'd been fully strapped in with seat belts, that kind of full-speed crash would put them in the hospital for a few days or longer.

Will eased his foot on the brake, gradually slowing to a stop. The two men looked back at the scene of the wreck, then over at each other.

"That worked out pretty well all things considered." Will kept his gaze fixed on the spot where the other vehicle had disappeared.

Dak finally caught his breath and stared over at the driver. "Worked out?"

"They're gone, aren't they?"

"How in the world did they find you? Do they know where you live?"

"No. No way. They must have followed us from the airport. It's the only explanation. Tracked me somehow. Maybe they'd been watching the airports. But don't worry. We'll be safe at the house. And we aren't staying long. We'll catch a few hours of sleep then head back to Lisbon. Jimmy is meeting us in the morning."

"You sound pretty sure."

Dak never liked to make assumptions. He wasn't going to simply assume that the men who just smashed their car were dead, and he still had questions about whether or not he could trust this pilot character, Jimmy.

They needed a pilot who wouldn't ask too many questions, or already knew the answers. According to Will, it was the latter, and Jimmy was a guy he'd worked with before.

That required a little faith on Dak's part. But checking to make sure their pursuers were dead only took a short walk over to the guardrail.

"Turn around."

"What?" Will blurted.

"Turn around. We need to make sure they're dead."

Will's eyes glazed over as he stared at Dak with bewilderment in his eyes. "Dude. There's no way they survived that. Look." He pointed toward the back window. "See that crash?"

Smoke and steam spewed out of the engine block from under the crumpled hood, swirling and dancing until it mixed somewhere in the darkness above.

"Just do it."

With an eye roll and shake of his head, Will shifted the car into reverse, performed a three-point turn, and sped back down the road to the wreckage. Will eased the car to a stop but kept his foot on the brake without shifting into park.

"Keep it running," Dak ordered as he pulled the handle and opened the door.

"Sure. No problem," Will said with an uneasy tone in his voice. He gripped the wheel loosely, still confident he'd been correct about the fate of the chase vehicle's occupants.

Dak stepped out and cautiously approached the black sedan. Something sizzled from under the hood. An alarm dinged inside the cabin through the broken driver's side window.

As he approached, Dak saw that the car was empty. A closer inspection revealed that the two men had been ejected through the windshield and over the mountainside. He only relaxed slightly as he drew close enough to see every detail inside the mangled vehicle.

A pistol magazine lay in the floorboard on the passenger side. Dak considered opening the car and rifling through the interior to see if he could get more info on the men who'd tried to kill him and Will but thought better of it.

No need to turn the scene of an accident into a crime scene by leaving a few easily found fingerprints.

Instead, Dak walked over to the retaining wall and looked out over it. A hundred feet down the hillside, he spotted the two North Koreans, their bodies illuminated by moonlight. Even from that distance, Dak knew the men were dead.

One's head was twisted at an impossibly awkward angle, along with his arms and legs. The other lay against the base of a huge boulder near a row of grapevines. A dark stain smeared the side of the rock where the man's head had struck first, killing him on impact.

Dak sighed, both from relief and from knowing Will was going to rib him about having predicted the men were dead.

He turned and ambled back to the rental, where Will waited patiently. When Dak reached the door, Will raised both eyebrows and tilted his head. "Well?"

Dak inhaled sharply and bobbed his head without saying a word.

Will cleared his throat, unsatisfied with the response.

Dak climbed in and shook his head as he closed the door hard. For a second, he ignored his annoying friend and stared through the windshield.

Will refused to let up and cleared his throat again. "I'm sorry? I couldn't hear you. What did you say?"

Dak angled his head slightly toward his friend and met Will's judging eyes. "You were right. They're dead. Now, let's get out of here before another car comes along. Pretty sure that Mercedes has GPS tracking and crash sensors to alert first responders if there's an accident."

Will grinned a goofy, smug grin. "I wouldn't worry too much about the first responders. We'll be at my house before they arrive."

He turned the car around and drove away from the scene.

"I'm still concerned about these North Koreans knowing your whereabouts. You're sure your home is secured?"

"If anyone was at the house, my security system and my cameras would have alerted me already. These guys found me. We'll just have to be on the lookout when we head back to Lisbon. Since we're chartering a plane, I don't think they'll be able to find us again. If they try at all."

Dak accepted the reasoning. After all, he didn't have a choice. "Okay. Maybe next time let me know you've pissed off North Korean nationals before I ask for your help with something."

Will hummed a laugh. "Oh, I'm sure there are plenty more people on that list, my friend."

He pressed down on the gas pedal, and the car accelerated into the night, leaving the scene of the crash behind.

16

Will slowed the car down as they approached a gate with a rock wall on either side. The stones and mortar looked as if they were a hundred or more years old, though the black metal gate looked brand new.

Dak figured it was one of the many updates his friend must have needed to refurbish the old farmhouse.

The driveway connected to the main road they'd been on since entering the valley and wound down the hillside with a series of switchback curves until it paused at the gate. Through the iron bars, the car's headlights illuminated a rustic stone house. It was two stories tall with a covered patio on the right side supported by timber posts.

Will rolled down his window and reached out to a keypad fixed to a stand-alone post. He entered the four-digit code and leaned back into the car as the gate slowly rolled away, opening the path onto the pebble driveway.

Once the way was clear, Will drove through the opening and parked in front of the entrance. Two stone slabs served as the steps up to the light brown door. Two gas lamps burned on either side of the doorway, their flames flickering steadily within the glass cages.

"Nice place," Dak commented. "Authentic for this part of the world."

"I like it. Although I made some changes to the interior. Needed some updating."

The two men climbed out of the car and collected their things from the trunk. Dak followed his friend to the door where Will unlocked it, stepped inside, and disarmed the alarm system. Before entering, Dak noticed a camera in the left corner under the portico, remembering Will's reference to his security system from before.

Dak closed the door and locked the deadbolt in a habitual manner as he would if he were in his own home.

Will flipped on some lights, allowing Dak to fully survey the room.

The interior's open floor plan looked much like a cabin or lodge in the Smoky Mountains. Timber beams supported the ceiling overhead, with matching posts in the corners. The small kitchen to the right housed a steel Viking gas stove and matching refrigerator. The countertops were formed concrete atop black cabinetry. In the living room, a light brown leather sofa and two matching lounge chairs sat facing a silent fireplace.

"Nice place," Dak noticed.

He walked past the bar at the kitchen counter where three wooden stools sat underneath, and through the living room to the huge window on the far side. A covered porch beyond offered a place to sit and enjoy the view of the valley spreading out beyond.

"Thanks," Will said. He set his bag down and walked over to the fridge, opened it, and took out a glass bottle of water. "Thirsty?"

Dak nodded, still staring out through the window.

The house was perched halfway up the mountainside where the gradual slope above suddenly steepened. It wasn't a drop-off, but hiking up from below would have been a workout.

Will joined his friend by the window and handed him the proffered bottle. "Here you go."

Dak thanked him. "You can really pick the spots. Although I thought you were more of a beach guy."

"I'm both. I love the mountains and the coast."

"Same," Dak said with a tired grin and clinked his bottle against the side of Will's.

"This place has an old winery out back. Real old-school. Not a big operation. Family thing."

"That's so cool. Like with the thing where they stomp the grapes with their feet?"

"Yep." Will took a sip from the bottle. "The kids didn't want to have anything to do with it, so when their parents died, they put it up for sale."

"Shame to let good grapes go to waste."

"Oh, they don't. I pay people to tend the vines for me, harvest the grapes, and make the wine. The barrel house is out back, too."

The answer surprised Dak. "Seriously? You're a wine maker now?"

"Not me. I just own it. I don't know that much about the process, honestly. And I'm not here consistently enough to learn all the ins and outs. I will eventually, when I decide to slow down my business."

"Retirement?" Dak huffed at the notion.

Will had plenty of money if he wanted to call it quits at that very moment. But Dak knew it wasn't the cash that kept him going in the gun smuggling trade. It was purpose. Sure, Will might have been a little addicted to the adrenaline that came with his occupation. There were those types out there, almost always in illegal markets of one kind or another, who didn't really need the money but loved the rush, the chance of getting caught, and the feeling of triumph when they weren't.

Power also had a role in all that.

Drug dealers, gunrunners, and illicit artifact dealers liked the sense of control they had over others and the feeling of invincibility that came with it.

Dak felt fortunate to never hear the call of things like that. He'd grown up in the suburbs of a midsize Southern city where that sort of thing was either kept under wraps or nonexistent. Then again, Will grew up in much the same way, but Will's journey was different in that he did it to help those who couldn't help themselves. The money was almost a byproduct.

"I can't do it forever, Dak," Will said, going back to the question of retirement.

"Yeah, but you're not even forty yet."

Will chuckled. "I know. But this isn't the kind of gig you want to do until you're fifty-seven. Or whatever retirement age is now."

"You haven't been watching what's going on with the economy and inflation, have you?"

The two shared a laugh.

"Yeah. I've seen it. But you get my point. I wouldn't want to do any job for that long. But this is more of a mission, so I don't know. Maybe I'll keep at it. It's dangerous, but people got to be able to stand up to oppression. Know what I mean?"

Dak nodded and said that he did.

He'd been thinking about that very thing for a while now, particularly with what was going on down in Cuba. One dictator died, and another fascist regime took its place. The citizens weren't permitted to have guns, and so their oppressive rulers remained unchecked.

Dak had spoken to his friend Ricardo about this very issue. Rick was in his late sixties and had escaped with thousands of other Cuban refugees in the early 1980s, much like their predecessors in the '60s.

They had been at a cabin in the Smoky Mountains, sipping on Willamette Valley Pinot Noir and staring out at Mount LeConte across the valley under a clear moonlit night not dissimilar to the one in Douro.

"What are your thoughts on the situation in Cuba right now?" Dak asked.

Rick shook his head. "They're going to kill all those people who disagree with them or don't get in line. Someone needs to get them some guns. But our dear leader won't do that. He's too busy funneling money elsewhere."

Dak knew Rick had way more intel on the situation than he did and trusted the statement. And it made Dak wonder if there was a way Will could help. Perhaps he'd bring it up once this ordeal was through. For the time being, though, Dak had to focus all his energy on doing whatever it took to get Nicole back.

"So, where is this weapons stash you told me about?"

Will took another slow sip of water, then gradually turned his head. He wore a cryptic grin on his face that held both secrets and mischief.

"What?" Dak pressed. "Where is it?"

"Let's take a walk outside. You need to see the barrel house."

17

From the way Will said it, Dak knew the barrel house contained much more than just wine.

Exhaustion beckoned him to get some sleep, but Dak knew he'd struggle to get some shuteye without a weapon by his side. That wasn't always the case, as he knew it was with some guys who'd been in his previous line of work. But after the attack by the North Korean assassins on the road, it seemed prudent to at least have something on the nightstand or under his pillow, just in case.

He followed Will through a laundry room on the main floor and out across the wraparound porch. They descended the steps and walked across the pebble driveway to a large wooden building a hundred feet off from the house. The barrel house was at least three times the size of Will's house.

The structure looked similar to a barn in many ways, with angled roofs and a siding much like Dak had seen on the farms near where he grew up. But with additional sections jutting out from both sides.

Will stopped at a door to the right of the big barn doors and inserted a key.

"You really that worried about someone breaking in up here?" Dak asked. "I'd think this is a low-crime area."

"It is," Will said and turned the key. The lock clicked, and he retracted the key, then turned the knob. "But you can never be too careful."

"I had a feeling you'd say that." Who was Dak kidding? He'd have done the same thing. Even in the most remote place in the world, he'd probably lock his front door.

Will pushed the door open and stepped inside, flipped on a light switch, and watched as the cavernous room lit up.

Long wooden planks ran from one end to the other, making up a narrow walkway between the racks stacked three barrels high. Dak noticed thick wooden beams overhead supporting a similar floorboard above. The smell of aged oak filled Dak's nostrils. He likened it to a combination of the scent of an old log cabin and a library. Light bulbs hung from the ceiling every ten feet, lighting the way down to the other end and a closed door.

"This is impressive," Dak said as the two walked toward the end of the row. "Does the upstairs above have this many barrels, too?"

"Yeah. But again, it's a small deal, honestly. Most wineries have more than one barrel house like this. And they're usually bigger. We're able to produce about fifty barrels a year, though."

"Wow. That's what you would call small output?"

Will shrugged. "It really depends on the acreage and how many grapes you get out of that acreage. A ton of grapes produces about two barrels."

"Sounds like you're rolling out a ton of barrels."

They stopped at the door on the far wall. This one wasn't locked, and Will pulled it open, stepped inside, and flipped a switch on the interior right wall. Dak joined him in the next room and looked around.

"A storage room?" Dak asked, confused at Will leading him into a 20 x 20 room with various tools, cleaning supplies, and maintenance equipment. The floor wasn't made from the same aged wooden planks as the rest of the building. Instead, huge rubber tiles with tiny, raised grooves covered the floor. "You don't have to give me the full tour, man. Besides, the two of us need to get some sleep." Dak glanced at his watch and shook his head in disappointment. He knew they were going to get little better than a nap in before heading back to Lisbon.

He didn't care. Making sure Nicole was safe outweighed everything else, including his own base needs.

Will cracked that same mischievous grin from before and closed the door behind him. "Yeah. Supply closet." He walked over to the wall to his right, where a gray panel hung, set into the wall.

Dak recognized it was a breaker box but noticed the peculiar keyhole fixed within the door.

Will produced another key, this one smaller than the one that allowed entry into the barrel house, and inserted it into the lock.

He turned it, then flipped up the latch above to pull open the breaker box.

Dak's weary eyes widened. Instead of rows of fuse switches inside, there was a clear piece of glass about the size of his palm. Next to it was a rectangular piece of glass with a tinted cover.

"Is that—" Dak began to ask.

"Retinal scanner and biometric access panel?" Will finished. "Yes. Yes, it is."

Will leaned close and pressed his thumb to the glass square while staring into the scanner.

His thumb activated the device, and a nearly undetectable laser panned across his eyes. "Welcome back, Will," a female voice with an English accent said.

"Thanks, Molly," Will answered. "Oh, Dak, you might want to join me over here."

Dak sidled close to his friend, though he still wasn't sure what was going to happen next.

"Okay, Molly. Take us down."

"Yes, sir."

The floor shuddered, then slowly began to descend.

"Okay. Okay," Dak said, impressed. "Now you're just showing off."

"Can't be too careful," Will reminded. "The closet hides the way to the goodie room."

"Molly, huh? There a story behind that?" Dak plied his friend with a deliberate, judging glare.

Will merely rolled his shoulders. "Girl I met in Vegas once. Really cool woman, actually. Has a big red dragon tattoo on her leg."

"Well, she can't be that cool if she hangs with you."

"You hang with me."

"Never said I was cool."

Will pursed his lips together, accepting his friend's willingness to burn the bridges. "Touché."

When the secret elevator reached the floor below, three rows of bright fluorescent lights automatically flickered to life, illuminating steel walls around the entire room. From what Dak could tell, this basement was the same size as the storage closet above.

"Molly, open the racks, please."

"Of course, Will."

Before the two men stepped off the lift platform, the metal walls dropped into the floor, revealing rows of weapons. Sniper rifles, LMGs, a variety of pistols, and tactical rifles hung from racks on the walls. Beneath the firearms, hidden drawers ejected from the walls. Inside the drawers sat rows of magazines. Beneath those were shelves stocked with ammunition cans. Dak figured Will probably had tens of thousands of rounds of ammo in those containers.

Dak whistled. "I do love a good goodie room," he drawled.

"I thought you might. Although it's a shame we can't take some of the good stuff with us. Gotta pack light. Know what I mean?"

Dak said that he did as he continued to sweep his gaze across the cornucopia of weapons around him. "You certainly have been busy compiling all this."

Will responded with a snort. "This is just my personal collection."

"You have light machine guns for your personal collection? What are you prepping for? End of the world? Zombie apocalypse? World War Three?"

Will flashed a toothy grin. "As a good friend of mine once said, why choose if you don't have to?"

Dak's face twisted as he assessed the statement. "Well, I can't say

I'm the only one who thinks that way. A friend of mine in Atlanta says that, too."

Will made his way over to the racks of pistols and took a 9 mm SIG Sauer off the wall. "Take a couple of each. Help yourself." He inspected the weapon, ejecting the magazine then pulling back the slide to take a look into the chamber and barrel. Then he slid the mag back into the well and set the firearm down on an empty shelf that served as a table.

"You don't happen to have any goodie bags do you?" Dak asked, approaching the wall of sidearms.

"But of course," Will said in that snooty British accent from the Grey Poupon commercials in the '80s.

He walked over to the other side of the room, opened a metal door under a rack of Heckler & Koch submachine guns, and pulled out a small black duffel bag. Will tossed it over to Dak, who snatched it out of the air.

"Thanks."

It wasn't the kind of bag he wanted to take into a firefight, but it would do well enough to carry a few weapons back up to the house. Sort of like a reusable grocery tote, but for guns.

Dak selected twin .40-cal. Springfields from the rack. He inspected both weapons the same way Will had, and satisfied with the choices, laid the pistols in the bottom of the bag. Then he scooped up eight magazines, four for each gun, and carefully placed them in with the guns.

Will took another SIG from the wall and eight magazines, same as Dak had done. "You think that's going to be enough rounds?" Will half joked.

Dak's chuckle echoed around the metallic room. "I would hope so. If we need more, we're probably screwed anyway."

That reminded him. "I do wish we could have gotten at least the name of this guy. Then we would know more about him, kind of what to expect."

"Or maybe a home address?"

Dak blew derisive air through his lips. "Yeah. Wouldn't that be lovely?"

His brain swam in a fatigue-induced fog. He knew people that might be able to help with that. But he'd been so focused on getting Nicole back, so emotional about it, that Dak hadn't been thinking completely straight.

The realization was discomforting to say the least.

Almost nothing put him off his game. But this was different, and the consequences of his actions would affect him in a very personal way.

"I might know someone who can help," Dak realized. "I'll text her and see what I can learn."

"Her?"

"Yeah," Dak nodded. "Her."

18

MARSEILLE

Cameron Tucker stood by the door of the abandoned countryside church, looking out over the rolling hills beyond the city of Marseille. To the southeast, Mont Puget and the shadows of the Marseille-Cassis Calanques Mountains stood out against the backdrop of the rising sun.

He raised a metal mug to his mouth, inhaled the scent of the dark roasted coffee, then took a long sip.

Tucker liked how the French made their coffee. It was bold, unconventional, and in your face. Some people might say it reminded them of French people, but he'd never had any issues with them. As long as you weren't an annoying tourist, they were lovely. At least to him.

But he wasn't here to make friends or to socialize. He was here to take out an enemy, and to make enough money to live comfortably and under the radar for the rest of his life.

He took another sip, admiring the view from the little stone hilltop church.

During the secularization of Europe, including many parts of France, churches like this one saw their memberships dwindle over the course of decades until they were finally unsustainable. Some parishioners simply transferred to larger houses of worship in the cities. Others simply gave up their faith altogether.

The humble cemetery outside had fallen into disrepair over the years. Most of the tombstones remained upright, though many of the older ones had long since toppled or were leaning more than that tower in Italy.

Grass and weeds had taken over, covering portions of the headstones. But wildflowers had taken root, too, and colored the resting places of so many with beautiful colors of yellow, white, red, pink, and purple.

Tucker did like it here in Marseille. The food, the culture, the weather, the ocean—all beckoned him to make this his permanent residence once Dak Harper was dead. He could find peace here, and maybe a good woman to share his new life with.

His mind flashed back to the bartender from the mercenary den.

He wouldn't describe her as *good,* per se, but he was certain she would make life interesting.

He let the idea float away and join the silky clouds drifting overhead, cutting through the hues of deep purple and blue as the bright rays of sun pushed back the darkness toward the west to begin a new day. A woman like her would kill him in his sleep if he so much as forgot to put the toilet seat down.

But what a way to go, he thought.

Tucker lifted the mug to his lips, held it there for a moment as he allowed his mind to wander, and then took a drink.

"Any word from your contact, sir?" Lee's voice interrupted his moment of serenity.

Tucker didn't immediately turn around to acknowledge the man. Instead, he finished his sip, then lowered the mug down to just above his waist, and shook his head.

"Not yet. She knows we're working on a time frame, though."

"The forty-eight hours you mentioned for the phones?"

"That too. But patrons don't often go in there with a five-year plan. They know the hitters in those places can take care of things quickly."

Lee thought about it for a second, nodding as if his employer needed the acknowledgment. "I was wondering—"

"No. You can't get access to the network of dens unless you're recommended, and vetted."

The bodyguard's expression darkened with disappointment. "How did you—"

"Know that you were going to ask that? Because you're a merc, Lee. And you'd be stupid not to get glittery eyes with the amount of coin that passes through these dens and into the hands of the hired killers. Or were you going to ask how I got in there?"

He rounded on the man slowly but only half turned his body. A cool morning breeze swept up the hillside and into the archway over the door where they stood.

Before Lee could respond, Tucker answered the unspoken question. "I got in because of who I am. And because I knew someone on the inside. So, just like everyone else, I had a referral."

Lee accepted the answer and didn't dare to ask anything else. He could tell he'd already irritated the colonel. He didn't want to push that irritation to anger.

So instead, he raised a green metal mug to his mouth and swallowed a dose of coffee to keep himself from saying anything else.

"How's the prisoner?" Tucker asked. He said the words without empathy. They were hollow, callous syllables. The only reason he cared about her well-being was in case they needed to use her for leverage, or if—in the most unlikely event—they had to trade her for the Rembrandt Dak Harper was hunting.

"Alive," Lee answered. "Not as feisty as before. Despair does that to them, though."

Tucker grunted at the response. He didn't expect her to be dead, so her being alive was a given. If she wasn't, he'd have heard about it before then, and his entire plan would have changed in a heartbeat.

He knew, too, what Lee meant about despair. At first, prisoners felt like they would find a way to escape and make those who captured them pay for their insolence. It was always the same. Eventually, that fire died out with no fuel to feed it and left the captive wallowing in a hopeless well of darkness from which there was no escape.

"She's eating, right?" Tucker asked.

"Not at the moment. But yes, she's been eating what we give her."

The rations they doled out consisted of better food than most people in her situation would probably get. Tucker, after all, wasn't a barbarian.

Nicole had been given the same provisions Tucker and his men received, all from local places down in the city.

Croissants, eggs, fresh fruits and vegetables, bread with a hard crust, and even a little butter to go with it.

"Make sure she stays hydrated. Can't have her passing out from lack of water."

"Yes, sir," Lee said, unmoving.

Tucker started to take another sip of coffee, noticed his guard still standing there, and then looked at him over his shoulder with an irritated glower.

"As in now, Sergeant."

"Yes, sir."

Lee awkwardly stopped in mid-sip with the coffee and nearly spit it out as he spun around and went back through the door into the church.

Tucker shook his head in disdain as he continued waiting on the church steps for the bartender to contact him.

He hadn't hired Lee for his brains. The man had his moments, but far and away wasn't brilliant in any sense of the word. He was an expert at killing, though, and could do it without conscience. That kind of soldier was the best kind to have on your side. So, Tucker tolerated the former sergeant's obvious lack of social acumen.

The other three men Tucker had hired were much the same, though of lower ranks in their previous roles in the military. All dishonorably discharged, they were an interesting bunch and came from a variety of backgrounds and from all around the country.

Before Tucker's thoughts dug too deep into the subject, the phone in his back pocket started vibrating.

"About time," he grumbled. He reached into the pocket, pulled out the device, checked the number out of habit, and flipped the phone open.

"Yes?" he said, holding the phone to his ear.

"She has accepted your offer and has your details."

Tucker recognized the den handler's scintillating French accent. He didn't know what it was about it, but the sound drove him wild.

"Excellent."

"She will be in touch as soon as I get off the phone with you. As you know, once direct contact is established—"

"This phone will be destroyed. Yes, I know the rules."

"Good luck, then. Thank you for your business."

The call ended unceremoniously and abruptly.

Tucker appreciated that, and it roused his senses all the more.

He sighed, anticipating the next call from one of the most dangerous people on the planet. Her reputation was unrivaled. Rumors abounded, of course. Some said she was raised by a family of assassins in the Far East. Others claimed she'd grown up in Russia, learning the deadly arts from the early age of six.

None of that sounded plausible to Tucker. Especially the last part. He'd seen six-year-olds, though he didn't have any of his own. They were tiny, innocent, incapable of such a thing. The rest of the stories sounded just as fantastical.

There was, however, one eerie component to her mystique. No one had seen her face.

Unlike the other mercenaries that hung around the dens, she had never once made an appearance. And all her arrangements, contracts, payments, everything, was done remotely and anonymously.

It actually surprised Tucker somewhat that so many underworld killers *would* congregate, but he supposed everyone, even the darkest among us, felt the need for companionship now and then.

His phone buzzed again, and not wanting to appear desperate, he picked up after two seconds without looking at the number. Flipping open the phone again, he raised it to his ear.

"Hello," he said. It took remarkable focus to stymie the quiver in his voice. No one made him nervous. No one. And yet this apparition with whom he was about to converse snaked tendrils of apprehension through his veins.

"Hello, Colonel," the woman answered.

She knew who he was. Protocol would have required the handler allow the two to make personal introductions. The handler wouldn't have told this woman who he was. Come to think of it, he realized he'd never introduced himself, either, which was also standard.

He wrestled with how this stranger on the phone knew who he was after such a short amount of time had passed.

Was it possible the security cameras inside the den had identified him and passed that intel along? He hadn't noticed any cameras and believed the reason for that could be as simple as no one would be foolish enough to try to take out an entire den of the world's deadliest people. If they could even get in through the door; and they'd have to know where to look to do that.

For now, he had to accept the fact that he was in the dark with an incredibly deadly person.

He squeezed a swallow through his throat, trying not to wonder if she had eyes on him and the church at that very second.

"Thank you for calling me so quickly."

"You made an intriguing offer. Two hundred is a healthy sum, even in today's economy."

He forced an uneasy laugh. "So, you agree to the contract?"

"If you have sought me out, then you know I only do... certain deals."

He wished he could place her accent. Not that it would give him any intel that could assist him in figuring out who this woman was. Still, he thought there was something to it, but faded. French? Spanish? Portuguese?

"Yes. I am aware."

"Then you know of my unique interests."

"I do. You only take jobs that involve rare pieces of art."

"Correct. And what piece are we talking about here?"

Tucker knew that question was coming. Not that he feared it. But now that he had her on the line, he felt a sense of apprehension.

By giving her the target, and the painting, he'd have no leverage, which meant he'd have to lean entirely on the integrity of the den network to make sure she didn't simply kill Harper and take the painting for herself.

Without any other options, though, it was a risk he felt he had to take. "It's a Rembrandt," he said.

"I'm listening." Her frigid voice sent a tingle across his skin.

"*The Storm on the—*"

"*Sea of Galilee,*" she finished. "I've heard of it. Disappeared in the early 1990s. No one knew who took it, though the authorities claimed two men were involved. Who has it?"

"The man you're looking for is named Dak Harper. I doubt he has the painting yet, but I believe he will soon."

The statement froze the conversation. She paused for a moment, and he wondered if she was even still on the line. Tucker wasn't about to ask if she was still there. He tried to hear her breathe, but the sound of the breeze washing over the hillside and whistling through dilapidated window shutters kept him from the subtle sound, if she was making it.

Tucker figured what he said must have confused her. This wasn't a traditional sort of hit, but she wasn't a traditional sort of killer.

"So, you don't know who has the painting?" she asked with only the slightest twinge of confusion in her voice.

"No," he said, opting for total transparency. "I don't. But he does." Okay, not total transparency. But a little lie never hurt in situations like this. He needed her.

"This is more layers than I would prefer, Colonel. I like things to be direct."

"I know. Which is why I have an additional fee I'm willing to pay for your services. And your discretion."

Another pause, this one shorter than the last. "You know that is not permitted. Any negotiations must go through the handlers. Without order, we have chaos."

"I am aware. If you wish, let the Marseille branch know of the new arrangement. It doesn't matter to me. That's less money for you."

He hoped that would veer her toward seeing things his way. But truly, it didn't matter. The money out of his pocket would be the same. He just wanted to get her full commitment.

"What is this... additional fee."

"Call it a bonus if you like. I leave that to you. My offer is this: If you bring me Harper alive, as well as the painting, I'll double the original contract."

She exhaled audibly through her nose this time, and he knew the offer had caused her to think. It was an incredible amount of money. Nearly a half million.

"I could sell the painting for twenty times that amount," she said.

"And you would have every bounty hunter and assassin in the world after you for doing so." He knew the threat wouldn't scare her as much as it might others. So he added, "But you don't just do it for the money. You do it for the art. To lay your eyes upon something that hasn't been seen in so long by the rest of the world. You love it."

Tucker hoped he knew what he was doing here. This play was like trying to tickle a rattlesnake. He didn't want to get bitten.

"The additional funds will be in cash. No wire transfers. No funny business. Large denominations."

"So, we have a deal?"

"Yes. When you change phones, send me a message to let me know the new number. I'll contact you when I have the mark—and the painting."

"Thank you." He listened, but she said nothing. Then he checked the little screen on the top portion of the flip phone and saw that the call had unceremoniously ended.

Tucker allowed a slight grin to crease his lips. Dak Harper didn't know it yet, but he was in a world of trouble now.

19

LISBON

Will walked out of the rental car office and into the baking morning sun. Dak leaned against a pillar supporting a covered walkway that ran along the line of various rental places adjacent to the Lisbon airport. The sunshine radiated against his skin, heating it like a low-temperature oven—not unpleasant since it was dry here, but he also didn't want to be there too long.

The rental office Will had used was located out of view of the main entrance to the terminal and ticket counters within. Dak knew that had not been by accident.

The Aeroporto Humberto Delgado Lisboa wasn't as titanic as some of the larger international airports in Europe, much less the United States, but its façade of curved glass surrounded on both sides by stacked white stone gave it a modern, clean look that held up against any of the others in regard to design.

"All done," Will said with a satisfied smile. He dusted his hands.

"And the damage to the vehicle?"

"Nothing a little cash couldn't fix. And a little more for them to not ask questions."

"Gotta love countries where you can take part in the corruption,"

Dak said with a little snark. He'd said it before and figured he'd say it again whenever, if ever he returned here, or to other countries like it.

"Indeed," Will agreed.

Cars zoomed by, ferrying their passengers to the nearest drop-off in front of the hotel, while others sped by to go find other fares throughout the city.

On a warm, clear day like today, the blue sky overhead mocked Dak. He'd much rather have been on the golden sands of the Algarve, or perhaps the beaches up near Will's old place in Nazare, or even São Marinho do Porto with its underrated crescent bay right on the town's doorstep.

A few beads of sweat crawled down Dak's neck from the back of his hairline, and he wiped them away with his palm mere seconds before they evaporated into the parched air.

"Where are we meeting your guy?" Dak asked.

"It's a bit of a walk. Private hangar way over there at the other end of the airfield. He should be there waiting for us."

He pointed toward the runways at no specific place. A few palm trees rising from a grass median stood between them and the main airport. If there was a hangar there, they couldn't see it through the terminal and other ancillary buildings.

"It would take us a while to walk, so I say we cab it over there," Will suggested.

"Fine by me. The more time we save, the better."

The two walked around the rental car parking area and turned right onto the sidewalk. They reached the main drag and hailed a taxi and informed the skinny, middle-aged man behind the wheel where they needed to go.

The guy gave them a disparaging look at the short drive. Dak and Will both knew the look. The fare would barely be worth the man's time.

Dak handed him a crisp ten and told him he could keep that on top of the fare.

The man accepted the money with a *might as well* shrug and drove them around the airport to the private hangars.

He dropped them off outside a row of the arched metal buildings, collected his fare, and drove off happy.

Dak stared up at the hangar closest to them and then down the row. "You're sure your guy is up for this?"

Will scowled at him. "Seriously? You're asking that now?"

"I did ask before, too."

"And I answered. Yes. I'm telling you, Jimmy is good. He's better than good. Would you just relax? I don't want you spooking him when you meet him."

"Why not?"

Will rolled his head around and threw up his hands. "Because people don't like to be spooked? Especially pilots who run smuggling operations."

Dak disarmed him with an easy, accepting smile and put out his right hand to calm his friend down. "Okay. Okay. Relax. I trust you. And if you trust him, that means I do, too."

"Good enough."

Will led the way over to a gate where a tall, skinny guy with a trucker cap and aviators stood talking to one of the security guards. He looked American in every way, from the loose-fitting khaki cargo pants to the gray T-shirt under an unbuttoned, dark green button-up shirt with the sleeves rolled up to his elbows.

"Speak of the devil," Will said when they were within earshot of the two men at the gate.

The security guard said nothing but looked over at them with cautious suspicion.

"Well, look who it is," Trucker Cap said in an English accent. "I was starting to think you weren't coming."

"I've never bailed on you yet, Jimmy," Will countered.

Dak shook off the surprise at the guy's accent. He'd thought for sure Jimmy would have a Southern drawl, or at the very least a sharp Midwestern tone.

"Good to see you, mate," Jimmy said, extending his hand.

Will clasped him by the forearm, and Jimmy did the same. They shook twice, then let go.

"This is my friend, Dak Harper," Will said, stepping aside so the two could shake hands.

"Nice to meet you, Dak." They shook hands the more conventional way, but Dak noted the man's firm, hardened grip like he'd been a rower most of his life.

"I really appreciate you helping us out on such short notice," Dak said.

"Not a problem. I wasn't doing anything at the moment, so I figured I might as well help out an old friend."

He cast a glance at Will. "You should watch yourself around this one, though. Friend or not."

"And there it is," Will jumped in, shaking his head. "Don't believe him for a second, Dak. He's getting paid to do this."

The two let go, and Jimmy did his best impression of looking insulted. "That hurts, Will. I thought you were different than the others."

Will reached into his back pocket and produced a white envelope. He handed it over to the pilot, who accepted it with a smile. After flicking it on his palm, he nodded. "I mean, yes, I gotta eat, right? But I would have done it for free, but only for you, Will."

"Uh-huh."

Jimmy pried open the envelope and started flipping through the bills.

"You're counting it in front of me?" Will asked. He actually sounded insulted.

Dak thought it was hilarious.

"You're like two of my ex-wives. You know that? I'm not counting it because I don't trust you." He flicked his head sideways toward the security guard standing ten feet back by the guard house. "I gotta give him something to look the other way."

"Oh," Will said at the realization.

Jimmy removed five hundreds from the envelope, stuffed it into his back pocket, and sauntered over to the guard. He planted the money in the guy's palm and said a few words to him.

The guard nodded, looking appreciative for the money.

Jimmy looked at the other two over his shoulder and motioned for them to follow.

They obeyed the silent instruction and walked on either side of the pilot through the gate and then to the left along the row of hangars.

A passenger jet roared as it flew over the start of the runway. Others like it waited, stacked at intervals in the sky, lining up to make their landing. It was busy, but nothing like Hartsfield-Jackson in Atlanta, or Heathrow in London. There, planes seemed to touch down every thirty seconds, nonstop, 24/7, and on multiple runways.

Most of jets carried cabins laden with tourists coming to Portugal for the good, cheap wine, the food, and a look at a unique country with a rich past. There would be new expats on some of the flights. Since rolling out the Golden Visa program, many foreigners had bought into the scheme by purchasing real estate in various places around the country.

Recently, the government shut down the visa program due to the influx of international buyers driving up the cost of rent in many of the larger towns and cities. At the time, however, Madeira—the destination for the two Americans—still allowed the process.

To be fair, the simplicity of the system had caused the flood of foreigners to invade Portugal, along with other nations who employed the Golden Visa such as Greece and Spain.

"Will tells me you're former military," Jimmy said.

"That's right," Dak said.

"Where were you deployed?"

"Middle East, mostly. Bounced around over there for a while."

"I had some friends over there a few years back. Messy situation, that."

"You got that right."

"But you're out now, yeah? Never going back?" Jimmy twisted his head slightly to the right, hoping he hadn't gone too far with the questioning.

"Nah," Dak answered. "Those days are done and gone."

"Do you miss it?"

Dak rolled his shoulders. "I miss the camaraderie. I guess I miss the simplicity of following orders now and then. Takes the guesswork out of life when you have a commanding officer."

The last few words speared his mind with images of Tucker. The most prominent ones were of the man lying in the meadow during the firefight with the rogue Russian battalion. Dak had thought the colonel was dead, and due to the intensity of the fight and the necessity to chase down the German, he'd had no time to confirm Tucker's demise. It was only when he returned to the meadow that he found the colonel was gone.

Regret gnawed at him. A single quick shot to the head, just to make sure, would have saved him from all of this—saved Nicole from the hell she was enduring at this very moment. And the question of whether he'd led Tucker to her still nagged him like a bad cough.

He batted those thoughts away. They would only throw rocket fuel onto the fire inside him.

"I know what you mean," Jimmy said, but he left it at that as he turned toward a hangar to their right. "This is us. I've already run through my preflight checks. So as soon as you boys are buckled up, we can take off."

Dak checked his watch and noted the time. "If you don't mind, I just need a minute to make a phone call."

20

In a perfect world, Dak would have been able to make the call in the dark hours of morning. Then again, in a perfect world none of this would be happening.

He had to take what he could get for now.

Dak took out his phone and walked away from Will and Jimmy, leaving the two to catch up on business or whatever it was those two talked about.

Dak tapped on the top of the screen, opening the search function, and typed in the letters E and M.

The name *Emily S* appeared in the contacts list, and Dak tapped on it to begin the call. The screen changed over to Calling Emily S with the digital options for audio appearing below that.

He held the phone to his ear and waited.

The call connected after three rings, and he was greeted with a pleasant "Hello, Mr. Harper."

"Hey, Emily. I'm sorry to bother you without warning."

"You're no bother, Dak." She sounded tired.

"I hope I didn't wake you."

"You didn't. I get up early. I just put on a pot of coffee a minute ago." She yawned, and he pictured her stretching in a T-shirt and pajama pants, though he had no reference for such a vision. "For you to call at this hour, though, I suspect you need something pretty badly."

Emily Starks was as smart as they came. Resourceful, clever, and a natural leader, it made sense that she was the director of the Axis Agency, a redacted government organization based in Atlanta. She answered only to the president, and her operation only had a dozen agents on the roster at any given time.

Keeping things within such a tight-knit group prevented leaks, among other problems. When special agencies or branches of the military claimed to only take the best of the best, Axis added one more layer to that deciding factor.

The training was rigorous to say the least. The regimens had been put together by former CIA, US Navy SEALs, Green Berets, Delta Force operators, and some of the best martial arts experts in the world.

It was no surprise to Dak that Sean Wyatt was so good in a fight, or in any kind of battle. He'd gone through all that training and been a field agent for an undisclosed number of years before calling it quits to go work for his friend at the International Archaeological Agency.

On the surface, Sean probably thought that would be a less stressful, less dangerous gig. But it had proved otherwise.

"I need a favor," Dak said. "And I know it's early, so you might not be able to get to it right away."

Another jet flew by and touched down on the runway.

"Where are you?" Emily asked. "Sounds like you're at an airport."

"I am. Just outside the Lisbon airport, actually."

"Oh, I do love Lisbon. Lovely city. I suspect, though, you're not there for a vacation. What's the favor?"

"If I send you a picture of someone, do you have the tech to identify them with facial recognition?"

"Sure. That shouldn't be a problem. What did this person do to draw the attention of someone like you?"

Dak ran a hand through his thick dark brown hair and narrowed his eyes behind the aviator sunglasses perched on his nose.

"He hasn't done anything to me. He's a black-market art dealer. I need to know who he is. I'm hoping he can help me track down a painting."

"A painting?" She sounded surprised. "I didn't realize you'd become a collector?"

"I'm not. It's... for another person."

He realized how that sounded. To her, it came across as though Dak had moved over to the dark side and was buying illegally obtained art to sell it for profit.

"I'm in a difficult situation," he added. "I can't elaborate more than to say it's a painting that was stolen three decades ago. I'm trying to get it back."

Dak rubbed his forehead. He was still tired from the night before, and the night before that. He knew dark patches probably hung under his eyes, a sign he could do with more sleep. He hadn't been a deep sleeper for a long time, ever since he was deployed to the Middle East. The constant threat of attack, or mobilization, kept him and everyone else on their toes—including throughout the night.

After the events of the last few years—hunting down the men who betrayed him and trying to evade, then locate, Tucker—Dak was always in mortal danger.

Especially when he slept.

He knew the risks that came with a lack of sleep. Higher levels of stress, hormone imbalances, depression, hypertension, and even muscle hypertrophy were all affected beyond the obvious fatigue that plagued every waking second.

Dak told himself when Tucker was dead, he'd finally be able to rest. That, or he'd go insane.

"Three decades ago," Emily said with a whistle. "I wouldn't know the first thing about even finding something like that. If the authorities, teams of investigators couldn't locate it—"

"I don't have a choice," Dak cut her off. "I need to find it. I can't elaborate more than that right now. When... it's all over, I'll fill you in on the details if you want."

"Okay, Dak. No problem. So, you believe this black-market dealer knows where the painting is?"

Dak inhaled a breath of warm, dry air through his nose. He exhaled it slowly, both to keep himself calm and to collect his thoughts.

"I hope so. A friend is helping me out too. A guy I trust, and that's a pretty short list. We know the dealer lives on the island of Madeira in the town of Funchal."

She let out a curious hum. "Interesting. How do you know that?"

"I had someone hack his computer and take a screenshot of him through his webcam."

"Really?" Emily sounded truly impressed. "Remind me not to piss you off. I didn't know you were friends with hackers, especially at that level. So, you have a picture of the guy, but you don't know anything about him, and yet you know where he lives?"

"Sort of," Dak conceded. "My friend recognized the beach in the background. He's spent a lot of time in Portugal, including Madeira. Owns a place in the Douro Valley now. You and President Dawkins should visit sometime when you're not so busy."

Emily laughed at the unexpected invitation.

Her relationship with the former president had drawn scrutiny from some. Most of the American people embraced the couple, though they had no idea who she truly was, or what she did for a living.

"I'll run it by him. The only thing he's busy with these days is doing book signings and working on his short game out on the golf course."

Dak allowed a short chuckle. "I'd say he's earned it."

"Back to the reason for your call, do you have the image handy?"

"Yes. Okay to text it to you now?"

"Yeah. Go ahead. I'm not at the office yet, but I'll be heading there shortly. Once I'm logged in to my computer, it shouldn't take long to get what you need."

Dak felt a ripple of relief trickle across his chest, like someone drawing a feather along his skin.

"Thanks, Emily. I owe you one."

21

ATLANTA

Emily parked her black Infiniti sedan outside the Axis building in downtown Atlanta, climbed out, and locked it with a push of the button on the key fob.

She looked around the mostly empty parking area, as she did every day when she came to work. The concrete columns supporting the building overhead and a lone white Toyota Corolla were the only companions she could find.

Emily knew the other car belonged to the night watchman, Carl, who roamed the halls of the complex through the haunting hours of the night and early morning.

Normally, he would have already gone by the time she arrived, but today she got to the office a little earlier than normal.

She didn't harbor resentment over that fact. It's not like she was losing sleep over it. And as she'd told Dak, John was already up in Adairsville, Georgia, for a weekend golf trip.

Her short-heeled black shoes clicked on the concrete underfoot as she walked across the garage to the elevator that would lead up to the lobby. She stopped at the lift, pressed the button, and waited for fifteen seconds for it to descend to her level.

The machine dinged, and the doors opened.

She stepped in and pressed the button for the lobby and watched out through the opening, taking a brief second to appreciate that she didn't have to share a parking garage with the rest of the city. Just the people from her agency. Those were few in number, and often most of them were out of the country, leaving only the logistical, strategic, and analytical teams to occupy the precious parking spots.

When the doors opened at the lobby, she stepped out and cast a sweeping glance around the room with its brushed steel pillars, gray tile floors, and white walls that wrapped around the entire area, only interrupted by a black desk in the middle of the left-hand wall.

A man in a security uniform sat behind the desk. He had gray hair and a matching mustache—one of those that looked like he'd come straight out of the 1890s. He stood as she walked off the lift, and for a split second Emily wasn't sure if he was going to salute her or piss himself for being caught slacking on the job by the boss.

"Good morning, Carl," she said, disarming him with a pleasant smile to go with the greeting.

"Good... morning, Ms. Starks. You're here early?"

She noted the cup of coffee sitting next to a half-eaten strawberry-iced doughnut atop a paper wrapper.

"How on earth do you drink coffee in the morning when you sleep during the day?"

The question seemed to rope him like a calf in a rodeo, binding his mind for a few seconds until he could find the words. "Oh. I guess old habits and all that, Ms. Starks. Is everything okay?"

"Yes. Thank you for asking. I'm just trying to get ahead on some things for the week. Have a great rest of your day."

He nodded appreciatively at her. "You, too, ma'am. Thank you."

Emily strode away from him to the double doors at the end of the lobby. Carl was a good guy from what she could tell. He always showed up on time, and more importantly, never asked too many questions.

But she knew that he provided very little actual security. At most, he'd be the second call to emergency lines were someone to infiltrate the fortress that was Axis HQ. Carl didn't really even represent the second line of defense. He was a figurehead, much like a British monarch.

That said, Carl understood the importance of the agency and its secrecy to some degree. He didn't know the full extent. Very few did. But he operated under the knowledge that they were a secret branch of the government, and no one was to know who he worked for or what he did.

The latter was easy enough. But an entire story had been prepared for him to share with friends or family should they get curious and ask what he did for work.

"Night guard at an actuarial agency," she'd told him and given him documents with letterhead, business cards, and other items that would help sell the story.

She stopped at the double doors, pulled up the access card hanging from her clutch, swiped it across the RFID scanner, then entered her six-digit passcode.

The doors clicked then opened automatically.

Emily drew in a quick breath of the sterile air and then disappeared into the next room. White walls surrounded her on all sides, and the panels on the floor were no longer the gray tiles from the lobby, but white with black seams between them. The doors closed behind her, and she stepped up to another pair of doors.

This time, the panel fixed to the wall on the right of the doors was a black box with a glass surface. She leaned forward, nudging her eyes close, and waited. The scanner swept over her eyes, and the doors unlocked. Like the ones before, they swung open on their own, clearing the way into a white hallway with multiple gray doors lining either side.

She strode purposefully down the corridor, passing the doors until she reached the intersection where it branched off left and right, then turned left and continued to the open office door at the end.

Emily entered her corner office, closed the door behind her, and set her things down on a cabinet in the right-hand corner before sitting down in her plush, black leather seat.

She pulled the chair up close to the Elton black executive desk. Its façade featured a metal trapezoid embraced by pieces of angled glass. Two computer monitors occupied the shiny surface, along with a wireless keyboard and mouse.

Emily clicked on the mouse, and the screens blinked, then presented black backdrops with a white button requesting her login information inside two blocks.

She quickly entered her ID and password, then clicked the button.

The screens changed in an instant. The one on the right opened a map of the world with multiple red, yellow, and green pins positioned in various countries.

The monitor directly in front of her displayed a desktop with her most frequently used application icons.

She brushed her fingers over the mouse and then gently laid them on top of the smooth, curved surface before swishing the digital arrow across the screen to a database-access application.

Her right finger clicked on the left mouse button twice, and the program expanded to fill a large box on the screen.

She took out her phone, found the image Dak had sent her, and AirDropped it into the computer. A message popped up in the top-right corner, asking her to confirm she wanted to allow the device to transfer the image.

After clicking okay, the picture of the art dealer dropped into the bottom of the screen where downloads displayed. Emily clicked and dragged the image into the dialogue box and then clicked a blue search button.

Technology had come so far, even in the short time since she joined the agency. She couldn't imagine how long something like this would have taken her predecessors fifteen or twenty years before. And prior to that would have been a completely different ballgame.

Emily shuddered at the thought.

She sat back against the chair for a moment and watched the screen change. The box in the center flashed as the system searched through the database for the identity of the man in the picture.

The setup was fast, but she knew it could take a few minutes before anything was produced, so she pushed herself up from the chair and walked over to the bar to her right.

A collection of various coffee bags sat neatly on the corner of the bar next to an OXO coffee maker with a double-walled stainless-steel pot. Boxes of green tea, black tea, and matcha occupied the right-hand corner.

She picked up a bag of Seven Hills Coffee—a local roaster in midtown Atlanta—and turned to the black Fellow Opus coffee grinder, dumped in the amount of beans she wanted, and then closed the bag. She pressed the button on the grinder and listened to the whirring and grinding sound that filled the office for a few seconds until the beans were just the way she liked them. Then she took a filter, dumped in the fresh, aromatic grinds, and set it into the coffee maker. After pouring in a dose of filtered water from a nearby pitcher, she pushed the brew button, and returned to her desk.

The routine of making coffee probably seemed mundane to billions of people around the world, but not to Emily. It was a part of her necessary routine, yes, but also something she enjoyed. The grinding, placing the filter, pouring in the water, all of those were simple tasks, easy to complete in just a few minutes.

Her job was anything but easy.

Every single day she was tasked with finding the world's most dangerous people, people who were very good at not being found. And when she did locate them, she had the macabre privilege of ordering either their capture, or most often, their execution—and by doing so, putting her agents in the greatest of harms' way.

She stood over the desk, staring down at the screen. The box continued searching. That wasn't all that surprising. Sometimes these things took longer than others, especially if a suspect was exceptionally good at covering their tracks.

In those cases, it was usually a result of multiple aliases and layers upon layers of manufactured identification. Passports, driver's licenses, even utility bills were incorporated into the most creative masks. But eventually, the computers sorted through it.

Emily wondered what the advent of artificial intelligence would do for this kind of thing. While many people feared what it could bring to humanity in regard to the singularity—the cataclysmic event where machines decided humans were the problem and needed to be removed—Emily preferred to look at how AI could help humanity become more productive and improve the quality of life around the world for billions of people. Eventually, she surmised that the machines could even help humans reach farther into the cosmos than ever before.

The coffee machine hissed and bubbled as it dripped fresh brew into the steel pot. The warm, toasty scent from the brown liquid spilled into the air and reached into every corner, filling her senses beyond that of smell.

Her mind, instinctively, begged for the sacred morning ritual. The perfect cup, though, could not be hurried, and so she turned away from the computer screen as it continued its search for the mysterious art seller.

She distracted herself by stepping over to the panoramic window that stretched across the back wall of her office and gazed out upon the city she'd come to love.

Her building was on the invisible border between downtown and midtown, and her office provided sweeping vistas of the latter and of the Buckhead skyline in the distance beyond, just a few miles away.

Rush hour hadn't yet begun, but the streets were already brimming with cars carrying their drivers along their commute to work. She'd heard that since the COVID pandemic, fewer people were going into work in lieu of working remotely from home or other locations.

What she saw every day from her window contradicted this. Then again, she had never really taken any sort of measure of the before and after, but the evidence before her suggested more people than not were still driving to work every day of the week.

The coffee pot beeped, signaling that her brew was ready.

She turned to the bar and took one of the white mugs from the four sitting upright in the center of the counter, then picked up the pot and filled the cup nearly to the top. After replacing the pot on the warmer, she heard another beep, this one from her computer.

"I do love synchronicities," she mused and spun slowly around to the desk.

She eased into the seat to keep from spilling the precious, hot coffee, and set the mug down near the keyboard.

The box on the screen had changed and now displayed multiple images of the man in question, along with the original, all arranged in a neat set of two columns on the left-hand side. Textual information filled the other two-thirds of the box, starting with the dealer's name at the top in big, bold font.

"Marial Juncao," Emily read out loud.

22

FUNCHAL, MADEIRA - PORTUGAL

Dak and Will barely jostled as the King Air twin-engine plane touched down on the tarmac.

"That was a smooth landing," Dak noted to his friend sitting across the aisle.

"Jimmy's very good," Will added. "I've used him before, and his landings are always perfect. Well, almost always."

"Almost? Why do I feel like there's a story there?"

Will cracked a smile and shook his head. "Some other time, perhaps."

"All right. Fine. Be that way. But I am not going to forget."

The pilot turned the plane off the main runway and taxied toward a row of hangars off to the right of the main terminal and gates.

Dak looked into the cockpit at the skinny guy from Portsmouth in England. The headset covering his ears pressed down on the shaggy light-brown hair atop his head. He wore khakis and a plaid shirt with multiple hues of yellow, blue, and white in between.

The conversation with him had been brief earlier that morning when Dak and Will arrived at the airport. Part of that brevity had been due to the fact neither of the Americans had slept very well the night before in Will's home, despite several reassurances from Will that no one knew he owned the place.

During the flight, Will explained how he'd met Jimmy several years before. The pilot was former British RAF and now spent most of his time ferrying businesspeople around Western Europe.

That gig paid well enough, but Will had convinced him to join his smuggling operation. Nothing permanent or consistent. Just a little extra cash here and there to move some weapons to people who really needed them.

Jimmy had been happy to jump on board, and Will got the impression the thirty-seven-year-old pilot would have done it for free, simply so he could help in the fight against oppression and tyranny.

When they arrived at the lonely hangar, he cut the engines and ran through the multiple steps he performed at the end of every flight before hanging the headset to his left.

"How was the flight?" he asked as he opened the door and unfolded the stairs.

"Great," Dak answered. "Thanks again so much for doing this."

"Happy to help," Jimmy replied. "There's a rental car waiting for you in the hangar. I hope it suits your needs. Nothing fancy. You won't win any street races with it."

"All we need are wheels," Dak said with gratitude.

"Still the cheapskate, huh?" Will countered.

The pilot pretended to be offended. "Aw, now. Come on, Will. Is that any way to talk to your old pal? Or would you prefer to walk?"

Will stood and picked up his rucksack. "You know I'm only messing with you, Jimmy."

He'd already given the pilot a generous stack of cash for his trouble before they took off from Lisbon.

Jimmy said he knew and added a friendly wink. He held out his arm to invite the two passengers to exit the aircraft. "Age before beauty."

"Then Dak should go first on both counts," Will quipped.

"Hilarious," Dak muttered as he slung his bag over his right shoulder and made his way to the exit. "You hanging out here on Madeira for a bit, Jimmy?"

"Just for a few days. I'll hang out here, gorge myself on the local cuisine, maybe enjoy the beach one day. Then head back to the mainland. From there, I'm going to Marseille to pick up a couple of folks to take them to Madrid for some corporate merger or some nonsense. Those types can be annoying, especially if they decided to toss back a few before they come on board. But they pay well."

"I'm sure."

A warm breeze slapped the three men as they descended the stairs and stepped onto the tarmac. The sun warmed their skin from a cloudless blue sky.

Dak inhaled a deep breath of the salt-infused air and held it for a few seconds before exhaling. No matter where he went, he always caught himself doing that.

"Thanks for the lift," Dak said. "I'm sure you have few checklist things to do before you can head out."

"Yeah. Safety is on the list," Jimmy replied. "There's a road out behind the hangar that will take you into the city. Shouldn't be any trouble. Navigation apps work fine here, so I doubt you'll get lost. And I don't think anyone will ask many questions on your way out. One of the benefits of flying Jimmy Air." He pointed at a door in the back of the hangar—the general direction of the prescribed road.

Not much in the way of security, Dak thought, grateful for the discretion.

"Thanks, man," Will said, clasping the pilot's hand firmly. "I'll be in touch."

"I know you will. And you're welcome."

The two Americans left Jimmy to do his thing with the plane and made their way toward a red Mazda hatchback parked in the shade from the hangar's curved roof.

"Where should we begin looking for this guy?" Dak asked. His voice echoed around in the hangar, bouncing off the metal walls.

"I know the general area where the image was taken," Will said.

"We can start there and snoop around until we find it. Shouldn't take too long."

Dak hoped his friend was right. Time wasn't exactly a luxury they had at the moment. He remembered to switch his phone back on out of airplane mode, though Jimmy hadn't really said anything about doing that in the first place.

Within seconds of him reactivating the device's full functionality, it buzzed and the screen displayed an alert that he had a text message from Emily. He tapped on the green icon, and the screen opened the texting app. The message from her was short and to the point.

"Call me."

Dak stopped by the car and tapped on the number. "Hey, Will. I got a message from Emily. Wants me to call her. I'll just be a second."

"Great," Will said, as he stuffed his gear into the trunk and then climbed into the driver's seat. He took out his own phone to kill time while Dak made the call to the Axis director.

The phone rang four times before Emily picked up. "I guess your flight from Lisbon was okay," she said.

"Uneventful. Just the way I like flights to be."

"Definitely. Well, I found some interesting information about our guy. His name is Marial Juncao."

"That's an interesting first name for a guy."

"Apparently, it's more common than you might think over there. Everything about him looks clean. Too clean if you ask me. Doesn't even have so much as a traffic violation on his record."

Dak understood what she meant by too clean. If someone's record was so spotless, they were either a saint, or they'd doctored things behind the scenes. Since he was trying to deal black-market art to Boston, Dak automatically figured it was the latter.

"What else do you have on him?"

"He runs a legit business, or at least that's what the database says. Pays his taxes. Has a salary. Nothing remarkable."

"Sounds like a very normal guy."

"They often do. The one thing I couldn't find was the home

address for that property in the image. It could be a leased office space he's using."

"Could be. I'll have to check it out."

"He does have a residence on file, but it's not in Madeira. It's back on the mainland in Porto."

That wasn't helpful. Maybe Will had been wrong about the picture of the beach in the background. He'd seemed sure it was here on Madeira, but perhaps it had actually been Porto.

He hoped that wasn't the case. If so, they'd gone a long way in the wrong direction, and Dak didn't have that kind of time.

"Any aliases?" Dak asked.

"Not that I see. Which is also odd. Someone in his line of work who doesn't have some alternative monikers is either very sloppy or very ignorant."

That, Dak thought, *is indeed unusual*. As Emily suggested, Juncao not having other identities would expose him to multiple threats, both from authorities and from potentially dangerous criminals. Still, the fact the guy operated in the black market online suggested he was somewhat aware of the dangers.

"What's his salary like?" Dak asked, his mind drifting to the real estate overlooking the coast he'd seen in the picture. "Property like that isn't cheap, no matter what country you're in."

"Nothing remarkable. Eighty thousand a year."

"That's a nice round number. Keeps him in a certain tax bracket, I'd imagine."

"Yep. I was thinking the same thing."

Dak considered the information she'd given. It was helpful to put a name to the face, but not knowing the exact address would eat away at more of that precious time. He only had four more days to track down the painting and get it to Tucker, and hopefully liberate Nicole.

"Thanks for all your help on this, Emily. I really appreciate it."

"No trouble at all, Dak. Happy to help any time if I can."

"We're heading into the city now, so I'll let you go. Thanks again."

"You're welcome."

He ended the call and shoved the phone back into his pocket, then stowed his bag in the trunk, closed it, and joined Will in the front of the car.

"Well?" his friend asked.

"I got a name but not much else."

"That's something at least."

"Yeah. Something." Dak couldn't mask his disappointment, but she'd done all she could. Either Juncao was extremely good at hiding things or really bad at it. Either way, they were going to have to do this the hard way.

23

Outside the airport, the two drove into Funchal. Dak had no idea where he was in the city other than the name of the café Will had given him as a place they could grab something to eat and have one of the local coffees.

Will found a parking spot four car lengths away from the café, expertly worked the hatchback into the tight opening, and killed the engine.

As he'd done for years now, Dak gave a quick survey of the immediate area—the street straight ahead and the opposite sidewalk, plus a look in the rearview mirrors. He didn't notice anything suspicious.

The two stepped out of the vehicle and up onto the sidewalk.

Beige buildings with terracotta rooftops crowded the street. A white sign with a picture of a baguette and a coffee cup hung out over the sidewalk sixty feet away. They watched as the front door opened and a pretty young woman in a pale blue dress carrying a paper coffee cup stepped out and turned down the sidewalk. Her long cocoa hair fluttered in the breeze, mirroring the bottom of her dress's movements.

"How did you know about this place?" Dak asked, turning to face the café. Behind it, the steep slopes of the island climbed upward, filled with more buildings that offered higher vistas of the sea beyond their lower neighbors.

"Dude. It's my go-to here in Funchal. Good food, coffee, pastries. And it's not far from where I think that dealer's house is. You want to get a coffee before we head over there?"

Dak's stomach grumbled at the thought of food and a jolt of caffeine. Despite time pressing against them, he knew he'd be better off having a quick bite and a cup of coffee.

Surrendering to his base needs, Dak followed his friend into the little shop and grabbed a coffee, some crusty bread, slices of white cheese, and a banana.

The two scarfed down the simple meal in short order, saying nothing until they were both finished eating.

After shoving the last piece of bread in his mouth, Dak finally spoke up as he chewed. "How far do you think it is from here?"

Will shrugged, taking a sip of milky coffee. He swallowed then set the cup down. "Ten-minute walk. Maybe fifteen. But you can see how congested the homes are here. It could be right behind us and we wouldn't see it until we basically tripped over it."

Dak nodded. "Okay. We best get moving, then. You good?"

"Yep. I'm ready."

The two set out from the café and turned left, heading toward the coast. The sidewalks twisted and turned, rolling up and down the undulating hillside town.

Will led the way down several streets that branched off from the main one where they started, but didn't find the art dealer's house.

An hour passed, and with every minute that ticked by, Dak grew more impatient. His friend seemed lost in the maze of streets and buildings.

"You sure you know where this place is?" he pressed as they turned down another street that ran parallel to the main one.

"If I knew where it was, we would already be there," Will huffed. "Like I said, I know it's around here somewhere. But where, exactly, I'm not sure."

Dak didn't like the answer. They were wasting time. But there was nothing he could do. He tried to remind himself to be grateful for Will's help, that without him, Dak would basically be screwed.

"Maybe we should split up," Dak suggested. "Could cover more ground that way."

"Yeah. Maybe you're right."

They reached the end of the street where it branched off to the right and left. Just as Dak was about to tell his friend to go one way and he'd take the other, he looked down to the right and stopped the words before they were spoken.

"Or maybe not," Dak said, changing his mind.

Will followed Dak's stare to the end of the street two hundred feet away where a tall white mansion stood out against the rest of the homes. Through the narrow gaps between buildings, the Americans saw the coast beyond—the same view from Boston's screenshot.

"Well, well, well." Will raised his hand to his forehead to shield his eyes from the bright sun. "Would you look at that."

A white wall stood out in front of the mansion, providing both a buffer from the street and a courtyard for the homeowner.

Through a wrought-iron gate, a driveway made of gray brick pavers split off to the right and left. Little green shrubs lined the path to two sandstone steps. The wooden front door was painted a pale hue of grayish blue. Round white pots stood on either side, each containing a two-foot-high tree with branches shaped to look like a ball.

On the right side of the gate, the front of a white sports car stuck out just beyond the wall.

Dak took a couple of steps toward the home and then stopped next to a red door of another resident.

He crossed his arms and thought. Will looked at him, then to the house again.

"You're thinking there isn't any security. Aren't you?" Will realized.

"Not as much as I would have thought," Dak admitted. "He does have cameras up. One in the right corner. Two over the front door. One at the gate. One in the left corner of the house."

"Probably others around the other sides, too."

"Yep," Dak agreed.

Still, something didn't sit right with him.

"I would think a guy so deeply involved in the dark web and selling illicit art would have at least a few guards around."

"Maybe he keeps them all inside."

"Yeah. Maybe."

Will kept his gaze fixed on the house. "How do you want to do this? Discreet? Or bust down the doors?"

Dak surveyed the quiet street. "Looks like somebody is home," he observed. "Unless they're a homebody, the guy will probably leave at some point. Maybe to get dinner or drinks."

"Or both."

"Why choose if you don't have to?"

"That's always been my motto," Will said with a chuckle.

"Same." Dak checked his watch. They had four days until the deadline. It felt more like minutes counting down to a nuclear blast. "I don't want to wait for him to come out. Could be hours, and he still might not appear."

"We don't have that kind of luxury."

"No. But getting killed by a couple of guards inside that place won't help Nicole either."

"True. So, I guess we're waiting?" Will ventured, still gazing at the front gate to the mansion.

"We give it until dark. If he doesn't leave by then, we go in."

24

Dak had hoped things would play out the easy way, though he knew such hopes were fanciful and foolish.

Nothing had ever seemed to be easy in his life. Now, his days presented never-ending challenges from the mundane to the occasional life-threatening crisis. Just because he was good at surviving, and at passing such trials, didn't mean he enjoyed them.

Hope taunted him now and then, giving him false glimpses into a future Dak knew he would probably never have: Family vacations. Trips to amusement parks. Picnics. Holidays with loved ones. Relaxing by a pool or at the beach. Hosting cookouts. Making love to the only woman he'd ever truly loved.

None of those things felt like real, possible outcomes for him. Dak figured he probably had a better shot at winning the lottery than any of that stuff playing out. But he had to try.

His mind rifled through those thoughts as he sat in the rental car, staring out the windshield at the white mansion at the end of the street. The impending realization that they were going to have to break into the house grew stronger by the second as the sun descended toward the horizon to the west.

Dusk quickly approached, and with it came Dak's self-imposed deadline.

He didn't like the idea of breaking into the mansion. Too many variables he couldn't foresee or control. When he was in Delta, there were plenty of unknowns, but they very often had enough intel to make semi-informed decisions and take precise action.

Here, there was no way to know how many people were inside the house, whether or not they were armed, or what kind of training they might have had.

Way too many unknowns for Dak's taste. But there was nothing to be done about it now. They were here, and time was peeling away.

"You gonna call it?" Will asked, his voice slicing through the silence like one of those television knives through an aluminum can.

"Afraid so," Dak answered. Reluctance littered his voice. He spent a precious few seconds trying to think of another way, hoping that circumstances would change. The man in the house was dangerous; of that Dak felt certain. The dark web wasn't a place for those with a faint heart. With the exception of his young employer, the underbelly of the internet brimmed with those bent on evil, hawking sinister wares and services.

If that was the place where the owner of this home made his living, Dak could only assume the man himself was just as dark.

Dak pulled the handle next to him and opened the car door. He set foot on the asphalt next to the vehicle and took a deep, calming breath. The salty air tickled his nostrils and cleansed his mind. By the time he exhaled, Dak felt ready.

He walked around behind the car, meeting Will at the trunk, and flipped open the lid. The two men removed a pair of pistols from their bags, one for each of them, along with a spare magazine. Including the mag in the well of both weapons.

"You still think two mags are enough?" Will asked with a cautious glance over at the mansion.

"We went over this before, Will."

"Just checking. Seems like maybe we should have more firepower is all."

Dak stuffed the SIG Sauer 9mm in a holster under his armpit. The short suppressor on the muzzle made it a little trickier to slide in, and Dak knew drawing it would offer the same sort of resistance.

He only planned on keeping it in the holster until they were inside the gates, at which point he'd pull the weapon and have it ready.

"You got a plan for the cameras?" Dak asked as he finished getting ready by throwing on a black leather jacket to cover the pistol. As he did so, he leaned around the car and checked the street just to make sure no one was watching. Nothing like getting arrested because some random pedestrian happened to see him and his friend strapping up with an illegal firearm.

"Not really. If I had an infrared light, I could momentarily disable them. But I didn't think I'd need anything like that."

"So, we're just going to go in guns blazing?"

"Hey, I'm winging this just like you, man."

It was becoming abundantly clear how little Dak had thought through this ragged plan. "Can't go in through the front gate. And going around will take time, though that might be the best play. Less chance of being noticed if we hop over the wall in the back."

Earlier, they'd taken thirty minutes to hike around to the ocean side of the mansion. The opulent home perched on a rock cliff with a short forty-foot drop down to another row of homes below. A narrow path snaked behind the mansion, winding precariously along the rocky edge.

The wall around the house continued but stopped at the lip of an infinity pool that hung out over the precipice.

Dak made sure he and Will didn't linger too long as they reconnoitered the area and kept moving beyond the mansion in case their target inside happened to be standing by one of the enormous windows.

Dak stole casual glances at the house as he and Will passed, doing his best not to look suspicious—as much as two people walking along the goat path behind a private residence could.

He didn't notice any figures in the home or any movement. As they passed beyond the view of the mansion's interior, Dak started questioning himself as to whether he'd misread the situation or not.

Maybe no one was home after all, and if that were the case, they'd wasted the entire afternoon on a stakeout of an empty residence. Still, it wasn't like they'd had a better option.

He wasn't about to attempt a break-in without the homeowner present. Dak wasn't good enough to pull off a job like that. He'd need someone who could hack into the security system and disable the alarm. Will wasn't the one for that kind of work, either. Dak's friend had a plethora of tools and resources and was handy in a number of other ways, but cybersecurity and breaking and entering weren't his strong suits.

During the rest of the afternoon, the two friends had come up with few ideas other than barging straight in.

Dak reflected on their recon until Will was ready. Then he closed the trunk and faced the mansion.

To the west, the setting sun painted hues of orange, pink, and purple across the sky—stained only by a few gray clouds here and there. A crescent moon hung in the looming darkness approaching from the east, smearing the black backdrop with a pale glow.

"Still want me to take the back?" Will asked without looking over at his friend. A sense of apprehension frosted his words.

Dak confirmed with a nod. "I don't have to tell you to be careful. Without good intel, or maybe a thermal camera, we won't know where they are, or how many."

Will's shoulders slumped. "Crap."

Dak broke away from staring at the home and peered at his friend. "What?" The long look on Will's face told him everything. "You have a thermal camera in there. Don't you?"

"I didn't think about it. I brought it in case—"

"In case we needed to get a warm body count on the guards in this place?"

"Actually, I was thinking more along the lines of operating at night."

"Which we are," Dak piled on.

"Yeah. I meant more night. Like total darkness."

Dak rolled his eyes. "Would you mind getting it out so we can have a look?"

Will bobbed his head quickly, opened the trunk, and unzipped a pouch on his bag. He pulled out a FLIR thermal scanner, pressed the button, and flipped open the screen on the side.

"Seriously," Dak said. "I can't believe you had that in your bag this whole time. We could have been in there already."

"I know. I'm sorry." He pointed the camera at the front gate and watched it appear on the display in various shades of blue. He turned the lens to the right, then back to the left, but no human forms in red, yellow, or orange appeared.

"Doesn't look like anyone's home," Will announced. "So, maybe you can take it easy on me about forgetting I had this?"

"Maybe," Dak allowed but said nothing else. He could have added that knowing no one was home would have at least given them a little leeway in terms of taking a break over the last few hours, or perhaps taking more time to survey the place. But he left it alone. There was no sense in holding something like this over his friend. It wouldn't help. And Dak could have made the same mistake. It was highly unlikely, but anything was possible. The thought amused him, though he didn't show it.

"So, we have an empty house," Dak mumbled. "I wonder if he's even going to show up."

"Yeah. In hindsight, coming here was a pretty big risk. I mean, this dude could be on the other side of the planet by now, sipping margaritas on the beach or at a club on an island somewhere."

"You're thinking of Ibiza, aren't you?"

Will flashed a cheeky grin. "You know it."

Headlight beams sprayed through the darkness ahead of them, originating from the street to the left of the mansion where the pavement curved away and down the next hill.

"Over there. Quick," Dak ordered.

Before Will could comply, Dak ducked into a recessed entryway to a home and tucked in close to a red wooden door with squares carved into it and raised with a type of trim to accentuate the design. Will joined him a second later, just two breaths before the car appeared at the end of the street.

Dak leaned out and spied the vehicle as it slowed, nearing the gate. It was a white Mercedes-Benz G Wagon, AMG edition. Dak resisted the urge to whistle at the expensive vehicle, knowing that it cost more than some people's homes back in the States, and most certainly here in Portugal where the cost of living was comparatively cheaper.

The metal barrier creaked as the motors behind the hinges slowly began pulling it to the right. The wrought-iron gate shimmied and bounced slightly on its wheels until the path onto the driveway was clear.

"I'll say this," Will whispered, looking past Dak's right shoulder, "I like his choice of SUV."

"Yeah. He's got style. And clearly money to blow." Dak peered harder at the vehicle as it passed through the gate. The windows were tinted so dark they were nearly impossible to see through. Back home in the States, he knew people who got pulled over by the cops for having windows tinted less than that. Then again, maybe here that wasn't an issue, or even a law.

But what he could see through the nearly black glass was another figure in the back. And he thought perhaps there were two.

Making sure the gun was tucked inside his jacket and out of sight, Dak emerged from the entrance and hurried down the steps, cutting left on the sidewalk toward the mansion.

His abrupt move caught Will off guard, but he quickly caught up and walked a half step behind Dak as they approached the huge home.

The gate began rolling back to its original position again, which caused Dak to quicken his pace slightly.

He and Will were still a good thirty yards away, which they could have covered in under five seconds but not at a brisk walk.

Dak felt the need to risk it, and the temptation to break out in a sprint nearly overwhelmed him as he neared the corner across from the gate. In seconds, it would be closed, and then he and Will would have to go over instead of through. Doable. But not preferable.

Instead of making a break for it, Dak froze there on the corner, as if unable to make a decision.

That wasn't a problem he'd experienced in a long time. Decision-making was one of his strengths. In his past life, and indeed in the current one, the ability to decide on what actions to take in a quick and confident manner had saved his neck more times than he cared to recount.

Now, however, he couldn't make himself move.

"What's the matter with you?" Will hissed. "We need to—" He stopped himself in midsentence. He followed Dak's stare through the gate where the SUV had parked off to the side of the other car.

Neither man could say a word as they watched a woman and two children step out of the SUV with the art dealer.

25

Dak shifted for the first time in what felt like minutes, though in reality he'd only been standing on the corner for five or six seconds.

He turned, ambled across the street to his right as if making his way to his own home, and kept an eye on the family as they walked up the wide steps to the gigantic front door.

Will walked close behind him, not daring to speak. Even if he felt it safe to do so, he wasn't sure what he could say. The sight of the family had taken both men by surprise. Considering their backgrounds, that was saying something.

Dak made sure his speed was slow enough to be able to see the family enter the home and the door close behind them. Then he moved faster until the wall in front of the mansion blocked him from view.

He exhaled and realized he hadn't been breathing since he noticed the kids in the SUV.

"Who are they?" Will demanded, extending his left hand toward the wall and the home behind it.

"I don't know," Dak confessed. "At first, when I saw the outlines of figures in the G Wagon, I figured it was his guards. Emily didn't say anything about a woman and kids."

"Yeah. Those are not guards."

"You think?"

"They look like the guy's wife and children, Dak. Just what did we get ourselves into? I thought this dude was a black-market art dealer."

"He is," Dak insisted.

"Really? How many of those types do you know with a wife and two kids? I bet they have a golden lab somewhere in the house, too."

Dak thought for half a second before the conspiratorial side of him took the wheel. "Would be the perfect cover."

"What?"

"No one would suspect. Could be that the wife and kids don't suspect, either. That's how these things usually go."

Will wasn't sure if Dak was being serious or not. "Do you really think that's what's going on? Because that's messed up."

"Maybe," Dak said. "We can't rule it out. And from the way the kids were laughing, and the smile on the woman's face, I'd say they're not being held against their will."

"Doesn't appear that's the case," Will agreed, albeit begrudgingly. "What should we do?"

A gray compact car rolled by slowly on the street to their left. The engine rattled. The tires looked as though they'd seen as many years as the vehicle itself. The wear and tear on the old car was evidenced by flaking and faded paint in several spots. The windshield had a crack that ran from the bottom-left corner to the top right. Still, the thing was running, and it apparently still got the driver where he needed to go.

The vehicle only took a moment to drive by and disappear around the corner at the top of the rise, but something about it caught Dak's attention. He wasn't suspicious of the driver, or fearful that something would come of the car's passing.

Rather, it caused him to reflect in a way he rarely did, looking at his own life as if he were a shiny new car that would someday look weathered and beaten, just like the vehicle that had passed.

Dak didn't feel that way yet. He was still in his thirties, but time passed quickly. He'd always heard older people say that. His parents. Their parents. Aunts, uncles, teachers. They all made the same claim.

As a young person, life seemed like it would never end, as if it would go on forever and you had all the time in the world. Then you were thirtysomething, and you realized it's moved faster than you thought. But you still had plenty of time. You could still live forever, do all the things you planned when you were young.

The realization that none of that was true only grew with every passing year.

Dak wasn't sure why he felt these emotions all of a sudden. He'd had similar thoughts before, but not as heavy as they seemed now, weighing down on him like a yoke strapped with anvils on either side.

Perhaps it was seeing the art dealer's family. This criminal had created a life with a beautiful woman and two healthy kids. Of course, because of the man's occupation, all of that could—and would—come crashing down.

Eventually.

Dak found himself feeling sorry for the kids. He pondered whether the wife knew about her husband's illicit activities, but figured she didn't. Most likely, he'd been hiding everything from her, living a lie about some legitimate business he ran out of his home office.

Probably told her it was e-commerce, Dak mused.

"What now?" Will asked, interrupting Dak's wanderings.

The question snapped him back to reality in an abrupt and jarring way. Dak wasn't often given to daydreaming, or letting his thoughts drift. For a second, he wondered how long he'd been standing there staring at the car and then the empty street, allowing his mind to roam.

"We still have to go in," Dak said.

"Okay. But what about the wife and kids?"

The family certainly complicated everything, but it was still doable. The hour was early, so Dak doubted the kids were off to bed just yet, though that would probably be soon. Especially given the week was about to begin the next day. He wasn't sure they'd be in school, but what little Dak knew about parenting, he figured the mom and dad probably kept the kids on a consistent schedule.

"We can either wait until the kids are asleep... or we can go in now."

"In? You mean like break down the door and go in with guns out?"

"No." Dak almost laughed at the thought. "I don't think traumatizing a couple of innocent kids is a good idea."

"Oh." Will puzzled over what plan his friend might possibly be concocting. "So what then?"

Dak spied the keypad fixed to the wall next to the gate. He figured it had a call button to ring the home's occupants for deliveries or visitors.

Dak's lips stretched on the left side of his face. "I have an idea."

26

Dak sat on a rock outcropping that jutted up from the cliff overlooking the beach. Juncao's house was only a few buildings down, and if the man happened to sense something was amiss before Will could execute the plan, there was only one way for him to escape.

Dak had effectively blockaded the path down to the ocean, and the other way would lead back to the streets. Admittedly, that would be more difficult to track were he alone, but with Will covering the other side, Dak knew there was nowhere for the Portuguese art dealer to run.

The plan was to flush him out the back, if he were willing to abandon his family, and get him away to question him about the Rembrandt.

It was a long shot. Dak knew that. But it was the only lead they had right now, if he could even call it that.

Boston had seemed confident that this guy could provide answers, but what if he couldn't? The trail would go cold, and leave Nicole dangling like a sail in a doldrum.

Perched on the hard, jagged surface, Dak kept his firearm hidden for now in case any of the neighbors happened to go outside for a bit of fresh air and saw a crazy-looking guy with a gun in his hand.

Heat was something he didn't need right now.

Alone in the night, under the stars with the wind tossing strands of his hair around like short ribbons on bicycle handlebars, he had nothing but his thoughts to occupy the time as he waited.

He ran through the gambit of possibilities in his head, hoping they really had cordoned off Juncao. Was it possible the guy had another way out, perhaps a secret passage? Dak doubted as much, though with the kind of money the dealer was working with, anything was truly possible.

Then there was the other unlikely scenario. If Juncao, for whatever reason, decided to try to leave out the front door, he'd make an easy getaway.

Dak chided himself for disparaging his own plan. It would work. It had to work.

He peered out across the ocean into the wet, roiling darkness that merged with that of the sparkling sky. Whitecaps rippled across the ocean's churning surface. Dak wasn't a sailor, but he imagined this was the kind of night those types really appreciated. The wind was good, from what he could tell, and no storms lurked on the horizon.

He wished he could say the same about his life.

The last few years felt like nothing but one storm after another, with only false breaks that seemed as if he were standing in the eye of a hurricane. Just long enough to catch his breath before the next battering began.

Part of it was of his own choosing. He'd taken the job with Boston McClaren as a way to earn some serious cash and to stay on the move while he tried to find Tucker—and while Tucker hunted him.

The cat-and-mouse game had lasted this long, but now it felt like things were coming to a head.

Dak hoped so.

For a moment, he wondered what he might do if all of this worked out the way he wanted. If he made sure Nicole was safe, and Tucker was gone for good, could he settle down and start a new life?

That question haunted him almost every night, and the answer never seemed clear—like the murky waters of the deep beyond the shore.

And then there were the people he'd helped along the way. That part bothered him, too. He'd saved lives, untold numbers of them, by his actions over the last few years. From Peru to the United Kingdom, to the southeastern United States, Ukraine, and even India, Dak had made a difference to the lives of total strangers, people he would never have met if he hadn't been willing to put his own life in jeopardy.

His young boss called him the Relic Runner. It was a moniker Dak thought sounded cool but was maybe a bit grandiose for his tastes. In reality, recovering the artifacts he'd hunted down had been a byproduct of a greater purpose—helping those who couldn't help themselves.

He'd never been able to spend much time in charitable works—donating time to feed the hungry or house the homeless. Sure, he'd volunteered during high school, but that was also part of what was expected there. Everyone was doing it.

Not everyone could do what he could now.

He had a unique set of skills that both enabled him to recover priceless pieces of human history for future generations, and to give others a chance at a better life.

Could he walk away from all that?

It almost felt selfish to consider it, despite the imminent dangers that lurked perpetually around every corner.

Another gust of wind splashed into his face, spraying a moist cloud of salty air against his cheek.

The gun pressed into his ribs just slightly, reminding him it was there. Dak hoped he didn't have to use it, not here, not in this instance. He knew almost nothing about this Juncao character, but with a family so close by, killing the man would have grievous repercussions on more lives than one.

He sighed and refocused on the moment, figuring the answers to all the questions and the scenarios would eventually come with time. Right now, he had a painting to find.

27

Will didn't like the plan, but he agreed with Dak that it was the only way they could flush out the dealer without causing extensive childhood trauma to the man's kids. They were innocent in this whole thing, no matter how guilty their father might have been.

Standing next to the keypad now, Will knew the built-in camera was staring at him and had probably alerted the homeowners to his presence. He imagined they got an alert on their phone, something these kinds of systems often provided.

Either way, they'd know he was there the second he hit the call button. Will glanced to his left down the street leading toward the waterfront, then back up the hill. "You in position?" he asked into the radio. The tactical mic and earpiece were state of the art, nearly undetectable from a distance of more than ten feet. Up close, someone would notice, but the device was far more discreet than most he'd seen on the market.

"I'm good. Make the call."

Will reached out his right index finger, hesitated, then pressed the button.

The sound of a phone ringing came through the speaker on the keypad. He waited. One ring. Two. Immediately after the third, someone picked up.

Moment of truth, Will thought.

"Hello?" the man said in Portuguese.

Will felt a spark of relief at the sound of his voice. If the woman answered, he would have needed to change the plan.

Fortunately, the dealer had been the one to take the call.

Will moved into phase two of the operation and made a show of pulling back his jacket to reveal the pistol holstered under his armpit.

"I've been looking for you," Will said, doing his best sinister voice. Working in the world of illegal gunrunning, he'd been forced to use that tone more than once, and it was never fake in any of those scenarios.

For a second, all Will heard were the sounds of the quiet streets of Funchal—a cat meowing somewhere, muted conversations, cars driving by on the adjacent street behind him, and air conditioners humming.

Then the call ended without warning. Just as Dak said it would.

MARIAL JUNCAO SET the phone down quietly on the kitchen counter. His wife was upstairs getting the kids ready for bed. He'd already kissed and hugged them goodnight and was about to sit down for his routine beer as he caught up on the latest Portuguese premier league scores.

He'd thought the call from the front gate at this hour to be strange. No one would be out delivering things other than food at this hour. And he had not ordered any food.

Juncao had feared this day ever since he got into his trade. It was a dangerous world, fraught with sinister people who could chill even the most hardened imagination. While the money was more than he could have ever dreamed of in his previous life as a curator, his current profession brought with it far more risk than reward.

He'd made millions grifting black-market dealers for their

corruptly earned money and had expertly cleaned it, scrubbed it, and cleaned it again through various laundering operations.

That part was easy enough, and he often wondered how or why people got caught laundering money. Carelessness? Sure. Greed? Definitely. He'd fallen prey to neither, other than the fact he had a target amount he wanted to make before he called it quits.

Juncao believed he had the final piece on the line when he'd been connected with a potential seller the night before. As a precaution, he always tried to backdoor a seller or buyer, and last night had been no different. But before he could pinpoint the seller's location, the mysterious user had dropped offline.

After a few minutes of trying to reconnect, Juncao assumed the seller got cold feet and changed their mind about the deal. It was a shame, and the money lost from that one could have set Juncao and his family up for life. But he'd learned early on that getting too attached to a transaction was a dangerous thing to do—particularly for his mental health.

He'd adapted and taken lost revenue in stride as much as possible and over time had developed a good reputation on the dark web—a fact he found hilarious.

But now, the humor was crumbling around him like a sandcastle against the tide. He'd spent countless nights without sleep, hoping that he'd plugged every possible leak, made everything as clean as possible to avoid the boogeymen he saw in his mind.

Apparently, though, he'd screwed up.

He had no way of knowing if the man at the gate was a disgruntled customer or the seller from the night before who had somehow tracked him down. There was, however, no mistaking the pistol the man showed within the confines of his jacket.

Juncao had planned for this. Well, sort of. He had a bugout bag he kept near the back door on a shelf in the laundry room. His wife had asked him about it a few times, and he blew it off, telling her it was just for walks in the mountains. The island of Madeira offered many trails around ancient volcanoes and calderas that had been dormant for millennia. She seemed to accept the answer, probably because he told her a few times he was going hiking and took the bag with him for good measure. But he'd never actually gone up into those mountains on any of the occasions he'd used the excuse.

The lies had worked, though he felt a little bad about telling them.

Still, it was better she didn't know the truth, especially with the kinds of people he dealt with.

Juncao made up his mind. He couldn't deliberate on the issue. Every second he spent in the house, contemplating his next move, could prove deadly to his family. Better to leave and try to escape with the chance of maybe getting in touch with them later. Though he doubted that.

It would hurt his kids. His wife would be confused, destroyed. But they could live. Whoever was here wanted him. If he escaped. Fine. If he died, at least they would be safe.

The best he could hope for was that they learned of his murder and placed blame on someone else.

He hurried to the back of the house, walked through the open laundry room door, and reached up to grab the bugout bag from the top shelf. He slung the maroon pack over his shoulders and pushed open the back door.

Stars glittered in the darkening sky above, and the crescent moon cast a dim light down on the steps leading to the infinity pool in the back and the deck surrounding it.

He looked out for what he thought would be the last time at the ocean beyond the cliffs and the beach that rippled alongside it.

There was no time to reminisce. Nostalgia could be a deadly vice at a time like this.

Juncao eased the door shut, still fighting the guilt that ravaged his mind, and hurried down the steps.

He wondered how he'd been found as he scuttled across the stonework pool deck, passing the infinity pool glistening in the moonlight. His children's laughter echoed in his memory, reminding him of the warm days past they spent out here playing, romping in the water, enjoying life.

He thought, perhaps, after some time had passed it would be safe to call his wife, to talk to his kids again. But abandoning them felt almost too difficult to bear. He paused near the back gate and looked back at the house again, like Lot's wife from the Bible as they left their home in the city.

Juncao only vaguely recalled hearing the tale as a child, but the part about Lot's wife turning into a pillar of salt stuck out in his mind. He wondered, for a second, if that was some kind of metaphor for never giving a second thought to running away from danger.

The notion floated away on a warm, gentle breeze, and he pushed the back gate open, turned left, and froze.

A man stood before him, blocking the trail. He wore jeans, a white Soulcrush T-shirt, and a lightweight gray jacket. He looked distinctly American, but Juncao wasn't concerned about the man's nationality or his stylistic choices of clothing.

What did concern him was the pistol in the man's steady right hand, pointing straight at Juncao's face.

28

A ridiculous notion flashed through Juncao's mind like lightning in a field. Within two seconds, he visualized spinning around and running the other direction, but as soon as the vision ended, he knew it was nothing but fantasy.

"Going somewhere, Marial?" Dak asked.

"You're American." It wasn't a question.

"And you're astute, though not smart enough to think of another way out."

Juncao swallowed a chunk of fear. It caught in his throat like a piece of unchewed steak, and he had to gulp it down with effort.

"Who are you?" Juncao asked. "What do you want with me? How do you know my name?"

Dak inclined his head, eyeing the man carefully. He didn't appear to have any weapons on him. While ownership of firearms in Portugal was permitted, the process to obtain the license for one was rigorous. According to some statistics, there were a little over two million guns in Portugal the last time Dak saw some random stats pass through his feed. That didn't include the ones his friend Will imported and exported, though Dak figured most of the time the weapons didn't actually touch Portuguese soil.

Still, there were almost a million illegal or unregistered firearms in the country, and Dak found it surprising that this guy who made his fortune on the dark web selling illicit art didn't have something in the way of self-defense.

Sensing no danger, Dak lowered his weapon to his hip, still keeping it loosely pointed at the art dealer.

"I have connections," Dak answered. "Where are you going?"

The Portuguese man shook his head as if denying something he'd been accused of. "What are you going to do? Kill me? My wife and kids are in the house. Please. If you're going to kill me, don't do it here."

The response wasn't what Dak expected. The begging part he'd foreseen, but not the reasoning. It sounded as though the man actually cared about the woman and two children in the mansion.

That disproved the notion that they were a cover, or some kind of fake family.

Dak had no intention of killing the guy, but that could remain his little secret for the time being.

"You didn't answer my question," Dak pressed and made a show of shifting the pistol ever so slightly, just to remind the man it was there.

"I...I was going to leave."

"The city? Or just going out for some ice cream?"

The man shook his head, biting his lower lip. "The country. I knew sooner or later you would come for me."

"You have no idea who I am."

"No. That's true. I don't. But I knew someone would find me eventually."

"And why would you think that? Were you careless?"

Juncao shook his head. "I've been as careful as a man could be in my position. Call it paranoia."

Dak knew all about that. But he had the guy talking, so no sense in slowing him down now. "You speak excellent English. I suppose that's necessary in your trade."

Juncao's brow tightened at the statement. Questions dripped from his eyes. "Yes. It is. But I learned it as a second language growing up. Many of us did."

"So, you were going to leave the country. Just up and go without so much as a goodbye kiss to your wife?"

Pain streaked across Juncao's face. And Dak saw it as plainly as the moon in the sky.

"I... didn't want them to get hurt."

"They're going to hurt when they realize you're gone without a trace. Never to be seen again."

"They'll be safe, at least. But you haven't answered my question. Who are you? What do you want from me? Money? I have a stash hidden here in the city. And some in this bag. If you want it, it's yours. But I imagine you won't take a bribe from me. Someone else is paying you much more for my head."

This guy was making a lot of assumptions—all of them stemming from deeply rooted fears he'd been feeding for who knew how long.

"You don't think your leaving would devastate them?" Dak asked.

The man puzzled over the question. "What?"

"It was a yes-or-no question. Is it Portuguese tradition to ignore questions, or just unique to the island?"

"What?"

"We've established you like asking that question."

Juncao shook his head, confused.

"I know you operate on the dark web under an alias, or multiple aliases if you're smart. But you couldn't hide from me."

That much was true. Juncao had several online identities and fail-safes on fail-safes to prevent this exact scenario from happening. But he'd slipped up somewhere. Where, he didn't know. But clearly a mistake was made.

"I tracked you down, and if I can do it, I'd say others could, too, Marial," Dak said, motioning to the opulent home with a casual wave of the pistol. "I doubt some of your contacts would be as conversational as me."

"You haven't told me what you want," he said, choking on the words. "Who do you work for?"

"Okay, Marial. I work alone. And the only thing I need from you is answers."

Juncao's face darkened as the confusion mounted. "What kind of answers?"

"Are you okay? Because you seem a little like you're going to vomit, or maybe crap yourself. Either way, I want to be very clear. I don't have a lot of time on my hands for lies and nonsense. You operate on the dark web. So, I have to assume you're a real piece of work, and dangerous in your own right. Especially because you have a pristine record."

He watched his captive, gauging the man's facial expressions and body language.

"Please, can we move away from the house? I don't want my family to see this."

Dak glanced up at the second-story windows. Lights were on in multiple rooms, though he couldn't see anyone inside due to the dark curtains hanging just beyond the panes.

"Fine. We'll play it that way. Sit down."

"What?"

Dak tightened his trigger finger against the curled metal. " Sit. Down."

Juncao didn't hesitate. He plopped down on the trail with a jarring thud.

Dak lowered himself more carefully, assuming a cross-legged position as if about to enter a meditative state.

"You sell stolen art on the dark web, yes?" Dak began.

Juncao thought about it, and Dak saw him mulling over the answer. In the man's facial features, he could see that the guy was trying to decide whether he should tell the truth or brew up some lie in the cauldron of his mind.

"Look," he said. "I don't know who you work for. But if you want your money back, I can get it for you. What painting did I sell your employer? If you just tell me, I can make it right."

The statement confused Dak. "My employer is the one who

tracked you down. I won't tell you his name. But he never bought a painting from you."

It was Juncao's turn to look confused. "Then why are you here?"

"My employer located you on the dark web. I won't get into how he did it because frankly I don't understand much of that cyber stuff. What I do understand is that you sell art on the black market, art that has been missing or was stolen. I'm looking for a painting. A very specific painting. And I need your help to find it."

The worry on Juncao's face eased into a befuddled expression.

Dak watched as the man's lips parted and caught himself before he said "What?" one more time.

"I'm sorry?" Juncao said. "You want my help finding a painting?"

"That's right. And I don't have much time. I need to locate it before Friday."

Will appeared around the corner on the trail. He panted for air but relaxed when he saw Dak already had the guy they were looking for.

He trotted over to the two men and looked down at Juncao.

"Why are you two down there?" Will asked in a matter-of-fact tone that minimized the fact they were holding a man hostage.

"Didn't want the family to see," Dak answered.

"So, that really is his wife and kids."

"Who is this?" Juncao asked, looking up at Will.

"A friend," Dak said. "Look. I don't know much about you except what you do on the black market. What I do know is the painting we're looking for is a Rembrandt that was stolen over thirty years ago."

Juncao's face brightened in the kind of way a person's would if they'd been told they were growing a third arm. "A Rembrandt?"

"Yes. From what we know, it was taken by two thieves from a museum in Massachusetts."

"*The Storm on the Sea of Galilee*," Juncao finished.

Dak and Will shared a quick sidelong glance.

"That's right," Dak confirmed. "You know it?"

"Of course. That one has been requested many times in the...well, where I sell things. I never tried to locate it, though. No clue where it might be."

"You've never seen anything about it? Not one clue that might give you an idea as to who has it?"

Juncao thought for a couple of seconds. The waves crashed into the shore down below, spraying salty mist into the air to be carried away by the constant ocean breeze.

"No," he said, shaking his head. "I can't think of anything."

"Maybe if we start breaking fingers, you'll think of something," Will threatened.

Dak nearly laughed but choked it back. They had no intention of torturing the guy for information, especially now that they knew he had a family just eighty feet away inside the house.

Fear streaked through Juncao's eyes. "No. Please. I'm telling the truth. I don't know of anything that can connect to whoever stole that."

"There were two thieves," Dak stated. "That's what the authorities claim. They even suggested they had a lead at one point, but nothing ever came of it."

Juncao lowered his head for a moment, staring at the scree on the trail. He abruptly raised his eyes and looked into Dak's. "Did you say two thieves?"

29

BARCELONA

The sleepy streets of Barcelona roared back to life after the sun went down—an after-effect of the siestas enjoyed by so many.

The Black Lotus sat quietly in the corner of a tapas bar, sipping on a fine red wine from the Rioja region in the north of the country. She held the glass in her right hand, tilting it and spinning it slightly to allow the liquid to swirl around within. The alcohol legs drained down the sides slowly with every pass, another sign that this wine was an exceptional one.

Not that she needed further proof. A connoisseur herself, she knew the good from the bad by name and year. This one was one of her favorites.

She eased against the seat back and crossed one leg over the other —watching the windows at the front of the bar as people passed outside, their revelry increasing by the minute.

So it was in many cities in Spain, where the days were long, and the nights were longer. Some people stayed up into the witching hours of the morning, past two a.m. on a regular basis. She figured that sort of ritual may have been the original cause of the siestas traditionalized in this part of the world.

Work. Take a nap. Stay up late. Repeat.

She'd never known that life from personal experience.

Hers had been spent in a very different upbringing, full of discipline, learning, and often discomfort.

She didn't regret it. It had forged her into what she was—clever, lethal, adaptive. She hadn't expected to get the call regarding Col. Cameron Tucker. Then again, she never planned on calls from any of the den handlers.

Those were few and far between—exceedingly rare instances when her services were called upon. And when she was requested, not even the handlers understood the real reason why she took a job or not.

She raised the glass, lowered her nose into it beyond the rim, and inhaled slowly, appreciating the scent of the wine as it circled up into her nostrils. Then she tilted the rim to her lips and took a long, slow sip, savoring the drink as it splashed over her tongue and into her throat.

The server, a young male, probably in his early twenties, she suspected, exited the kitchen on the far side of the room and made his way across, carrying a small round tray loaded with her order.

He held the tray in his palm as he unloaded the three plates of food—*patatas bravas* with a spicy garlic aioli, *espinacas con garbanzos*, and *croquetas*.

"Will you be needing anything else?" he asked, staring down at her with young lust in his eyes.

He was attractive in a youthful sort of way—dark, wavy hair down to his ears, a well-groomed dark brown beard to match it, and slender like a footballer.

"Just the bill," she replied in a curt but polite way.

He nodded once and set a black vinyl folder down on the table next to the food.

"Thank you," she said in Spanish.

"You're welcome. Have a lovely evening." His voice trembled as he offered the words. She could tell she made him nervous, and the thought humored her.

Not that she was interested. Boys like that had never swayed her. She was too cold-blooded, a shark swimming among minnows. And only a man of equal cunning and strength could have her.

The thought brought a smile to her dark red lips, and she took another sip of the wine to wash it down.

She ate the food slowly, first tasting the potatoes, then the croquettes, and finally the spinach and chickpeas, then rotating back through again until the plates were empty.

In the corner near the window, four young men, probably a few years older than her server, laughed loudly, much to the irritation of some of the other customers.

She also noticed them stealing glances over at her in the corner. She recognized the looks, had seen them before. As an attractive woman, men of many ages snagged their eyes on her, much the same way the server had.

But these four were different. They had the look of trouble about them. It wasn't in their clothing—ordinary shirts, trousers, jeans, shoes. They were all clean cut, and didn't look like they were strung out on drugs.

These types were the ones that had other vices on their minds, and she could sense it with every obvious glance they fired across the room. They, like her, were predators. Just of a very different kind.

She imagined they preyed on females, or at least thought about it, and the notion disgusted her to the point that her usually calm thoughts burned with a silent fury.

She finished her meal, pretending to pay them no mind, and when she was done, downed the rest of the wine. After leaving a few notes to cover the bill and a small tip, she stood, collected her black clutch, and headed for the door.

As she moved, she kept her eyes forward on the exit while also monitoring the absurdly obvious gazes of the four men in the front corner. They may as well have been catcalling her.

She ignored them, and stepped out the front door and into the cool, stagnant evening air. She turned right and walked by the front windows of the bar, giving one last view to the four men as she passed.

The only breeze on the street came from her movement and caused her long, dark brown hair to flap behind her ears, and if she'd been wearing a dress instead of the white, quarter-zip long-sleeved golf shirt and tight jeans, it would have done the same.

Before she reached the corner of the bar, she heard the door creak open behind her amid the cacophony of sounds on the street and sidewalk.

A young couple passed her, talking about where they should go to eat a late-night snack and have a couple of beers.

She paused, twisted her body in their direction, and looked back over her shoulder. To no surprise, the four young men were standing there on the sidewalk just outside the tapas bar entrance, every one of them ogling her hungrily, like a lion would a T-bone.

They froze for a second, and then she ducked into the alley next to the tapas bar, knowing full well what would happen next.

She walked straight ahead into the shadowy thoroughfare, her shoes barely making a sound on the pavement, partially so she could hear them approaching but also in part because that was just her nature—to be quiet, stealthy.

Their laughter preceded them, echoing through the alley before they reached the corner. She heard their feet shuffle to a stop. A few of them shushed the others, but their drunken giggles managed to slip through to her ears.

She didn't stop walking, though she slowed her pace enough to allow them to catch up.

"Hey," one of them shouted in Spanish. "What's your name?"

She paused, huffed quietly to herself at the thought of him asking her name. Why? Did he want to know that about someone he intended to victimize? She wondered if they'd done this before, followed a woman—probably younger—into a dark alley, a quiet side street, or maybe the edge of a forest.

She heard them approaching but still didn't turn around. Instead, she stood perfectly still, staring straight ahead, listening to their clumsy feet shuffling and clomping on the pavement.

She'd noted the blue dumpster eight feet behind her and the putrid smells that worked their way out of its seams and into the air around it. A few dim lights hung from the stucco walls on either side of the corridor, but they were spaced out and allowed huge gaps of shadows between.

That didn't bother her. She wasn't afraid of the dark. In fact, she embraced it as an old friend, an entity she could lean on in times of need.

"Don't want to talk?" another said.

'She's scared," added a third.

"Are you scared?" the first continued. "You might enjoy this. I know we will."

They were close now, probably fifteen, maybe twenty feet away. She'd give it three more seconds.

"She is definitely scared," the second stated with a laugh. "I do like an older woman."

That one caused her to raise an insulted but amused eyebrow. Three seconds.

She rounded on them slowly, dropping her right foot back as she twisted to face them. They slowed to a halt, one of them tipping forward as though he might fall on his face.

"Do you not speak Spanish?" the one in the front and middle of the pack asked. He had a broad, clean-shaven face and looked like he spent a good amount of time at the gym. Not a bodybuilder-type frame, but stronger than the average guy.

The others looked athletic, too, each in the prime of their lives. Two of them had light blond hair, one dark blond, and the one who'd asked the question, deep brown.

"I speak Spanish," she replied in the language. Her words were fluid, calm. No sense of being threatened quivered her voice, and her eyes remained steadfast, locked on them like a hawk circling a rabbit.

The alley ended at a wall thirty feet behind her. She'd considered allowing them to follow her all the way there but decided here was a better place. More ways to hurt them in this spot.

An old mop leaned against the back door of the tapas bar. Its dirty threads still looked wet from the last time it was used. Two boxes of empty wine bottles sat nearby, stacked against the wall. And then there was the dumpster.

"What do you want, little boys?" she asked, her Spanish fluid and demeaning.

The leader pulled his chin back toward his neck, both shocked and infuriated she would insult them in such a way.

He ventured a step toward her, closing the gap to only eight feet. "Oh, you're about to find out what we want."

They moved forward as one semi cohesive unit, their drunken wavering steadying with the focus of rage and desire.

"I think I know what you want," she said. "I hope you like it rough."

For a second, the confusion danced across the leader's face, and then a sadistic sort of satisfaction replaced it, easing his cheeks and jaw into a pleased smirk.

"Why do you get to go first?" the dark blond asked from behind him.

The leader didn't take his lust-filled eyes off her. "Because I said so." His gaze went from head to toe and back, as if sizing her up, judging her. "I think she likes the idea, boys," he mused.

Then he spoke to her again as he stepped within a few feet of her, just beyond arm's reach. "Take off your—"

She snapped her right hand out at his throat, sending her fingers deep into the skin, crushing the larynx.

He staggered back a step for a second, but that was as far as she would allow him to retreat. She grabbed his shirt near the collar and pulled him closer, jerking him toward her right elbow as she swung it forward.

The bone met his nose with a sickening crunch. Before the blood burst out of his nostrils, she struck again, crushing the appendage in such a way that no plastic surgeon on earth would ever be able to make it look like it had before.

Then the blood flowed, out of his nose and down over his mouth. His eyes glazed in an instant, and he didn't know which injury to grasp for—the one that cut off his airway, or the demolished nose.

She twisted her body, leaning back as she kicked out her right leg and drove her heel into his abdomen.

The shoe sank deep into his gut and sent him stumbling back-ward onto his hindquarters. Unable to stop the fall, his head whipped back and smacked against the pavement.

He writhed around slightly like a fish on dry land in its dying moments. Both hands covered his face, the dark red liquid sopping his fingers.

For a long, awkward moment, his three amigos didn't know how to respond. It all happened so suddenly. One moment, they were getting ready to look the other way and watch the alley for any witnesses or Good Samaritans brave enough to venture into the shadows with the idea of helping the woman.

Then, out of nowhere, she'd attacked their friend. Within seconds, he was on the ground, immobilized by the blinding pain of a shattered nose, blood oozing all over his face and fingers, and desper-ately gasping for air through a windpipe that had been closed in an instant.

Their paralysis seemed to last minutes, though it was only ten seconds, maybe fifteen before they were able to react.

They wouldn't suffer the same fate as their friend. And now, sex was the last thing on their minds.

She'd pay for what she'd done.

30

The next one in line, a blond guy, swore at her—calling her a few choice names before he charged ahead.

His attack was bold. She had to give him that. But it was just as reckless, fueled by righteous indignation and too many beers. He raised his right fist and reared back to strike, telegraphing his move. It may as well have been on one of those digital billboards so bright you can see them from two miles away.

She stepped to the side as he lunged at her, his body following the fist. She stuck out her right foot, catching him on the ankle, and watched him trip. He tumbled to the ground, shoulder first, and rolled to a stop. As he collected himself and scrambled to his feet, the other two rushed forward.

They weren't going to take it one at a time like the other two had.

She noticed the movement to her right and waited, centering herself between the two men.

They slowed down as they neared her, splitting out wider so they could each take a side. Their strategy was better than the other two. Divide and conquer was always a good plan. It had worked in battles throughout history, as well as in modern politics.

When both of them were on either side, they paused for a second, then gave a nod to each other as a signal to attack.

She jumped into the air, twisted her body slightly, and kicked out her left leg, catching the guy on that side under the chin with the tip of her shoe. His head snapped upward, and he fell back against the wall—momentarily stunned.

The other on her right grabbed at her, but she ducked down so all he managed to grasp was the air above her head. His momentum carried him into her fist that she buried in his groin.

He yelped, then groaned as he dropped to his knees, all thought of a night of fun lost to the nauseating agony radiating from between his legs.

The guy she'd tripped had recovered and was diving back into the fray, rushing forward to aid his compadres.

She shook her head at him, and he slowed his pace, apparently having learned his lesson from the first failed attempt.

That didn't stop him entirely. The nonverbal warning merely stemmed his approach to a more cautious, strategic attack. As much as that was possible for someone like him, and in his condition.

He positioned himself in a boxing stance, with his left shoulder in the lead, and bounced on the balls of his feet as if ready to go a round with her.

She saw his eyes twitch to the left, just a little. It was barely noticeable, but she noticed everything. She didn't need the visual clue to know that the guy she'd driven into the wall was barreling toward her from behind, probably to wrap his arms around her neck, possibly pull a knife, and then put her on the ground before they finally had their fun. Thanks to the butt kicking she'd handed out, that fun might include a beating before... other things.

If she were some poor, weak soul.

But that was not the case.

She waited a second, noticed the boxer ease his stance by a fraction in anticipation of the rear assault, and then she dropped to one knee, spun to her right, and kicked out her leg to catch him on the shin with her heel.

He tripped into the guy she'd toppled before. The men clashed together in a clumsy tangle of arms, the one previously in a boxing stance trying to keep his friend upright.

The one she'd hit in the groin was struggling to his feet, but gravity wasn't helping him as it should. She glanced over at him and whipped her right foot at the side of his face with a roundhouse kick. The top of her shoe struck him across the jaw and temple before he could reach his feet, and he fell to the pavement like a sack of dirt.

Two out of commission, she thought. *Amateurs.*

The other two untangled themselves. One reached into his back pocket and pulled out a knife. It was a small, pathetic thing, and it was all she could do to keep from laughing.

"Do you use that to open love letters from each other?" she asked.

The barb went over both their heads at first, but when they realized what she meant, a burning fury sent them into a blind rage.

They rushed her at the same time, the one with the knife approaching from the left.

She sidestepped toward him. He swiped the blade at an angle from shoulder to hip, catching nothing but air as he lost his balance. She grabbed his wrist, twisted it toward his leg, and shoved the blade into his upper thigh. She received a pain-infused yell as her reward.

She grabbed him by the back of the neck, walked him over to the dumpster a few feet away, and slammed his head into the top edge, where the plastic lid met metal. He fell to the ground like he had a concussion, out cold, leaving only one assailant remaining.

The guy looked uncertain now. He stood there surrounded by two unconscious friends and one whose face looked like the gymnasium floor in the final scene of *Carrie.*

Doubt filled his eyes, drawing the dark circles under them down toward his quivering jaw.

The sounds of the street at the end of the alley beckoned to him. He could run. He could escape relatively unharmed. She saw the conflict in his eyes. Leave his friends here? Or avenge them?

"Big men, you are," she taunted, tilting her head slowly to the side. She stood inches away from the two boxes of empty wine bottles. "Picking on a poor, helpless, innocent woman." She punctuated the adjectives with a sharp staccato, tipping her head from one side to the other with each word.

His lips still trembled, and she knew before he moved what he was going to do.

He turned and started running toward the busy street. His arms flailed, and his legs kicked out behind him as he tried to put as much distance between him and the woman as possible.

She had already decided what to do if that was his play. He'd only taken a few steps when she quickly reached down and grabbed one of the empty wine bottles from the box near her feet, gripped it by the neck, turned like a baseball pitcher, and flung the glass as hard as she could.

The dark green bottle cartwheeled through the air. Her aim was true, the velocity was good, but if and how the projectile struck the target was left to chance. If she missed, she could probably chase him down. Or let him go. Either way was fine. He could go on to tell the cautionary tale to others, and she doubted any of them would ever think about attempting what they tried here this night.

The bottle, however, did hit the target. And as was the case on so many occasions, luck was on her side.

The dense base of the container smashed into the back of the man's skull. The blow dazed him, and his right toe caught on the pavement, sending him tumbling down. His arms swung forward as he tried to catch himself, but she knew the strike to the head had thrown off his coordination.

He crashed to the ground, his hands impotently crumpling under his weight. He skidded a few inches, his face grinding on the rough alley stones.

She took no time to appreciate the throw. Instead, she stalked toward him like a cat to a cornered mouse. He moved, planting his arms on the ground in an attempt to push himself up, but now he was weak. She knew his head must be throbbing, his vision probably blurred.

He raised his left elbow again, then the right, once more trying to shove the earth away so he could stand and make his escape. He managed to get a few inches off the ground before she reached him.

She towered over him, hovering for a moment to allow him to appreciate the impending sense of doom, the gravity of what was to come, and the lesson he would forever carry with him until his last breath.

Bending her knees, she crouched down next to him and grabbed a fistful of hair just above his neck. She jerked his head up, and he winced. Then she turned his face toward her so he could look her in the eyes through the fog in his.

"I trust you and your friends won't do anything like this ever again. And as for my name... you may call me the Black Lotus."

She turned his head so his face was aimed at the pavement, and then shoved it into the hard surface with a thud.

The woman stood upright, looked down at his motionless figure, and then walked back toward the busy street.

31

FUNCHAL

"Yes," Dak said. "Two thieves." Sensing no immediate threat of Juncao trying to flee, and also detecting no sign of a weapon on him, Dak tucked his gun back in its holster. Will hesitated, but after a subtle nod from Dak, he did the same.

They saw the gears turning from Juncao's expression. It was momentarily distant, focused on something deep inside his memory as if trying to recall a detail he'd collected at some point but given no thought to in a long time.

"What do you know?" Dak asked. "We need your help, Marial."

Juncao tore his mind away from the distant thoughts, and he looked up at Dak, then over at Will. "Are you police? Interpol?"

"No," Dak said with a turn of the head. "We're not with an agency or organization."

"We're private investigators," Will offered.

Dak almost chuckled at the statement, but in reality, he knew it was kind of true.

"I don't suppose you would tell me who you work for?" Juncao risked.

"Not a chance," Dak answered. "But we need to find that painting, Marial. An innocent life is at stake."

He leveled his gaze at the man, allowing him to see the sincerity of the statement, and a little of the pain that it caused.

Dak had no way of knowing if the art dealer had any sense of empathy, any touch of humanity within him. After all, he'd just abandoned his family to try to escape a perceived threat. Had that been simply out of self-preservation? Or was it also to protect them? Dak decided to find out.

"Why were you leaving?"

Juncao searched Dak's eyes, and the expression the dealer offered didn't present a lie. "I thought you were here to kill me."

Self-preservation then, Dak thought. Unfortunate.

"I've been prepared for that," Juncao went on. "I knew the risks involved in what I was doing. But my family... I didn't want anything to happen to them. And I certainly didn't want them to see me killed. I made an escape plan. As much as it hurt to do it, to even plan it, I had to. To protect them. You can kill me if you want. All I ask is that you don't let them see it."

Dak had been wrong about him. The guy did have a sense of right and wrong after all. It surprised him, especially considering how he made his fortune. Still, Dak wasn't entirely ready to give Juncao a pass just yet.

"We're not here to kill you, Marial. As I said, we need your help finding that painting. When we mentioned the two thieves, something sparked in your body language. You know something. I saw you thinking about it like you were trying to remember. What can you tell us? Please. I have to find this painting."

Juncao took on a puzzled look. His eyes narrowed with concern. His brow wrinkled. The corners of his lips dipped slightly into a frown.

"You say someone's life is at risk because of it?"

"Yeah. I care about her as much as you do that family in there. It's her for the painting. That's the trade I have to make. She was taken by the worst sort of person you could ever meet. Let me ask you, Marial. What would you do if someone took your wife, your kids, and demanded you turn over a rare painting for them?"

Marial let out a long sigh. His lips flapped as the air blew through them, and his shoulders slumped.

"I would do the same thing. I mean, I wouldn't hold someone at gunpoint. But I don't own a gun."

The last part didn't surprise either of the Americans.

"But," he added, "there's something you should know."

A sense of concern swelled in Dak's chest. He didn't like the way that sounded.

"What do you mean, there's something I should know?"

Juncao looked at Will, then back at Dak. He was nervous. It was written all over his face, widening his eyes. Dak knew he wasn't going to like this.

"The paintings I've moved in the past...." He faltered.

"What about them?" Dak insisted.

"They... were forgeries."

32

A t first, the words didn't really set in. A natural reaction might have been relief at knowing that this guy wasn't really a criminal, that he was selling fake masterpieces to the real criminals, and thus ripping off the bad guys.

But the confession brought with it another, deeper problem—one that Dak quickly realized could unhinge everything, and that would mean their trip to Madeira, and all the time it took to get here, had been wasted.

If Juncao didn't have connections who could help them locate the real Rembrandt, they were now farther behind, with only three more days to go. And one of those days would need to be a travel day. Time, as it seemed so often, was Dak's petulant enemy.

Dak needed clarification.

"What do you mean, forgeries?"

The wind blew stronger from the ocean, bringing with it moist, salty air spraying across their faces.

"I... have a guy. He was a former expert in the field."

"Like a curator?" Will asked.

Juncao shook his head. "No. Not exactly. I believe he may have done something like that at one point, but he was a freelancer—

someone who museums and auction houses hired to analyze the masterpieces they brought in."

"So, a researcher," Dak clarified.

"Yes. Researcher. I worked in a museum in Lisboa. That's how we met. I stayed in contact with him over the years, and then he told me of a plan he had, a way to make a lot of money from criminals. Sort of like... How do you say, your Robin Hood?"

Dak snorted at that. "Except Robin Hood didn't keep the proceeds he took from the nobles. He gave it to the poor."

"I do some of that," Juncao defended. "I donate to charities."

"You must have quite the money-laundering setup going to pull that off," Will said. "I imagine that's what your company is for."

Juncao nodded. "Do not be mistaken. I pay my taxes, and I always make sure to pay a little more than I'm required so the government doesn't get suspicious. But they are so tied up with all the newcomers moving here for the Golden Visa scheme it will be a decade before they get caught up. By then, that money will be clean."

Dak listened to the explanation. He had to admit, he was impressed. But it was a dangerous tightrope Juncao was walking, with the worst kind of people in the world.

"I bet you don't get much sleep, knowing that if one of the guys you sold to figures out they bought a fake painting they'll come after you."

The dealer bowed his head and bobbed it once. "Yes. It has been difficult. Especially with a family. But I had to take the risk. My children will never need anything. Nor will their children. I've been careful, and my friend is one of the best in the business."

"You said he's a researcher and an analyst," Dak noted. "But you have to have someone creating the paintings."

"Of course. He does both. He was an art student. That's what his degree is in. He understands how to create the perfect forgery, including how to age a painting so that another expert won't be able to tell. That's the real trick. Anyone can copy a painting. Not everyone can make it look the correct age."

Dak hadn't considered that part. He'd been focused on simply making the correct brush strokes, using the right combination of colors. It had to be an excruciatingly painstaking process. And to add on top of it, this guy had to make the age of the painting look authentic? Dak wouldn't even know where to begin.

His mind simmered with an idea. It was a long shot, but he had to ask. "Is it possible this friend of yours could create a replica of the Rembrandt I'm looking for?"

Juncao shot it down with a shake of the head. "No. We're talking about a process that takes months to complete. Maybe half a year."

"Worth a shot," Will commented.

"Yeah," Dak groused.

That put him back on the trail to finding the thieves who took the Rembrandt in the first place, and the original reason they were here in Funchal.

"You sounded like you knew something when we mentioned the two thieves who took that painting thirty plus years ago. Do you or don't you?"

Juncao swallowed a gulp of the salty air and wiped his brow with the back of his hand. The movement caused Dak to instinctively reach for his gun again, but he thought better of it. This guy was unarmed, and too passive to do anything stupid like pull a weapon.

He slowly brought his hand back down, palm facing out so Dak and Will could both see he meant no harm.

The wind howled up over the ridge, whistling over the jagged rocks, blowing through strands of tall grass that stood near the trail. Off in the distance, dull yellow flashes of heat lightning roared on the horizon, but here no clouds appeared in the sky. Only vast numbers of twinkling stars, and the moon nearly at its zenith.

Juncao nodded his head. "About a year ago, my friend said he had the most unusual meeting with two men. They were older, probably in their sixties. He said they were dressed in expensive suits and arrived in cars that cost more money than most people make in a decade. He said they were interested in selling a painting, but that they didn't want to do it through an auction house."

The hairs on Dak's neck stood up, and his arms crawled with goose bumps.

"My friend thought the request was strange. At first, he suspected they were police in fancy clothes. But he had never seen cops in Ferraris and Versace."

"Flamboyant," Will chirped.

Juncao agreed with a nod. "Yes. So, he decided they were probably legitimate sellers."

"Legitimate sellers who didn't want to use an auction house. Sounds sketchy," Dak said.

"Yes. Exactly."

"So, what happened?"

"My friend asked about the painting. Said he would need to verify it before he could reach out to me about moving it. They call me the facilitator since that is my primary job. I find buyers, usually of our own creations."

"But this one was for a real painting." Dak made the statement with an element of concern in his voice.

"Which is why we turned it down. It was a lot of money. They offered a generous sum for us to help them sell it."

"What happened when you told them no?"

"They left. Went their separate ways. And I mean that literally. According to my friend, these men drove away in different directions, just like they arrived. I guess they didn't want to be followed, and figured it would be difficult for someone to do so if they split up."

"Pretty smart," Will noted.

Dak hummed his agreement. But the news also brought with it a sense of impending doom for his situation.

"I don't suppose your friend would be willing to describe these two guys," he reached.

The question caused Juncao to tilt his head to the side and look at Dak as if it was a silly request.

"Perhaps he could. But it would be easier to look at the pictures he caught on camera."

Dak fended off the hope that surged through his chest and into his brain. "Camera?" He glanced over at Will, who looked as if he were impressed.

"Yes. My friend was always careful, just as I am on my end of the business. He knew he was dealing with... How do you say, shady characters? So, he brought video cameras with him and set them up around the meeting place just in case anything bad happened."

"Like the two sellers killed him?" Will asked.

"Maybe. Yes. Eventually, someone would find the cameras and be able to take the footage to the police."

"Clever," Dak said. "Is it possible your friend still has the footage?"

Juncao nodded. "Yes. I mean, I will have to ask him. If you will allow me to do so. But yes, he should still have it. I think he held on to it in case anything bad happened after the meeting. He was worried they would come for him when he told them no for the deal."

"I would be, too. So, will you contact this friend and ask if he'll help us?"

Juncao glanced over at Will, who crossed his arms and inclined his head a little. Then the dealer looked back to Dak. "Yes. Of course. I will help you. Does... this mean you're not going to kill me?"

"Killing you was never really the plan, Marial. Unless, of course, you left us no choice."

Juncao swallowed a dose of relief. His body relaxed visibly, shoulders loosening, head drooping just a little.

"But if you try to screw us," Dak added. "I will personally throw you off this cliff."

33

BARCELONA

The hotel elevator gave a ding, and the golden doors split open. The Black Lotus drew a breath through her nose and stepped out into a small atrium with a window to the left offering a sweeping view of the city. Lights sparkled throughout the darkness, though fewer than just an hour before.

The city couldn't party forever.

She turned right and walked to the T-shaped intersection where the corridor stretched right and left. The carpet design featured a base of light brown, with various darker shades of the color swirling in and out in the shapes of wide, wavy lines. They were contrasted with white dots of varying sizes, interspersed across the matted fabric.

The walls were covered in black-and-white-striped wallpaper, which she thought an odd combination with the floor.

Brass sconces with faux-candle light bulbs hung from the walls every ten feet, casting a dim but adequate light throughout the hallway.

She turned left and walked down the corridor, passing four doors before she reached hers on the right, room 831.

She scanned the key card, waited for the narrow light strip on the top of it to turn green, and when it did with the accompanying click of the lock, she turned the handle and pushed the door open.

As was her routine, she paused for a second with the door slightly ajar. Hotel security was almost nonexistent, including the locking mechanisms on the doors. They were more difficult for an ordinary thief to break into, but all one needed was a job and a master key card to have access to the entire building's collection of rooms, and the treasures that awaited within.

A random hotel worker stealing her things was the furthest thing from her mind. Her cautionary practice was to protect against a far worse threat.

Over the years, she'd made enemies of the most dangerous sort. Mafia, Russian mobs, Chinese syndicates, human traffickers, drug kingpins, and moguls who dabbled in a little of everything.

She danced on the thinnest of wires, one that spanned a chasm with no net beneath her. So tenuous was her public persona, the game she played across every continent. A single failure would shatter everything she'd built like a Ming vase on stone.

Should anyone ever find out the truth, both about her and her methods, her motives, lives would unravel in a catastrophic way.

Fortunately, she maintained the utmost secrecy and knew how to —for the most part—steer clear of that kind of trouble.

Satisfied no one lurked immediately behind the door, she nudged it open wider until she could see into the hotel room.

She slipped through the opening and allowed the door to close quietly behind her with the subtlest click. The light on the wall to her left was still on, just as she'd left it, as were the twin lamps, one on either side of the bed just beyond the corner wall that housed the bathroom to the right.

She always made it a habit of leaving the lights on when she was in a hotel. If someone were to have broken in and been waiting for her return, they likely would have switched off at least one of the lights to conceal their presence in the darkness. And if they didn't, they'd be exposed.

It was far from foolproof, but every little bit of caution exercised added up to fewer incidents.

She returned to the door, twisted the additional lock above the handle, and then flipped the metal doorstop out so that if someone were to try to barge in, they'd probably end up with a severely injured shoulder.

With the door secure, she returned to the bedroom, set down her handbag, and retrieved the laptop from under the pillow on the far-right side of the bed—another cautionary practice.

Sure, everything on her computer was password protected, and the most sensitive documents were encrypted at a base level of 128 bits—not as strong as 256 bits but far above the standard nonetheless.

She took the laptop over to the desk in the front corner of the room next to the wall-length window and placed it on the polished black surface.

After flipping open the computer, she entered her password and waited as the machine revved to life. The monitor lit up and displayed a picture of the island of Capri on the desktop.

She did love that view.

Now wasn't the time for sentimentalities, though. She had a mark to find.

She sat there for just over an hour, scouring the databases she could access without much trouble. The programs buried within her computer were midstage AI, able to scan passenger manifests and street camera feeds from cities around Europe. The United States feeds were trickier in that there were far fewer of them, but she didn't need those.

Thirty minutes into the search, she'd located Dak Harper's last known point of travel—arriving in the city of Lisbon.

But where had he gone since then? And whom did he know there?

Her first inclination was to search for relatives or friends, but that would be too obvious, and could take up precious time.

She considered brewing a cup of coffee since these things could take time to complete, but decided against it since it was so late at night. She'd just have to soldier through it.

The computer continued flashing through images of people on streets around the continent.

There were no other flights listed with Dak Harper on them, and none of the rental car companies had anything on him either. So, she deduced he had either stayed in Lisbon, or taken a train to wherever he might have gone.

But the facial recognition software included train station camera feeds, so if he'd gone that route, she would know it soon.

Something bothered her, though. She didn't need to scan through the dossier the handler had sent to know that Harper was a resourceful person. He could have flown out of the country on a privately chartered aircraft, one that was less than thorough when it came to filing passenger manifests.

She'd used such methods on multiple occasions to keep from being followed.

With the idea teetering on the front of her mind, she minimized the recognition software, allowing it to keep running in the background, and pulled up another database.

She scanned the list of flights that had left Lisbon in the last twelve hours, and noted several private ones.

One had gone to Nice in France. Two to Monaco. Another had flown to Macao. A fourth to Luxembourg. And one to Miami. The last one caught her eye.

It was a King Air twin turbo aircraft, and it had landed in Funchal on the island of Madeira earlier that day.

The other flights had been on more expensive jets, and to locations that were known playgrounds for the uber elites. Funchal was more subdued—a quieter island with smaller towns.

It had a thriving digital nomad community thanks to upgraded internet services, affordable housing, and low cost of living. On top of that, the scenic island featured spectacular mountain views, hiking trails, beaches, and an overall good quality of life that appealed to those who could work remotely for their careers.

None of that explained why Harper might visit the island. But if her instincts were right, as they often proved to be, the scant evidence suggested that was where he went.

She looked up the name of the pilot, Jimmy Dewild. The information on the screen said he was a former RAF pilot from the United Kingdom. The other details she scrounged up were disconnected, and seemingly random. It also seemed like things were missing, hidden deliberately from prying eyes.

He offered private charter flights through his antiquated website, but there was no way to book one online, and he'd provided no contact number. There wasn't even an email.

"Doesn't look like he wants to be in business," she noted.

Strange facts were adding up to a compelling conclusion that Harper may have indeed gone to Madeira. But why?

She tagged the plane with her Echelon clone application—a copy of the program used by the American government to track every plane on the planet. It had been implemented decades before, and creating a similar system proved simpler than she might have imagined—thanks to a friend who was a former hacker turned coder.

She exhaled slowly, both from fatigue and to reset her mind. She raised her fingers to her brow, and pinched the top of her nose—massaging it gently. Then she rubbed her eyes, and clicked on the web browser to open a new window.

Her fingers pecked rapidly across the keyboard, and when she hit the Enter key, an airline website appeared on the screen.

She entered a query for Lisbon and found several flights leaving the next morning—the earliest in five hours.

Another exhausted sigh escaped her lungs. The airport was a twenty-minute ride from her hotel. That gave her enough time to take a shower and a short nap. The flight from Barcelona to Lisbon was only two hours, which meant by the time the plane reached altitude, it would only be half an hour or so before it began its descent.

Getting additional sleep on the flight probably wouldn't happen.

That didn't matter. She had a lead on Harper, thin as it might be, and needed to pursue it.

She entered the details she allowed airlines and governments to see and purchased the ticket. Then she searched for travel from Lisbon to Madeira, found multiple flights, and booked one that took off forty-five minutes after she arrived in the Portuguese capital.

Satisfied she'd done all she could for now, she closed the laptop, went into the bathroom, and turned on the shower to let the water heat up.

In a few hours, she would find out if her hunch was right, or if she would have to go back to the drawing board.

34

FUNCHAL

Juncao paced back and forth in his basement office. He walked to the wall on one side, paused, spun around, thumbed his chin, and then crossed back the other way. His feet clicked quietly on the gray ceramic tiles made to look like wooden boards.

The spacious room contained a large white desk designed in a modern style with a glass top. Juncao's leather chair positioned behind the desk matched the color. Two shelves stood behind the workstation, each brimming with volumes on the subject of art history. Two steel lamps sat on either side of the wide-screen computer monitor atop the shiny desk surface.

Off to the side, a black sofa and two matching chairs wrapped around a glass-top coffee table, angled to face a flat-screen television mounted on the wall in the corner.

Abstract art hung from the walls, minimally placed so as to add to the ambiance but not dominate the simplicity of the room's design. The front wall was made of glass to give a full view of the pool and the sea beyond, interrupted only by the glass sliding doors.

Dak and Will watched him carefully but with an unconcerned air about them. There was nowhere for the dealer to run if he was lying or trying to pull one over them. The man had told his wife via text message that he had some work to catch up on down in the office and that he'd prefer not to be disturbed.

Dak wasn't sure how well that request would hold up, but without many options, he had to go with it.

They'd been waiting in silence for thirty minutes. The quiet was only dispelled a few times by Juncao to apologize for it taking so long or to check his phone and relay that he'd received nothing yet.

His connection, a man he called Braga, had initially responded quickly to Juncao's request for the video footage.

But since promising to deliver the recordings to Juncao's email inbox, they'd heard nothing.

Dak stood by the enormous window with his hands behind his back, looking out into the night. He loved being by the ocean. Despite growing up in southeastern Tennessee—a landlocked region—he'd always felt a call to the water.

Sure, he enjoyed being out on the river or one of the many lakes in his hometown, but there was something about the ocean that made him feel calmer, more at peace with everything. He'd never been able to fully explain it.

One friend suggested it was because he was a Scorpio—a water sign—but Dak didn't buy into that stuff. Then again, he wondered sometimes about ancient teachings such as those, especially after some of the things he'd witnessed when helping out the crew from the International Archaeological Agency.

The agency even had a division now—albeit only operated by two agents—dedicated to discovering the wonders of the unexplained mysteries of our reality, the paranormal incidents and places that were often swept under the rug by classical science, or skeptics with a fervor for always being right.

Dak checked his watch and noted the time, then peeled himself away from the window to look back at the pacing homeowner.

He didn't have to ask if Juncao had received anything yet. When Juncao did get something, Dak and Will would know it.

"How long have you lived here?" Dak asked, deciding the silence was too overbearing to allow to continue.

Juncao stopped in the middle of the floor, just in front of his desk. "What?"

Dak leaned against one of the black steel frames supporting the massive window, and crossed his arms. "How long have you had this house?" He twirled his right index finger to indicate the building.

"Um... two years now, I think. Getting close to three. We move here from Porto."

"Lovely city," Will commented, looking up from the chair over in the corner near the television. He sat with his elbows resting on his knees, leaning forward. "I enjoyed visiting it when I lived in Nazare."

"You lived in Nazare?" Juncao asked, suddenly a touch more cheerful than a moment before.

"Just for a short time. I have to move around a lot."

"And what do you—"

"Can't answer that one, chief," Will said, cutting him off before he could finish.

"Oh. So, it's some kind of—"

"I said... I can't answer that. Let it go."

Juncao closed his mouth and swallowed. He knew he was already on thin ice with the two Americans, and pressing his luck on any front didn't seem like a good idea.

Fortunately for him, his phone vibrated in his left hand before he could check it for the umpteenth time.

He looked at the screen and tapped the text message preview.

Dak and Will both perked up, focusing their attention on the device and the man holding it.

Juncao spoke before either could ask what the message said.

"My friend sent the video footage," he said and hurried over to the workstation.

He leaned over the keyboard, clicked the mouse, and wiggled it around a few times to spark the monitor to life.

The two guests joined him behind the desk, hovering just behind

Juncao on either side, both looking over the man's shoulders as he worked.

Juncao eased into his chair and clicked the secure email, entered a passcode, and then double-clicked on the video file.

The video player opened a new box and displayed an empty parking lot. Straight ahead, a dilapidated concrete building blocked the view beyond. Broken windows dotted the façade. No doors were within sight.

"This was an old knitting factory," Juncao informed them. "Abandoned. No one around to see the meeting."

"Seems like your friend was taking a pretty big risk there," Dak suggested. "Public place would have been better."

"He didn't have anything of value on him. All the money was in a Bitcoin cold-storage wallet. Without the keys, it's just another flash drive and basically can't be hacked."

"Smart," Will said.

He'd recently employed the same kind of payment system. Working with Bitcoin allowed him to do things without being watched. There were people in various governments around the world who claimed cryptocurrency was used by many people in illegal markets. Their primary target usually tended to be cartels and lower-level drug dealers.

Will knew that to be untrue. While those types, including himself, used the crypto platform to keep their transactions clean and secure, that stuff only comprised about 5 percent of all the money moved through the digital currencies.

Juncao allowed the video to keep playing. Two minutes passed, and Dak was about to suggest they fast forward to the part where the thieves showed up, but he didn't have to.

Headlight beams raked across the screen, blurring the view for a moment before the camera adjusted and refocused.

The fronts of two cars appeared on the screen, just as Juncao had described.

"Awfully ostentatious to bring a couple of super cars like that to a meeting in a derelict parking lot," Dak observed.

He knew that most thieves had expensive tastes. That, combined with the fact many loved the thrill of both the job and the chase, led them to an inevitable career conclusion behind bars.

These two, however, had managed to steer clear of the authorities for decades.

More lights switched on from the left side of the screen, Dak surmised from Juncao's partner's vehicle.

Ten seconds later, he appeared on the screen in front of the lights. Soon after, the two thieves stepped into view on the right.

Juncao's friend was average height and bore an unremarkable build. He was probably around 190 pounds with a balding head that retreated back to a half circle of short, dark hair.

He strutted with a long gray coat that flapped behind him and reached down to the knees of navy-blue trousers. The black shoes on his feet shined brighter than a pair of sports cars on the showroom floor.

The other two men were older by at least twenty years. One was tall and skinny with a long nose that dipped down slightly at the tip. His graying hair was pulled back in a ponytail. He wore a burgundy windbreaker and khakis.

The shorter one was thirty pounds heavier. His face and neck were thick, and he had broad shoulders and a barrel chest that continued down to a belly that caused his untucked white long-sleeved button-up shirt to stick out over his black pants.

Dak leaned closer, watching carefully as they met in the middle between the facing cars. The three discussed the terms of the deal. The conversation turned sour, and even though he knew the outcome of the meeting, Dak still wondered if one of the men would produce a firearm and end the discussion with violence.

That didn't happen, though, and the three men departed, spinning around to return to their cars.

"Freeze it right there," Dak said when the two thieves had turned halfway to their vehicles.

Juncao did as told but was a split second slow.

"Rewind it."

The host set the video back a few seconds so that the two thieves' faces were highlighted in the car beams.

"Take a screenshot of that," Dak ordered.

"Way ahead of you," Juncao answered. He tapped a couple of keys on the keyboard, then dragged boxes around the men's faces. The computer made a clicking camera sound.

"Can you send me that?" Dak asked.

"Yes. You just need to connect your phone to my network, and I can drop it into your phone directly."

Dak glanced at Will, who nodded that it would be okay, and then entered the information for Juncao's Wi-Fi.

"I see you now," the host declared. Then he tapped on Dak's device on the screen and moved the file.

Dak's phone buzzed, and the screen filled with the image of the two thieves.

He peered into the two men's dark, irritated eyes. They weren't happy about the deal going awry, but there was more to it than that. It looked like a sense of disappointment, born from... Was that desperation?

It was difficult to tell from one picture and without any background context. Dak had become adept at reading body language, and he understood voice tone the same way. This was just an image. But these two guys had shown up expecting to make a bunch of money and then were turned down.

"Looks like I'm going to have to ask for another favor," Dak said. He tapped on the share button at the bottom of the screen, then found his previous message with Emily, typed out another quick request, and sent it.

He didn't know how long it would take for her to get back to him, but for now, all he could do was the hardest thing of all.

Wait.

35

The Funchal airport was clean, somewhat modern, and nowhere nearly as busy as Lisbon's.

The Black Lotus carried her rucksack over one shoulder as she walked through the terminal, past the baggage claim, and out into the open air where taxis and rideshare drivers offered their services to new arrivals.

She'd already made arrangements for ground transport.

Instead, she kept walking, turning right out of the building, and continued along the sidewalk to a corner. She looked both ways along the street, then hurried through the crosswalk to the other side and into a rental car parking area.

One in the lot, she cut to the left and found the rental company she'd chosen. It, like all the others, occupied a strip in a single-story building adjacent to the lot. She stopped outside the glass door and looked in through the wall-to-wall glass. The rental counters were only separated by dividers, each staking out the different companies' claims to that portion of the interior.

She pulled the door open and stepped inside.

The area smelled sterile and of cleaning chemicals that the night crew had used hours before to prep the room for another day of business.

A few people waited at various counters for their keys. Some filled out paperwork. Most were younger couples, though there was one family with a man, woman, and two small children waiting in a line to get their car.

The counter she was looking for was off to the right, next to last on the end, and walked across the room.

Her shoes made no sound on the short-pile, dark gray carpet. Abstract black swirls blended in with the base color and provided the only semi remarkable attention to aesthetics in the place.

Her destination counter was empty, save for the clerk—a woman an inch or two shorter than she was and probably around 150 pounds with long dark chocolate-brown hair that draped down to her shoulders. She wore a white button-up, a loose-fitting shirt with the top two buttons undone so the golden crucifix hanging from her neck was visible against her tanned skin.

The clerk smiled politely, having no clue as to the true identity of the woman approaching her.

"Welcome to Funchal," the clerk said.

The Black Lotus mirrored the smile, putting on her friendly mask to look more like a tourist, or one of the many digital nomads arriving in the city.

"Thank you," she replied, keeping her bag tight against her shoulder. She produced a passport and a credit card and set them on the counter.

The clerk thanked her for the expedient passing of the needed items and quickly typed up the name on the passport.

"We have your car ready. Will you be needing insurance for your stay?"

"Yes. You never know, right?"

The clerk forced a chuckle as if she hadn't heard that same line a thousand times in the last month.

The process was over in a few minutes, and the clerk explained where the car could be found in the lot.

Once all the documents were signed and the keys were in her hand, the Black Lotus thanked the clerk one more time and made her way outside, back into the lot.

She found the gray five-door Hyundai hatchback exactly where the woman described, unlocked the car, and set her bag in the passenger's floorboard before starting up the engine and doing a quick routine check. Then she entered the details of the hotel, hit Go, and allowed the GPS to set up the directions.

With everything in order, she pulled out of the parking space and onto the street.

Earlier that morning at the Barcelona airport, she'd done some digging and learned where the pilot was staying.

According to the GPS, the Funchal de Luxe Hotel was only fifteen minutes from there.

Whether the pilot would be in his room or not, she didn't know, but if she had to wait around in the lobby until he appeared, she'd play it that way.

The streets of Funchal were brimming with people. Cars, motorcycles, and scooters moved along like ants, all keeping in line with the exception being the two-wheeled vehicles that would occasionally, and somewhat recklessly, pass between a car to their left and the curb on the right.

Pedestrians walked casually along the sidewalks. Some carried bags from bakeries, cafés, or shops, while others seemed to simply be out for a leisurely morning stroll, admiring the architecture, the colorful buildings, and the offerings of the island's capital.

Fourteen minutes after she left the rental car place, she spotted the hotel just ahead on the right.

It was a six-story building. The exterior was covered in huge white tiles with black windows and balconies for every room. The rooftop offered a bar and patio that could be seen from the street. From her prior research, she knew the place offered gorgeous views of the ocean to one side and the hilly city on the other.

She flipped on the turn signal and pulled into the circular drive in front of the hotel, then peeled off to the right, opting to skip the valet service. She found a parking spot near the back of the lot, parked the car, and got out, slinging the rucksack over her shoulder once more.

As was her habit, she surveyed the area, checking the other cars to make sure no one was lurking or paying attention to her. Palm trees lined the space behind a hedgerow that served as the property's boundary.

At the moment, it appeared she was the only person there.

She locked the car and walked around the building to the entrance, where two uniformed valets waited behind a podium. The two young men smiled pleasantly at her as she passed and entered the hotel through two automatic sliding doors.

Once inside, she kept walking, passing the concierge counter to the left and a seating area with plush, light-blue velvet sofas and chairs. A few patrons sat discussing the plans for the day.

The black tile floor was interspersed with huge white and blue rugs with the hotel logo surrounded by outward leaning palm trees in the center.

Another collection of people loitered at the coffee stand in the far-right corner, just beyond a bar with a lonely bartender standing behind it.

Too early for most people to start drinking, she guessed.

Near the coffee stand, a dozen tables and chairs offered a place for people to eat their breakfast and sip their drinks.

She found a table near a tall, slender window in the corner and plopped down, keeping her bag on the floor next to her feet.

She checked her watch, noted the time, and settled in for what she knew could be a long wait.

36

Thirty-six minutes passed while she sipped on a double espresso from a white porcelain carafe.

She'd expected it could be several hours before, and if, she spotted her mark, but it was nowhere near that long.

Every time the automatic doors at the entrance opened, she watched as hotel patrons entered the building. And she did the same whenever the elevators dinged on the other side of the lobby as people exited the lifts.

Her patience and planning were duly rewarded when she saw the pilot James Dewild walk through the front doors of the building.

The second she spotted him, she casually reached down, grabbed her rucksack, and stood.

She watched as he ambled through the lobby toward the elevator, and when he neared the lifts, she made her way toward him.

He pressed the button to go up and stepped back to wait for the next lift. A few seconds later, she joined him, saying nothing and appearing not to pay attention to him.

Dewild carried a small paper bag in one hand. The markings on the bag proclaimed it to be from Leonardo's bakery.

The bell signaled the elevator's arrival, and the two silver doors split open. After waiting a second to see if there was anyone on board, they saw an empty lift.

The pilot stepped inside, reached out to hold the door for her, and she entered, thanking him with a grateful smile and nod.

He pressed the button for the sixth floor, and then looked over at her.

"What floor?" he asked in an English accent.

"Six," she replied.

"Oh, that's convenient."

The doors closed, and the lift ascended to the top of the building.

When they opened again, he made a motion to allow her to exit first, and then followed behind her.

Once in the atrium outside the elevator, she stopped and took her phone out of her pocket to act like she was looking at something important, allowing him to continue on his way before falling in line behind him.

She kept her distance, remaining fifteen feet back so he wouldn't become suspicious. Then again, why would he?

They were in a hotel where many people stayed on vacation, and based on the location, the clientele in the lobby, and the design of the place, she guessed few sketchy characters ever set foot in here.

She kept looking at her phone as she walked, glancing up now and then to keep an eye on him.

He stopped at room 615, pulled out his card key, and swiped it in front of the magnetic reader.

She slowed her pace only slightly, as if about to pass him. He pushed down on the handle, then shoved the door open.

Once his right foot touched the floor inside, she took four more hurried steps, cut to the right, and barged into him, knocking him forward and deeper into the room.

"What the—"

He turned around, his face flushing red with anger, though his eyes widened with bewilderment.

For a wildly confusing second, all he could do was stare at her. It was the woman from the elevator.

She was beautiful. Her dark brown hair was pulled back into a tight ponytail. The tight white tank top with a symbol of a circle within a triangle and a line through it accentuated her upper physique, as did the snug dark blue jogger pants held up by a white drawstring.

It was easy to see his immediate thought was that one of his wildest fantasies was about to play out in the most unexpected way, and in a place he probably never imagined.

But as he stared at her, trying to figure out if this was going to be pleasurable or painful, he sensed those lustful fantasies would not be playing out here.

She took a step toward him, her expression that of a predator bent on feasting.

"What are you doing? Who are you?" He took a defensive posture, but also retreated a step backward.

She allowed the door to close behind her, set the bag down on the floor to her left, and inclined her chin. She met his gaze with frozen brown eyes like pools of cacao.

"Hello, Jimmy," she said. "We need to have a little talk."

37

Marial Juncao woke up from a dream.

He'd been walking through the streets of Genoa, one of his favorite cities in Europe. He didn't speak Italian, but the people all around him spoke the beautiful language fluidly, carrying on pleasant conversations over cappuccinos and pastries. The sidewalks were lined with café tables with colorful umbrellas shading the customers as they forked rolled webs of pasta into their mouths.

Vespas scooted by, interspersed between the cars. Music drifted out of the restaurants as he passed.

The sun warmed his face from a cloudless sky.

All was right with the world as he strolled along the sidewalk.

And as quickly as the dream began, it ended with the first beams of sunlight pouring in through the window and brightening slivers of the wall near his bathroom door.

He smelled coffee again, but it wasn't the same scent he'd detected in his dream. Or was it?

Juncao closed his eyes again, rolled over, and tried to will himself back to sleep.

He dared not look at the clock. Once that happened, there'd be no slumber for him.

The dream began piecing itself together again, as if it were a faded painting that was recoloring itself back to its original glory.

He saw the winding streets again. The smells started to return to his nostrils. The sounds of cars and scooters driving by and people chatting oozed into his ears.

"Marial," someone said from across the street.

He turned and looked over at a man standing on the curb. He looked familiar and strange at the same time. He was wearing an army-green button-up jacket and khakis. He had a blue T-shirt on underneath. The man's quaffed brown hair and matching beard didn't move in the breeze produced by the passing traffic.

Marial couldn't see the man's eyes beyond the aviator sunglasses.

Then he heard his name again. "Marial."

Juncao turned to his left, and to his shock, found the man standing before him only a few feet away.

Whipping his head around, Juncao looked across the street, but the man was gone.

"Wake up, Marial," the man said.

Juncao faced him just as the man reached out and touched his shoulder.

"Marial. Wake up," Dak said, shaking his host gently on the shoulder.

Juncao's eyes peeled open by a few millimeters, closed lazily, then shot wide as he realized the man from his dream was standing there in his bedroom.

He panicked, thoughts immediately rushing to his wife and children. The latter would be in their bedrooms, probably still asleep even.

But his wife would be in bed to his right.

He sat up like a bucket of ice water had been dumped on him. His bare chest swelled and collapsed with desperate breaths.

When he looked over at his wife's spot on the bed, though, he found it empty.

A terrible thought stabbed fear through his chest. "What did you do to her?" he demanded. "Where are my children?"

Dak held out a calming hand, grinning at what must have been a shocking wake-up call. "Relax. They're fine. They went out to get some breakfast. Lovely woman, your wife."

"What?"

Juncao rubbed his forehead with a cluster of fingers, then both eyes. He shook his head as if that would loosen the cobwebs from his brain.

"You... met my wife?"

"Of course," Dak said in a matter-of-fact tone. "I explained to her that you probably needed to sleep in a little since you were so kind to hang out with us late into the night. I may have added that we were all drinking. She didn't seem to mind."

Juncao's throat pulsed as he swallowed. "You spoke to my wife?"

"It would have been awkward if I hadn't since you didn't explain to her that we were here."

"I couldn't. She was already asleep when I got up here."

"That's what she told us. By the way, your coffee is really good. We saved some for you downstairs. Come on. We have work to do."

Dak turned and walked back toward the open bedroom door, leaving Juncao in utter astonishment.

All he could do was sit there and watch as the American walked out and disappeared around the corner.

"What a nightmare," he muttered.

"Could be a lot worse!" Dak shouted from the hallway.

After dragging himself out of bed, slipping into some blue jeans and a gray T-shirt, Juncao plodded down the stairs, around the corner through the foyer, and into the kitchen.

It was tasteful and modern, with white cabinets and walls accented with a black stone backsplash behind the sink and a steel ventilation over the stove like the ones found in many restaurants.

The black granite countertops glistened in pendant lights that dangled from the ceiling above the kitchen island.

Dak was leaning up against the counter with a white coffee mug in his hand. Will sat at a counter on the other side of where the L-shape design housed the dishwasher, four drawers, and four doors below that concealed pots, pans, and other items.

"You really did speak to my wife, didn't you?" Juncao asked, still fixated on that detail.

"Well, someone had to," Dak explained. "Imagine if we'd tried to sleep in like you did, and then she came downstairs to your guest room and found two dudes in the two beds."

Will chuckled as he raised his coffee mug. "If Dak didn't wake you up, the screaming definitely would have."

Juncao shook his head, still in a fog from the dream and the unwelcome awakening. He stumbled over to the pantry, pulled out a coffee mug, and lifted the pot. After the mug was filled nearly to the brim, he put the pot back and shuffled over to the counter where Will sat.

He eased into the seat at the end, keeping a chair between them, then hovered his face over the steaming cup as if the smell and heat could disperse the haze.

"My connection got back to me," Dak announced.

Juncao looked surprised. "Really?"

Dak had allowed only a half hour to pass before he decided they needed to get some rest. He was on a deadline, and a tight one at that, but refusing to give the body what it needed would only cause more problems.

Juncao had shown them to a small guest room on the downstairs floor that contained two full-size mattresses complete with pillows, sheets, and blankets. There was also a full bathroom with a shower and toilet just one door down the hall.

Dak had fallen into a troubled sleep. It seemed like that was the only variety of sleep he could manage recently, especially the last few days since Nicole's abduction. In all honesty, he knew it was a minor miracle he'd achieved any slumber at all. But the guest bed at Juncao's place had been comfortable, and tumbling off into dreamland had taken no effort.

"My connection gave me the info on the two thieves that your guy met with," Dak said.

Juncao took a sip and burned his tongue. He winced and cursed himself for being impatient.

"Who are they?"

Dak passed a subtle nod to Will, who slid a piece of paper over to their host.

Juncao looked dubiously at Will, then down at the sheet, and pulled it over in front of him.

"Their names are Marco Rothschild and George Sorovski," Dak explained. "Seems what we have on our hands is a couple of spoiled brats turned high-end art thieves."

Juncao stared at the sheet for a minute, his eyes poring over the text in an attempt to understand what he was reading.

"How were you able to get all this information?" Juncao asked, his eyes still focused on the paper.

"I have friends who can get that sort of thing," Dak offered without going into too much detail.

The concise dossier included information about their similar pasts.

Both members of prominent, wealthy families, the two had gone to the same exclusive private schools in the United Kingdom.

Sorovski's grandparents relocated to London before his parents were born, and Marco's family had lived in the United Kingdom for much longer—though there were no definitive details on the dossier that could connect his immediate family to the prominent global financiers of the same surname.

Juncao read through the rest of the information with a look of disbelief painted on his face.

"I don't understand," he confessed after finishing and raised his head to meet Dak's gaze.

"Why two uber wealthy kids would take to a life of crime?" Dak finished the thought.

Juncao nodded absently. "Yes. They had everything handed to them."

"On a literal silver platter, probably," Will added cheerfully.

The host set the paper down and lifted his mug again, this time being more careful with the drink as he sipped it.

"Could be anything," Dak said. "Sometimes people who grow up like that are never happy. They could be thrill junkies. Or it might be the old rebellion-against-the-family story. That happens all the time. Saw it back home with some kids I knew who grew up with a lot of money."

"But thieves?"

"High-end art thieves," Will corrected.

Dak nodded. "Kids who come from wealthy families have expensive tastes. That only goes one of two ways. They can turn minimalist, give up all their possessions, and transition into a life of simplicity when they realize all the material things in the world won't fill the void in their soul. Or they constantly seek more. These two, it seems, went the latter route. And if it's combined with one of the other paths, the thrill seeking or rebellion deal, well, there you go.

"They were both, oddly, left out of their parents' wills, too. That must have served as the last straw for them. Once that happened, it was a life of crime for them from then on."

Juncao stared blankly at Dak, then back down at the dossier. "You think they've stolen more than one painting?"

"You said yourself they were trying to sell you one. I'd guess they probably branched out into other forms of thievery—artifacts, sculptures, rare gems, and jewelry."

"Or they might have stopped with only a few," Will theorized. "You said they were trying to sell you one. Sounds to me like maybe their little elite-kid hobby turned into a need for cash. Maybe they ran out of money."

"That's definitely a possibility. Especially if the families cut them out. Guys like that burn through millions in no time, like so many lottery winners."

"So," Juncao said, trying to clarify "you think they wanted to sell that painting because they needed the money?"

"Sounds right. And they fit the mold for the types who would end up in that situation."

Juncao listened and then looked down at the sheet again. "But this says that Sorovski died a little over a year ago."

Dak nodded. "In a car accident."

"You sound as if you don't believe it was an accident."

"Seems convenient. You said they tried to sell that painting to you, what, a few months before that? Maybe as many as six?"

Juncao bobbed his head, his eyes vacant as he tried to remember the timeline. "Yes. That does sound correct."

"So, the two go broke," Will concluded. "And when they couldn't move that painting to replenish their accounts, Rothschild takes out the other. Now he owns everything outright."

"Is this really his home address?" Juncao asked, tapping the paper with his index finger.

"We believe so," Dak said. "We've double-checked it to confirm. That's the place. It's a mansion."

"More like a fortress," Will corrected. "Getting in is going to be extremely difficult, and based on what we were able to glean, the security system is virtually impregnable."

"On top of that, he has a massive safe built into the basement. It's basically bank grade, made in Switzerland by Schuster and Fillauer, one of the top safe experts in the world. As far as we know, no one has ever been able to crack one successfully. The company even pays people to try."

"How did you find that out?" Juncao asked.

Will's mischievous grin preceded the answer. "Realtors know things," he said. "And they know people." Noticing Juncao's confusion, he elaborated. "Construction crews, contractors, architects, interior designers, and even unique items. Like a really expensive safe. I reached out to some people I know in the real estate business in that area. Didn't take them long to find what I needed."

Juncao inhaled sharply and shrugged. It wasn't his problem anymore. At least that's what he hoped. He'd done his job for these two, and now it was time for them to move on. He could get back to his life and perhaps retire from his illicit activities. This whole thing had been one huge close call, and he didn't want any of those ever again.

But his curiosity held him in the conversation like tentacles, squeezing him and refusing to let go.

"If no one has ever been able to break into one of those safes, how do you two think you can do it? Are either of you experts in that sort of thing?"

That was the rub, and Dak knew it. Neither he nor Will had ever done anything like that. They hadn't even researched how to do it. Which meant they were either going to have to learn fast or find an expert. The latter, Dak knew, could prove difficult.

"No," Dak admitted. "I've never done anything like that. Neither has Will."

"So, what are you going to do?" Juncao wondered.

"I'm not sure. I don't think we have enough time to learn how to do that ourselves. The kind of thief necessary for this job would need a ton of experience. It's half art and half science."

"Where are you going to find such a person?"

"Yes," a woman's voice said from behind the corner of the archway. "Where, indeed?"

Dak froze for a second. He and Will had left their weapons hidden in the bedroom downstairs. A foolish mistake he now cursed himself for making. How could he have been so stupid?

She'd entered the house with such stealth none of the three men had heard her. And now, she had the drop on them.

He knew Will was thinking the same thing as the silhouette of the woman remained in the shadows.

Dak searched the kitchen counter for a knife, or anything he could use as a weapon. As a last resort, he could always throw a fastball with the coffee mug clutched in his fingers.

"Don't look for a weapon," she warned. "I already found your guns downstairs. That wasn't smart to leave them there."

Juncao looked at the woman's figure. The light touched the side of her dark brown hair, pulled back in a ponytail, but refused to illuminate her face as though afraid of her.

Crap, Dak thought, again reprimanding himself for the error.

"Who are you?" Dak demanded. He decided to play it cool, still holding the coffee. If he was going to die, it wouldn't be like a coward. And he certainly wasn't going to waste good coffee if it was his time to go.

"Tucker sent me," she answered. "I go by many names." She stepped into the light after that, letting the splinters splash across her face to show her true identity. "But my friends call me Adriana."

38

Dak's head dropped forward. Relief and disbelief battled for his choice of emotion as he stared at the Spaniard standing in the light under the archway.

Juncao stared at her, then Dak, then back again. He looked like he needed to change his pants, or would need to in the very near future.

"You gotta be kidding me," Dak finally managed. He shook his head back and forth, then set down the mug and walked over to where she stood.

Adriana lowered the pistol she'd been aiming over their heads just in case the thing went off, though she'd removed the round from the chamber before climbing the stairs from the basement.

She smiled at him and handed the gun over, placing it in his palm. "The pipe is empty," she said. "Didn't want to accidentally shoot a friend."

"What about on purpose?"

They shared a comical stare for a few seconds. "That's funny," she allowed, and cracked an even broader smile. "I see you brought Will along for the ride."

Will signaled her by raising his coffee mug. "Good to see you, too."

Juncao was lost. Like a child in the deepest and darkest of forests, he had no clue what was going on.

"Excuse me," he interrupted. Everyone turned to listen to what the host had to say. "Is anyone going to tell me who she is?"

"This is Adriana Villa," Dak said, then turned to her. "Or do you go by Wyatt now?"

"Either is fine," she said.

"Yes, I gathered what her name was," Juncao retorted. "But why is she here?"

Dak explained what he knew about her, which admittedly wasn't all that much. He'd spent limited time with her husband, Sean Wyatt, and the team from the IAA, but he knew a little.

He told Juncao how she specialized in tracking down artwork that was stolen by the Nazis during World War II, and how that had translated into the search for lost artifacts with Sean.

When he was finished, he asked her if he'd missed anything.

That, she knew, was a loaded question if ever there was one.

Only a few people were privy to the truth about Adriana's past— how she'd begun martial arts and self-defense training when she was only a child, about the man who'd trained her, and the work her father did in the intelligence community.

And then there was the death of her mother. A victim of her mother's cancer in her own way, a piece of Adriana's soul had been ripped away by the disease—a piece she wondered if she could recover. For the most part, she believed she had. Her new family with Sean and the rest of the IAA crew had created something that, while it could never replace her mother, created a new space in her heart for love and acceptance.

"No," she answered Dak's question. "I think you summed it up nicely."

"Okay," Juncao said. "But that doesn't explain why you're here. Unless you knew about the painting. Were you already searching for it?"

"No." She looked to Dak. "Tucker went into the merc network. He requested me."

Dak inclined his head, peering down at her over his nose. "Interesting." He turned, laced his fingers on the back of his head, and stretched. His spine cracked a few times before he lowered his hands and faced her again. "Which den?"

"Marseille."

He flicked an eyebrow, and his lips curled upward slightly for a half a second. "Some good ones there."

"I don't believe he hired anyone else from that location," she continued. "He wouldn't have called for me if he did."

"I'm sorry," Juncao interrupted again. "Hello. What is a... What did you call it? A merc network? And what are these dens you're talking about? Did you say Marseille?"

Dak wanted to ignore him, but he figured scaring him might work to shut him up for a moment. "Merc dens are underground temp agencies for assassins and mercenaries. If you're a soldier, or a killer, for hire, those are the places you go to get work. They're all over the world."

"And usually right under your nose," Will added. "There could be one anywhere. Even here, in Funchal."

The statements did seem to frighten the man, but he had one more question. "So, if those are places that... hire killers, and she was hired from one of those, does that mean...."

He trailed off.

Adriana saw where he was going. "I operate under a strict code," she said. "I only kill in self-defense. My primary objective is retrieval, not murder. But due to the nature of the things I hunt, I often find myself in... threatening situations. If someone wants to hire me, they know that I will likely turn them down."

"So, people hire you to steal artwork from other thieves?" Juncao asked.

"No. The artwork is my payment, along with an upfront fee, of course. They hire me to eliminate someone, but as I said, that comes as a byproduct of my search for the lost art."

Juncao tread carefully with the next question. He wasn't sure he wanted to know the answer. "And... how many people have you... let live on these jobs?"

"I have never met someone with one of those paintings that wasn't despicable in some way. That said, I let them hang themselves. If they try to kill me, then the gloves, as they say, come off."

Their host seemed somewhat satisfied with the answer, if not a little disconcerted. But he sealed his lips, unwilling to venture any further into that line of questioning.

"So," she said, turning to Dak, "it seems your old boss is looking for a stolen Rembrandt."

"Yeah, except if he sent you that means he's just as happy to kill me as get the painting."

"I thought the same thing. I found you as fast as I could." She walked over to the counter where the coffee machine still warmed a half-full pot, picked up a mug from nearby, and filled it.

Adriana held the cup close to her face, smelled the aroma, and then took a careful sip. It was hot, but she liked the heat. It woke her up, and she needed the pick-me-up after a short night of sleep and a fitful nap on the plane.

She nodded approvingly at Juncao, lifting the cup toward him to let him know she liked how he made his coffee.

"How much of our conversation did you hear?" Dak asked.

"Enough to know you're up against a serious challenge. Particularly with the safe."

"Have you ever cracked one of those before?" Will said.

"I've seen them," she answered. "Studied them. That company uses a combination of technologies for their safes. Obviously, the locking mechanism will be difficult to beat, though without knowing the exact model, I can't be sure. It's probably a combination, like most of them."

"How would you break into a safe if you don't know the combination?" Juncao wondered.

All of this was new stuff to him, and his curiosity had replaced most of his concerns at this point.

"Normally, I would drill it," she said. "I have a set of tools for that sort of thing. But with a Schuster and Fillauer, that technique can be tricky."

"Why's that?" Will asked.

She took another sip of the steaming coffee before answering. "They build a sheet of glass between the metal plates where the locking mechanism is housed. It's to prevent thieves from using a drill to bypass the lock. If you break the glass, it prevents a thief from being able to unlock the safe. But this company also uses an additional security measure. They build a series of lasers into the casing. So, if the glass is broken, it will trigger an alarm."

"That... sounds like an impossible task," Juncao said. Disappointment drew his jaw toward the counter.

"I guess we'll find out," Adriana countered.

"What about the security system in the house?" Dak asked. "Cameras. Sensors. Alarms. All that stuff is going to be tricky to get by *before* we even see the safe."

"I'm pretty good with those things. But I would prefer not to take any chances. You don't happen to know a good hacker, do you? I would normally outsource this part of the job, but on such short notice I doubt I can get my usual assistants."

Dak thought for a minute. Who did he know who was good with computers and could possibly hack a security system?

Only one name came to mind. He wasn't sure he'd be able to get him in time, but he had to try. Otherwise, they'd have to lean entirely on Adriana's skills, and while capable, she sounded like she'd prefer to have someone who was a true expert in the digital field.

Dak took his phone out of his pocket. "I may know someone who can help."

39

MUMBAI

The cell phone rang on the coffee table, pumping out a Daft Punk song as it danced like one of the players from the electric football game that was so popular in the 1980s.

Chester glanced at the number, then muted the call by pressing the volume button on the side.

He refocused his attention on the computer monitor in front of him. This was no time to be interrupted.

He'd been glued to the screen for just over two hours—a modest amount of time compared to his usual sessions. His eyes burned and watered, and he had to rub them more than once to stem the irritation. But he didn't dare look away. Not right now. The stakes were too high, and distraction would cost him everything he'd worked so hard to build.

The phone started dancing again, playing the tune again.

This time, he didn't even look at it as he reached over with his left hand and muted the call.

He moved the mouse quickly, clicked a few times, and then tapped on the hot keys on his keyboard to execute the next command.

"No, no, no, no, no," he blurted out in frustration. "Come on."

He watched as his sorcerer was killed by an overwhelming number of demons and lower-level minions.

Chester released the mouse and leaned back in his red-and-black gamer chair, ran his fingers over his nose, rubbing it for a moment before moving on to his eyes. He sighed, scratched his short green hair, and shook his head.

"Unreal," he complained.

He took off the gaming headset and placed it on the desk next to his phone and stared at the screen.

The game counted down and then returned him to the last checkpoint, informing him his equipment had taken a 10 percent hit in the process.

Shaking his head, he left the game, returning it to the house screen and the image of the demon Lilith featured in *Diablo IV*.

He dragged his eyes away from the screen and looked at the phone and frowned. "Guess it wasn't important enough for three—"

Before he could finish the sentence, the phone started ringing again. "Oh, for the love of...." He pressed the green button and held it to his ear.

"Yes?"

The snappy answer sounded all the sharper with his British accent.

"Is that any way to talk to a friend?"

Chester recognized the gruff voice, the serious tone, the straight-and-to-the-point manner.

"Dak? Is that you?"

"Yeah. It's me."

Chester spun around in his chair and looked back at the open door to his studio.

Light bars illuminated both sides of the doorframe in a futuristic red hue. The same colored lights glowed under and around his desk, bathing the entire room in the color of electric cherries.

Pictures and posters from his favorite movies, shows, and books adorned the walls, along with shelves of collectibles he'd accumulated through the years—some of which were original vintage.

"Are you... watching me?" Chester asked.

"Through your computer monitor. Yes."

Chester spun around again and faced his computer. He leaned forward toward the display, staring into the tiny camera embedded in the top of the frame.

"Are you really?"

"No," Dak said. "Not really. I wouldn't know the first place to begin with something like that."

"Right." He relaxed, slumping into his chair a little deeper, holding the phone so loosely between his fingers the slightest jarring from behind might have knocked it out of his grip. "What's going on, mate? Haven't heard a peep out of you in a while."

"I need your help with something."

"That much I figured. You haven't kept in touch since last I saw you, so I doubted this was a check-in to see how I was doing."

"I've... been busy."

"Aren't we all, mate?" Chester reached over to a bag of chips sitting on the left edge of his workstation and pulled out a handful. He stuffed one into his mouth and bit down. The crunch echoed around the room for a second. "I'm fine by the way," he said while chewing. "Tamara and I have been together going on two years now. Not that you care."

Dak sighed audibly through the line. "I know about you and her. I've spoken to her more recently than I have with you. But I'm glad to hear things are going so well."

"Oh. What you mean, you've spoken to her?"

"I don't really have time to get into it, but don't get jealous, Chester. I'm not interested in your lady friend. I needed her help with something back in the winter. I didn't want too many people to know about it. Now, I need your help."

"Really?" Chester said, extending the word out to emphasize his dubiousness. "And what, pray tell, do you need my help with?"

"I don't have much time, so I'll be blunt."

"I didn't know you were any other way. Go on."

Another exasperated sigh. "Someone very dear to me has been kidnapped by my former commanding officer."

"Whoa!" Chester cut him off. "That's messed up. The same guy from before? I woulda thought you'd have killed him by now."

He lowered the phone away from his mouth for a second, covering the microphone to mute himself as he listened. No sound came from the hallway beyond the door, so he raised the device back to his ear.

"I almost did, but he got away."

Chester detected a sense of regret in Dak's tone.

"Now," Dak went on, "he wants me to track down a stolen painting, retrieve it, and give it to him in exchange for her."

The gravity of the situation took all the joking wind out of Chester's sails. "That's bloody awful, mate. What painting does he want?"

"It's a Rembrandt," Dak said.

"What?" Chester nearly yelled. He covered the mic on his phone again, and looked back over his shoulder as if he was worried his mum might come stomping down the hallway and demand to know why he was being so loud. "A bloody Rembrandt? This guy sure has expensive tastes."

"That's right," Dak confirmed. "The painting was stolen back in the 1990s by two men. One of them died last year. We have the identity and location of the other."

"Wait a minute." Chester sat up, his curiosity spiking. "Are you telling me you're going to nick the painting from the ones that done it?"

"The one. But yes. That's the plan."

Chester was intrigued, but he failed to understand how he fit into this and why Dak would call him about helping with what for all intents and purposes sounded like a heist.

"All right, Dak. So, you're going to steal a painting from a thief. What does that have to do with me?"

"The man who has it will have cameras and security systems that need to be bypassed. We need someone who can do that. I know your main business is in crypto, but I also know you've done some hacking in your time."

"Some hacking?" He sounded insulted. Whether it was real or not, Dak couldn't tell. "Some hacking? Son, you're talking to the person who was accused of hacking into a British satellite."

"Accused?"

"That's right. Of course, I can neither confirm nor deny that I did it. And the British government couldn't either."

"Really? I didn't know that."

"You never asked, did you?"

"You said they accused you but couldn't confirm it."

Chester twisted the chair halfway around and then back again. "Yeah. They saw that everything had been encrypted. Bloody clever, whoever it was that did that. So, they couldn't really pin the crime on anyone. That didn't stop them from making threats about obstruction of justice and all that. Made me help train their surveillance and intelligence teams, and their cybercrime divisions for a year. Without pay, mind you. Had to work side jobs to get by until that was over."

"Well," Dak said, "it sounds like whoever the person was that hacked into that satellite would have no problems getting into a little home security system."

"I see what you're doing."

"Is it working?"

"Of course it is. Sounds like fun. And besides, I owe you one."

"No one owes me anything," Dak corrected. "But I appreciate it."

"No problem. When and where?" Chester stood up, closed down his computer, and walked over to a shelf on the left-hand wall, where he kept a laptop plugged in, and a backpack underneath the bottom shelf.

"It's short notice," Dak said with hesitation. "So, if you can't—"

"When and where?" Chester interrupted. "I didn't ask you to tell me how short notice it was."

"The painting is in Nice."

"France?" He returned to his desk, pulled out a drawer, and

removed two silver flash drives with little black-and-white skull stickers attached to the casings.

"Is there another one?"

"Not that I know of. Lovely city, Nice. Only been there once. Looks like I'll be making it twice. When?"

"We will be there tomorrow. I have to have the painting to Tucker by Friday, so I figure we'll arrive, recon the place where it's being kept, and make our play on Thursday."

Chester stood up straight for a moment, surprised at how soon this needed to go down. "You're right. That *is* short notice. But I can manage. I'll be there by tomorrow morning. Text me the address of where to meet you and what time."

"I... really appreciate this, Chester. I hate to put this on you. And you know, it could be dangerous."

"Danger? You should try living with Tamara."

Dak laughed through the speaker. "I'll be in touch tomorrow. Thanks, man."

"No worries, mate. See you in France."

He ended the call, set the phone down on the desk, and turned to go back to the shelf to collect the laptop. He sensed a presence at the doorway and looked over to find Tamara standing there.

She wore a tight black dress . The skirt barely reached the top of her knees. Her skin glowed in the red light, and her dark lipstick gave her the look of an exotic, Indian vampire come for her next victim.

She leaned against the doorframe with one shoulder, her right eyebrow arched in curious inquisition.

"What was that about living with me?"

Chester slid the laptop into his backpack and continued pretending to look for more items. "I was joking, love."

"Joking with who? And where are you going?"

He faced her, holding the backpack in one hand down by his shins. "That was Dak Harper. Said he spoke to you in the winter."

"That's right. I helped him with something. Why was he calling you?"

"Looks like he needs my help now. Got a job for me in Nice."

"France? You're going to France? Just like that?" Her exotic accent intoxicated him on most occasions, and it was something he'd never gone deaf to. "Yes. France. You can come along if you like. He needs me to hack a security system for him."

She straightened up at the confession. "Hacking? I thought you weren't going to do that anymore. You could get in—"

"I won't get caught. It's a private security system. And from the sound of it, the owner is a crook. Simple job for me, really. I imagine I'll be in a coffee shop when I pull the rug out. Safe as you like."

She took a step forward, letting her hips sway back and forth to accentuate her movements.

"You're sure you'll be okay? I don't want anything to happen to you."

He loved and hated it when she walked that way, when she talked that way. Odysseus and his men must have encountered similar temptation when they discovered the sirens.

"I'll be fine," he said, deepening his voice a little to sound more masculine. "But Dak needs my help."

"Well." She took one more step forward until they were standing nearly toe to toe. She reached up and tugged on the collar of his black T-shirt and pulled him close. "Then I guess I should give you a proper send-off."

He took an audible gulp, dropped his bag on the floor with a clunk, and kissed her.

40

VILLEFRANCHE-SUR-MER, FRANCE

"Wow."

That was the only word Will could conjure from the depths of his vocabulary.

He and the others stared down at Marco Rothschild's sprawling estate from the cliffside a few hundred feet above.

Dak's crew was concealed by trees in a thin forest between two other opulent properties, and with the occupants out of town on vacation, it was the logical spot to reconnoiter Rothschild's ridiculous home—or what Dak imagined was one of several.

It hadn't slipped past Dak that Marco had purchased this fifty-million-dollar château and its acreage in the hills of Villefranche-sur-Mer, which also happened to be the location where the more famous Rothschild family owned a palatial estate.

Perhaps it was his attempt to reconnect lost family lines, or establish himself in what he believed to be his rightful place with the lineage whose rise to prominence and extraordinary wealth seemed perpetual targets of conspiracy theorists.

Dak had heard some of those theories. The one he found most interesting was how Mayer Rothschild had used the nineteenth-century version of fake news to sway the Battle of Waterloo in the favor of the British, and how he hedged his entire family's fortune on the outcome. From there, Mayer had amassed so much money that he built a banking and financial empire that was larger than many sovereign nations combined.

True or not, Dak had to admit it was a doozy of a theory.

He twisted to the right, looking west at the crowded buildings along the eastern side of Nice, then swept his gaze back to the left along the coast.

Villefranche-sur-Mer was bursting with some of the wealthiest people in Europe, and from around the world, and their homes—in many cases, second homes—attested to their financial status. Lavish mansions of stone, brick, pastels of pink, blue, and yellow, and even a few with exteriors updated with a modern design, dotted the cliffside and slopes of the French Riviera, all the way down to the water's edge of the Mediterranean.

Nearby Nice was the second largest city in the Provence-Alpes-Côte d'Azur, and played host to vacationers from all points in Europe, particularly the United Kingdom, and was in its own right a luxurious getaway.

But by comparison, this town may as well have been a whole other country.

Dak refocused his attention on Rothschild's property.

The estate was built on two primary tiers, with another above the château filled with a dense grove of trees running all the way up to the rocky cliff and one that hosted a long, narrow swimming pool wrapped in a concrete deck. Small, sculpted trees stood in neat rows on either side of the pool's length, and a curved double staircase swooped down to the shallow end.

The stairs narrowed into one at the above tier and ended in a walkway leading up to a gazebo furnished with white chairs, an outdoor sofa, matching white metal table, and a chiminea. The roof of the gazebo looked like something out of a French circus with swooping support rods joining at a crown-like fixture above the tent-shaped dome.

A perfectly manicured emerald yard stretched out above the pool to one side of the gazebo, and toward the driveway and another series of steps on the other.

Next was what Dak had figured was originally a greenhouse, but based on photos he'd found from a real estate company had been converted into a massive home gym.

And then there was the château itself.

Painted in a putrid yellow color, the three-story mansion overlooked the sea from multiple rooms, as well as from a rooftop patio with a viewing tower providing shelter from the hot midday sun or the occasional rain that could drench the area.

Dak had studied the various rooms on the flight to Nice, as much as was possible. The kitchen was decorated with white marble floors and handcrafted cabinetry and molding, and there were parquet floors in the living room, sitting room, and bedrooms, and even in the bathrooms with their extraordinary tubs, showers, and vanities.

Palm trees above and below the huge lawns swayed in the brisk sea breeze, tossing their long, broad leaves from side to side, gently testing the strength of the trunks.

The wind reached up to where he and the others crouched in the undergrowth and blew through his hair, tickling his scalp.

"You know what a real criminal is, Will?" Dak asked. Before his friend could answer, Dak continued. "A moron who defaces a work of art with that color yellow. They oughtta have their butts removed."

Will and Adriana chuckled.

Chester lowered his binoculars and looked at the other three. "Did you get that from a movie?"

"*The Rookie*," they all answered at the same time.

"Clint Eastwood and Charlie Sheen," Dak clarified. "Always wanted to use that line. Now I kind of hate that I had to."

"It's appropriate," Adriana consoled. "I was thinking the same thing."

"Talk about screaming for attention," Will added.

"Yeah," Dak agreed.

What they hadn't found in any of the online photos were pictures of the basement that housed the vault, the safe protecting the Rembrandt, or possibly other stolen works of art.

He hadn't been surprised by that. Such a thing would be kept secret, even if the owner was trying to sell the place. In that case, he'd have gone to great lengths to make sure it looked more like a gigantic man cave, entertainment room, or maybe even something ridiculous like a bowling alley.

Dak knew of a guy back in Chattanooga who'd made his fortune in the nursing home industry and built a basketball court in his basement.

He couldn't imagine what that kind of boredom must feel like.

"So, what do you think, boss?" Dak asked, directing the question at Adriana to his immediate left.

"I think he overpaid for the property. But then again, this is a one-in-a-million view."

Dak hummed his amusement at her wit. "Looks like no one is home right now. But from what I learned, Rothschild *is* in town. It will only be a matter of time before he comes back."

"He's probably out shopping for a gazelle or a giraffe or some other exotic animal to keep on the property," Chester joked.

"You might not be wrong," Will said.

"We're not going to have much to go on," Dak said. "Normally, I would want to recon the place, learn his habits, figure out an average timeline. We don't have that luxury for this. Feels like we're handcuffing ourselves a little."

"Then we assume the worst," Adriana suggested. "Figure on him being there when we do the deed. Which means we'll need a distraction."

The other two men turned their heads slowly toward her, and she drooped her head, jaw, and lips. "Not that kind of distraction, idiots. Besides, I'm the one cracking the safe. Remember?"

"What?" Will acted innocent. "I was just thinking you could pretend to be a pizza delivery girl or something."

"I'm sure that's what you were thinking, Will."

"What *do* we know about him?" Dak said, refocusing the conversation.

"He likes to gamble," Chester reported. "Sucks at poker. There's a high-stakes game here in town. From what I understand, he's lost a lot of money there, occasionally rakes a big pot or two, but is pretty consistent at losing."

"Well, that's something."

"He also never leaves the house without his two bodyguards."

Dak raised his eyebrows at this. "Only two?"

"Looks that way from what I've seen. He isn't shy about flaunting the fact that he has bodyguards. I doubt he actually needs them, well, except for the fact that we're about to rob him. But from what I've gathered, they likely make him feel important. Like he belongs in this part of the region."

"He's bleeding money from his accounts, too," Will said. "But it's probably too late to try and lock those down from the inside."

Dak nodded. "Yeah. It sounds like we need to find out if there's a poker game going on tonight or tomorrow."

"It's tomorrow," Chester said.

The other three looked over at him with wide eyes.

"What? Did you guys think I wouldn't do my research? I *always* do my research."

"All right, then," Dak said approvingly. "Well done, Chester. We need to make sure Marco attends that poker game."

"Shouldn't be that difficult. Like I said, he's a bit of an addict."

"Still, it would be nice if we had a little insurance."

Will cleared his throat, and the others directed their attention to him. "I think I might be able to convince him."

41

The group returned to their hotel suite in the Hotel d'Azur just ten minutes away from Rothschild's château.

They'd left the blueprints of the house spread out on a huge dining table surrounded by six luxurious chairs with beige upholstery framed by white wood. The balcony stretched from the living room to the master bedroom, allowing access from both by way of powder-blue French doors.

Matching blue sofas and chairs curled around a 72-inch flat-screen television above a weathered gray entertainment unit.

Dak and Adriana leaned over the schematics while Will stood out on the balcony, talking on his cell phone. Chester sat in one of the chairs in the living room, his laptop sitting on his legs as he worked on accessing the château's security system.

He'd managed to figure out the internet service provider and the security company, as well as the brand of cameras Rothschild had employed with a few quick searches and a couple of pictures he'd taken from the cliffside with a telephoto lens on his camera.

Now it was simply a matter of hacking into the system and making sure his intrusion wasn't detected.

"So, let's go over this one more time," Dak said, looking down at the schematics. Dark circles hung under his tired eyes. He propped himself up with his palms on the table as he leaned over, studying the plans.

"The poker game starts at eight-thirty," Adriana said. "But no one ever shows up then. The real money begins arriving about an hour later."

"Yep," Chester agreed. "These guys like to play late into the night. Sometimes all the way till sunrise."

"Thank you, Chester," Adriana drawled.

"You're welcome."

She rolled her eyes and smiled at Dak. "You okay? You look like you need to rest."

"So do you," Dak groused. He looked up at her, his eyes barely visible under his brow.

"You know you're not supposed to say that to a lady."

"Yeah, I know. But I figured you of all people could take it." He winked at her, and she smiled.

"So, Will's friends," she used air quotes with the last words, "will show up at eight-thirty at the château and tell him they're there to escort him to the poker game."

"And that story is going to check out? We're sure of it?"

"It's not uncommon," Chester chimed in again. "Sometimes those kinds of underground games send escorts to pick up and accompany the players. It takes away any doubts they might have about attending."

Dak and Adriana gawked at him.

"I'm sorry," she said. "Why do you know so much about this sort of thing?"

Chester giggled. "Because maybe my girlfriend runs an underground casino in Mumbai?"

Adriana looked to Dak for confirmation, who affirmed the statement with a nod.

"Well, all right then."

"She sometimes hosts high-stakes games, brings in some extra money to the club. Of course, a lot of it filters back to her by way of players buying drinks, food, that sort of thing."

"Women are the rake," Dak said, quoting a line from one of his favorite movies. "And in more ways than one."

Adriana snorted a laugh. "Love that movie."

"What movie?" Chester asked.

"Okay, when all this is over, we're all going to have a movie night together where we catch you up on some important flicks you obviously missed."

"It might take a few nights," Dak added.

Chester simply shook his head and went back to focusing on his laptop.

Adriana studied the plans for another thirty seconds then stood up straight, stretched her arms over her head, and yawned. "Are there any fire doors, anything that could lock us out of the basement or keep us down there should things go wrong?"

"Not that I can tell," Dak said. "But anything's possible." He rubbed his chin, poring over the blueprints one more time.

He'd been looking at it for so long he would probably see it in his sleep.

Will opened the doors to the balcony and stepped back inside. He momentarily blocked the afternoon sun that sent splinters of light through the glass in the door.

"They're good to go," Will announced. "They'll be at the château at eight-fifteen tomorrow evening, ready to knock at eight-thirty and get him out the door."

"Your friends aren't actual call girls, are they?" Adriana asked.

"No," Will laughed. "But they can play the part. I met them here a few years ago when I was... well, when I was conducting business. They're bartenders, so they know how to work a client."

"What if he—"

"I wouldn't worry too much about those two," Will cut her off. "They can handle themselves just fine. Dealt with way bigger trouble than the likes of Marco Rothschild and his two goons."

"Were you able to find out anything about the two bodyguards?" Dak asked.

"Only that they're both ex cops. Tough guys, probably know some pressure-point holds, self-defense, that sort of thing. But these girls know all that stuff, too."

"What bar did you say they work at?" Adriana wondered, putting her hands on her hips and peering at Will with dubious, brown eyes.

"I didn't. You two figured out the plan of attack yet?"

Dak shrugged, tilting his head sideways. "It looks pretty straightforward, which makes me think it's way too easy, like the vault has some surprises for us, something we're not seeing or anticipating."

"We've been over the plans a dozen times," Adriana exaggerated. "Chester is working on the systems right now. Once Rothschild is out of the house, it should be empty. His maids won't be there after dark. He doesn't have a butler, and based on our observations earlier today, it doesn't look like he has dogs we should worry about."

"You're right. It does sound too easy. Well, with the exception of you having to crack a nearly impenetrable safe. At least you should have some time to get that done. Unless Rothschild blows his stack in the first thirty minutes."

"It's happened before," Dak said. "We don't need to screw around once we're in. The faster we can get out of there, the better. Will, you got the wheels?"

Will nodded.

They'd decided he would be the getaway driver, which Will was more than okay with. He'd demonstrated a taste of his skills behind the wheel on the drive through the Douro Valley, evading the attacks of the North Korean nationals. Beyond that, Dak knew his friend was a skilled driver. Will had actually attended a racing school during the summer before his senior year of high school. He'd always had an interest in cars and in the limits to which they could be pushed—something Dak was grateful for during and after that harrowing ride through Douro.

"Yeah," Will said. "It won't be a fast getaway, but it'll have to do."

The vehicle in question was a small utility van he'd rented from a local company. The vehicle was built for skilled trade workers to transport their tools and materials from one job to another. Painters, electricians, plumbers... that kind of thing.

While it wasn't built for speed, it could be set up to look innocuous, and it had plenty of cargo room for the painting.

"Perfect," Dak said. "And us? A couple of Audi A5s?"

"Wouldn't that be lovely?"

Will let out a short laugh. "I got three of the vans. Same color, make, and model. We'll have to take the plates off, but that's easy enough."

The plan was simple, at least in theory.

Once they had the painting and were out of the château, they'd load it into Dak's van. If anyone tried to follow them, they'd be caught in the middle of a real-life shell game.

Dak got the idea from one of his favorite movies, *The Italian Job*. The thieves in that story used matching MINI Coopers to pull off the heist of several million dollars' worth of gold. In the movie, they had the advantage of a larger crew and more cars. Here, there were only three of them since Chester would be stationed remotely with his laptop.

The streets would be less busy at that time of night, though there would still be issues with traffic lights that would make the getaway much more difficult. And unlike in *The Italian Job*, Chester didn't have the ability to control the lights. He believed he could probably figure it out if given enough time, but with only a day to prepare, he had to focus only on the essentials.

"The vans will do," Dak said. "I doubt we'll have to deal with any kind of air support from local police if we do happen to trigger an alarm." Dak pushed aside the blueprints and revealed a map of the city.

Will joined him and Adriana at the table and listened.

Dak pointed to a street that ran in front of the château. "Two ways out from here. It's unlikely we'll encounter any resistance until we reach either this point"—he tapped on an intersection to the east—"or here." He moved his finger to another crossing to the west.

"Their response time would have to be pretty fast to get us there," Will said.

"Yeah. But that's a worst-case-scenario sort of deal. And I don't see them blocking both directions that fast. One? Maybe. An outside chance. Even less likely for both, though. That said, I think this is the safe zone we need to clear."

Dak picked up a red marker and circled a wider area surrounding the estate and several streets.

Adriana and Will studied the zone carefully, doing their best to memorize the French street names.

"Most of these *rues* are good, but there are a few one-way ones you'll need to be aware of. You don't want to go down one of those, or you might find yourself in trouble. If you do get caught, they won't have anything on you since I'll be the one with the painting. If I get nicked, so be it."

"I don't like that," Will said. "But I understand. It's your deal."

"Right. You two aren't going to take the rap for this."

The other two agreed silently.

" Let's do it then," Dak said.

"Um, guys?" Chester interrupted.

Dak didn't like the sound of his voice. Problems were contained within, and if Chester was encountering an issue with the surveillance and security systems, that would stop the whole operation in its tracks.

"What is it?" Dak asked, twisting his head to face their hacker.

"We have a problem."

42

D ak didn't need any more problems. He'd received his fair share, and now he was ready for something to be easy.

Was it too much to ask to be able to walk into the château through open doors, make their way down to the vault, lift the painting off an unprotected wall, and carry it back out?

It was going to be difficult enough to meet Tucker without getting himself, Nicole, or the rest of his team killed.

He'd already considered the last part. Once he had the painting, there was no reason for them to be involved anymore.

Dak knew they'd resist that sentiment. Well, maybe Chester wouldn't. He'd probably feel like he'd done his part and dip out back to Mumbai to the waiting arms of Tamara.

Dak wouldn't blame him. He wouldn't blame any of them if they departed once this part of the job was done. And there was no way he'd let them join him on the jaunt to wherever Tucker had in mind for the exchange.

Not that there would be an exchange. Dak had no misgivings about that. More likely, Tucker would set a trap, take the painting, and then kill Dak and Nicole. If she was still alive.

Of course she was. Tucker wasn't the brightest bulb in the lamp store, but he wasn't a total moron.

Nicole had to be kept alive to dangle that carrot in front of Dak until he had what he wanted. And what he wanted was the painting, and Dak's head.

Tucker would know he couldn't allow Dak to live because if he did, he'd never be safe. In a strange sort of way, the two men were living the same life, simply on different poles. Tucker needed Dak dead, and Dak needed Tucker dead.

Life was rarely so black and white as that.

Standing in the hotel suite, possibly the last hotel room Dak would ever visit, he stared over at Chester, awaiting the bad news.

He expected the young Brit to tell him that the system was unhackable, that the cameras were built on a secure platform unlike anything he'd ever seen.

Dak was ready for the worst.

"What's the problem?" he asked, bracing himself.

"This system is a little more advanced than I first thought," Chester said.

There it was. They were screwed. Dak's mind started running through other options. Most of them were brute-force ideas that involved a wrecking ball or a bulldozer.

"Can you get in?" Dak asked.

"Oh, I'm already in. That's not the issue."

A ripple of tentative relief rolled through Dak's head, easing the nonsensical solutions that ran amuck.

"So, what *is* the issue?"

"It seems Rothschild has a fail-safe built into the system. Maybe he didn't custom order. It's possible this was a factory upgrade. Hard to know."

"What's your point, Chester?" Dak pressed.

"Well, the cameras are easy enough. I can switch them on and off as I please. No big deal there. But the alarm system—that's a bit more complicated. See, it has a feature that if it gets shut down remotely, an automated text message will go to the homeowner after two minutes if it isn't turned back on. Basically, it acts as a secondary alarm. Probably in case someone tries to do what I'm going to do."

Dak listened carefully, and when Chester was done, he took a minute to process what he'd heard to make sure he understood correctly. "So, are you telling me that we have two minutes to get into the vault and get the painting?"

"Yeah. Basically."

Dak inhaled sharply. He ran his fingers through his hair and paced over to the kitchen counter where they'd placed a case of water bottles. He took one out, twisted off the lid to the familiar cracking sound of the cap's safety ring, and sucked down a long gulp. When he'd finished half of the bottle, he replaced the cap and set it down on the counter, then leaned against the edge next to it.

The others looked to him for answers, but Dak was tapped out. He was tired. Tired of hunting Tucker. Tired of coming up with crazy plans that no normal person on the planet would ever have to conjure. Tired of running for his life. And tired of.... He stopped himself there. He wouldn't let that one enter his mind. That, like all the other complaining thoughts, was a distraction, and not going to help the present moment.

"What do you think we should do, boss?" Will asked.

They all looked to him for answers he wasn't sure he could give.

There was one idea that simmered deep in his mind, but it would be nearly impossible to pull off. Then again, everything he'd done since leaving the military had proved near impossible.

He thought about the mission in Peru, the one in Ukraine and Romania, India, North Carolina, and London.

All of those things would seem impossible to a mere mortal.

Dak had no misgivings about his mortality. But he was also no ordinary human. He had a set of skills unlike most. He could figure this out.

They could pull it off.

"Well," he began. "That admittedly sucks about the system's lockdown mechanism. I assume that Rothschild can shut down the house and trigger the alarm remotely if he thinks something is amiss, which is what would happen if he got that automated text message."

"Correct," Chester confirmed.

"Hmm." Dak crossed his arms and stared down at the floor. "I guess that really only leaves us with one option. Or two, depending on how you guys feel about holding someone hostage in their own home."

Will sat down in the nearest chair, ready to hear more.

"Wait," Chester said. "Hostage?"

"Yeah. We could go in, hold Rothschild at gunpoint, and force him to open the safe for us. It would allow more time, and we wouldn't have to guess the combination."

"True," Adriana said, clearly on board with this idea. "Would be nice not to have to rush."

"Wait," Chester interrupted. "Are you serious? Don't get me wrong, I'm all for an easier plan, but he could have a panic button on him. If he hits that button, you'll come out of that vault and run straight into a bunch of police guns."

Dak knew he was right, which is why he leaned toward the other plan.

"I still like the idea of him going to the poker game with Will's friends. I think that's the safest route. But we'll need to buy ourselves some extra time inside the house without the alarm on, so that when Chester deactivates it, we'll be able to get clear before the alert is sent, or before he turns it back on."

"How do you figure on doing that?" Will asked, inclining his head.

An easy smile crept across Dak's face, stretching his cheeks slightly and narrowing his eyelids. "Same way the government pulls the wool over everyone's eyes all the time. With misdirection."

43

MARSEILLE

Tucker paced around the area that had previously been the presbytery of the little church on the hill.

He'd been stuck in this place for the last few days and longed for a comfortable bed, heating and air conditioning, and a meal at a nice restaurant. The colonel was getting soft.

It wasn't as if he'd been resigned to eating MREs the entire time they occupied the abandoned church, but it was still basically like camping.

He and his team had managed to rig a field shower in the bag to allow them to stay clean and not smell like Bourbon Street at two a.m. on a Saturday night. But that, and the cots they'd procured, were the only luxuries afforded to Tucker and his crew.

Soon, it would all be over. Within a few days, he'd be on a warm beach, maybe one close by, sipping expensive drinks, eating extraordinary cuisine, and letting the hard-won life he'd lived drift away into the distance of his memory.

He'd jumped through all the hoops in the military. Always followed orders, worked hard to get where he was, only to have it all unwound by Dak Harper.

In truth, Tucker had been fortunate to get the honorable discharge he'd been issued by the United States Army.

It could have been much worse.

Without much evidence, though, those who decided his fate leaned on his exemplary record prior to the accusations and let him off easy.

That didn't comfort him much.

And it certainly didn't add to his financial stability.

He'd accumulated a pile of money during his time in the military, moving weapons around the Middle East in exchange for gold that, he in turn, converted to cash in multiple banks around the world.

The advent of cryptocurrency had accelerated the growth of his monetary value. Untraceable and entirely built on decentralization, Tucker had used it to clean money across continents.

But the fact Harper remained alive had hampered all of that.

He'd spent more than he cared to consider in multiple attempts to eliminate Harper, but his former operator had proved more slippery than a greased toad.

Harper had evaded multiple assassins on top of killing every one of his former team members—all of whom were extremely skilled and well-trained men.

He was the last thorn in Tucker's side, an irritating, itchy splinter that needed plucking before he could finally feel relief.

Soon, though, it would be over.

Lee walked into the room and stopped, put his hands behind his back, and stood awaiting orders much as he would have if they were still in the military.

"Is everything in order?" Tucker asked.

"Yes, sir. The team is ready. Prisoner is secure. We can head out by nightfall."

"Good. Tomorrow is a big day. Are all the vehicles loaded?"

"Yes, sir. The men are just stowing the last of the gear. She'll be last, obviously."

Tucker nodded his approval. "Dismissed."

Lee spun around on his heels and walked back out through the front doors of the church, leaving Tucker alone with his thoughts.

He hadn't heard anything from the assassin he'd sent after Harper, but that was—to a degree—to be expected.

The Black Lotus was one of the most cryptic, mysterious killers in the network. No one knew anything about her, save the wild exaggerations he'd heard whispered in corners. He likened her legend to the stories of great heroes of the past who could shoot lightning bolts from their eyes and slay a thousand enemies with their bare hands.

There was at least a modicum of truth to her lore, but he was pragmatic enough to keep expectations in check.

He folded his hands behind his back and paced to the other side of the building. He stopped by a tattered window and looked out through the fragments of stained glass. The city of Marseille glistened in the waning afternoon sunlight. Tendrils of whitecaps streaked the inky Mediterranean beyond the city's ports and beaches.

While Tucker did appreciate this place, he knew he couldn't stay here. Being in this church for the last few days was the longest he'd remained in a single place for the last two years.

Soon, that would all come to an end. He'd be rich, and more importantly, he'd be free of Dak Harper once and for all.

44

VILLEFRANCHE-SUR-MER

Dak stepped into the steaming hot shower. The water stung his skin for a second, shocking his system momentarily before it quickly acclimated.

He let the heat soak his tired muscles and joints for a few minutes before scrubbing off, washing his hair, and closing the valve.

After drying off, he slipped on one of his favorite T-shirts, an army-green Pearl Jam one he got from a concert at Wrigley Field in Chicago back in 2018.

The fabric, thankfully, had held up well over the years. He was glad he had, too. He could still fit in it.

He finished getting dressed, brushed his teeth, and wandered into the bedroom. The town's lights twinkled in the darkness below. No stars mirrored them on this night. The black sky was marred with charcoal, broiling as if it might bring rain.

He couldn't see the Mediterranean well tonight, which he hoped wasn't an omen of bad things to come, but they'd done all they could to prepare for what would certainly be a difficult operation tomorrow evening.

. . .

DAK KNEW the next day's hours would pass like single grains of sand dripping through the tightest hourglass in the world.

He and his team had come up with a good plan.

They'd gone out and driven the streets, making mental notes of the names, and of the twists and turns. This was the kind of place a person could easily get lost in, and going the wrong direction tomorrow could prove to be an unforgivable mistake. At least for him.

The others would be fine. They wouldn't be carrying a priceless Rembrandt that had been missing for three decades.

After touring the town, they'd stopped at a nice restaurant Adriana had recommended. Dak wasn't sure if she'd been to the place before or if she simply did a quick internet search to find one with good reviews. Not that it mattered. The food had not, as French cuisine rarely did, disappointed.

He'd even allowed himself a glass of red wine to wash down the meal.

Dak thought maybe it would calm his nerves, but in truth it barely brushed them.

The others had gone to bed thirty minutes ago, and he realized that he needed a bottle of water for the nightstand in case he got thirsty in the middle of the night. Just in case, he pulled on some jogging pants and stepped out into the suite's common area.

To his surprise, he found Will standing out on the balcony, staring into the darkness.

Dak wandered over to the kitchen counter, took one of the bottles from the case, and walked back over to the balcony door. He pulled it open quietly, so as not to startle his friend, but Will heard him' and turned to see who'd come to join him.

"Hey, man," Will said. "Just out here breathing some of this good sea air."

"Mind if I join you?" Dak asked.

"You're an idiot."

Dak grinned at the response and stepped out onto the landing, closing the door behind him.

"I thought you went to bed."

"I thought the same thing," Will replied.

"I was about to, then remembered my water. I wake up thirsty most nights."

Will simply nodded.

"Euro for your thoughts?" Dak said.

Will shrugged. "I was just thinking about how much I love the sea."

"Don't tell me you were considering buying a boat when this is over."

"Actually..."

"Well, that's going to be a solid investment," Dak said dryly.

"Okay."

"No boat owner ever regretted that purchase."

"You know, I've heard all that stuff before, right?"

Dak chuckled and leaned over the railing, clutching the bottle with both hands. "I'm sure you have."

"Did you come out here to give me a hard time and question my financial choices, or did you have another reason?" Will asked, looking over at his friend with a mocking annoyed expression.

"No, I didn't have a reason. I guess... maybe I just didn't want to go to bed yet. Like if I stay up a little longer, this pause will continue indefinitely."

Will inhaled through his nose and nodded as he exhaled. "You have something to help you fall asleep?"

Dak shook his head. "No. Not with me. Besides, that medicine makes me groggy in the morning."

"Better than not sleeping at all."

"I'll be fine," Dak insisted.

In truth, he feared touching his head to the pillow. The demon insomnia had tortured him for years, but had doubled down on his slumber in the last few days. His mind wouldn't shut off, constantly forcing images of Nicole tied up in a basement or an abandoned building somewhere, barely given any food or water, and who knew what else.

The more tired he felt, the worse it seemed to get.

He fought off visions of how Tucker and his men had been treating her, what they might be doing to her right now at this very moment.

Dak shuddered at the thought.

Will stared at his friend, wishing sympathy alone could make it all better and ease Dak's torment.

"She's out there, Will," Dak said. "She's out there somewhere. Maybe she's cold or starving or beaten or—"

"Don't do that," Will cut in. "Don't do that to yourself, Dak. She's okay. She's alive. And we're going to get her back. All right? You don't need to go on haunting yourself with that nonsense. It doesn't change anything, doesn't make any of this better."

Dak nodded. He knew his friend was right. He'd used similar logic before with other people, telling them not to worry. All it did was ensure you'd suffer twice.

"You gotta keep your mind focused on the mission, Dak. That's the only way we have a chance at rescuing your girl—and all of us getting out of this in one piece."

Dak hummed quietly, musing over the statement. "She hasn't been my girl in a long time."

"She hasn't been anyone else's, either."

Dak turned his head and searched his friend. "How do you know?"

"I just know," Will said with a subtle laugh. "There aren't many men like you in the world, Dak. I'd be willing to bet my new boat I haven't bought yet on the fact that she's been waiting this whole time for you to come back."

"Meh." Dak blew off the statement. "Plenty of guys out there in the world. Better looking, more stable, richer."

"If looks mattered, she wouldn't have got with you in the first place." Will reached over and nudged Dak on the shoulder to go with the barb.

Dak let out an amused hum.

"I don't think she cares about money, man. She has her own.

Would she want more stability? Sure. Who wouldn't? But I have a feeling she loves you for who you are, unstable or not."

"You make it sound like I'm insane."

"Your words."

The two friends shared a laugh, and then the conversation fell silent again.

"It feels like the night before a big game," Dak said after a moment of nothing but the breeze filling their ears. "Except with very real stakes."

"That it does," Will said. "But the good news is we're on the winning team."

"I hope you're right." Dak paused. He wondered if their plan had the slightest chance of working. There were so many variables, he couldn't help but see a million ways it could go wrong. Doubt needled his mind and poked holes in every possible successful outcome.

"Do you think it will work?" he muttered. He spoke so quietly, it was almost as if he were asking himself.

"Of course it will, man. Don't let those doubts change your mind. It's going to work."

Dak straightened up and patted Will on the back. "Enjoy dreaming about your money pit... I mean boat."

"I will."

Dak opened the door and stepped back inside, while Will shook his head and leaned out over the railing, enjoying the view.

45

D ak woke up at 7:30 the next morning, about thirty minutes later than his usual time. He'd slept better than expected, and through the slumber-induced haze, he wasn't exactly sure why.

Falling asleep had been difficult—his mind a swirling tornado of problems, worries, and vain wishes that kept him from letting go and drifting off into the obscure darkness behind his eyelids.

After throwing on a pair of jeans, he stepped out into the common room, and found it quiet and empty—except for Chester sleeping on the pullout in the far corner. The doors to the other two rooms were closed.

Dak walked over to the counter, scribbled a note on a piece of paper to let the others know he'd gone out for coffee, and left the suite quietly.

Outside, the sun burned a deep yellow above the horizon to the east. The clouds from the night before had retreated to the north, leaving only remnants of wispy cirrus strands in their wake.

The waxing moon hung eerily over the horizon to the west. Dak loved it when he was able to see that. The rising sun on one side of the sky and the dipping moon on the other seemed oddly spiritual to him, as if the two celestial objects embodied a balance, the ebb and flow of life.

The air was cool, and he was glad he'd grabbed his jacket on the way out the door even though he thought it might have been unnecessary. It was summer, after all, but the mornings along the southern coast of France could be finicky at times, and more akin to fall back in Tennessee.

He strolled down the sidewalk, inhaling the scents of fresh baked goods—especially the bread the French were so famous for. Just smelling it took his mind to another sense—that sound when a baguette's crusty surface cracked when the loaf was broken.

The thoughts made him hungry, but he wasn't ready to eat yet. Dak always waited a few hours after waking before eating. Coffee, on the other hand, was a necessity.

He found a coffee shop in a light gray building two blocks away. A pink sign hung over the entrance and proclaimed the place to be Le Boulanger Fou. Dak's French was a little rusty, but he knew what a boulangerie was.

The entrance had offsetting white- and blue-framed stones around a pink wooden door. Three large square windows with white frames occupied the street side wall, allowing him to see the line of patrons inside waiting to place their orders.

"That's never a bad sign," Dak mused.

There was no need to check online reviews when the line was this long at this hour of the morning. The locals always knew what's up.

He pulled open the heavy door and was immediately welcomed by the smells of warm pastries and strong coffee.

His routine of not eating for a few hours after waking crumbled in an instant, much like the walls of Jericho.

Dak fell in line behind the other customers, knowing with every passing second his willpower continued to take a beating. He stared hungrily at the pastries, the cheeses, and fruits.

Yep. I'm having some of all that, he thought.

He ordered four black coffees, four croissants, and an assortment of cheeses and fruit, and walked back outside disappointed in himself for yielding but eager to get back to the hotel room and dive into the delicacies tucked in the pink paper bag.

It probably wasn't the healthiest way to start the day. But he let it go.

If the plan failed, he'd be in a French jail cell that night. And if it succeeded, he'd have to meet with Tucker tomorrow—a rendezvous he didn't expect to survive.

So, if it was going to be his last twenty-four hours on earth, he might as well enjoy what he could of it.

46

The hours crawled by the rest of the day.

After Dak's team devoured the breakfast he'd brought back, they spent the rest of their time making final preparations.

They went to the rental place and picked up the three vans—only after inspecting each one to make certain there were no significant differences. A dent, a huge scratch, a cracked window or windshield could all mean the difference between success and failure.

Chester ran through every systematic fail-safe he could think of to make sure everything went smoothly on his end. It seemed like a simple enough job, as long as Will's friends could distract Rothschild long enough to allow Dak and Adriana to get in and crack the safe.

Time was going to be tight, and there were no guarantees the girls could keep Rothschild occupied for that long without making compromises no one wanted them to make. They were bartenders, honest women for all he knew, and Will didn't want to put them in a situation where Rothschild would try to take advantage of them.

To make things worse, none of them had the benefit of weapons other than the two hunting knives Dak had picked up at a camping store in Nice. Will had connections in many places around the world, but Nice wasn't one of them. He tried one of his guys in Paris, but the contact was in London until the beginning of the following week.

Dak would make it work. He didn't have a choice. Though he wished they hadn't had to leave their firearms in Portugal.

The thought did make him smile, knowing that Juncao now had a stash of guns he probably didn't know how to use, but he'd seemed happy to hold on to them, perhaps in case he needed them in the future.

The sun plowed through the sky as if drawn by a slow, invisible mule. Dak must have checked his watch a hundred times while going over the details of the heist.

Part of him couldn't believe he was about to attempt this. Sure, he'd stolen items from villainous characters before—people who'd taken what didn't belong to them in the first place, but he'd never tried to break into a safe.

Having Adriana there made him feel much better about that. He knew there'd be little chance of success without her in on this. He'd have been relegated to driving a bulldozer through the château, or the subtler option of putting a gun to Rothschild's head and demanding the combination.

The hour turned over to 7:30 p.m. after the longest day of Dak's life.

Standing on the balcony, he removed the phone from his pocket and sent a quick text message before turning and walking back into the suite.

The other three sat around on the sofa and chairs, their tasks complete.

"Okay," Dak said. "This is it."

"You're not going to give us one of those speeches about how if we want out this is our last chance, are you?" Will asked. He lounged on the sofa with both arms spread out across the top.

"The thought crossed my mind," Dak confessed. "But no. I know you're in. The girls will arrive in forty-five minutes at the château. Adriana and I will be in place in the forest behind the house. Will has eyes on the front. When the girls go in, he'll let us know, and that's when Adriana and I slip in the back."

"And I'll have the cameras off before you leave the cover of the trees," Chester said, remembering his first objective.

"Right." Dak met the eyes of each one. "Once she and I are in, it's on Will to let us know if he sees anything going off the rails."

"Yep. The second I see movement at the front door, I'll give the signal."

Dak gave a nod. "Hopefully, they can hold Rothschild long enough for us to get into the safe. Unfortunately, there's no way to estimate how much time that will give us. Could be five minutes. Could be more or less. We'll have to work fast."

He sighed. The events of the week, the travel, the stress had all taken a toll on him. He figured the decent amount of sleep he'd had the night before came as a result of absolute fatigue. But one night wouldn't catch him up on several days' worth of lost slumber. He'd need a week for that.

Then again, Dak worked under the assumption that he'd be resting for good soon enough, though he didn't tell the others that.

"Thank you all for volunteering to help me with this. I really appreciate it."

"Volunteering?" Will asked. "I thought we were getting paid. I'm out."

He pretended to stand up to leave and then laughed. The others joined in. "We got you, man. This is going to work. So relax. Take that beleaguered look off your face, and let's get the job done."

Dak wished he shared his friend's optimism. For now, he faked it with a grin.

"Okay, then. Let's go."

47

Dak picked a spot in the forest where a copse of trees and shrubs provided cover from view. Even if someone had been really looking, they would have had a hard time seeing him and Adriana.

The two had left their vans about two blocks away from the château—far enough that they wouldn't arouse suspicion but close enough that they could get to the vehicles quickly if they sprinted and were unimpeded.

Will parked a little closer to keep an eye on the entrance, keeping an angled view from about one block away. Two palm trees provided a little cover for him, along with a few smaller trees sculpted to look like spheres.

Chester was the safest. He'd taken up a remote position and would easily be able to get away if things were to go south. While he was unlikely to be caught, by cops or other authorities, that didn't make his task any easier. His timing had to be spot on, and if it wasn't, his friends would pay the price.

In truth, the entire mission hinged on him, and he knew it.

"How we looking, guys?" he asked.

"We're good, Chester," Dak answered. "In position. Will's friends just arrived."

Dak watched through his binoculars as a black Bentley pulled up to the front of the mansion and parked at the wide steps that narrowed as they climbed toward the entrance. The super car had been a nice touch—picked up by Will from a high-end rental shop in town. It wasn't cheap, but they had to sell the whole package for this to work.

The women climbed out, both wearing tight dresses—one black, the other made of a red fabric. The outfits were revealing, but didn't give away everything. Just enough to make a man like Rothschild lose focus for a little while, which was the whole idea.

It was a fine line, as Dak had considered before. If things went awry, he'd have to improvise. His actions, his life, had put one woman in harm's way. He wasn't about to add to that ledger.

The girls ascended the stairs between alabaster pineapples that stood on wide newels every ten feet along the railing.

Dak watched them disappear when they reached the front entrance. From his vantage point, he couldn't see past the western right corner. He and Adriana could have taken a different angle farther down the tree line, but that would have meant a long run to the house, and time was more important than them seeing what was going on.

That part would have to be relayed by Will.

"It's on you now, Will," Dak said through the radio attached to his ear and the lapel mic concealed in his shirt.

"Eyes on," Will answered.

Dak breathed deliberately, trying to calm himself.

Adriana looked over at him and touched his shoulder. "Relax, Dak. You've been in way worse."

"Yeah. But not with so much at stake."

He felt better about the two of them having hunting knives strapped to their belts, even though they seemed like impotent weapons compared to his usual choice.

"The girls are at the door," Will said.

"Kill the cameras," Dak ordered.

"Killing them now, boss," Chester said. "Aaaand you're clear."

"Go," Dak said. He sprang from his position and ran, picking his way along the edge of the trees just inside the shadows in case anyone happened to be stationed by a window on the west side of the mansion. Adriana stayed close, right on his heels as they ran toward the back entrance.

Dak hoped it would be unlocked, but he'd already bet on that not being the case—Adriana's first test.

"Front door is opening," Will said. "It's one of the bodyguards."

Dak had expected as much.

"Twenty yards to the back," Dak said between breaths.

His heart raced. His legs warmed from the run.

The day had gone from a cool, autumn-like morning to a wet heat he hadn't thought possible in this part of the world.

"Girls are in the building," Will announced.

Dak cut away from the trees and darted across a small patch of lawn to reach the back corner of the château. He stopped near the rear door and waited one second for Adriana to catch up.

He crouched down and removed a telescoping aluminum compass fitted with a black suction cup on one end and a diamond glass cutting tool on the other.

Dak handed the tool over to her and stepped aside near the back door, glancing up at the camera over the entrance.

"Did you want to try the door first?" she asked. "You never know."

Dak responded by stepping over to the entryway and pressed down on the button above a dark bronze handle.

To his surprise, the door opened easily. He winced, thinking there might be an alarm, or at the very least one of those annoying dinging sounds that so many people had fitted to their entrances to alert homeowners when someone came in.

But all he heard was silence.

Adriana looked surprised but was glad for at least one thing going their way.

She set down the cutting tool and followed Dak into a short

hallway lined with black-and-white-striped wallpaper and crown molding along the top, where it met the eggshell-white ceiling.

The two of them had spent hours memorizing the layout of the mansion, but looking at rooms and corridors in 2-D was much different than in the third dimension.

Dak pushed ahead, moving carefully so his shoes didn't make a squeak or a click on the hard marble floor.

The hallway ran into a laundry room with white cabinets above the machines.

The two intruders passed through there and into the next portion of the corridor that stretched another twenty feet before it appeared to open into a much larger room.

Dak heard the girls' voices, though he couldn't understand what they were saying. He figured they were flirting with the guards at this point, which would turn into flirting with Rothschild before—he hoped—they escorted him out of the mansion.

If he was really lucky, Rothschild would forget to arm the alarm system, but Dak figured that responsibility would fall on the guards, and there was no way he was that lucky.

They reached an intersection in the corridor, and Dak turned left, recalling that the stairwell down into the basement would be in that direction.

He was rewarded with another door and a set of stairs leading down a stairwell painted in cherry red.

He bit his lip to keep his initial reaction from escaping vocally. *My eyes,* he thought.

The two tiptoed down the stairs, reached a landing, and then continued down around one more flight to the right.

Dak was surprised at how deep this basement went, but remembered the place had been built in the nineteenth century —a time when secret passages and massive underground chambers were occasionally built into the homes of the wealthy aristocracy.

"Still nothing out here," Will said.

Dak didn't answer. He and Adriana were on radio silence now, and they had to remain that way until they were on their way out of the building.

They had to trust Will's friends were okay, and were handling the situation the way female bartenders always did with men. Let them think they had a chance, but kick them to the curb and shut the door when it was time.

Dak and Adriana arrived on the basement level in a giant red room. Abstract art hung on the walls around the entire place. There was a bar with a black marble top in the far-left corner, with champagne glasses hanging from slots overhead.

To the right, a huge flat-screen television loomed high in the corner with black leather club chairs and a sofa pointed at it.

A billiard table stood in the center of the room atop the parquet floor. A pool hall-style green-and-white stained glass lamp hung over the table.

Dak frowned. "I thought this was the vault," he whispered to Adriana.

She responded by pointing to the back wall, where a door led into a dark corridor.

He nodded and motioned for her to take point.

Adriana led the way around the billiard table, the seating area, and the bar in the back. Colored nightclub lights hung in the right corner opposite the bar, and Dak realized it was a small dance floor.

The parties this guy must throw, he thought.

They left the man cave behind and entered the hallway, passing a bathroom on the left before they stopped at a closed door at the end.

Adriana tested the doorknob. It didn't move.

It was too much to hope all the doors would be unlocked.

She removed a lockpicking tool from her belt and got to work.

She eased a tiny rod into the keyhole and then inserted a second, flat piece. The door only resisted for fifteen seconds before it clicked, allowing entrance beyond.

Adriana stood, tucked the tool back in place, and pulled the door open. She hesitated for a second, wondering if there would be an alarm, but no Klaxons sounded to foil their plans.

She pushed the door open farther and met a much bigger problem.

Dak and Adriana stared at another door six feet away in a small room. Unlike the door she'd just unlocked, this one required a code entered on a key panel to the right.

Dak's heart sank. He hadn't accounted for this possibility. And there was no way he could have. This barrier wasn't featured on any of the blueprints he'd pored over.

"Will, what's going on up there?"

"Not sure, boss. Still no visual. What about you?"

"We have a problem."

48

"There's a keypad access panel to get into the vault," Dak explained.

"Didn't expect that," Will answered. "My real estate contacts didn't say anything about another door."

"No."

Dak silently chided himself for not thinking of this before. He'd been so focused on the safe, the possibility of another barrier standing in their way had slipped his planning. The only comfort he took from the problem was that there was no way he could have known. Their recon had been as thorough as possible with the amount of time they had.

That didn't make the issue go away, though.

"Can you figure out the code?" Dak asked Adriana, keeping his voice low. He glanced back over his shoulder but didn't see or hear anyone approaching.

"No," she said, but set her bag down and unzipped the front pouch.

Dak hoped she was going to pull out a device that could break the code, but instead she removed a small fabric coin purse.

"But I can narrow down the numbers that have been used."

That was something, but depending on how many digits the keypad required, it might not help. Even a four-digit code had ten thousand possibilities.

"Hey, guys?" Chester said in their ears. He didn't wait for a response. "You do have a hacker on your team, in case you forgot."

"Can you do something like that?" Dak asked, feeling a thread of hope.

"Of course I can. Those things are usually connected to the home network. Not typically Wi-Fi, but it's possible. Especially if the owner is sloppy."

"What do you need?"

"Nothing except a few minutes, hopefully. I already have the router and ISP information. Can you tell me the brand on the keypad? It should be on the bottom somewhere."

Dak leaned close and found the logo of the company on the bottom right corner. He gave the name to Chester and waited.

After ten seconds, Chester said, "Okay, I see it. Hold on."

Dak turned around and stared through the door they'd just come through. He considered closing it, but not until this one was open. If any of Rothschild's goons, or the man himself, decided to check the vault for some reason, Dak wanted to know about it. Even if they were being careful, the men would make some kind of noise. At least with the element of surprise, Dak and Adriana could get the drop on them.

If that happened—particularly in the case that Rothschild showed up—they could force him to give them both entry to the vault and to the safe.

Unless he proved unwilling to cooperate. In that case, Dak would have to use tools of persuasion he'd not put into action very often.

Adriana looked back through the door, too, their minds on the same thoughts.

The seconds ticked by like a blacksmith's hammer on an anvil.

Dak felt certain at any second one of Rothschild's guards would appear around the corner with a gun aimed in their direction.

"Chester?" Dak said, his patience drained.

"One second." The reply didn't fill Dak with a load of confidence. But there wasn't much he could do about it.

Dak was about to suggest Adriana use the powder in her pouch to narrow down the passcode possibilities when a beep from the keypad stopped him.

The door clicked and swung open.

Dak felt a rush of relief. He and Adriana stood and hurried to the door.

"That should have done it," Chester said.

"It did. Good job, Ches," Dak replied. "What kind of security measures are we dealing with on the inside?"

"None now. I disabled the laser system a few minutes ago. You should have a clear path to the safe. It's just on the other side of that room. It should be, anyway."

Dak pulled the door open wider. He saw the next room through the doorframe and motioned for Adriana to go first.

She stepped inside, wary that there might be some other trigger in place but didn't see or hear anything to suggest that was true.

Dak followed behind her and eased the door shut.

They stood inside a room that was twenty feet wide and thirty feet long. Paintings hung on black walls around the entire space. Dak didn't recognize any of them, but he knew each one was probably worth a considerable sum of money.

He wondered if they'd been stolen, or if Rothschild had come by them honestly—or semi-honestly. If the man had bought them, it was probably with money that didn't belong to him in the first place.

The floor was made of sturdy concrete panels, and Dak figured they were probably reinforced by more concrete below to prevent thieves from digging their way in.

"Most of these are priceless," Adriana whispered. "All stolen works of art from various museums and private collections around the world."

He knew what she was thinking. Adriana wanted to steal all of the paintings from this vault, but that wasn't on the table. Not now.

Straight ahead, at the other end of the room, was the reason they were here: the front of a steel safe that reached from the floor nearly to the ceiling was fixed into the wall.

49

Dak and Adriana hurried across the room, stepping lightly as they moved. They stopped at the safe and inspected the surface, the combination lock, and the wheel that opened it once the mechanism was unlocked.

He noted the name of the manufacturer down on the bottom-left corner, emblazoned in black cursive on the shiny metal surface.

Adriana placed her bag down on the floor and removed something that looked like a modified stethoscope with two bells instead of one. It had a black box attached to the central rubber cord above one diaphragm and bell.

Dak didn't need to know how it worked, just that it would.

"I'll cover you at the door," he said.

She acknowledged with a nod as she inserted the earpieces into her ears.

Dak walked back across the room and took up a position by the wall near the handle. He removed the knife from its sheath and held it by his side. If a threat came through that door, they wouldn't see him until it was too late.

Once the first threat was incapacitated, he'd take their firearm and go from there—assuming they would be armed.

There was no reason to think otherwise.

He looked back across the room and watched as Adriana placed the two bells against the steel surface near the combination lock.

He'd seen this sort of thing in movies but never in real life. Then again, he'd never been involved in a heist before either.

Dak figured it was an upgrade to the older version that probably amplified the sound from within, or perhaps sent a sort of sonar signal into the steel door. He was only guessing, and could have been way off.

If they got out of this alive, he might ask her about it.

She turned the dial deliberately, the movement so subtle it was barely noticeable. Dak didn't dare make a sound, and he hoped the urge to cough or sneeze didn't suddenly arise and cause him to throw her off.

He occupied his worried mind by pressing his ear to the wall and listening for signs of anyone approaching.

Nothing.

Dak twisted his head away from the wall and saw that Adriana was turning the dial in the other direction. Had she already gotten the first number of the combination?

He knew she was good, but that was impressive. Still, there were more to go, and he knew better than to get his hopes up with a big lead.

That thought had barely left his mind when he heard Will's voice through the radio.

"Movement at the front door," he announced.

Dak waited for a second, not wanting to miss a detail by asking what was going on.

"I have eyes on one of the guards. The girls are coming back out."

"Is Rothschild—"

"Yeah. He's with them. Guard number two is behind him."

Crap.

Dak knew everything had been too good to be true up to that point. The back door being unlocked, the ease of access into the vault, even Adriana getting over the first hurdle with the combination. Everything had gone swimmingly.

Now, they were about to be up against the clock, and he had no way of knowing if Adriana could figure out the rest of the combination with that short amount of time. Not to mention the two of them acquiring the painting and escaping undetected.

"Chester?" Dak said.

"Nothing yet, chief. I'll let you know the second the system is armed."

Dak forced himself to breathe slowly, keeping his heart rate steady as he'd practiced so many times before in intense circumstances.

Adriana didn't appear distracted by the conversation. She kept working as she had before, patiently turning the dial on the safe door.

Every second crawled by, even slower than before. Each moment hung over a thousand-foot drop, dangling Dak by a frayed thread.

He knew Chester would give the warning but didn't know when. Will had eyes on Rothschild, but that only went so far.

"They're getting in the car," Will said, as if cued by Dak's thoughts.

Any second now, Dak guessed.

Adriana was still turning the combination dial the same direction, trying to guess the next number.

Then things went from bad to worse.

50

There'd been no way to anticipate the lights going out in the vault. Not based on the limited recon Dak and his team had been able to perform.

Chester might have been able to tell them this was part of the security system, but Dak figured his tech expert hadn't known.

"The system is armed," Chester said. "I can shut it down. Then you'll have two minutes."

The room went pitch black for one second. Then, an instant later, a series of tiny red lights built into the base of the wall blinked to life a few inches above the floor.

"Adriana?" Dak said.

"I see them," she replied without moving so much as an inch. "You have a canister in your pack. If you can move enough to get to it, you can spray that along the floor to see the lasers better. Or you can just not move. Up to you."

"I think I'll stay put."

"The car is leaving," Will informed.

"Well, that's good news," Dak grumbled.

It was the dimmest of hopeful rays, and an expected one at that.

He looked down at the floor and the laser emitter nearest him to the right. His foot was a scant few inches from interrupting the beam.

They hadn't seen the lights beforehand due to nearly seamless panels that retracted upon the system's activation.

Across the room, Adriana was turning the dial back in the original direction.

"Two down," she whispered.

Adrenaline pulsed through Dak now, and he could only imagine how Adriana felt with all the pressure squarely on her shoulders now.

He didn't know how she did it, how she kept her fingers steady with one hand holding up the two bells against the safe's surface while the other gently turned the dial one millimeter at a time—and all while she knelt between the wall and a beam that would probably lock the two of them inside this vault until Rothschild and his men showed up.

Dak wondered if the system would alert the police, but knew that wouldn't be the case. The last people Rothschild wanted coming around would be cops—unless he'd bribed enough of the local authorities.

That was doubtful. There were too many, and while Rothschild may have had a few of the locals in his back pocket, all of them would have been a tall ask for almost anyone—save his distant, estranged relatives.

More than ever, Dak felt the very real sensation of the metaphor *waiting on pins and needles*. His skin crawled with every subtle sound the building emitted. And he felt like even his breaths could set off the alarms that would alert Rothschild of their presence.

A click echoed through the room, and Adriana stopped moving.

"I got it," Adriana announced.

Dak didn't dare move, no matter how much his emotions begged him to.

He wanted to run across the floor, spin the wheel on the door, and fling the safe open. But he resisted all of that and remained perfectly still. The only change was the pace of his heart ramping up by ten beats per minute.

"Chester?" Adriana said. "Kill the system."

"Done," he replied.

His response was appropriate. There was nothing else he could do to contribute to the mission, as far as his capabilities allowed. He'd told them once the system was deactivated, they'd have two minutes, and there was nothing he could do to stop that countdown once it was initiated.

The only action he had left was to turn it back on once they were clear and on their way to the vans.

The lights overhead blinked on, and the slits inside the walls slid back across the laser emitters.

"System is down," Chester confirmed what they'd seen.

Dak set the timer on his watch and hurried back across the room, his eyes darting left and right in case the lasers reactivated for some unknown reason.

They remained concealed and he reached the safe as Adriana stood, removing her device.

She spun the wheel, and when it stopped with a clank, the safe door swung open. Dak pulled on it while Adriana stuffed her equipment back in her bag.

Lights along the top walls and the floor flickered on inside the eight-foot-deep safe.

Three-foot-high stacks of gold bars imprinted with Chinese characters lined the left side. Dak ignored that and the six briefcases propped up on the right. He assumed those were stuffed with cash or some other kind of monetary denomination. He didn't care. What he was there for was right in front of him, propped on a black display easel.

The fabled lost Rembrandt stared back at the two thieves from within a gilded frame adorned with random swirling reliefs.

Dak stepped over to the painting with Adriana by his side.

He reached out to pick up the frame, but she held out a hand to stop him.

"Wait," she ordered.

He didn't say anything, but the question as to why seeped from his eyes as he looked at her.

She took one step closer and inspected the back of the frame. "It's rigged," she said.

A new fear tugged on Dak's chest. "Rigged?" He checked the back of the painting and saw what she was talking about. Two wires—one red, one black—stuck out from the back of the frame and into the easel.

She nodded and retrieved her bag within five seconds. "It's a remote alarm system. If we pull this off the easel, it will probably lock down the vault and alert Rothschild. I can bypass it, but it will take a minute."

"We have less than two," Dak reminded.

"What do you guys mean it's—"

"Not now, Chester," Adriana scolded.

She removed a tiny black box no larger than her palm from the bag. Red and black wires with small copper clamps stuck out from the top.

Dak observed while he kept a keen eye on his watch as the seconds dropped away. The sense of urgency overwhelmed him, but there was nothing he could do to rush her. That would only make things worse.

She carefully clamped the red wire to the matching one coming out of the frame, then repeated with the black wire.

Adriana exhaled and then raised a pair of wire cutters, slid them over the wires near the back of the frame, and squeezed.

Dak held his breath almost involuntarily as he watched.

The two listened and waited for two seconds.

"I think we're good," Adriana breathed.

"You think?"

"Only one way to find out."

She wrapped both hands around the frame and hoisted off the easel.

Nothing happened.

Dak checked his watch.

"Seventy seconds," he said.

She nodded, handed the painting to Dak, and headed for the door.

On the way out, Adriana grabbed her rucksack and slung it over her shoulder. Dak followed close behind her, certain at any second unseen Klaxons would start blaring, piercing their ears as the system alerted the château's owner of the theft.

Adriana reached the door to the vault, scooped up Dak's rucksack, and opened the door. She peeked out through the opening and then held the door wide so Dak could get through.

Again, he thought an alarm might sound as they exited the vault, but once more he was pleasantly disappointed to hear only silence.

Dak passed through and stopped short of the next door to allow her to go by and open it.

This time, she turned the handle and shoved it wide, more concerned with the amount of time they had left than the threat of one of the guards coming in. If anyone had returned to the home, Will would have seen it and alerted them to the danger, and he'd been silent on that front.

Adriana held the door for Dak as she had before, and he stepped through and into the basement near the staircase.

"Lead the way," he said, clutching the painting tight with both hands.

He glanced at his watch as she began the ascent.

"Fifty seconds."

That was more than enough time. Not much more, but they could do it.

He followed her up the stairs, taking each one more carefully so as not to trip and fall. Damaging the painting would be problematic enough, but slowing down and not making it out of the château would be just as bad.

Dak reached the first landing by the time Adriana was halfway up the second set of stairs. He rounded the railing and continued, taking one step at a time. At the top, Adriana paused and peered around the corner of the open door, then motioned for him to hurry.

He arrived at the top in a few seconds and then followed her to the right, down the same corridor they'd used before.

Dak snuck another peek at his watch. Thirty-five seconds remained.

When Adriana arrived at the back door and flung it open, they still had twenty-four seconds left.

Dak didn't want to test the system down to the last second.

She pulled open the door, stepped aside, and let him pass before following behind him and closing it again.

"We're clear," Dak said as relief flooded his chest.

The air felt fresher than anything he'd ever inhaled in his life. The sun's rays warmed his skin.

The two checked the back corner and kept moving at a steady pace. They neared the back corner of the converted greenhouse and slowed down slightly.

The plan now was to skirt along the tree line, around the property's perimeter, and to the vans where they'd make their getaway.

Things had gone so well—save for the two surprises in the vault —that Dak started to think the shell game bordered on the verge of overkill.

"Okay," he said into the radio. "Last leg."

The words had barely escaped his lips when he stepped around the corner of the building and froze.

His heart dropped into his gut and a chill of fear swept over his skin as if he'd just run headlong into a coiled viper.

The snake would have been preferable.

Standing twenty feet away was the man who'd caused him so much trouble for the last few years.

51

C ameron Tucker grinned like the devil over a fresh batch of souls. He held a pistol in his right hand. His left was firmly wrapped around Nicole's waist.

Dark bags hung under her tired eyes. She looked as if she'd been crying for days. Her usually creamy, coffee skin had turned ashen, and her hair was frazzled in a million directions. She appeared weak, almost to the point of being unable to stand.

Five men stood around the colonel, two on one side, three on the other. Each held pistols aimed at Dak and Adriana. One of them clutched a metal briefcase in his left hand. Off to the left of Tucker's men were Rothschild and his two guards. The château owner wore a smug, disdainful expression.

A lump in Dak's throat kept him from saying anything.

"Nice of you to fetch that for me, Dak," Tucker drawled. "I hope it wasn't too much trouble."

Dak's nostrils widened and receded over and over again as fury pulsed through his veins.

There had been few times in his life he'd been left speechless without a clue as to what to say. This was one of those moments.

"I can see by the look on your face that you're surprised," Tucker went on. "I suppose you should be."

"Let her go, Cam," Dak demanded.

"Or what? You have no leverage, Dak. I hold all the cards, son. You lost."

"It's not her you want. It's me."

He watched Tucker's eyes narrow to slits as the man grinned. Dak sensed Adriana next to him, tensing like a cheetah ready to spring forward and attack.

"Oh, you're right about that, Dak. I don't need her. But someone else does."

The comment caught Dak, and he felt a pain in his chest at the anticipation of whatever Tucker was about to say next.

It wasn't what he said. It was who appeared.

From around the corner, Will stepped into view, a pistol in his right hand.

"Will?" Dak spewed.

"That's right," Tucker said, delighted at Dak's obvious misery.

Will walked up behind the colonel and sidled next to Nicole. "Sorry, Dak," Will said. "Nothing personal. But I was never going to get that yacht without doing a deal with the colonel. Not to mention I can take better care of Nicole than you ever could."

Tucker released her and she tried to step toward Dak, but Will grabbed her by the shoulder and yanked her back.

"Not so fast," Will warned and pressed his gun into her side.

"If you hurt her—" Dak started.

"Save it, Harper," Tucker snapped. "Your time is done. You stabbed me in the back, along with all the men you served with. Only they were too stupid to think you wouldn't come after them. That's on them."

"And Rothschild?" Dak asked, deciding to keep the conversation going as long as he could. Every second he could delay the inevitable might open a window.

"He was very willing to part with the painting for the price I offered," Tucker answered.

Dak knew Tucker didn't care about the painting. He'd probably sell it off the second he was out of the country.

"Speaking of, Colonel," Rothschild said, "my money?"

"Of course, Marco," Tucker replied. He motioned to the mercenary carrying the briefcase. "Pay the man, Lee."

The one named Lee pivoted and took a step toward Rothschild. He extended the briefcase, and as Rothschild reached out his hand, Lee raised his pistol and fired at the nearest guard.

A hole opened in the man's temple at the same time a pink mist erupted behind his left ear. Lee quickly adjusted his aim and shot the second guard in the forehead before the man could get his gun turned even a quarter of the way toward the threat.

Rothschild's smug "gratitude" vanished in an instant, turning to confused rage.

"What are you doing? You just killed my—"

Lee fired a single shot through Rothschild's left eye, ending the sentence before it was finished.

Nicole jumped at the gun's reports, but Will held her tight in his grip.

Rothschild fell prostrate on the grass between his two men.

Tucker grinned as Lee leveled his weapon at Dak again.

"No sense in paying for what you can get for free, eh, Dak?" Tucker took a step forward, out ahead of his men. "You really were my best, you know. And you've proved that over the last few years. You were a real pain in the—"

"You think you can trust him, Will?" Dak interrupted before Tucker could finish. "He'll do the same thing to you. There isn't a place you can hide on this planet that he won't find you."

"The difference between you and me, Dak, is that I don't have anything he wants," Will fired back. "I helped him get what he wants most."

Tucker glanced over his shoulder at Will and nodded. "He's right. There isn't anything he has that I want."

"You're a loose end, Will. You know that as well as anyone."

Will remained unflinching. "He's stalling, Colonel."

"Oh, I know he is," Tucker said with a chuckle. "Same old Dak. I already transferred a healthy sum to your friend there. With that money, and your girl, I'd say he's going to be a happy man."

"What happened to not paying for what you can get for free?"

Tucker edged closer, narrowing the gap to ten feet between him and Dak. "Oh, you I'm happy to pay for."

Will took a step back, pulling Nicole with him. "Enjoy your prize, Colonel. I fully intend to enjoy mine."

He leaned in close, getting his nose to Nicole's neck, and inhaled through his nostrils.

Dak couldn't hide his anger. "Will. If you—"

"Enough!" Tucker snapped, raising his pistol at Dak's head. "I have had enough of your games, Dak. Enough of the problems you have caused me over the last few years. Go on, Will. Get out of here. I trust I'll never see your face again."

"Yes, sir," Will said.

He dragged Nicole away from the group. She barely had enough strength to offer even a meager protest before the two of them disappeared around the corner of the building.

Tears teased the corners of Dak's eyes. He'd failed, and he knew Tucker could see it written all over his face.

"This one looks feisty," Tucker said, motioning to Adriana with a slight wag of the pistol. "Where'd you find her, Dak? I thought you were a one-woman guy."

"Leave her out of this, Cam. Take me, and do what you want with me. Let her go."

"You know something? You are really bad at the art of negotiation. See, Dak, I can do whatever I want. I may just let the boys here have their fun with this one before I dump her body over a cliff."

Dak couldn't hold back the rage anymore, and he ventured a step forward. Tucker brandished the pistol and halted Dak in his tracks.

"Don't," Tucker warned. "I'm going to make you suffer for what you've done."

"Why bother, Cam?" Dak asked, positioning himself so that the guard named Lee was directly behind the colonel. "You have a clear shot. Why don't you take it?"

Tucker snorted in derision. "I'm sure you'd like that, wouldn't—"

Blood sprayed across Tucker's back, followed a half second later by a rifle report echoing across the property and off the cliffs above.

Tucker flinched, leaning forward out of sheer instinct before he looked back and saw the crater on Lee's forehead an instant before the man dropped to his knees. His eyes stared forward, the life gone from them.

The other four gunmen spun around, each taking aim at an unseen enemy.

Another shot rang out. The high-powered round exited through one of the men's backs, having entered through his chest. The impact knocked him down onto his back where he lay writhing and clutching the catastrophic wound in the center of his rib cage.

Tucker swore and looked back toward Dak just in time to catch a fist squarely on the nose.

The colonel fired the pistol impotently under Dak's armpit—the round diving into the grass a few feet away from where Adriana stood.

She sprang from her position and charged the gunmen on the far right while ripping the knife from its sheath at her side.

The second the sniper took out Lee, Dak dropped the painting and charged Tucker, landing a hard fist in the center of the colonel's face.

He reached down, gripped the handle of his knife, and drew it as Tucker staggered back. Blood gushed out of the colonel's crumpled nose, but he steadied himself and raised his pistol, desperately trying to aim through the blinding haze in his eyes.

He fired. Dak ducked to the side, but the round still caught him just below the ribcage on his right.

The sharp, burning pain screamed through Dak's nerves. He saw Tucker aiming again, but knew the man was struggling thanks to the broken appendage.

His vision wouldn't be stunted for long. And Dak knew he had to end this now.

52

Tucker's three remaining men clustered together, each aiming their pistols out toward the field—completely unaware of the threat that approached from behind.

Adriana grabbed the first gunman, wrapping her left hand around his forehead as she deftly slid the tip of the long blade up through the back of his neck and into his cerebellum.

His body gyrated for a moment, then abruptly went limp. The knees buckled, and he fell forward as she pulled the knife from his head.

The guard to the left caught movement and saw his comrade fall. He reacted fast and spun around to meet the enemy. He fired one shot and missed over her shoulder as she dipped below his aim and swung the blade around, driving the tip into his abdomen. Only the hilt stopped the momentum.

The man yelled in pain but managed to muster enough focus to twist the pistol toward Adriana.

She was faster.

Already sensing the desperate counter, she pulled on the knife, slicing through the man's gut while grabbing his wrist.

She pressured his hand up in an awkward motion the moment he fired. Two rounds went up through his torso and never came out.

He gurgled, standing immobile for a second.

Adriana tore the gun from his fingers and whirled him around at the last gunman before he could get off a clean shot.

Adriana aimed the pistol and fired two shots as the dead man fell in front of the lone gunman.

But he dove out of the way and let out three of his own volleys before he hit the ground. She responded by diving as well and fired back four more times.

Both missed their target, but the gunman rolled to one knee before she hit the ground. His pistol's muzzle popped over and over. She rolled backward like a child rolling down a hill in the summer grass.

Bullets exploded in the ground, missing by inches each time as she rolled away from him. He took two steps forward to point-blank range, lined up his aim, and accounted for her momentum.

His finger tensed on the trigger, ready to end this nonsense once and for all.

He never knew what happened.

The right side of his face exploded an instant before the rifle echoed from the other side of the field.

Out of habit, Adriana kept her weapon trained on the man until he fell over on his side.

"Nice shot, Chester," she said.

"Thank you," he chirped.

"Could have taken it a second or two sooner."

"It did the job, didn't it?"

She rose to her feet and looked to the left, where Dak had been engaged with Tucker, but neither man was in sight.

53

Dak clutched his side as he darted around the corner of the old greenhouse-turned-gym. He'd seen Adriana lunge at one of the guards with her knife drawn, and knew that man was dead before he realized it.

She could handle the other two as well. Dak wasn't sure there was anyone as deadly as her, and based on his career, that was saying something.

A split second after he found cover, Tucker fired his pistol. The rounds ricocheted harmlessly into the metal corner post.

Dak looked down the length of the building. He could try to run to the next corner, but that wouldn't do. It was too far to be that exposed. Then it would come down to a Wild West-style shootout with him and Tucker in a final duel. Except that Dak had brought a knife to a gunfight. He'd be resigned to throwing the blade at his nemesis while Tucker had a nearly full magazine of bullets to unleash at him.

On top of that, Dak was severely injured, and the wound was already taking both a mental and physical toll.

His hand felt warm and wet against his side where the bullet had gone through.

His face felt clammy. And he hunched over slightly from the pain.
Even if he had a pistol, Dak didn't like his chances.

He needed to level the odds.

Dak reached out to the door, hoping it was unlocked. If it wasn't,
he'd be forced to face Tucker out in the open—the weighted coin flip
he needed to avoid.

He grasped the handle and pulled down, fully expecting it to
resist. Instead, it went down easily, and Dak barged through, closing
it behind him and flipping the lock.

He knew that wouldn't hold Tucker for long, but every second he
could buy was crucial.

Dak surveyed the room quickly. A row of dumbbell racks lined
the wall beneath windows that ran the length of the building to the
left. The sun shone through the glass, illuminating the entire room in
its natural light. The dumbbell racks stopped halfway down the wall
where modern workout machines took over and filled the rest of the
floor space to the end.

More machines lined a wall to the right—two treadmills, an ellip-
tical, a rower, and two exercise bikes.

That wall divided the building in half. Dak didn't know what was
on the other side, but standing here, with a clear view outside
through the glass, he was still an easy target.

An open door straight ahead invited him to take refuge, and he
hurried through it, easing it shut behind him.

Dak took quick inventory of the new space.

There was a cedar sauna to his right. And a bathroom parti-
tioned by walls and a door next to it, complete with a shower and
toilet. There was a steam sauna to Dak's left, constructed of black
tiles and a glass front wall. Two teak benches provided seating
inside for those wishing to spend more time in the relaxing wet
heat.

The ceiling was made from a white material that looked like plastic. The curved material diffused the light and cast a white glow
throughout the entire area.

A kitchen occupied the other end of the room. Dak figured it was there for supplements such as protein shakes and for keeping other necessities conveniently located for whoever used this place.

Based on his physical appearance, it certainly wasn't Rothschild.

A steel refrigerator stood to the left of a white cabinet and white marble countertop, a sink, and dishwasher. There was a notable absence of a stove, which reinforced Dak's assessment that the kitchenette was primarily used for hydration and supplementation.

Dak heard the sounds of gunfire outside and hoped desperately that no one from his team had fallen. If he got out of this alive, he'd never forgive himself if one of them died.

A distinct gun report popped from the front of the building. It was followed by a metal clank. He felt a change in air pressure, the kind of subtle movement that only came when someone opened a door and a draft pushed in.

He moved behind the cubicle steam room. The tiled wall would give him cover, and when Tucker came through the door, Dak could get the drop on him.

"Daaaak?" Tucker taunted. "Come out, come out wherever you are."

Dak slowed his breathing. He tried to ignore the pain radiating from his side, but to no avail. It had started getting sore, stiff to the point that he wasn't sure how agile he'd be a few minutes from now.

Blood continued to leak through his fingers covering the wound, and he felt weaker than he had a few minutes before.

"You're bleeding, Dak," Tucker said, loud enough to be heard clearly through the thin walls. "You can't hide from me anymore."

Dak cursed the wound in his side.

An idea pushed him out of his hiding spot, and he stepped around to the steamer shower, opened the door, and pressed the power button in the panel fixed to the wall.

The machine gurgled as he retreated back behind the tile again.

TUCKER EASED the door shut behind him, leaving it slightly ajar with the mangled handle and lock no longer functional thanks to the .45-caliber bullet he'd blasted through it.

He'd spotted the drops of blood on the floor, most of which had collected around the entrance.

Dak stood here, trying to decide what to do.

That much was obvious.

He was wounded and probably getting desperate.

Tucker doubted he'd bleed out, not in the next few minutes. But if given enough time....

The colonel had no intention of letting that happen. He'd make sure Dak Harper was dead before he had the chance to bleed out.

Sounds of gunfire, muted by the walls around him, roared from outside the building. Tucker heard the thunderous boom of the sniper rifle from the other end of the field. He had no way of knowing how many of his men were left, if any.

How had this gone so wrong?

The thought tortured him.

Tucker was a man who planned everything, who accounted for every possibility. He never left anything to chance.

Yet somehow, Dak Harper had thrown a monkey wrench into his well-thought-out plan. Someone would have heard the gunfire, especially the rifle. A shootout in this quiet resort town would stick out like a Baby Ruth in a swimming pool.

He needed to leave. He could take the money, and the painting, and get out of here if he left now. There was still time. And that temptation tugged on him, dragging him toward the door.

But Tucker wouldn't abide that.

Sure, Harper could die from his wound, but he doubted it. The pest would survive like the cockroach he was, and he'd turn up again sooner or later to cause trouble.

No, Tucker had to end this today, right now.

He told himself he had time. The police response time would be slow enough that he could eliminate Harper and still get out with the money and the Rembrandt.

He'd calculated his taunts, letting Harper know he'd seen the blood on the floor. It was a game of cat and mouse.

Harper would think that Tucker following the trail of blood would make him desperate, and possibly flush him out into the open.

Tucker knew he had the advantage in that kind of showdown. Dak would be weakened from the loss of blood and from the pain that was surely pulsing through his body.

The colonel hadn't seen exactly where the bullet struck, but he knew it was in the upper body. Perhaps it *was* a mortal wound, but he doubted it. There would have been more blood, and Harper likely would have been on the floor somewhere in this building.

There was no place to hide in this room. Tucker could see all the way from one end to the other, past all the exercise machines and free weights.

He didn't know what was on the other side of the wall dividing this area from the other half of the building, but he knew Harper had to be there.

Tucker followed the trail of blood to a door leading into the next space and stopped with his fingers on the handle.

He heard something on the other side, but couldn't tell what it was. It sounded like a fan, or a vent, perhaps? Maybe there was machinery beyond the door. He pressed his ear to the door and listened.

That didn't clarify anything.

Tucker figured Dak was probably waiting for him to open the door and walk through. He shook his head. So obvious.

He turned the handle and flung the door open wide, ducking back behind the wall for a second, thinking Dak would charge through, wielding his knife.

But that didn't happen.

Tucker kept his back against the wall another second and then stabbed his pistol through the door, checking the right corner, then sweeping to the left.

Fog billowed out through the open glass door of a steam room, blurring his visibility toward the other end of the building. He saw what looked like a kitchenette at the other end, but no sign of Harper.

"Where'd you go, you little rat?" Tucker mumbled to himself.

He stepped forward, pointing his pistol into the steamer in case Harper had taken refuge in the fog.

The steam room was empty, which left only one other place for his quarry to hide.

Tucker saw nothing on the other side of the dry sauna to his right, so that left the nook behind the steamer.

He grinned, predator anticipating the kill, and sidestepped around the corner of the steam room.

The wet air enveloped him for a moment, but when he reached the far wall of the wet sauna, he found no sign of his prey. He couldn't see the blood trail through the fog around him, but he knew there was only one way Harper could have gone.

Coward.

"You can't run forever, Dak!" he shouted. "Come out and face me like a man. I won't make it hurt... too much."

"Neither will I." The familiar voice reached Tucker's ears from behind.

For an instant, an overwhelming sense of dread shot through Tucker's mind. Goose bumps fluttered across his skin, and his stomach turned upside down.

He started to turn around but felt a sharp point stab through the back of his neck and puncture through the front, cutting through his Adam's apple and severing his windpipe.

His body tensed. His face contorted in a panicked, fear-stricken grimace.

Tucker tried to turn around, but Dak wrapped his arm around his face, and squeezed hard.

The colonel flailed his arms, desperately trying to free himself. But to what end? He'd been outmaneuvered, and there would be no surviving the wound Harper delivered.

He gurgled, unable to speak or breathe.

In a last, vainly hopeful act, he twisted the gun around and held it upside down as he fired over his shoulder.

The sound was deafening, and the immediate ringing in his ears overwhelmed his senses. But he kept shooting. He'd only be deaf for a few more seconds until he lost consciousness. And then he'd be dead. He might as well take Harper with him.

But Dak had ducked to the side, still holding the man's head as he emptied his magazine. The rounds burrowed into the walls. One shattered the glass door to the steamer. But none found their mark.

Dak's ears rang, but he held on until the pistol clicked.

Then he squeezed a little harder.

Tucker's legs buckled, and Dak felt him become instantly heavier as gravity overwhelmed the former colonel.

In one last, involuntary protest, Tucker toppled forward, and Dak released him, gripping the knife so that as the man fell away, the blade retreated back through the wound and into the open.

Tucker hit the floor with a thud, his twitching body shrouded in steam.

His wide, unseeing eyes stared at the interior wall. Blood seeped from the wound in his throat, soaking the floor underneath. The twitching in his arms and legs grew less frequent by the second until every ounce of life had left Tucker's body.

Dak winced as he grabbed his side.

He didn't need to check the body. Finally, Tucker was dead.

But now, Dak had one more person to find.

His mind's eye filled with Will's face, and he turned and hurried through the door.

54

Outside, Dak limped around the corner of the converted greenhouse and found Adriana standing alone, surrounded by unmoving bodies.

She saw Dak and immediately rushed toward him.

"Dak. Take it easy." She looped her arm around him to help support his weight.

He shook his head. "I'll... be okay. Where's Will?"

"Just rest," she said. "Sit down. We need to get you an ambulance."

The sounds of sirens blaring in the distance reached her ears. "Maybe they're already on the way."

Dak shook his head, staring down at the grass. "Nicole," he muttered, "where are Will and Nicole?"

"Right here, buddy," Will said, stepping around the back corner of the building.

Dak looked up and saw his friend. Will's arm was looped around Nicole under her armpits to support her weight as the two slowly made their way forward.

Dak grinned through the pain. A surge of strength pulsed through him, and he moved toward the two, wincing with every step.

Nicole was exhausted, but she offered a weary smile as he approached. Then she saw the blood soaking his shirt and his hand covering the wound. Worry streaked through her eyes.

"You're shot," she realized as they met. Her voice cracked.

Their eyes swelled with tears.

"I'll live," he said, hoping that was true.

The sirens drew closer.

"Chester?" Adriana said through the radio.

"Already on my way out," he said.

The cops would have to dig around to find the sniper rifle Chester left buried in the dirt under a copse of trees on the other side of the lawn. They might locate it, and the shell casings he'd scooped into the hole with it, but that was unlikely.

Will busily wiped his fingerprints off the pistol with the bottom of his shirt before placing it in one of the dead men's hands.

"I'm going to head out, too," Will said. "If you're going to be all right."

Dak nodded. He wrapped his hand around the base of Nicole's neck and stared into her eyes. He wanted to hug her, wanted to squeeze her forever, but he didn't want his blood getting all over her. He could hold her soon enough. And when he did, he would never let go again.

55

Dak lay in the hospital bed, staring at the television hanging from the wall. An intravenous tube connected to a bag hung from a rack to his left.

The cold metal handcuffs on his left wrist kept him from even thinking about trying to get out of the hospital, though at the moment he was too weak to even attempt such a thing.

The local police had arrived moments after Will had disappeared in the van. An ambulance was only a few minutes behind.

The cops had been shocked at the discovery of so many bodies, and two Americans—a man and a woman, at the scene.

To say they were suspicious was beyond an understatement, especially since Dak was covered in his own blood from a gunshot wound.

Dak had lost a lot of blood, but he was feeling a little stronger this morning—the day after the heist.

Nicole had been treated for dehydration and was, as far he'd been told, in a room nearby being kept for observation.

The cops had balked at nearly every piece of the story Dak relayed to them when they'd come to visit him in the hospital room.

But there was no denying the part about the painting they'd found lying on the lawn near the thicket of bodies.

Experts had been called in the moment the police seized the Rembrandt. They'd been blown away by the revelation that it was indeed the real thing, the missing masterpiece stolen more than three decades earlier.

The machines to his left beeped. He didn't know what it meant, but Dak had gotten used to it.

The door cracked open, and someone knocked on it.

"Can we come in?" Will's familiar voice caused a smile to crease Dak's lips.

"Would you leave me alone if I said no?"

Will stepped inside, followed by Chester. "Probably not," Will answered.

He closed the door. Chester walked over to the window side of the room. Will stepped over to Dak's left side.

"I told you the plan would work," Will said with a cheesy grin.

"Yeah, you did." Dak rolled his head to the right on the pillow. "I had no idea you could shoot like that, Ches."

Chester shrugged. "I'm a man of many talents," he joked.

"That you are."

"But let's keep that part between us, yeah? I don't want Tamara knowing about that particular skill set."

Dak chuckled and immediately wished he hadn't. The laughter hurt his side where the doctors had patched up the bullet wound.

"Did you get the briefcase open?" Dak asked.

Will nodded. "Yep. And the money has been deposited in the account we set up."

"Looks like you're going to get that yacht after all. What are you going to name it?"

"I haven't decided yet. But I'm thinking *Magnolia*."

Dak's eyebrows lifted slightly at the name. "Wow. You really are a sensitive type."

"Shut up," Will laughed.

Dak wearily closed his eyes for a second.

The plan had been a long shot, at least as far as he reckoned. Will had contacted Tucker to let him know where the painting was under the guise of selling-out his friend for a handsome payout, along with Nicole.

The last part had enticed Tucker the most as it would allow him to witness the betrayal tormenting Dak just before he killed him.

It was too good to resist. And Tucker had fallen for it.

"Where's Adriana?" Dak asked, suddenly noticing her absence.

"She had to head back to the States," Chester said. "But she sends you her best."

Dak knew the Spanish-American woman was probably on her way home to see her husband, Sean Wyatt. *What a duo those two were.* Dak could only imagine how exciting the holidays were in their house.

The door opened, and a man in his mid-thirties wearing a white button-up shirt and black tie walked in. His matching black pants swished as he moved. He was of medium build, with a slight bulge around his midsection.

Dak recognized him as one of the detectives who'd questioned him before.

"It looks like you're a free man, Monsieur Harper," the cop said. He produced a set of keys, inserted one into the handcuffs, and turned.

The metal clasp dangled loose for a second before the man scooped up the restraint and repeated the process on the one wrapped around Dak's wrist.

"You have... influential friends, it would seem."

"Oh?" Dak wondered.

"Yes," the detective said with disgust. He ran a hand through his short brown hair.

Dak wondered who the guy might be referencing but could only think of one person with the ability to pull those strings—Emily Starks.

The three watched as the investigator sauntered back out of the room without so much as a goodbye or good luck. He closed the door and disappeared into the hallway outside.

"Influential friends indeed," Chester commented. "Might I get that person's phone number, whoever it is?"

"Probably not," Dak teased. "She doesn't do requests. Not often, anyway."

Chester's expression turned crestfallen. But he understood.

The door opened again, and the three turned their attention back to it.

How many more people could there be coming to see him?

The cynical question vanished from his mind the instant Nicole appeared in the doorway.

The color had returned to her skin, and the dark circles under her eyes had disappeared. She was in a T-shirt and jeans, and a pair of black fabric sandals.

She stood there, staring back at him with a grateful smile on her lips, and tears in her eyes.

He smiled back at her, but his voice failed him.

"Come on, Chester," Will suggested. "Let's give them some alone time."

The Brit followed Will out the door. Both of them nodded to the lady as they passed and then pulled the door shut behind them.

She glided across the room and stopped next to the bed, hovering over him. She ran her slender fingers through his thick hair and stared down into his eyes.

"I'm so sorry," Dak said, finally able to find his voice again. "I'm sorry for everything."

"It's okay, baby. You saved me."

A tear trickled down his right cheek. "I was the reason you were in this mess to begin with. It's all my fault. And... I should have never left you."

Her smile cracked a little wider.

"You were trying to protect me. It's okay. I know."

He shook his head. "No. I was wrong. But if you'll give me the chance, I swear I will never leave you again."

"We both know that's not true."

The answer stabbed him in the heart, and he had a bad feeling he knew what was coming next. He'd wanted to tell her he loved her, and that they should give it another chance.

"But," she said before he could protest, "I know whenever you leave, you'll always come back to me."

Hope blunted the knife that had stuck in his heart and replaced it with a warm, radiant sensation that pulsed through his body.

"Does that mean..." he faltered.

She nodded. "Yeah."

She leaned down and pressed her lips gently against his. They felt like plump rose petals. He raised his right hand and cradled the back of her head, lacing his fingers through her hair.

Dak didn't know what the future held. But right now, nothing else but this moment mattered.

And it was everything he could possibly want.

THANK YOU

Thank you for taking the time to read this story. I love a good heist story, and I hope you enjoyed this one.

The story of the missing Rembrandt is a true one. Back in the 1990s, two thieves really did steal The Storm on the Sea of Galilee from a museum in Boston. As I suggested in the story, investigators claimed they had leads on the identities of the thieves, but no arrests were made.

I always thought that to be an interesting piece of the tale. If the authorities truly did have an idea about who could have stolen the painting, why not make an arrest? Or had the culprits already slipped away, changed their identities, and taken up residence in a place with no extradition agreement?

More questions than answers, it seems. But it was fun to speculate on possible scenarios.

If you enjoyed the story, please consider leaving a review on Amazon. Those reviews help authors get noticed by new readers, and they help new readers better decide whether a book is right for them.

And if you haven't joined the Relic Runner VIP reader list and received your free Dak Harper origin story, you can do that here: https://readerlinks.com/l/3492924

That's all for now. I'll see you in the next story.
Your friendly neighborhood author,
Ernest

OTHER BOOKS BY ERNEST DEMPSEY

The Relic Runner - A Dak Harper Series:

The Relic Runner Origin Story

The Courier

Two Nights In Mumbai

Country Roads

Heavy Lies the Crown

Moscow Sky

Thief's Honor

Sean Wyatt Adventures:

The Secret of the Stones

The Cleric's Vault

The Last Chamber

The Grecian Manifesto

The Norse Directive

Game of Shadows

The Jerusalem Creed

The Samurai Cipher

The Cairo Vendetta

The Uluru Code

The Excalibur Key

The Denali Deception

The Sahara Legacy

The Fourth Prophecy

The Templar Curse

The Forbidden Temple

The Omega Project

The Napoleon Affair

The Second Sign

The Milestone Protocol

Where Horizons End

Poseidon's Fury

Adriana Villa Adventures:

War of Thieves Box Set

When Shadows Call

Shadows Rising

Shadow Hour

The Adventure Guild (ALL AGES):

The Caesar Secret: Books 1-3

The Carolina Caper

Beta Force:

Operation Zulu

London Calling

Paranormal Archaeology Division:

Hell's Gate

Guardians of Earth:

Emergence: Gideon Wolf Book 1

Righteous Dawn: Gideon Wolf Book 2

Crimson Winter: Gideon Wolf Book 3

ACKNOWLEDGMENTS

As always, I would like to thank my terrific editors, Anne and Jason, for their hard work. What they do makes my stories so much better for readers all over the world. Anne Storer and Jason Whited are the best editorial team a writer could hope for and I appreciate everything they do.

I also want to thank Elena at Li Graphics for her tremendous work on my book covers and for always overdelivering. Elena rocks.

A big thank you has to go out to my friend James Slater for his proofing work. James has added another layer of quality control to these stories, and I can't thank him enough.

Last but not least, I need to thank all my wonderful fans and especially the advance reader team. Their feedback and reviews are always so helpful and I can't say enough good things about all of them.

Made in the USA
Middletown, DE
29 August 2023

37613973R00196